"King David: 'My Life as I Remember It'"

"King David: 'My Life as I Remember It'"

* * *

R. Furman Kenney

authorHOUSE®

AuthorHouse™
1663 Liberty Drive
Bloomington, IN 47403
www.authorhouse.com
Phone: 1-800-839-8640

First published by AuthorHouse   07/15/2011

ISBN: 978-1-4634-2829-7 (sc)
ISBN: 978-1-4634-2192-2 (dj)
ISBN: 978-1-4634-2828-0 (ebk)

Library of Congress Control Number: 2011910622

Printed in the United States of America

DEDICATION

This work is dedicated to all Bible students, especially to those who love to read the story of King David as portrayed in the pages of the Old Testament.

CONTENTS

PREFACE

Told herein is the life story of the great King David as told by him. He tells the good and the bad that occurred in his life, that is, it pictures him "warts and all".

It collects the many historical events in David's life and brings them together in story form in order that his life might "wake up and live" in our imaginations. It reveals him to be a flesh and blood person who faced many of the temptations which the reader faces. In this presentation of his life we see a person who faced his problems on his knees before his God. It tells how his humanity was "heavy upon him", and how he dealt with it.

By telling the story of the life of the great King David in first person the reader is made to realize that David had his imperfections of character even as present day people do. More especially it tells how he met the temptations and hardships along life's journey so that he was able to survive that journey.

Although this book is a compilation of the historical facts of the life of King David, it reads like a modern day novel. That is true because its characters are portrayed as characters in a novel.

It reveals that King David was a completely human being in spite of the fact that he is glorified by people of our day. He would be embarrassed by the esteem with which he is held in our day. The reader will come to the realization that David's "greatness" is due not to his own abilities but to the fact that he "walked and talked" with the Lord daily.

R. Furman Kenney

CHAPTER 1

DAVID, THE SHEPHERD LAD

"It's so hard to be the youngest child in the family!" young David mused to himself. "My big brothers are always fighting among themselves, but I've noticed that they stand together when they start picking on me. 'Hey, runt, go and fetch me my bow and arrow', or 'Get out of my way, you sorry little twerp'. Sometimes they knock me around simply because they are bigger and can easily do so. They treat me like I was an animal of some sort, a person of no value. They are rough with me in speech and in behavior. Well, all I can do is 'grin and bear it'. I must say that I am not good at 'grinning', but I am good at 'bearing it', not because I want to, but because I can't help myself . . . . I'm forced to.

It's just not fair! My father gives my seven older brothers all the important things to do such as tilling the soil on our land, taking care of the donkeys and camels, going to the market to make purchases for the family, going to the livestock sales to buy or sell cattle, sheep, goats, donkeys and camels. He doesn't trust me to do important stuff like that. Often I ask him why he never allows me to do the kind of work like they do; he always says, "Son, you are just too young; that's man's work." My brothers often work together in doing those big jobs; they laugh and talk . . . and sometimes argue and fight . . . . and seem to have a good time while working because they have the companionship of each other. What is the job that my father gives me to do? He says to me, "Little David, you are to take care of the family's flock of sheep. You are to see to it that they have sufficient grassy spots on which to graze, and you are to see to it that they get a sufficient amount of water to drink. You'll have to search for water and grassy areas, because you know very well that there is a great scarcity of streams or pools of water in these parts and that there are very few grassy spots on which they can graze. Above all you are to protect the sheep with your very life."

At first I was very proud of the fact that he thought that I was able to do the work of a shepherd for the family's big flock of sheep. Later, however, I thought about the assignment he gave me and said to myself, "Hey, he's giving me that job, because it is considered too menial for my big brothers to do. It's just not fair!!! One of these days I shall become a man, and then I won't have to be a lowly sheepherder. If there's a war I can join the men of our nation and fight the enemy with all my might and main. Some of these days . . . ."

It's hard being a shepherd. I'm not talking about the physical labor involved, for my trusty sheep dog is a big help in keeping the flock together. Most of the time I sit on a big rock in the midst of the flock and watch my sheep as they graze so that I can be certain that a sheep does not wander away as it moves from one grassy patch to another. Yes, much of my time I sit, but I'm sitting unprotected from the rays of the sun. My ruddy colored skin has long since turned to a dark brown due to being baked in the rays of the Palestinian sun. When I realize that my sheep have nibbled up all the grass in one spot, I call to my sheep and cause them to follow me as I lead them once again in search of another grassy spot on which they can feed. All too often my sheep and I have to walk miles before we reach such a spot.

The hardest part of being a shepherd is the awful loneliness. Though my sheep and I may have to trudge a great distance to find a desirable grazing spot, a spot that is miles away from my home and from the family's sheep fold, that is easy compared to the great loneliness I have to endure. Often I have to go days on end without seeing my family and another human being. When occasionally I cross paths with another shepherd, there is no time spent in fellowship. We have to keep some distance from each other to prevent our flocks from mixing and mingling with each other. Also, there is a bit of competition with those shepherds I chance to encounter because we are each vying for the best grazing spots. So much for fellow-ship with other shepherds!

Night and day and day after day there is that heart aching loneliness for us shepherds. However, the up side of the great loneliness which I have to endure as a shepherd is that it has certain benefits. For instance at night I sit on a rock where I can have a full view of all of my sleeping sheep. While they are sleeping I gaze at the night sky and see the beauty and majesty of God's great universe. The moon is sometimes full and sometimes on the wane; the stars are twinkling down at me as though they were sending me a coded message of the might and power of the God I worship. How wonderful is the handiwork of my God. Indeed, how majestic is the Lord Jehovah Himself. At times like these I cannot refrain from singing . . . my heart almost bursts within me as I meditate on the awesomeness of His majestic person and on the wonders of His great creation. In such moments my heart almost bursts within me as I meditate on the wonder of His majestic person and the wonders of His great creation. At such times as these poetry seems to flow through my mind and my heart. I grab my harp and begin to strum on its strings until I find just the right key in which to play and sing. The following words just seem to vent my emotions concerning the attributes of my great God:

"How majestic is thy name, O Lord my God!
The sun, moon and stars are handiworks of Thy great power.
The sky arching over me is a testimony of Thy home above
And of Thy great protective love which hovers over helpless man.
I see the awesomeness of Thy power and of Thy great love for mankind
When all about me I see the beauty of the earth,
The pride and joy of Thy great creation.
Then I wonder, 'What is man that Thou art mindful of him?'
Helpless and sinful man stands in great contrast to
The power and purity of my Lord and my God.
Then my soul cries out, 'O Lord my God, how great You are!'"
—By R. F. Kenney

If I had not given voice in song to the deep emotions stirring within my breast, I believe that my heart would have burst within me.

In moments like these poetry seems to flow through my mind and heart. After giving voice in song to the results of my meditation, I scramble to my feet and search through my crude shepherd's pouch in which I keep life's necessities until at last I find a piece of parchment and the crude writing instrument which I use. Then, I sat back down and let the verse flow once again from my mind and heart down to my finger tips and thence onto the piece of parchment.

When the moon is on the wane the darkness of the night surrounds me and causes me almost to be afraid. But I am not afraid, for the Lord is my light and my salvation. Thus, of whom should I be afraid? On many of those lonely nights my heart wad indeed filled with a love and understanding of God that I had never before sensed. I look at my innocent and helpless sheep reclining at my feet and think to myself, "How dependent on me are these poor sheep." I have to lead them to green pastures, and I have to lead them to streams of water that move slowly and quietly (I learned early on that my sheep seemed to fear a fast moving stream, perhaps fearing that to drink from such a stream might cause them to inhale water). I use my staff to fight off animals of prey that may attack them. I use my shepherd's crook to reach down into a crevice in the rocky area to pull out the sheep that have fallen into it. My sheep seem to look at me with a look of faith that I their shepherd will provide all their needs and will protect them from all danger. Then I muse to myself, "How like the relationship between my sheep and me is the relationship of my God with me. Indeed, He is my good, loving and protective Shepherd who provides my daily needs and protects me from all harm."

On one occasion such thoughts seemed to burn within me until I wrote them down on that piece of parchment. It began with "The Lord is indeed my Shepherd, therefore, I shall not lack anything that I need.'" That thought seemed to flow right out of my heart down to that piece of parchment. Yes, just as I was the shepherd or caretaker of my flock of helpless sheep, so was the

Lord Jehovah the Shepherd of us helpless human beings. The following words flowed from my head and heart down my arm and to my finger tips as I wrote them down:

"The Lord is my Shepherd; nothing shall I lack,
For He causes me to lie down in verdant grassy spots
And leads me to drink from quiet, slow moving streams.
He gives me rest for my tired body and worried soul.
He guides me in paths of the right kind of thinking
And action so that I can be like Him.
Even when I walk in the dark and dangerous valleys,
I shall sense no fear in my heart that death is lurking in wait for me,
Because I have the assurance that my heavenly Father is right beside me.
I know that His powerful rod and staff can and will protect me
Just as I use my rod and my staff to protect the sheep of my flock.
He sets before me a feast of wonderful blessings in the presence
Of those who endeavor to harm me.
He pours on my head the sacred oil of salvation.
Realizing His great love for me, I am overjoyed by the
Knowledge that His righteousness and love will always be with me.
How wonderful is the assurance that I shall forever live with Him
In His heavenly home."

—An interpretative paraphrase of Psalm 23 by R. F. Kenney

In those quiet moments I would pick up my harp and play and sing to my heart's content. Out alone under the night sky there were no big brothers to complain about my early efforts to play on the harp. My harp of course was a small one that I could, with the aid of a leather thong, sling over my shoulder and easily carry with me as I moved from one grassy area to another. The sheep did not seem to object to the discords I produced in my early efforts to play. I noticed that little by little I was able to get a more beautiful and more soothing sound out of the harp. Now, I must admit that if I had been at home in the midst of the family circle my big brothers would have teased me unmercifully about playing on a harp. 'That's not a manly thing to do! You are a sissy!' Part of their teasing would probably have been due to their jealousy of my ability to play a musical instrument. Little did I know that some time later I would be asked to use the music I produced on the harp to soothe the troubled spirit of the first king of our nation, the great King Saul.

Some time at night as I sat watching the sleeping sheep lying all around me my eyes would get very heavy. In fact sometimes I would become so sleepy that I dozed a bit. On an occasional night I would sense some movement on the outer circle of my flock, or I would hear a low growl from my faithful sheep dog. I would become wide awake and tense as I listened and watched such a movement. Quietly I reached for my sling and for one of the small round rocks which I kept 'at the ready' for just such occasions as this. In the quiet moments of each day I had been practicing the use of my sling. Little by little I had gotten to the point that I could hit a very small target with the stone hurled from my sling. In those moments when I sensed a movement not made by a sheep, a movement on the periphery of the flock, I would quietly pick up my sling, insert a stone and whirl it around my head and let go of it in the direction of the movement. I knew that I had succeeded in hitting my target when I heard a yelp of a wolf or the growl of a bear or mountain lion.

Unfortunately there were times on a dark moonless night when there was no observable movement on the outer circle of the flock, but there was observed a commotion among the sheep in a certain area. On such occasions I knew that to use the sling aimed in the general direction of the commotion would be dangerous, for I could possibly kill one of my sheep instead of an attacking wild beast. With that in mind I would run (almost fly) in that direction and encounter first handed a snarling wild beast. Immediately I would attack it with my bare hands (if in my haste I had not grabbed my shepherd's staff). So angry was I at the wild beast that I would literally tear it limb from limb with a strength that I had not known that I had. Later I realized that God had empowered me through a rush of adrenalin to have almost superhuman strength. My strength at that moment was due to my ardent desire to protect my beloved helpless sheep . . . . a strength empowered by God. Afterward, I would rehearse that event in my mind and would realize that my God is a mighty fortress of protection around me just as I was the protector of my sheep.

After a while of serving as a shepherd lad in many lonely situations I realized that I was no longer lonely. I came to know that the Lord Jehovah was my constant companion. I walked and talked with Him day by day. I came to realize what great love He had for me, just as little by little I showed more and more concern and protective love for my sheep. Often I sang to them songs or psalms which I had written down in my mind. I learned the peculiarities of each sheep, and gave a name to each one, a name based on the peculiarity of each one, such as 'pokey', 'pushy', etc. Eventually I could call each by the name I had given it. In spite of my keeping a close watch on my flock on rare occasions a sheep would wander off without it being noticed. At sundown I would draw the flock into a fairly tight huddle for their time of sleep. Just before dark I counted the sheep, naming each one as I counted it off. On rare occasions my heart would almost stop beating when I realized that after counting the members of the flock two or three times that one was missing. On such occasions I would quietly slip unnoticed from the flock and go out into the gathering dusk to look for that lost sheep. As the darkness of night approached I would became more and more frantic, searching over the mountainside. When at last I heard a weak bleat I would cautiously move in that direction until I came to a crevice in the rocky mountainside. There in the darkness I could barely discern a light colored object which emitted a faint bleat. Ah, my lost sheep had been found! Using my rod, I reached down and inserted the crooked end down beside the white object and slowly worked the crook of the staff around and under it. Slowly and gently I pulled the sheep upward until I could reach it with my hand. Grabbing the sheep by the scuff of its neck I twisted and turned its body until it came loose from the clutches of the jagged sides of the crevice on the sheep's wooly frame and pulled it up and into my arms. I smothered that wooly animal with kisses and patted it gently. I looked up to heaven as I held that lost sheep in my arms and called out, "'Thank you, Lord of heaven and of earth, for leading me to my lost sheep. I rejoice that the sheep which was lost has been found." At that moment I felt that the "joy bells of heaven" were loudly ringing, because my sheep which had been lost was now found!

Slowly I quit complaining about my lowly task of being a shepherd to my father's flock of sheep. I had come to enjoy those long days and nights of not having fellowship with human beings, for I had come to learn what it meant to have uninterrupted fellowship with my God. Out on those lonely hillsides with only the sheep around me I keenly felt the presence of God. I came to know Him better and to love Him more each day. I sensed that He was talking to me under the beauty of the night sky and in the warmth of the noon day sun. God revealed Himself more and more to me as the days went by.

Finally after many weeks away from the family circle I realized that my father would be worried about me, for there had been no communication between me and the family during the weeks in which I had been away from the family tent. Although my father was not a man to show affection, I knew in my heart that he loved me and that he probably missed me. Slowly I led my flock of sheep over the hills and through the dark valleys in the direction of my father's tent in which our family lived.

After several days of herding the sheep in the general direction of the place I called "home", I was able to see in the distance the family's huge tent and to see the herds of donkeys, camels, and cows milling around. My heart quickened at the sight. Questions scurried through my mind: would my father be glad to see me; would he show any affection for me; would he check to see if I still had the same number of sheep with which I had left home those many weeks earlier; would my big brothers show me any respect for having been able to herd the flock of sheep successfully, or would they still tease and taunt me unmercifully?

Finally I was able to herd my sheep across the remaining distance and to get them into my father's sheep fold, counting them off one by one in order to be doubly sure that I had brought them all back safely. Out of the corner of my eye I saw my father slowly walking in my direction. When he came face to face with me, he simply stood there and gave me a long look. Finally he patted me on the head and gave me a slight hug. He said matter of factly, "Son, you did all right. Come on into the tent and get some water and food.'

As the sun was setting my big brothers, having finished their various chores, came drifting into the family tent. When they saw that I was back in the family circle, they called out, 'It's about time you dragged yourself and the sheep back home. What took you so long? Don't you know how to herd sheep in the proper way?' Most of them came over and gave me a punch that knocked the wind out of my lungs. No, they had not changed. They still treated me like a little kid. I wondered to myself if any of them could kill a wild animal with their bare hands. I wouldn't be surprised if their talk wasn't bigger than their actions.

Eating a home cooked meal of boiled mutton and lentils once again was a very pleasant experience after living on dried rations for weeks. Suddenly the weight of responsibility for the flock of sheep which I had so carefully tended for the past several weeks rolled off my shoulders figuratively speaking. For a while after the evening meal I sat on the outer circle of the men and listened to their chatter concerning things they had seen and heard that day. Soon my eyes grew so heavy that I crawled over on my pallet in a dark corner of the family tent and soon was fast asleep. Dreams of bleating sheep, the growls of wild animals, the beauty of the night sky, etc. filled the hours until suddenly the rays of the morning sun found their way through a tent opening and into my eyes. It was so refreshing to have a night's sleep in which the burden of responsibility for the family's flock of sheep had been lifted from my shoulders.

I awakened to the sound of the voices of the family members who had just finished eating their morning meal and were preparing to leave to tend to their various chores. Well, everything was back to normal. Each of the big brothers had tasks of responsibility to which they were hurrying off to do. There seemed to be no such task for me now that I had brought the family's flock of sheep safely back to the fold. I muttered to myself, "Oh, will I ever be big enough to do anything that is important, or will I always be the little brother who is too small to do any of the big things?"

CHAPTER 2
ALMOST LEFT OUT

Sometimes I heard more than my family members thought that I did. Well, I guess it would be more correct to say that I "overheard" more than they thought I did. It's not that I intentionally eavesdropped; it's just that I had good hearing, and my brothers talked loudly because my father was rather hard of hearing. Well, the oddest thing happened the other day. All my big brothers were doing the jobs that had been assigned to them for the day, jobs which were in areas scattered from the family tent. I had overheard the assignments which my father had given to each of my brothers. As usual I was tending the sheep ("will I ever get big enough to do something besides herding sheep"???). Suddenly one of my father's servants came running up to me and asked, "Where are your brothers working today? Your father told me to go and fetch them, but he seemed to be so excited that he didn't bother to tell me where they were working today. Your father mentioned that the great priest Samuel was coming to the area of Bethlehem to hold a religious sacrifice and feast." Excitement must be contagious, for the servant seemed to be very excited also.

I thought to myself, "What is going on??? He said that my father was very, very excited, and it's very obvious that the servant is greatly excited also. Something unusual seems to be happening. Could it be a meeting of the clan members? Could it be a meeting of the men in our area to hear some new law that King Saul has ordered to be relayed to the local citizens? If that is what the meeting is to be about, it is surprising that my big brothers would be included in the group which has been invited, for most of my older brothers are not yet considered to be men. Although the great and revered Samuel is a prophet and priest, he is also the one who had been the political leader of Israel before the great Saul had been anointed king. No, it is not likely that he is calling men together to share a new law with them. After all the words of the breathless messenger were that Samuel will be holding a religious sacrifice and feast, so it must pertain to matters of religion. It's obvious that Samuel and my father must think that boys my age are too young to be religious and, more especially, too young to know about the great God of Israel, the Lord Jehovah, and too young to revere and worship Him. He must think that boys my age would not know how to behave themselves at such a great religious service." All such thoughts flitted through my mind in an instant after hearing the breathlessly issued message from the lips of the messenger.

"Slow down and catch your breath. Then I will tell you where my father sent them to work today. First, tell me what you think caused my father to be so excited? Did you see any strangers at my father's tent this morning? If so what was said by that stranger that caused my father to be so excited." "Well, yes I saw one who was a messenger. I overheard him tell your father that Samuel, the priest/prophet, was coming to Bethlehem to offer a sacrifice unto Jehovah God and that he was inviting your father and all your brothers to be guests at the feast accompanying the sacrifice." So that's what the excitement is all about! I thought, "My father and brothers are invited, but I am not! Again I am left out of all the interesting stuff. I would give anything to be allowed to attend the sacrifice and especially the feast that follows also. But, NO! It seems that not only my father and big brothers but also the messenger who came to my father's tent with the invitation think that I am too young to do anything but herd sheep, not to do the important and interesting things. I surely would like to attend the sacrifice and feast which the great prophet Samuel is conducting. Well, that's that! Now to answer your question, I'll tell you what I overheard my father tell each of my big brothers where they were to work today."

I stood there watching the servant running at top speed to give to my big brothers the message that they were invited to the sacrifice the prophet Samuel was conducting. I muttered to myself, "I'm not too young to worship the Lord Jehovah. I can't understand why they would not let me go to that great worship service! All they think seem to think that I am old enough to do is to take care of my father's flock of sheep. Well, that's that! One of these days I'll grow up; then I will show them that I can do all the interesting stuff that they are allowed to do." Then I turned to my sheep and started leading them to greener pastures.

Some hours had passed when suddenly I glanced up and saw in the distance one of my father's servants running toward me. I asked myself, "Now what is the matter! Did I not give proper directions as to where he could find my big brothers? Just look at him run! He is in a bigger hurry that he was a few hours ago." Suddenly the messenger arrived and gasped, "Your father said to tell you to join him and your big brothers at the sacrifice and feast Samuel is giving . . . . and to hurry as fast as you can. I'll take your place herding the sheep while you are gone." With that he sat down on a nearby rock to watch the sheep. I almost shouted, "Oh, goody, I am invited to attend Samuel's religious service of the sacrifice and feast after all. Let me get there as fast as my legs will take me!"

What a strange sight! There milling around the great prophet Samuel (I recognized him, because he was the one in the group that looked like a prophet ought to look . . . he almost had an otherworldly appearance) were many men among whom were my father and my brothers. I would never admit it to them, but I thought my brothers were such fine, handsome looking young men . . . . tall and of good countenance. In that moment I was so proud of them as they stood with my father in the presence of Samuel. Rushing up to the group I went directly to my father's side. I heard him say to the great prophet, "Here he is." Why would he say that about me to Samuel? Suddenly Samuel said to me, "Come over here, lad." His servant handed to him a big ram's horn which he took and lifted up over my head and said some words that I didn't understand, only two of which I grasped, 'anoint' and 'king', but I really did not understand what he was saying or what he was doing. He tilted that horn over and poured some oil from it on my head. There was a quiet murmur among the men present indicating they understood the meaning of Samuel's actions, but that they had to be quiet about expressing

13

their approval or disapproval about what had just happened. I would have thought that Samuel's action was that of anointing someone to an important task like becoming a king or some such matter. However, we already had a king of whom we were proud most of the time. Therefore, that surely could not be the meaning of his action. Oh, well, the important thing to me was that I had at long last been accepted to mingle with grown men at an important religious function.

As the crowd dispersed I observed that everyone quietly went his way in a secretive manner. Although I did not grasp the meaning of what had just happened, I sensed that the great prophet Samuel had instructed the men who had gathered there not to tell anyone about what they had witnessed. I recalled that some time ago I had overheard my father and some neighboring men who had gathered at dusk outside my family's tent talking in low tones, saying that there had been hard feelings between the prophet Samuel and our great king, Saul. I had not tarried long enough to hear the cause of the rift for fear that my father would catch me eavesdropping. Well, I suppose that was no concern of mine as to what I had just witnessed and experienced. I was just such a happy fellow to have been allowed to take part in the sacrifice and feast. At long last they had treated me like a man . . . well, almost. One thing I could not understand . . . why did all of those men who were present look at me in such a peculiar way after Samuel had poured oil on my head and muttered some strange sounding words?

After that event I was instructed to go back and take care of my father's flock of sheep. Back to the old grind so to speak, but I was one happy fellow that for a few hours I had been permitted to mingle with my father, big brothers and a lot of other grown men, men who had treated me almost as if I were a man. In fact after that odd ceremony in which the prophet Samuel had poured oil on my head the men in the group, including my big brothers, looked at me in such an odd way. It made me feel that I was now different. I had a feeling that some sort of power was surging through my being. I could not explain it . . . I just 'sensed it.

After that exhilarating experience it was good to get back to the life of solitude with only my sheep as my companions. During the long, quiet hours with my sheep I had time to meditate on the meaning of the event which had just transpired. Just what was the meaning of the prophet pouring oil on my head? There seemed to be an understanding on the part of Samuel, my father, and those present as to its meaning. I seemed to have been the only one who did not grasp the significance of the occasion. Oh, well, I supposed that in due time its meaning would become clear to me.

Suddenly I came out of my reverie with the strangest feeling. I had a feeling that some sort of power was surging through my being. I could not explain it . . . I just 'sensed' it. Was it a realization of my having arrived at manhood at last or was it something more? Somehow I felt that a superhuman strength had been poured into my veins, that I was ready to handle any situation that might arise in the future, be it mental, spiritual or physical. I recalled that when I was at the sacrifice that my father was looking in my direction with an odd expression that I had never seen him have. Something was different . . . but what?"

At the end of the sacrifice and feast which followed my father had given me a stern look which I interpreted as a message that I had better get back to my flock of sheep. Obviously my father was indicating to me that practical matters must prevail, that is, that I needed to hurry back to the task of minding the sheep. Regretfully I left that scene where I had been singled out for special attention and hurried back to the dull life of minding my sheep.

Having arrived back at the grassy area where my sheep were peacefully grazing, I relieved the servant who had filled in for me as the herdsman of my father's flock of sheep during my absence. I settled down to watch over my sheep which were peacefully grazing. In the solitude of that lonely spot I took my small harp out of my backpack and began to play some familiar tunes and to sing with only my sheep as an audience. My heart was very happy over the events that had transpired a few hours before. It's true that I did not understand all that had taken place at the sacrifice and feast to which I had belatedly been invited, but I "sensed" a lot of meaning concerning those events which had occurred there in the presence of the great Samuel and all those grown men. Yes, I seemed to feel that some new spiritual knowledge had been imparted to me by the religious service in which I had participated only a few hours before. Also I seemed to feel that a new power of mind and body had been given to me through that spiritual experience. Yes, that sacrifice which had been offered up to Almighty God by the great Samuel had been very, very meaningful to me. As I admitted earlier I did not understand all that had happened, especially that part in which Samuel had poured oil on my head, but I understood enough to feel that I had been in the presence of Almighty God, that His love and power had infiltrated my mind, body and soul. Was it just a feeling which had been created due to the excitement of that service, or did God truly enter my heart in a new and special way?

On into the late evening hours I continued my reverie concerning that awesome experience I had had at the sacrifice and feast. Only when I heard an uneasy stirring among the sheep did I suddenly come back to the present moment to check on the problem. As was my habit in such times after reaching for my staff and checking to be sure that my sling was still hanging from my shoulder and that there were rocks in my "ammunition bag", I stiffened and waited for an audible sound such as a growl or grunt, a commotion among the sheep, or some other signal that there was a prowling wild beast endeavoring to attack one of my sheep. Zeroing in on the spot where the commotion was occurring I "loaded my sling" with a smooth stone, whirled it over my head and let it go. Suddenly there was a "yelp" heard and the sound of a wild animal running from the area, knocking pebbles here and there as his feet raced from the area.

Thus, my reverie over the great event which had happened in my life a few short hours prior to that moment gave way to the reality of the present in which my technical skills were demanded in order to provide safety to those innocent sheep which had been entrusted into my care and keeping.

Chapter 3
Medicine for the King

As time passed I began to notice that the sheep of my flock were staying healthy and becoming fatter. Their wool was longer than when I first assumed this task. I didn't know how that condition had come to pass, but I strongly suspected that it was due to the fact that I was very careful to take them to new grazing areas as soon as they had closely cropped the present one. I could not refrain from being a bit proud of my work with them. Already I had come to feel that although I had been assigned the task of caring for the sheep because I was the youngest and smallest of my father's sons, my task as herdsman was actually a very important one among the family's business enterprises. My sheep provided the main entrée at most meals served in the family tent, and my sheep's wool was important in that it keep us in warm clothes and in bartering material with the townspeople. Yes, I finally began to take pride in my lowly task.

During those long days in the sun and during those long and lonely nights I had become more proficient with my weapon. No, it was not a sword or a javelin such as soldiers use. Instead, it was a lowly sling. In the dullness of those days I practiced its use by placing a pile of small smooth round shaped rocks beside me, "loading" my sling with one of them, picking a small target many feet from me and aiming at that target. I slung the loaded sling several times around my head before letting it loose to seek its target. As the days passed by I came ever nearer to the target's bull's eye with the stone slung from my 'weapon'. At last I had to admit to myself that I was very good at hitting the target and good at hurling with such power that the stone made its imprint on its target.

Another thing I enjoyed doing to while away the long hours of tending my flock of sheep was to play on my small portable harp which I almost always brought with me on those long stretches of days while tending my flock of sheep far from the family's tent. Little by little I became proficient at causing the music from it to be soothing to the ear, mind and heart. It even seemed to lull my sheep to rest when the shades of night approached. Little by little I began singing as I strummed on the harp's strings. I began to write beautiful and worshipful poems depicting the love and righteousness of the Lord Jehovah and of my love for Him. After a while I learned to play tunes that matched the poems I had written. Sometimes when I was back at the family tent for a few days I played the harp and occasionally sang in the presence of my family members and of neighbors who had dropped by our tent in the late evenings. I noticed that they seemed to enjoy my playing . . . . even my older brothers although they never admitted it to me.

Occasionally on such evenings when the neighboring men who came to have fellowship with my father and my big brothers I lingered nearby in order to overhear their conversation but far enough away so that my big brothers would not notice that I was eavesdropping and give me a bad scolding. Lately I began to notice that their conversation quite often mentioned that King Saul was not in the best of mental health, that at times he was in a very "blue mood". They said that no one seemed to know what to do for the king when he was in such a state of depression.

One day a messenger came to my father's tent and said that he was there on behalf of King Saul. My father replied, "Is that so? How can I help you?" "'Some of the people at the king's court have noticed that when the king is in one of his "blue moods" music seems to help him to come out of that condition. The people of the court said that rumor had it that one of your sons could play the harp. Is that true?" "Well, yes, my youngest son does play on the harp. However, I don't know anything about music, so I don't know whether he plays well or not." "Sir, may I 'borrow' your youngest son and take him to the king's court and have him in readiness when King Saul goes into one of his spells of depression? Well, I will do anything for our great King Saul; I will allow my son, David, to go with you and remain there for a short while to determine if his playing the harp helps the king when he has one of those attacks."

"Thank you, sir. Tell young David to come with me and to bring his harp with him." And so it was that I was sent by my father to play my harp (a much larger one that I used in earlier years) for the great King Saul, the very first king that our people of Israel had ever had. Before that we had been ruled by "judges" who were men of God (well, there was one woman, Deborah, a prophetess who led our people victoriously in battle against the Canaanites) who ruled us under the direction of the Lord Jehovah. This was the way it was until the people of Israel wanted to be like the neighboring nations, that is, have a king to govern them but more especially to lead them into battle when our nation went to war.

Well, what could my father do but obey the will of the messenger, for he had come on behalf of King Saul. And so it was. My father sent a servant over to the place where I was watching over my sheep in order to bring me back to the family tent so that I could go with the messenger. My father did not want me to go empty handed into the presence of King Saul, so he loaded one of his donkeys with a skin of wine, a big load of bread and a goat to be presented to the king. When I arrived at the palace and was introduced to King Saul, I realized that he gave me a critical visual inspection. "'Isn't David a fine looking young man and doesn't he speak well?", said one of the king's courtiers to him. The thing that impressed me most was that they saw me as a 'man' who could speak well, not as a 'boy' as my father and brothers thought of me." After, all I had lived through sixteen summers already!

Hardly had I arrived at the palace when King Saul went into one of his periods of depression. The men of the court referred to it as an "evil spirit from God". The king's assistant motioned for me to begin playing on my harp. The music which I produced on the harp sounded more soothing than ever . . . was God empowering me to play in that fashion? After a long period of harp music it was obvious to all that the king was feeling good once again. I overheard one of the king's messengers telling his fellow members of the court that the king was sending him to Jesse, the harpist's father, to ask him to allow his son, David, to remain in King Saul's service, for I had pleased him. Evidently my father felt that he had no choice but to obey the king's request, for I was told to continue in service there at the king's court. Since there was no position in the king's court called 'musician' or 'harpist', I was given the title of "armor-bearer".

As time went on King Saul seemed to be having less frequent spells of depression. Therefore, I was allowed to return home to tend my father's sheep. Now I had even more things to think about when out on those lonely Palestinian hillsides with only my sheep as companions. What memories I had of life in the great palace of King Saul! His court officials were always coming and going as they carried out the king's business. The army officers were often in conference with the king; I assumed that they were conferring on the 'state of the nation', such as, which enemy would probably be the next to threaten Israel; the state of readiness the army of Israel was in at that particular time, etc. I realized that the king didn't really know me as a person; he simply looked upon me as a "doctor" of sorts, one who could assist in bringing him out of those times of great depression by playing in a pleasing and soothing manner on the harp. Well, that was all right as far as I was concerned. I was just glad to be of assistance in his time of need. As I continued to muse to myself in those quiet hours alone with my sheep I concluded that I was simply 'medicine for the king's ailment.'"

In many ways it was a relief to be back with my sheep. They were defenseless creatures who needed me to lead them to grassy spots on which to graze, to slow moving streams from which to drink, to protect them from marauding beasts of prey, etc. More especially it was so good to be back in the solitude of the hills and plains of Judea. In the distance I could see sitting atop the hill which rose up out of the valleys surrounding it the little village of Bethlehem. At that time it bore not even the remotest suggestion that some day it would be known world wide as the "City of David" and where the great Messiah would be born. It was simply just a nondescript village.

Though some time had passed from the day when I was sent out to tend my father's sheep, it seemed like only yesterday. The beautiful azure colored sky during the cloudless day time hours and the night sky with its myriad of twinkling stars and the moon in its various sizes depending on the seasons of the year . . . . all filling my mind and heart a great sense of awe of the Lord Jehovah God who had created such scenery by His simple command of "Let there be . . . ! I could never seem to get enough of the awe that the knowledge that He was not only the Creator but also the Sustainer of His beautiful and awesome handiwork. In the solitude of the night hours when there were only the dim light of the waning moon and the twinkling stars I al-most felt that the Lord had created such peace and beauty for me alone. In fact the solitude of those night hours seemed to be given to me alone that I might feel more keenly the presence of my loving heavenly Shepherd who was right there with me. It enabled me to talk with Him in a normal tone of voice with no human being there to overhear my conversation with God and to declare that I had gone "daff". Oh, the joy of those hours in which I could spend with my God! What a privilege it was to have all that time alone with Him in which I could talk to him and could listen to Him with the ears of my heart! Oh, to be sure, my sheep could hear my voice, but they seemed to take no notice . . . . and they certainly could not "tell on me" to my family members and neighbors.

At times it caused me to wonder if I was a bit "strange", for I never noticed my older brothers of others of my age seeming to have an expressed fellowship with God. Was I a peculiar person? Was I going off the deep end? Why did not my brothers and neighbors of my age not seem to commune with the Lord Jehovah? Did they have a close fellowship with God but were ashamed to let others know? Oh, if only they had the opportunity of solitude in which they could come face-to-face with Almighty God in a personal experience with Him! By this time in my life I had come to count the solitude of a shepherd's life as being a blessing. What a change from my attitude when first I was sent out into the lonely plains with my sheep as my only companions.

From the viewpoint of "hind sight" I realized other great values gleaned from a life of responsibility for a herd of defenseless sheep. It gave me the opportunity to develop a fearless attitude toward danger. Hither-to-fore in my young life I had had the usual set of fears such as the fear of darkness, the fear of being alone, the fear of wild animals, the fear of the inability to handle the ordinary needs of daily life, etc. As a shepherd I had quickly realized that it was myself and myself alone who must meet the needs of my sheep and myself. I realized that the greatest fear was fear itself. I learned that although there was not another human being in the sound of my voice when shepherding my sheep out on those desolate hills and in those dark valleys that I was not alone. My Lord and my God was always there with me. If human fear took over in me and caused me to become afraid of something there in the darkness of night, I quickly reminded myself that I was never "alone", that my powerful God was right there with me.

The solitude of a shepherd's life gave me an opportunity to gain some abilities that doubtless I would never have achieved. The art of playing on the harp was developed because there were no human ears to hear and to make fun of my poor ability when first I began to learn that art. What a blessing my grasp of that art was in the calming of the "blue moods" of my great king, King Saul! The solitude of a shepherd's life gave me time in which to practice the art of using a sling. Day by day I practiced that art until finally I had it perfected. Without having learned that skill I could never have slain the great giant, Goliath. The life of a shepherd taught me the responsibility of taking care of those under area of my responsibililty. If there came slinking up to my improvised sheep fold in the darkness of the night hours a marauding animal, with a sense of fearlessness I attacked it with my staff of at times with my bare hands. What good training that was for later days when I went to battle against the enemies of Israel!

CHAPTER 4
"IN THE NAME OF THE LORD"

My routine of life changed somewhat after I began to minister to King Saul with my music on the harp when he was in one of his blue moods. I loved to play for him, but I regretted the cause for my musical time with him. When in those periods of severe depression he had a glazed look in his eyes, a scowl on his face and what appeared to be an attitude of hatred toward anyone who was in his presence. He would glare across the huge royal court room at me when I was playing on the harp. It caused me to watch his actions out of the corner of my eyes for fear that he might throw something at me. Fortunately, his periods of depression did not occur very often at the onset of his problem. It was much later that his actions were that of a deranged person when all in the room had to watch for their personal safety.

The early agreement that my father had had with King Saul concerning me was that I would be at the king's palace for certain periods of time and at home taking care of my father's sheep during certain periods of time. On one of the occasions when I was at home minding the sheep my three older brothers had been conscripted to serve in King Saul's army. The members of the Israelite army had been called back into active duty because the relations became Israel and the Philistines had gone sour. King Saul realized that war between the two nations was imminent, and as a consequence he needed many of the able bodied young men of Israel to become trained into a strong fighting force."

After a while my father felt it wise to send some food to his three sons and to the army in general, for the quartermaster corps was probably running very low on rations. He called me in from the area where I was minding the sheep and instructed me to carry a large container of roasted grain and ten loaves of bread to my three brothers who were in Saul's army. Also, he instructed me to take ten 'heads' of cheese to my brothers' unit commander for him to share with the troops under his command. "Now, son, listen to me carefully; what I really want you to do is to visit a while with your brothers and determine how they seem to be faring in their army life. Hopefully you will be able to bring back to me encouraging news about their health and their attitude toward army life." "'Yes sir, I shall do as you say." Secretly I was saying to myself, "Oh, goody, for a change I am getting to do something interesting. I am sure that I shall enjoy seeing how the soldiers go about engaging in battle with the Philistines. That should be very interesting and exciting!"

After a long walk I came at last to King Saul's army's encampment in the valley of Elah. I arrived at the camp area just as the soldiers sounded their war cry and were in the process of taking up their battle positions. I hastily ran to the quartermaster's location and left with him the supplies I had brought for the unit commander. Then I moved among the troops until I found my brothers. Of course they were anxious to hear all the news concerning our father and the rest of the family. All the time I was wondering why the soldiers of Israel were not advancing toward the Philistine army. I wanted to see some action, that is, I wanted to see how the two opposing armies went about fighting. I had never seen such a sight, but I imagined that battle action would be very interesting. I knew better than to ask my big brothers why they were not engaged in battle, for I knew they would give me a resounding scolding if I asked too many questions. Suddenly I saw our soldiers retreating from their battle positions and running to the rear. I could not help but blurt out the question that was on my mind, "Why are our soldiers running toward the rear? That seems to me to be a cowardly act." To my surprise my brothers did not scold me for asking that question. Instead, they said, "Look over at the Philistines' battle line. Do you see that huge man standing in front of their line, and can you hear him shouting, 'You cowardly Israelites! I am representing the Philistine army. Instead of the two armies fighting each other, I will fight a man from your army. If I kill your soldier whom you select, your army will surrender to the army of the Philistines. If you kill me, then the Philistine Army will surrender to the army of Israel." Then I began to understand the situation as to why a battle was not in progress. I stepped away from my brothers and walked out among the other Israeli troops. I asked one of them, "What will King Saul do for the soldier of our army who kills Goliath and by so doing remove this disgrace from our nation. That huge fellow standing in front of the Philistine army is defying the power of the God of Israel. That is a disgraceful insult to the one true God, the Lord Jehovah?" He answered, "King Saul has promised that the man who succeeds in slaying Goliath will be given great wealth and the king's daughter will be given to him in marriage. Also, the father of that soldier who succeeds in killing Goliath will be exempt from paying taxes in Israel." I had not noticed that my oldest brother, Eliab, had walked up just in time to hear me asking that question. He became so angry with me for asking that question that he scolded me loudly, saying "Just why did you come down here? And did you walk off and leave your sheep without someone to look after them . . . . I just bet you did, you young good-for-nothing kid. I bet father did not send you, but you ran away from home just to satisfy your curiosity about how a war is fought! I know how conceited you are and what a wicked heart you have." Now I had thought that I had asked a fair question of that soldier with whom I was speaking, for I had already overheard bits and pieces of the answer to my question from other soldiers around me. "Now what have I done, Eliab? Can't I be allowed to talk with people? You have always scolded me about everything I have done. You have always belittled me because I am the baby of the family!"

What neither Eliab nor I had realized was that people were listening to our 'squabble', especially the question I had asked about the rewards the king was offering to anyone who could kill the huge Philistine whose name was Goliath, the question which upset Eliab so much. He had jumped to the conclusion that I was thinking about doing that big job myself. I must admit that even that early in the game I had wondered about my doing that, but I certainly had not at that time made a decision to be the one who should assume that responsibility. After all, that task should be done by a trained soldier from the ranks of the army of Israel, not by a person who was too young to be in the army. My big brother Eliab was acting as though he was my parent. I resented that.

Evidently the eavesdropper gathered from my question about the rewards which the king had offered to anyone who was able to kill the giant, Goliath, that I was thinking of being the one to win that great reward offered by King Saul. I had simply inquired about that matter so that I could use the news about the great reward to cause some of the soldiers to want to kill that giant who for days had been taunting the soldiers of King Saul's army. Well, it seems that the eavesdropper went directly to the king and told him what I had said; only he gave to the king his interpretation to what I had said. The result when the king heard that story from the eavesdropper, he immediately sent for me.

By then I came to the conclusion that it was obvious that none of the trained soldiers were willing to fight the giant single handedly. When I came into King Saul's tent there on the battlefield, I immediately felt so sorry for him. He seemed to be very afraid that there would be a negative outcome to the battle against the Philistine army. He stood to lose a lot personally and the army . . . yes, and the entire nation of Israel . . . . stood to lose everything because no one of his soldiers was willing to fight the giant. I could not help myself, but suddenly I felt compelled to offer my services to the king as the representative of Israel chosen to fight Goliath. I really thought that King Saul would laugh at my offer and tell me to go home and tend my sheep as my brother Eliab had told me. Instead he looked at me for a long time. There was no evidence that he recognized me as being the one who had played the harp for him during his periods of depression. Finally in his desperation he gave a long sigh and said, "All right, young man, you can fight the giant Goliath and do so with my blessing. However, you cannot represent my army dressed as a shepherd lad. Put on my tunic and coat of armor and put this bronze helmet on your head. Also, use my sword." When I got dressed in all of the king's equipment, I walked around for a few moments in order to 'get the feel of it'. I discovered that I could hardly take a step due to the weight of the king's armor. After a while I realized that I could not fight in all of that unfamiliar apparel. "King Saul, I don't want to offend you. You have been so generous to offer your very own tunic and fighting equipment to me, but by your leave I prefer to fight in the only way to which I am accustomed. I have fought many successful battles with vicious animals using only my staff and sling. Those are the only kinds of weapons with which I am familiar. Please understand, sir, that I shall not be fighting Goliath alone, for my God, the Lord Jehovah, will be fighting in and through me." "Well, have it your own way." So with his permission I removed all of that heavy equipment and put back on my shepherd's robe, picked up my staff, and slung my pouch over my shoulder. Then I picked up my sling, but even as I did so I thought to myself, the soldiers will ridicule me for going out to meet Goliath with just a shepherd's staff and a sling as my weapons. Well, that's their problem! Again, King Saul took a long look at me and finally said, "Go and the Lord be with you."

The next morning when the two battle lines were drawn facing each other out stepped Goliath in front of the Philistine battle line. He gave his usual challenge as he leered at the army of Israel. My three brothers along with the rest of Saul's army stood in stony silence in their battle formation without showing any sign of anyone breaking ranks and going forward to meet the giant head on. True to my promise to King Saul I stepped forward and squeezed through the Israelite's battle line and walked slowly and deliberately in the direction of the big Philistine. Loud whispers were heard in the ranks of the Israelite army behind me, "Who is that going forward? He looks like a kid, is dressed in a shepherd's garb, is carrying a shepherd's staff, and has a shepherd's pouch hung across his shoulder. Do you suppose he is a shepherd lad who is looking for a lost sheep and does not realize that he is the heart of the battle line? Somebody ought to run out there and grab him and drag him out of danger's way!" Obviously no one was willing to come forward and drag this shepherd lad out of harm's way, so I just kept walking toward the enemy. As I crossed the little stream that meandered down through the valley between Socoh and Azekah I stooped down and scooped up five round stones and put them into my shepherd's pouch. About that time Goliath began stepping forward with his armor bearer in front of him and came closer and closer to me. As he scrutinized me and saw that I was but a young lad who was approaching him and saw that I was wearing no armor but was carrying a shepherd staff and a sling, he became very angry. "Am I a dog that you are about to attack me with sticks?" He began cursing me in the name of his heathen gods. "Come right on to me, and I shall give your flesh to the birds of the air and the beasts of the fields." I responded by saying, "You come against me with a sword, javelin and spear, but I come to you in the name of the Lord Almighty, the God of the army of Israel whom you have defied. This day the Lord will hand you over to me, and I'll strike you down and cut off your head. Today I will give the carcasses of the Philistine army to the birds of the air and the beasts of the earth, and the whole world will know that there is a God in Israel, and, also, all those gathered here will know that it is not by sword or spear that the Lord saves."

As Goliath began to move nearer me, I ran toward him and quickly whipped out my sling, loaded it with a rock, slung it around and over my head several times to gather speed and strength and then let it fly. It flew straight toward the one spot on Goliath which was not covered with metal armor, a spot in the center of his forehead just above his eyes. The stone sank into that very spot on his forehead, and he fell face downward to the ground. While the armor bearer and soldiers of the Philistine army stood as though frozen in their tracks, I quickly ran forward, removed Goliath's sword from its scabbard and killed him and cut off his head. Immediately the soldiers of the Philistine army began to run like scared rabbits with the soldiers of the army of Israel in hot pursuit. The bodies of the Philistines were scattered all along the escape route. At eventide the soldiers of Israel came back and pilfered the tents of the Philistine soldiers. As for me I wanted as my booty in payment for my efforts the head of Goliath and his armor. King Saul readily granted my wish, so I took it and put it in the army tent lent to me.

Even as I had suspected earlier King Saul did not recognize me as being the harpist who had played many times for him in his times of depression. He was overheard asking his army commander, Abner, who I was. Abner was heard to answer, "As surely as you live, O King, I do not know." "Then let us find out. Go and bring him to me." Perhaps as a young teenager I had had a "spurt of growth" which had greatly changed my appearance since I had last played the harp for the king. Whatever the reason neither King Saul nor Abner now recognized me. When I arrived in the king's presence I was still holding in my hands Goliath's head. "Whose son are you, lad?" he asked. I replied, "I am the son of your servant Jesse of Bethlehem." That question really accentuated the fact that neither of them recognized me and, therefore, had no clue as to my identity. Well, that didn't matter so much, because I was reasonably certain that he would remember who I was from that point on due to my having slain Goliath.

The soldiers of King Saul's army now looked at me in awe. They referred to me as the "young giant slayer" and treated me, a simple shepherd lad, as though I stood tall among them. The news soon traveled to all parts of the kingdom about my having slain the giant. All the adulation which the people were paying me made pride swell up in my heart, a fact that caused me to recall what my brother Eliab had said to me a few hours ago . . ."you are conceited and have a wicked hear". I stopped in my tracks at the memory of that. Was I a conceited person who thought he was a notch or two above other people? Had all the praise heaped upon me about my great bravery and great ability with a sling and a stone dimmed my memory that the honor for that deed should go to the Lord Jehovah, the God of Israel, who had empowered me to accomplish that feat by causing the stone from my sling to hit the one small vulnerable spot on the huge frame of Goliath and thus causing him to be struck down? Had the flattering praise of the people of Israel caused me to accept the credit that was due God? I was brought to my knees before God in a great spirit of humility.

One of the great results of that episode concerning the slaying of the giant was that I met for the first time a fine young man about my age whose name was Jonathan. Oh, I had seen him passing through the court on those occasions when I was playing on my harp for King Saul, for he was the King's son and was often in and out of the palace. I first met Jonathan at the time when I was called by Abner to come to the king's tent so that he could inquire concerning my identity. Young Jonathan and I were introduced to each other by the king himself. It seems that due to my slaying Goliath I had suddenly been transformed from the lowly status of a sheep herder to a young man of stature, one who was considered as a proper person to be a friend of his son Jonathan. Immediately we two recognized that we had much in common as pertained to our personalities. I soon discovered him to be a young man in whom there was no guile. He did not have a jealous bone in his body. After a while we became close friends.

CHAPTER 5

UNDER THE KING'S WING

I thought to myself with a great sense of pride, "King Saul must have really been pleased with me for slaying the giant, Goliath." However, I knew that it was not so much me as it was the Lord Jehovah who struck down the giant. The Lord saw to it that my practicing day in and day out with my sling paid off on that special day; He really blessed me. Now, I admit that it was I who rushed in and cut off the giant's head with his own sword. I knew that he was more than likely just greatly stunned by the blow on his head with that rock from my sling and that he might regain consciousness at any moment. Therefore, I did not run any risk of that happening . . . . I made use of Goliath's huge sword to severe his head from his body.

Yes, King Saul must have been pleased with me because of that event., for he told me that I was to remain in his service and that I was not to go back home to my father. I never knew whether he actually bothered to 'ask' my father to allow me to assume a full time position there in the court with him, or did he just allow father to 'hear about it' as time went on. He was, after all, the king of the land and had the power to draft anyone into his service. Well, be that as it may, I was thrilled that I no longer had to herd my father's sheep or be at home where I would continue to be brow-beaten by my older brothers. The king never said what my task would be while I served under him in the future. I felt that no doubt he intended that in addition to soothing his nerves during his "blue moods" the king decided that though I was a stripling of a lad that I should serve as one of his soldiers. Now that type of job was something that I could sink my teeth into, for I liked all that I had heard about the work of a soldier. I wondered if I would be 'lost in the crowd' as my big brothers seemed to be when I visited them in the battle against the Philistines.

Call it pride, conceit, or simply a matter of personal curiosity or whatever you will, but I could not help wondering how my father took the news of my slaying Goliath when my brothers finally got around to sharing the news with him No doubt that was in itself a hard task for my brothers who always belittled me . . . at least to my face. My father was an unusually quiet and taciturn sort of man. However, when he finally said something I noticed that people stopped talking and began to listen to what he had to say. He was not an outwardly affectionate person, but I always felt that he loved his family members deeply. How would I ever learn of his reaction to the news of my slaying Goliath with a simple sling, for I was quite certain that my brothers would not share such news the next time I saw him. That caused me to wonder if my new position in the king's court would allow me to visit my family or to allow any of them to visit me. I could not fathom what my future held for me. I could only guess. Would the king keep me house-bound for the purpose of being "at the ready" with my harp on those unpredictable occasions when he would have his "blue moods"? In spite of the fact that I had accomplished a great act of heroism (an act that not one of his trained soldiers would undertake) would he feel that for yet a while I would be too young and immature to go into battle with the rest of the soldiers in his army? All such thoughts raced through my mind as I contemplated my future. Well, I guessed that I would just have to wait and see how the king looked upon me as to my abilities in spite of my youthfulness.

Word of the slaying of Goliath by me quickly spread throughout Israel. I discovered that "word of mouth" communication worked just fine, for in no time it became the chief subject of conversation not only among relatives, friends, and neighbors but with strangers who met each other while traveling to and fro in Israel. Unfortunately it unwittingly became a sore subject with King Saul when the news of the slaying of the giant became the lyrics of songs sung by admiring women. They made up a song concerning the event which went something like this: "Saul has slain his thousands and David has slain his ten thousands."

In their effort to express their sincere appreciation for my toppling the huge giant off his throne of self assurance and pride and sending him to have fellowship with his various idols in the nether world.

I began to wonder about the reaction of my three soldier brothers who saw my slaying of Goliath. They did not come seeking me out to congratulate me. However, in all fairness I personally was caught up in the thrill of the moment and walked about in a bit of a daze and was not aware of much that was going on about me. Oh, I, almost forgot . . . . my three brothers were not there to congratulate me nor to scold me, for they were rushing madly along with the other members of the army of Israel as they chased after and slaughtered the members of the Philistine army. In the meantime I was rushed to the tent of King Saul and had an audience with him. He informed me that in spite of my youth he was inducting me into his army with the title of "armor bearer". The army did not have a marching band nor any kind of slot for a musician. I suppose he gave me the only title that he could think of at the moment.

One of the best things to come from the history making episode in which the giant Goliath was killed was that I officially met Jonathan, one of King Saul's sons. My friendship with Jonathan grew day by day. No doubt one big cause of that was that I was lonely for companionship when I first went to the king's court to live. It was hard to admit it, but I actually missed my big brothers and their constant teasing and 'rough housing' me. Surprisingly, Jonathan also seemed to be lonely. I strongly suspected that it was due to the fact that those there in the court near his age were commoners who felt that it was improper for them to associate with the king's son. I was certain that it was not because Jonathan was a vain person who held himself aloof from the common folk. For whatever reason the friendship between the two of us strengthened as the days went by. Soon we came to feel that we were like brothers who had come to respect and to love each other as such Jonathan, the kind and generous person that he was, decided that I should not wear in the court area the nondescript clothing which I had worn as a sheep herder. He took off his royal robe, tunic and belt and gave them to me along with his sword and his bow and arrow. I suppose that he felt that these gifts when worn by me would give me proper status in the eyes of the citizens who went in and out of Saul's court. When I remonstrated about his great generosity, he replied, 'I can easily get more where those came from.' Knowing in our hearts that we could easily be separated as each of us would be fighting in different areas of wars to come, we decided to declare our undying respect and love for each other. Therefore, we made a covenant that we would always be there for each other. Let me pause here and say that neither of us ever forgot the covenant we made with each other.

As time passed my question as to what King Saul would be having me to do as "armor bearer" was answered. He gave me one military assignment after another. In each of these God led me to success. Because of this the king gave me a high rank in his army. I learned by the "grape vine" that his doing that greatly pleased the officers of the army as well as the citizens of the area. However, as mentioned earlier, the women who sang or shouted a refrain in honor of my success in slaying Goliath, a refrain that went like this, "Saul" has slain his thousands and David his tens of thousands" got me into trouble with the king. When he heard about the refrain that the women were singing he became very, very jealous of me. From that time on, although he used me in his various battles and gave me a high rank, he kept a jealous eye on me. Outwardly he was so nice to me that I did not suspect that he was seething with jealousy. In his times of depression he said to himself that the people of the kingdom were paying much more respect and adulation to me than they were to the king himself. In such moments he ranted audible, 'What more can he get but the kingdom?' A comrade at arms overheard those words spoken by Saul and reported them to me. From that time on King Saul seemed cool toward me and stared at me as though he was up to no good concerning me.

Unfortunately, the king's periods of "blue moods" seemed to come more often. At their onset I would move rapidly to my special seat across the great court room from the king, sit down in the proper position at the harp and begin strumming on the strings of the harp. Earlier I had learned that I needed to keep an eye on the movements of the king while I was playing. He would glare across the room at me during those periods of near insanity as if to say that he was going to throw something at me. Finally, on one of his "blue mood" occasions, he actually did pick up his javelin and hurl it across the great room with such force that it stayed steady on course right toward me. Seeing the direction of the approaching javelin, I dived to one side. Due to my quick response in dodging to one side the javelin landed with a heavy thud, burying its dagger-like point into the wall right behind where I had been sitting. During the days following that episode I continued to keep myself at "ready", yes, ready to dart to one side of the place where I was sitting. Obviously everyone around him was in danger of being hit by the king's sharp pointed javelin. Everyone in the great court room seemed to be constantly in a state of fear and of readiness to jump to one side if the king should turn his wrath upon them. I knew where I stood with King Saul. To the observing public, the king was always kind to me. They could not believe that he could be guilty of seeking to pin me to the wall with his javelin. After that first time when he threw that sharp tipped piece of armor at me, I was aware that I was not on his love-list . . . . just the opposite.

I had always endeavored to be submissive, courteous and even kind to King Saul. However, all my efforts in that direction had come to naught. In spite of it all, however, I continued be a loyal subject and continued to show my allegiance to him.

That day when I slew Goliath turned out to be a "red letter day" for the members of the army to gain some loot from the receding army of the Philistines. In the Philistine soldiers' effort to beat a hasty retreat before the pursuing members of the army of Israel, they abandoned their tents and all their possessions which they had with them. At nightfall the members of the army of Israel left off pursuing the Philistines and returned to take plunder from their tents. Yes, the members of Saul's army considered the day that I slew Goliath to be a "red letter day" for them because they had conquered their enemy that day and had gained a lot of loot from the receding enemy.

Let it be understood that the custom of soldiers of that day was to gather and hoard the possessions of the slain or escaping members of the enemy army in order to add to their earthly possessions. I learned as I became accustomed to the ways of army life that it was a matter of "finders keepers" as concerned the possessions left behind by the fleeing soldier of the enemy camp. Such loot provided the major amount of pay which the soldiers received during the course of their enlistment. The pay by the king was minimal (customs never seem to change), and the food provided to the soldiers of Israel by the quartermaster was unappetizing and sometimes stale. The families of the soldiers in the king's army felt the necessity of sending food for their family members in order to have the assurance that they would not starve on army rations. I can attest to that, for my reason for being there with Saul's army on the occasion of my slaying Goliath was to bring the food which my father took from his storehouse and send by me to my three brothers who were in King Saul's army.

Later on in my army career I learned the advantage (or should I say "necessity") of taking "loot" from the enemy at every opportunity. While still in King Saul's army I *thought* that I could understand that practice, but later on when no longer fighting under the banner of Israel's army I really did learn the art of taking "loot" due to the necessity for survival of my men. At first such a practice "went against my grain" to take the possessions of dead soldiers or of enemy soldiers who had fled before my approaching army, but later I became hardened to that practice for the very existence of my fighting men. Without taking "loot" from the enemy who had been slain on the field of battle or who had fled from our approaching renegade soldiers the men under my command would have surely starved to death.

Chapter 6
Dodging King Saul's Anger

As I have previously mentioned there were many occasions when I wondered about the mental and emotional state of my beloved King Saul. While in his presence there in the palace I observed that he was given to fits of anger, of depression, and of great jealousy. Of course my background was that of a simple sheep herder, and, thus, I had little understanding about matters of the mind and emotions of mankind, but from a common sense standpoint I could not help but notice his great mood swings. While playing the harp for him in order to ease his times of great depression, I watched him out of the corner of my eye. He often fixed his eyes on me with a look of great hatred. I instinctively knew that those were times of danger for me. In my mind I wondered if he really hated me, or was that look of hatred intended for anyone in his range of vision. I also wondered if such hatred was real and lasting, or was it simply a passing mood. As time passed I learned that his look of hatred was based on real hatred and that it was aimed directly at me. Realizing that to be the case I had to be on guard constantly when in his presence in order to avoid harm from him.

Now, as I said earlier, I was but a lad who was a simple sheep herder when Saul was anointed to be the first king of Israel. It was said that he showed some odd signs of personality back when he was being set apart to serve as the king of our nation. As the story was told to me, Saul and a servant were sent by Saul's father, Kish, to search through the surrounding hill country of Ephraim and the area around Shalisha for his father's lost donkeys. They searched here, and they searched there, but finally they had to admit defeat . . . . his father's lost donkeys were not found. Saul said that they should return home before his father started to worry' about him, for he might think that not only were his donkeys lost but also his son. The servant replied that perhaps they should first seek the aid of a "seer", as the prophets of God were originally called. In desperation the two of them agreed that perhaps they could secure help from such a person. The servant suddenly remembered that in the town near where they had stopped their search there was a "seer" who was a man of God, one who was highly respected; "everything he says comes true. Let's go there now. Perhaps he will tell us what way to take."

As best I can recall the one telling the story to me about the young Saul and his servant went on to say that they did find in the nearby town a "seer", a man named Samuel. To make a long story short it was said that when the prophet Samuel saw the two of them approaching he was told by God that the tall young man whom he saw before him was the one the Lord Jehovah had chosen to be the first king of Israel. Samuel followed through with the process of making him king . . . he had Saul to sit in a place of honor at a banquet he was giving. Later he anointed Saul's head with oil which was a ritual to indicate that before God and in the presence of the people Saul had been set apart by God to be the king of Israel. This anointing took place in secret. After this sacred service it seemed that there was an almost visible change in Saul at that point and in the days following the anointing service.

I was told that earlier Samuel had severely questioned the children of Israel about the advisability of their having a king. Prior to this time the nation of Israel from the time of Moses on to my time had been led by the Lord Jehovah, who was visibly represented to the people by His prophets who were earlier called "judges". In some instances those prophet/judges also were expected to lead the soldiers of Israel into battle. Most of them were also the priests of God for the people of Israel. There came the time when the Israelites decided that they wanted a king to govern them instead of a prophet/priest like Samuel. The Israelites wanted to be like the other nations who had kings to lead them in their in the affairs of state. Those kings led the armies of their nations into battle. The Israelites clamored for a king to lead them in that fashion. At that point in their history they became desperate to be like the other nations. In a sense they wanted 'to keep up with them'. While Samuel was questioning them about their demand to have a king he preached a powerful sermon to them about what it would be like to have a king. In essence he said that it would be very expensive for them, for the king would levy very heavy taxes on them in order to support himself, his national leaders, and his army. As time went on the king would practically own them body and soul. The Israelites responded loudly that even so they wanted a king over them. God saw that His beloved nation of Israel no longer wanted Him to be their leader and had determined in their hearts that at all costs they wanted a human being to be their national leader. Therefore, the Lord Jehovah instructed the prophet Samuel to select one for them.

So it came to pass when the time was set by God to allow the nation of Israel to have an earthly king to lead them He directed Samuel to select the son of Kish, a very tall and handsome figure of a man, to be the first king of Israel. As I think back on that choice I have come to believe that the Lord Jehovah probably selected Saul because of his fine looking appearance before the eyes of the people of Israel, not for his superior mentality, his emotional stability, nor for his character. Thus, it would seem that the Lord was giving them what they had asked for, not what was best for them. No doubt He wanted them to come to realize the cost of their turning their backs on His divine leadership. To young Saul's credit he remonstrated a bit to Samuel concerning his being chosen as Israel's king, for he said 'Who am I to be king of Israel? Am I not of the tribe of Benjamin, the smallest and most insignificant of all the tribes of Judah?" Samuel assured him that he was the one who had been chosen by the Lord Jehovah for that position. This selection and anointing of Saul was done in secret. A short time later Samuel made a public show of the selection of Saul for the position of King of Israel. He called the men of all the tribes of Israel to assemble before him. At a set time he had each tribe to march before him clan by clan and family by family. Finally each tribe had presented itself to Samuel by clans and families, that is, with the exception of the smallest and least popular of the tribes but with no obvious results. Finally, the small tribe of Benjamin marched before him clan by clan until the clan of Matri passed before Samuel. "Stop! Now let each family in the clan of Matri pass before me." Slowly each family within that clan marched by in front of him. When the family of Kish appeared before him, Samuel said, "Now, have each son of Kish pass before me." Samuel's dramatic selection of the future king had proceeded in good fashion up until this point, that is, until the last son of Kish had passed by. But alas, Saul was not in that group. Greatly puzzled Samuel inquired of the Lord as to the whereabouts of Saul. God revealed to Samuel that Saul was hiding in the pile of baggage belonging to the men who were assembled there. Was Saul hiding from the throng of people assembled there because of timidity, humility, or a sense of his inability for such a task as being the king of Israel? Looking back on it I decided that it was one of the 'quirks' of his odd personality."

At that point Samuel called forth Saul, son of Kish, and announced to the assembled throng that God had chosen him to be the first king of Judah. "Do you see the man the Lord has chosen? There is no one like him among all the people!" Then all the people assembled there shouted, "Long live the King!" It was later told to me that a great uproar arose from the assembled men as they applauded in order to show their approval of God's choice of such a fine looking young man, a person who stood head and shoulders above the majority of the young men who were present.

Looking back on the selection of Saul as the king of Israel, I often wondered in my mind and heart about that incident of Saul's hiding in the baggage of the assembled tribes and about his earlier ecstatic utterances when mingling with the group of men who were "prophesying," an act that caused the men of that part of the country who saw Saul acting in such a state of frenzy to ask, "Is Saul among the prophets?" I don't know why that event occurred, but Samuel had foretold that it would happen. As much as I loved and respected King Saul, the Lord's anointed, I secretly have harbored in my mind and heart through the years those events in Saul's earlier life. They seemed to me to be inconsistent with the usual type of person chosen for a leadership role in a nation, especially in God's chosen nation.

In those days after Saul became the king of Israel it was often my duty to play on my harp in order to soothe his nerves when he was suffering greatly during his periods of deep depression. As I said earlier, I was always careful to keep my eyes fixed on him, for he had a look in his eyes, yes, and on his countenance also, that caused me to feel that he was capable of doing harm to those in the palace who were serving him. Time proved that my suspicion that King Saul might do bodily harm to someone who was ministering to him was correct. On two occasions he suddenly lifted his javelin and threw it at me with all his might. Fortunately both times I saw the javelin coming straight at me and managed to dodge it just in time. Some of the attendants who were standing near him at those times overheard him mutter to himself, "I'll pin him to the wall". In my heart I felt that he was mentally deranged which caused him to do such a thing so openly. Therefore, I did not take his throwing his javelin at me personally; I simply attributed that wild action to his mental illness. After all, he was God's anointed whom I should respect and serve to the best of my ability. At first I loved him as my king and as the father of my best friend. I have to admit that as time passed and his hatred of me became more apparent my love for him and my respect for him gradually deteriorate, but I still respected him as God's anointed and as the king of my nation.

I was told by those who were present on that great occasion when Saul was publicly selected as the first king of Israel that when the applause from those assembled there had ceased, Samuel explained to the people the regulations and duties of the role to be played by the King of Israel. For the sake of clarity of memory Samuel took time to write down on a scroll those regulations, and in the presence of the great throng of Israelites he symbolically "deposited" the scroll to the Lord. Following that Samuel closed the meeting and dismissed all the people to return to their homes. Saul returned to his home in Gibeah, but before leaving the scene some of the men present were motivated by God to become followers of Saul; they followed him to his home in Gibeah. Others present gave or later sent presents to their new king. I was told that some of those present were overheard to say, "How can this fellow save us?" They paid no reverence to Saul and certainly gave him no gifts. Prior to that time, and I'm sure after my life is over there will continue to be differences of opinion concerning those in leadership roles.

I harbored in my heart all the bits and pieces of derogatory conversations I had heard or overheard and the facts (or was it gossip?) which had been given me about the character of King Saul. I had no intention of spreading such information among my contemporaries, for I felt that to do so would be demeaning to our king and would not help his condition in the least. My lips were sealed in regard to such information that I had gleaned through the past years concerning the background of King Saul. Rather I felt that the Lord would desire of me to honor the king and to speak well of him at every opportunity. After all, King Saul was chosen to be the first king of Israel and, therefore, deserved the respect of everyone in Israel. Secretly I admitted to myself and only to myself that it was not always easy to keep my mouth shut, especially some time later when he openly endeavored to hunt me down as though I were a common criminal.

CHAPTER 7

A GREAT KING, A PROUD PEOPLE

Now that I was in service for the king there were times when I was allowed to be free to "do my own thing". No doubt due to my early years as a shepherd boy out in the plains some distance from my home area of the small town of Bethlehem, (a name which I was taught literally meant "house of bread") I loved to meditate on life in general and on the goodness of the Lord Jehovah. Also, as a young lad I loved to sit in the evenings on the periphery of the circle of men who had gathered in front of our family's tent. I sat a good distance from the circle of men because I knew that the men considered that what they were discussing was for men's ears only. However, I must admit that from very early childhood I had an enquiring mind. I wanted to hear all the bits of news that were being discussed by my father and his neighbors. Most of them were shepherds who traveled about over the countryside, and in so doing they often chanced to meet other shepherds from miles away. During such encounters they carefully kept their flock of sheep at some distance from the others, but the shepherds could step aside from their flocks and share the latest news each had gleaned earlier from contact with other shepherds. That was the method used by shepherds to learn what was going on in the world as they knew it.

I recall that as soon as I had learned to eavesdrop on the conversation of my father and his neighbors during those evening gatherings outside my family's tent I made it a point to do so whenever there were such evening gatherings. I noticed that their conversation now centered around what our new king, King Saul, was to live in the same manner that he had always done. It was obvious that he did not have a clue as to what a king was supposed to do, so he continued to go out into his father's field and plow the land behind a yoke of oxen. One evening the men who were gathered in front of our family's tent seemed very, very excited. Since I was a bit too far away to hear what they were saying, I slipped over to a darker spot and sneaked up to the circle as close as I dared. It proved to be close enough to hear what they were so excited about.

One man was overheard to ask,

"Did you hear what King Saul did the other day?" "What, what!" the rest of the men almost shouted. Overhearing that great excitement in the men's voices, I crept even nearer. He said, "Well, it was like this . . . . the other day King Saul was plowing in his father's field with a yoke of oxen. At noon he came out of the field to eat his noon meal. He heard a strange sound from a group of men gathered there in Gibeah . . . . there were sounds of mourning coming from the group. Due to curiosity as to what was happening among those men Saul drew near. He saw that they were crying. He thought that such action on their part was extremely odd, so he asked them, "What's the problem?" The men in the group quickly informed him that a leader in the Ammonite army whose name was Nahash had led his army against the Israelite town of Jabesh Gilead and besieged it. Saul knew that Jabesh Gilead was a small town with few fighting men to defend it. The men of the group said, "The citizens of Jabesh Gilead feel helpless and are trying to bargain with Nahash. They are saying to Nahash, 'Make a treaty with us instead of destroying our town and its citizens, and we will be subject to you.' Nahash's reply was, 'I will make a treaty with your town only on the condition that my men gouge out the right eye of all of you. I know how you Israelites feel about a person with such a handicap . . . . you feel that it is a great disgrace.' The leaders of Jabesh Gilead made a counter bargain . . . 'Give us seven days to send the message about this to the tribes of Israel asking for help. If no help comes to us within seven days, then we will surrender to you.' A bit later he heard one of them say, 'We citizens of Gibeah have just received their message.'"

The way I overheard the story was that Saul became very, very angry over the situation. He killed his yoke of oxen and cut the carcases into pieces. He sent the pieces by messengers to all the areas of Israel and Judah with the message, "This is what will be done to the oxen of anyone who does not follow Saul and Samuel." Those who received Saul's message probably said to themselves, "Hey, at last we've got a 'take charge' person who is ready and willing to lead us into battle . . . we'll be glad to follow him." Also, no doubt Saul's threat put the fear of the Lord into the hearts of the people of Israel and Judah. As a result every able bodied man rapidly reported to Saul for military service. Quickly taking command of those recruits, he led them in the march toward Jabesh Gilead. In the meantime he told the messenger who had brought them the news to return and tell the citizens of the besieged town that by noon on the following day they would be saved from their attackers. Receiving that message the men of Jabesh Gilead resorted to a military strategy of their own; they sent word to the Ammonites that on the following day they would surrender to them. They knew that the soldiers of the Ammonite army on hearing such a message would let down their guard, a fact that would benefit Saul's army. Saul assessed the strength of his quickly acquired army and found that there were three hundred thousand men of Israel and thirty thousand men of Judah present and ready to march to the aid of Jabesh Gilead. He gave orders to his army to march rapidly toward their goal. During the darkness of that night he separated his army into three divisions in order to attack the Ammonite army on three sides. Just before dawn he led his army in a surprise attack on the enemy; the men of his new army fought as valiantly as though they were all well trained soldiers. The result of the attack was that the few Ammonites who were not slaughtered fled away with no two of them together.

In the jubilation of the moment some of Saul's soldiers asked, "Where are those citizens who sneered at Saul when he was made king? Let's find those traitors and put them to death." I was proud to hear of Saul's response, "No one shall be put to death today, for this day the Lord has rescued Israel!" When my young ears overheard what our new king said, I thought to myself, "He is a great king; I'm so proud of him." About that time one of my big brothers who was allowed to sit with the men and listen to their conversation spied me and started toward me with the obvious intent of giving me a slap across the face or even worse, that is, several hard punches to my body. When I saw him heading in my direction I ran like a frightened desert rabbit.

Samuel the prophet was obviously well pleased with Saul's victory over the Ammonites at Jabesh Gilead. He sent word throughout the land for all Israelites to come to Gilgal for the purpose of reaffirming Saul as king. No doubt not only Samuel but all the people of Israel and Judah were rejoicing over Saul's victory. A fledging kingdom had proved to the nations around them that now they had a king like other nations, one who knew how to lead his people to a great victory over a strong enemy. During the time of great jubilation over Saul's victory Samuel invited all the people of the new kingdom to assemble in Gilgal for a great celebration in which the people would have an opportunity to reaffirm Saul as King of Israel and Judah. Also, it was to be a spiritual celebration, a time of thanksgiving to the Lord for giving them such a great king and a time of rejoicing over his first victory in combat. They sacrificed peace or fellowship offerings to the Lord. At the conclusion of the sacred part of the celebration Saul and the members of his newly organized army had a time of military celebration over the great victory over the Ammonites.

When the jovial part of the celebration was over, Samuel spoke to the assembled crowd. He seized the opportunity to address the great assembly of the people of Israel, an address in which he shared with those present his farewell thoughts. He told them, "I have listened to everything you said to me and have set a king over you. Now you have a king as your leader. As for me, I am old and gray, and my sons are here with you. I have been your leader from my youth until this day. Here I stand. If you have something to say against me, say it here in the presence of the Lord and King Saul, his anointed. I ask you, whose ox have I taken? Whose donkey have I taken (stolen)? Whom have I cheated? Whom have I oppressed? From whose hand have I accepted a bribe to make me shut my eyes? If I have done any of these things I shall make it right." Those in the audience shouted out, "You have not cheated or oppressed us. You have not taken anything from anyone's hand." Samuel reminded them that the

Lord and Saul, the anointed king, were witnesses to what they said.

During his final public appearance among the children of Israel Samuel preached aother great sermon to the people. In it he reminded them how God had empowered Moses to lead their forefathers out of slavery in the land of Egypt; how during the years that followed God led them eventually into the Promised Land; and how God enabled them to take over the land of Canaan as their home land. Then he reminded them of those times when they sinned greatly by turning away from obedience to the Lord Jehovah and turned to the idols of the land; how that action brought disaster on them; and how the people were brought to their knees before the one true God who forgave them. Samuel then commissioned them and their new King to be obedient followers of the Lord Jehovah. If they were obedient, the Lord would prosper them.

Then, he brought his message back to that present point in history. "When you heard about Nahash the Ammonite besieging Jabesh Gilead you did not turn to God as your leader but insisted on following an earthly king. Well, here he is . . . .King Saul. If you and your king follow God, well and good! But let me caution you, if you fail to be obedient followers of the Lord Jehovah or King Saul fails to do so, God's hand will be against you."

Suddenly he redirected their thoughts by saying, "Here and now I am going to show you what an evil thing you did by demanding to have a king to rule over you. As you know we are in the season when the wheat is ripe unto harvest. I am going to call on God to send thunder and rain upon your wheat fields which will ruin your harvest." That jarred them into a state of true repentance. They earnestly called on Samuel to "pray to your God on behalf of your servants so that we may not die, for we have added to all our former and present sins this present evil of asking to have a king to rule over us."

Samuel replied that sin would be at his door if he failed to pray for them which was another way of saying, "Yes, I shall pray that the Lord will forgive you. Listen to my advice: Fear the Lord and serve Him faithfully with all your heart . . . . remember what great things He has done for you. If you persist in doing evil both you and your king will be swept away."

The things I heard from the lips of my father and his neighbors that evening as they sat in front of my family's tent were very valuable lessons to me. Those things they said that night gave me a mental picture of what happened on that day of great celebration in which the new king who had just led the Israelites victoriously into battle was being reaffirmed as king of the nation of Israel and in which the great prophet Samuel gave his farewell address to the nation. What I heard from the lips of those men who were huddled in that group that evening ended with Samuel's warning that if the people of our nation turned against the Lord Jehovah and began to follow other gods that the Lord would visit His punishment upon them. Those words greatly influenced my mind and heart so that years later when I was serving King Saul I remembered how he began his reign in favor with God and man.

Then my mind returned to the present time when he behaved so erratically, often looking with hatred toward me and even expressing that hatred by throwing his javelin at me. In order to give him the benefit of doubt I told myself that at times he was beset by emotional outbursts for which he was not responsible. I sincerely hoped that what I said was true.

CHAPTER 8

KING SAUL IN "HOT WATER"

As stated earlier in my "off hours" while in my role as armor bearer to King Saul I reminisced about life back home in the tent of my father Jesse. I thought about another occasion when as a small lad I eavesdropped on more of the evening conversations among my father and several of the nearby shepherds. Oh, the things I heard, or more correctly 'overheard', on those long evenings when the nearby shepherds and farmers gathered in front of my family's tent for fellowship and hot tea. I noticed that they seemed to like that tea, but it was so strong and bitter that I didn't like it at all. Let me hasten to say that I was never included in the group of tea drinking men gathered there. I learned about the taste of that strong tea by slipping back into the tent where the ladies of the family were brewing it, and, when they were not looking, I tasted some of it. I decided that if a taste for that stuff was required to be a man I just might never 'make the grade'!"

Well, back to what I was about to say .... some of the strangest news was being shared by those who had just arrived from the area near Micmash, a small town in the Bethel hill country. I heard one of those men talking over the hum of the conversation of the other men. He said, "I met a shepherd who had just passed by some soldiers who said that they were under the leadership of our new king, King Saul himself. That shepherd said that of the three thousand soldiers whom King Saul had selected two thousand men were to serve with him, while the other thousand men were to serve with his son, Jonathan. That soldier said that the two groups were scouting out the area looking for Philistine outposts. He went on to say that King Saul's son, Jonathan, was very young to have the responsibility for leading a thousand troops but that the King felt that his son could best be trained in military tactics by 'on the job training'. That soldier went on to tell the shepherd who was the contact person that young Jonathan soon got some experience, for he and his men came upon a Philistine outpost at Geba and proceeded to attack it. That soldier said that what happened could best be likened to a fellow knocking over a bee hive causing bees to come swarming after him. What that soldier said in essence was 'the fat is in the fire now'! When the head of the Philistine army heard how his outpost had been attacked by a group of Israelite soldiers, he became very, very angry. He let the people of all the area know that what that group of soldiers of the army of Israel had done to his men in their outpost had caused the army of Israel to be a 'stench to the Philistines'. That soldier went on to say that King Saul had the trumpet blown throughout the land to summon the men of Israel to come immediately to Gilgal to the aid of King Saul. That soldier went on to tell me, 'The reason you see such confusion is due to the fact that all of the able bodied men of Israel dropped what they were doing and came running to the defense of their country against the Philistine army."

For a while there wasn't a word spoken by my father and the men who were sitting in a huddle in front of our tent. By this time they had graduated from drinking to smoking their water pipes. I began to get nervous for fear that in this quiet time when they seemed to be meditating on the exciting news which they had just heard from one of their group they just might take notice that I had sneaked up close behind them with the obvious intention of eavesdropping on their conversation. I practically froze with neither sound nor movement coming from me. Finally, they appeared to come out of the fog of such earth shaking news and back to the present moment. Finally they turned to the neighbor who had brought that very interesting news to them and asked, "Is there anything more that you learned from that soldier whom you met as you passed through that area?" Obviously delighted that he appeared to be the only one with a current news event, he became almost dramatic as he continued with the news concerning King Saul and his army. "Yes, there is more which that soldier said." I noticed that the men in the group scarcely breathed until he continued with his story. "That soldier told me that when the men of Israel had assembled at the appointed spot, they looked across the way to the location of the Philistine army . . . and what a sight appeared before their gaze! In the distance they saw that the Philistine army had assembled three thousand chariots with six thousand charioteers. What an awesome sight that was! Then they looked a bit further into the distance and saw foot soldiers by the droves . . . . too many to count, for they were as numerous as the sand of the seashore. When the new recruits of Israel's army saw how critical their situation was, their hearts seemed to freeze within them. Suddenly in great fear they scattered like scared rabbits. Some hid in caves, some in thickets, some among large rocks scattered along the way, some in pits, and some even in old dry cisterns. Others fled beyond the Jordan River to the land of Gad and Gilead." There was an almost audible gasp among the men huddled there in front of my father's tent. Then there was another moment of silence which occurred among the members of his little audience. I began to wonder how much of what that soldier had told our shepherd neighbor was true and how much had been "interpreted" and passed on as "truth". There was no way of knowing, but whether it was total truth or truth spliced with fiction I didn't know and really didn't care, because what I heard ('overheard') was spine tingling.

There was another period of silence in which the shepherd story teller seemed to be resting his voice. Then, without any prodding from his small audience, he began again. "My soldier friend said that King Saul remained steadfast in his place even when he saw his new recruits fleeing at the sight of that huge Philistine army. His chosen group of two thousand trained men remained with their leader even though they were 'quaking with fear'. For seven days he and his two thousand soldiers waited for the prophet Samuel to arrive as he had promised that he would. King Saul knew that Samuel was a man of God and was able through the power of the Lord to bring order out of chaos. Early on the seventh day Samuel had not arrived on the scene at the scheduled time he had promised. King Saul saw that his men had been restless during those seven days but had obediently remained with him awaiting the arrival of Samuel. Obviously they entertained the faith that Samuel, the prophet of God who had called down a rain storm on their fields of ripe grain a short while before, could call down from the Lord Jehovah destruction on the Philistine army after he led them in a religious sacrifice. Realizing that Samuel had not yet appeared on the seventh day at the appointed hour, they seemed to have lost hope of help from him. Saul saw that they were beginning to forsake him."

"What was King Saul to do?" Suddenly he issued a command, "Bring to me the burnt offering and the fellowship peace offering." Then Saul assumed the sacred role of a prophet/priest and began offering up the two religious sacrifices unto God. Hardly had he finished the religious service when he saw the prophet Samuel arriving. After their greeting of one another, Samuel, who by this time had smelled the sweet odor of the sacrifice, sternly asked, "What have you done?" That soldier told me that King Saul began to stutter and to stammer as he tried to make excuses for his usurping Samuel's sacred role of priest whose role it was to offer sacrifices unto the Lord Jehovah. "Brother Samuel, it was like this; you were later arriving than the hour that you said you would be here at which time you were to offer the two sacrifices unto God to seek the Lord Jehovah's favor on our army. My soldiers were beginning to flee the scene even as the raw recruits had done earlier. I knew that I had to do something that would stop their forsaking me and leaving me helpless before the mighty arm of the Philistines." King Saul had failed to maintain the "separation of church and state," that is, he as a secular ruler had assumed power over the sacred. "What was I to do, Samuel?" The elderly Samuel answered in a thunderous voice which was overheard by King Saul's soldiers, "You acted foolishly; you have not kept the command which the Lord your God gave you!" It was reported that King Saul's face turned ashen gray when he heard Samuel say that. Samuel continued, "If you had kept His command, He would have established your kingdom over Israel for all time to come. But now your kingdom will not be a lasting one. The Lord has sought out a man who has a heart that is fixed on the Lord Jehovah, whose mind is stayed on the will of Almighty God. Such a man God has appointed to be the leader of His chosen people. He has done this because you have not kept His command." That soldier who reported this information to the passing shepherd who in turn reported to me what the prophet Samuel said to King Saul advised me that it surely would not be wise for one of the soldiers who overheard the conversation between Samuel and Saul or for anyone to whom it had been repeated to be the source by which it becomes known to the people of Israel. It would not bode well for any person in the kingdom of Israel to spread the story of the conversation between Samuel and King Saul. More especially King Saul's reaction to the words of rebuke by the priest/prophet Samuel to him, that is, how King Saul's face turned an ashen color at the words which Samuel spoke to him. The king's spirit seemed to depart from him. He suddenly looked old beyond his years."

From the time of the patriarchs and onward actions which were in the realm of the religious were not to be usurped by those of the secular world. It was understood that God's hand was on the prophet/priests just as they were on the king whom God had anointed.

When the shepherd who had shared all this news with the small group of men assembled there in front of my father Jesse's tent that evening had finally finished telling what he had seen and heard that day in his daily rounds among the neighboring shepherds, he became silent. One by one each of those assembled there in front of my father's tent that evening rose and made his departure. When the first one arose, shuffled his feet and appeared to be leaving the group for the evening, I silently and quickly crept from the edge of the group and slipped under the edge of the tent in order to prevent any of the elders, especially any of my older brothers who might have been in the group that evening, from being aware that I had eavesdropped on the shocking conversation that evening.

Coming out of my reverie of what had happened so many moons ago, I reverted to the present point in time. "Well," I said to myself, "that is just another piece of information that helps me to understand the nature of King Saul under whom I am now serving as armor bearer. That episode which happened between him and the prophet/priest Samuel paints another facet to the mental portrait which I was painting to myself of the characteristics of King Saul. He was obviously of an impulsive nature when he found himself in a 'tight spot' as he was on that occasion. It was clear that he was driven by fear to take hasty action when in a difficult situation, action which later revealed to be action that had not been thought through, action which seemed to meet the needs of that particular point in time, but action which showed that he had not concerned himself with the long term effects. His failure in this instance was brought to his attention in a graphic way when Samuel revealed to him the consequence of his action, that is, that his kingly dynasty would be short lived because of his sin of usurping the sacred to be used for secular purposes. Those words of Samuel obviously struck home to King Saul's heart for his face 'turned an ashen gray.'"

Little by little my memory of the past actions of the great King Saul whom I served wholeheartedly began to form a mosaic of the portrait which I was mentally painting in my mind of the kind of man he was. During the past several months when my services required me to be close to the king's throne so that at the first sign of one of his "blue moods" beginning to occur I could begin to play on my harp. I am the first to admit that I do not know how the human mind works, but never the less I was piecing together a collection of actions on the part of King Saul which caused me to know that he was not psychologically a "sound" minded person. Coming to that conclusion caused me to ask myself the following question, "Why had the Lord Jehovah selected such a person to rule over Israel???"

Chapter 9
A Poorly Equipped Army

Later on another "time off" from my daily routine in the king's palace I again found myself reminiscing about another time when I overheard my mother complaining loudly to my sisters, "Why do all those shepherds and farmers come to our home in the evenings after their day's work is done for their discussion of the news both local and national? While all those men sit out in front of our tent and talk and talk, drink tea and more tea, and smoke all those 'stinking' pipes, we women are inside working feverishly to be sure that we supply enough stuff so that my husband Jesse will appear to be a good host. I wish that Jesse were younger and could walk well enough to go to the tents of the other men for a change!" Well, that made it pretty plain to my young ears how she felt about that crowd of men gathering in front of our tent so often. I, on the other hand, was so glad that they chose to assemble in front of our tent real often for their talk sessions. I wanted so much to hear ("overhear" by eavesdropping) all the news that they shared with each other in the cool of the evenings. I had a very inquisitive mind when I was a "young sprout". I enjoyed hearing any sort of news which they might share, but especially did I enjoy any and all the news that they were sharing about my hero, King Saul.

That night in question those men had a very interesting news item about the problem which King Saul was encountering as he prepared to meet in combat the forces of the Philistine army. As usual I sneaked to a dark spot within hearing distance of the men some of whom seemed to mumble when they spoke. On this particular night a shepherd had heard from another shepherd about the plight King Saul was in. Earlier I had learned from this discussion group that Saul's men were slinking away from his command one by one. When he took a head count of his troops, he discovered that only six hundred men of the original three thousand were left under his leadership. It was heard that King Saul visibly shuddered when he learned how few men were left under his command. To make matters even worse he discovered that none of his men had weapons of any kind. I was too young at that time to understand the background as to why there were no weapons available.

Later I learned that after the Israelites' occupation of the land of Canaan many years ago they had settled down to an agricultural and sheep herding way of life. For quite a while the Philistines and Ammonites were at peace with the people of Israel. The people of those two nations pursued some of the more lowly occupations such as serving as blacksmiths. Those of that trade were so numerous and their prices were so competitive that the Israelites did not bother to dabble in that type of occupation. Before the Israelites realized it they were totally dependent on blacksmiths of those two nations. Because of the generally peaceful condition that existed in the land of Palestine, the Israelite citizens had not felt a need for weapons. What a terrible thing it was for King Saul to learn that those six hundred soldiers left under his command had no weapons of any kind with which to fight the enemy! The shepherd telling that story to the other men asked, "Can you imagine how scared the King was to learn that he was going to be forced to go into battle with one of the raiding parties of the Philistines with not a single weapon of war among his small group of soldier?" He added that only King Saul and his son Jonathan had proper weapons of warfare.

"Don't stop there . . . .go ahead and tell us what our poor king did when he had to face a well equipped outpost of Philistine soldiers." "Well, it seems that King Saul was sitting in the shade of a pomegranate tree with the soldiers of his rag-tag army scattered around him. They had been walking a long way toward the place where the king expected that they would encounter trouble with the Philistines. Naturally, they were very tired. I guess they were so tired that they were half asleep. Anyway, they did not notice that young Jonathan and his armor bearer had slipped away from the group. Much later it was learned that Jonathan and the armor bearer had decided on their own to do a little spying in the area around where they had heard that there was a Philistine outpost. Well, after they had gone a little ways, they came to a narrow passageway between two cliffs, one on either side. As they walked along that pathway they began to hear voices. The two of them figured that they were about to encounter the soldiers in the Philistine outpost. Jonathan quickly planned his strategy. He turned to his armor bearer and said, 'Come, let us go over to the outpost of those uncivilized fellows. Just maybe the Lord will act in our behalf. After all, nothing can prevent the Lord from saving, whether it be by many or by few.' The poor armor bearer was probably trembling in his sandals, but he was very loyal to Jonathan. He simply said, 'Do all you have in mind. Go ahead; I am with you heart and soul.' 'Well, here is my strategy. We shall cross over toward the Philistines whom we hear chattering, and we shall let them see us. That will startle them. They will see that there are only the two of us. If they say to us, wait until we come over to you, we shall do just that. However, if they tell us to come up to them, we shall climb up the cliff to them. That will be a sign that the Lord Jehovah has given them into our hands.' A few moments later the Philistines cried out, 'Look, the Hebrews are climbing out of their holes in which they were hiding!' Then they shouted to Jonathan and his armor bearer, 'Come up to us, and we will teach you a lesson!' Jonathan said to his armor bearer, 'Climb up the cliff after me; don't be afraid, for the Lord is going to give us the victory over them through the two of us.' Laboriously, Jonathan climbed hand and foot up the cliff with his trusty armor bearer right behind him. When finally they got to the top of the cliff they came face to face with those sneering Philistines. Like a mad man Jonathan started swinging his sword as he came face to face with them, and his armor bearer was doing likewise by using Jonathan's spear which he had being carrying. Before the sneering Philistines knew what was happening, the small area around the outpost was littered with dead Philistines, some 20 of them to be exact. The remainder of the Philistine soldiers fled the scene ahead of the sword swinging Jonathan and the spear jabbing armor bearer and raced as fast as their legs could carry them to the other outposts and to the main part of their army. The fearful story that those fleeing soldiers breathlessly told their peers must have put the fear of the Lord in their pagan hearts, for the ground literally shook as they fled back toward the land of the Phlistines."

"The way I see it is that the King's son, young Jonathan, is a very brave soldier who is a man of our God, the Lord Jehovah," he said as he ended his recounting of that piece of news. There where I was crouching in the dark shadows behind the circle of men gathered in front of my father Jesse's tent I almost shouted 'Amen' but caught myself just in time to prevent making a sound that would have revealed my hiding place. I said to myself, 'Our king's son is a young man whom I greatly respect. I would love to get to get to know him better and to become a friend of his.' This occurred before Jonathan and I had had the opportunity to get to know each other and later to become very close friends.

The shepherd who was relating to the others in the group the awesome thing that had happened went on to say that King Saul asked who of his small group of soldiers had caused that great victory. After mustering his men he discovered that there were two of his men missing, Jonathan and his armor bearer. Quickly the King issued an order that he and his men were to pursue the fleeing Philistine army even though none of his men had weapons with which to fight. Pursue the Philistines they did and what a victory was brought to pass. The Philistine army was in total confusion . . . . they were striking each other with their swords and killing each other. To King Saul's surprise there came running toward him Hebrew men who had been serving in the Philistine army; they were shouting that they were coming over to join King Saul's army. Also, when the Israelite soldiers who earlier had slipped away from King Saul's army due to their fear of going into battle against the Philistines without any sort of armor and had fled to the hill country, came rushing back to join the army of the Israelites in order to chase the fleeing Philistine soldiers. Not only had their bravery returned, but there was a strong likelihood that they wanted to get in on the taking of booty from the fleeing Philistine soldiers. What a battle that was on that day! It moved on to an area called Beth Aven." When the shepherd who had shared this wonderful news to the group and had finally become silent, the shepherds and farmers who were gathered there that night in that small huddle were beside themselves. "King Saul is a mighty king! Look what he accomplished with only a small group of men and with no weapons of war. What a great fighter!" "Wait just a moment; let us give praise where praise is due. Remember, it was young Jonathan who started the ball rolling with his brave attack on that Philistine outpost. Let's give him praise also." "Yea, and amen and amen to that!" Then I remembered what some of them had said on an earlier evening how it was that Jonathan was very young and had no military training, how King Saul said that the best military training for his son would be 'on the job trainin'. Well, the king seems to be right about that."

It was getting late, so the crowd of men gathered there that night began leaving and going over the hills and through the hollows back to their own tents. I couldn't help but notice that they left with a smile on their faces and a happier "Good Night" than usual.

While watching the neighbors leave, I said to myself, "One of these days I'll be big enough and old enough to be allowed to be a soldier. I believe that I could be a good soldier like the king's son, Jonathan, is. He sounds like quite a guy!" True, I did meet him on that great day when I slew the giant, Goliath. I recall the fact that he took off his tunic and had me to put it on and how he gave me with his armor. Thus, I had already realized that he was a generous person and now I realized that he was a fearless and powerful fighter in spite of the fact that he was very young. It revealed to me the fact that if the Lord Jehovah is on a person's side, that person can be almost invincible. Yes, I made a mental note right then and there as I was scurrying back through the dark shadows into the safety of the inside of the family tent that one of those days ahead I wanted to cultivate a friendship with young Jonathan, a young man in whom there seemed to be no guile.

Suddenly I snapped out of my reminiscing over the past and came back to the present. My great desire to become a friend of

King Saul's son, young Jonathan, had begun to be realized. We had had several opportunities to be together to talk about our views of life. It was uncanny how similar our outlook on life was, for he came from a king's palace and I came from a lowly sheep herder's family. Out past ways of life were so very different that earlier it had seemed impossible that we would ever have the opportunity to be able to come together for time of sharing our thoughts about life in general and our on personal thoughts in particular. I was one to be slow to take people into my confidence. That was probably due to the way my big brothers treated me. They were always belittling me about anything I did or said. Whatever I did was a source of criticism and ridicule as far as they were concerned. Their treatment of me in my earlier days had had a profound effect on my relationship with people in general.

On that day when I was called from minding my sheep in order to take from my father's "larder" food for my older brothers who were serving in Saul's army and to take an assortment of food to the quartermaster of the army, I was delighted to have an opportunity to go to the battle front to see how soldiers fight our nation's enemy .... in this case the Philistine. When in my boyish way I had begun to ask my brothers questions about the way of warfare and later posing questions to other soldiers, one of my big soldier brothers rebuked me severally by saying that I had a conceited mind. I recall momentarily pausing to analyze what he had said about my being "conceited". That was news to me, for I, a lowly shepherd lad, had never thought that I had anything about which to be conceited. I admit that I had a lot of curiosity about things about me with which I came in contact and about the modus operandi of people with whom I had come in contact, but conceited I was not! In the case of young Jonathan I admit that I did analyze his conduct and his character which shaped his conduct. I discovered that he was a man whose character was without flaw. He was certainly not conceited . . . anything but . . . and he was not selfish, for on that day when I first met him in his father's tent there on the battle field he proved to me that he was unselfish to the core when he literally gave me the shirt off his back, his tunic that is. Later when we became fast friends I judged him to be a person in whom there was no guile. I loved him as a brother. In the light of my relationship with my big brothers I guess I would have to say that I loved him more than a brother.

But back to what was said on that particular night when a neighboring shepherd told the assembled men there in front of my father's tent about what had happened to King Saul as pertained to his trying to wage war with an army from which the majority of soldiers had deserted and the remainder of which had no armor with which to fight the soldiers of a Philistine army outpost. That episode revealed to me other facets of King Saul's character. He was a man of great bravery! He dared to go into battle with a great shortage of manpower and a total lack of armor. Also, he was a man of determination, for he stuck to his goal of protecting Israel against the Philistine army outpost in spite of the impossible situation in which he found himself. Yes, that episode revealed to me other facets of the character and person of our great King Saul.

Chapter 10
A Taste of Honey

What had happened to me? There I was again reminiscing about the past. What was causing me to do so much of that? Was it pure boredom with my job as armor bearer? Was a touch of homesickness causing it? Was it subconscious desire to be out on the field of battle with King Saul? Was it due to a question in my subconscious thoughts as to why King Saul had not yet allowed me to go into battle with him in spite of the fact that I had accomplished something that none of his soldiers had done, that is, I had slain the that huge hulk of a man known as Goliath, from whom all of his trained soldiers had not dared to do? Well, whatever the cause I found myself reminiscing about the past when I was back in the family tent of Jessie, my father. But back to what had fascinated my boyish mind . . . . a time when the "huddle bunch" as my mother referred to the tea drinking group of men who were accustomed to gather in front of our family's tent many nights per week. It had been mutually agreed by them that since Jesse was very old and could not get about much anymore that it would be the kind thing to do to meet in front of his tent every time instead of taking turns among the tents of those men who were usually met for their evenings of enjoyment of sharing news of the day with one another. That agreement seemed to suit the men just fine with everyone with the exception of Jesse's wife, my mother. Who felt obligated to serve the hot and bitter tasting beverage which they referred to as "tea". Although she had been heard by the family members to complain about the extra work, she was secretly happy over the arrangement concerning the place of meeting. She realized that these men were paying respect and honor to her husbacn Jesse by agreeing to meet there every time so that he could be privileged to be part of their "bull sessions", for he greatly enjoyed them.

They usually sat in silence until one in the group suddenly remembered that he had a news item that he had not yet shared with the group. When he began telling that juicy tidbit of news, all eyes turned in his direction and all ears strained to hear what that person had to say. So excited were all of the members of the group concerning the news of Saul's great victory over the Philistine outpost were the men that they could hardly contain themselves. The Israelites had become a people of peace during the past decades, a people who had not been involved in military combat for such a long while. Thus, the news of King Saul's great victory in his recent skirmish with the Philistine soldiers in their outpost. It was the greatest news which any of them had had with which to entertain the thoughts of those in the "huddle bunch". As usual there was one at the periphery of the group who, though unseen by the men in the group, was listening with all of his hearing capacity. On the particular night of which I was thinking, the group of sheep herders and farmers had reassembled in front of Jesse's tent with the hope that there might be more news about King Saul's military prowess. The agreement each time in that location seemed to be very pleasing to everyone with the exception of Jesse's wife (and David's mother) who felt obligated to serve the hot and bitter tasting beverage which they referred to as 'tea'. Although she had been heard by the family members to complain about the extra work involved with that place of meeting, she was secretly happy over the arrangement concerning that location for their "huddles". She realized that those men were paying respect and honor to her husband Jesse by agreeing to meet there each time so that he could be privileged to be a part of their 'bull sessions', for he greatly enjoyed them.

On the occasion of this particular gathering of the men I had just arrived with my flock of sheep back at the family's sheep fold after several days on the outlying range and had safely secured them within the crude fence surrounding the area which was alluded to as "the fold, I came rushing into the family tent, grabbed a piece of bread which had just been baked on the hot rocks at the back of the tent. Like any boy I was always hungry, but especially was I hungry on that occasion, for I had worked up a good appetite while herding my sheep over the miles of grazing land for the last few days. Lucky me! In the gathering darkness of the approaching night hours I could see the men of the "bull session" group coming one by one from all directions. It wasn't long before it was dark enough for me to slip unnoticed into a spot back of the cluster of men. Above the hum of the quiet conversation among them I could hear one of them asking, "Does anyone have any late news from the battle front?" Finally one man slowly spoke up and said, "I had occasion a couple of days ago to be over in the area near Beth Aven and met a soldier who was sent on an errand by one of King Saul's officers. I chatted a bit with him and before long he began telling me some things that happened the day when the army of Saul was pursuing the fleeing Philistines. He said that the King was so intent on producing a complete slaughter of the members of the Philistine army that he proclaimed an edict, that is, he announced that none of his men should take time to eat anything until nightfall when it would be too dark to carry the battle further. He said that anyone who took time to eat anything before dark would be put to death. His followers heard him and acted accordingly. As the army of Israel went through a forest there was laying on the ground a bee hive which obviously had been knocked from a tree to the ground. So hungry were the soldiers that it was all that they could do not to take time to taste it."

"In the meantime Saul's son, Jonathan, and his armor bearer rejoined the other soldiers. As they passed through the forest they came across the bee hive. Jonathan stuck the tip of his spear into the hive causing the honey to ooze out onto his spear. He licked the tip of his spear, removing from it all the honey that had clung to it. Immediately, the honey was absorbed into his body, and he felt revived and was able to fight the enemy in a great way. One of the soldiers said to Jonathan, 'I regret to tell you that what you just did, that is, your eating a bit of that honey was off limits. While you were not present your father, King Saul, gave an edict that none of us were to eat anything until we had routed the Philistines at the end of the day.' 'Well, my father was wrong to make that edict. You can see that my eyes have a brighter look out of them. Would not the slaughter of the enemies been even greater if all of our soldiers had looted some of the food left behind by the Philistines and eaten it on the chase after the fleeing enemy?'

'At the end of the day when the edict was over our soldiers took some of the sheep, cattle, and calves and hurriedly slew them on the ground and immediately ate them blood and all. Some of Saul's soldiers said to him, 'Look, your men are sinning, for they are eating blood with the meat (from the early times Israelites had been taught that it was a sin to eat meat from which the blood had not been properly drained).' The King had told them to take the carcasses of the animals which they had slain and drape them over huge rocks so as to drain the blood before they ate the flesh. 'You men have sinned by eating the blood of the animals.'

'That soldier told me that King Saul did something that he had never done before. He built an altar unto God. The soldier said to me that he supposed that the King was trying to gain the favor of Almighty God on his military efforts. When he had completed a hasty religious service, he commanded his soldiers to chase after the Philistines in the darkness of night and seek to find those who were trying to hide from them. 'Let us slaughter every one of them.' 'Wait a moment,' interrupted the Israelite priest who was with the army, 'and let us inquire of the Lord whether it is best that we go after the fleeing enemy.' King Saul directly asked of God whether his army would be successful in that venture. He waited and waited, but God gave him no answer to his question. The soldier told me that soon King Saul decided that the reason that God did not give him an answer was that someone in his army had sinned. He announced that the one who was found to be guilty of disobedience to his edict, an edict that carried with it the penalty of death, would surely be slain . . . no matter who it was . . . 'even my son Jonathan!' Not one of his soldiers came forward to confess his guilt. 'All right, we shall find out who is the guilty one. All of you soldiers stand over there, and my son Jonathan and I will stand over here.' Obediently the soldiers took their places as requested. Then King Saul prayed.

'Give me the right answer as to where the guilt lies.' Eventually it was revealed that the guilt lay on his and Jonathan's side. The King commanded, 'Cast the lot between me and my son Jonathan.' The lot fell on Jonathan."

"The King said to his son Jonathan, 'Tell me what you have done.' 'I merely tasted a little of the honey on the end of my staff.... and now, you are going to kill me for that!' 'May God deal with me ever so severely if you do not die, Jonathan.'" Hearing that I said to myself that I didn't believe that my father, Jesse, would have treated me that way. But in the first place I don't believe that my father would have made an impulsive decision for his men not to eat and thus lose strength for the battle. It seemed to me that our King Saul had acted before he had thought through the curse with which he had accompanied his impulsive decision. Well, I guess no man is perfect even a great man like King Saul .... and so those thoughts raced through my mind when I heard that awful pronouncement on Jonathan by his father, King Saul."

"The shepherd who was relaying the news to the crowd which had gathered before my father's tent that night went on to say that suddenly the soldiers spoke up as one man and said sternly to King Saul, 'We must not put to death Jonathan who has brought about such a great victory for Israel against the Philistines. No, indeed, he shall not die. Not a hair on his head will fall to the ground, for he accomplished today's great victory with the help of the Lord!' There in my hiding place in back of the cluster of shepherds I made a mental note that King Saul surely lost face before his men that day .... and I bet that he was so glad that he did. He had taken an oath before his men that anyone who disobeyed his edict not to take time to eat as they pursued the enemy would be killed. When the one who unwittingly disobeyed his order was revealed to be his son Jonathan, no doubt King Saul knew that he had to carry out the curse he had earlier pronounced, or his word would not hold weight before his men ... BUT how his heart must have been broken to have to face such a dilemma as that! Yes, he lost face when the men of his army refused to allow him to carry out the curse he had pronounced on them earlier, but his son was saved by their doing so. I made a mental note that King Saul was impulsive and spoke before he thought."

"The shepherd who had heard all of this from one of King Saul's soldiers said that then and there a decision was made not to pursue the Philistine army any further. Consequently the members of his volunteer army disbanded and those of his regular army returned to the palace to be near the King until another crisis occurred. I thought to myself as I quietly retreated from my hiding place and slipped back into the family tent for the evening, 'How I wish that someday I could be a soldier. I would like to be a brave soldier like King Saul's son, young Jonathan. Well, unfortunately all my family thinks that I am good for is to tend the family's sheep. Some day, some day".... and I drifted off to sleep and dreamed of being a very brave soldier who fought the enemies of Israel.

About that time someone called across the court room to me and jarred me out of my reverie of the news I had heard during my eavesdropping on my father's and his friends' conversation a year or so ago. As always I was trying to characterize King Saul by taking bits and pieces of things I had heard concerning his actions and forming from those actions different facets to the true personality and character of King Saul. Unfortunately the episode which happened a year or so earlier and brought back to my mind through one of my times of reminiscing about the past revealed a facet of the character of my much loved King Saul that was not at all flattering .... impulsiveness resulting in rash decisions which was to play a great part in his later life.

CHAPTER 11
AN ODD DOWRY

The shepherd boy's slaying of the giant Goliath and the resulting victory over the Philistine army caused this young shepherd lad to be able to bask in the limelight not only of the King but also of the people of Israel. As is often the case I discovered that living in the limelight fades all too quickly. As mentioned earlier the ladies of Israel created a "hit song" with which to honor me, the young slayer of the great giant. They formed a large (and loud) chorus whose pleasure it was to sing a song of praise about me following my spectacular victory over Goliath. The chorus went something like this:

> "Saul has slain his thousands
> and David his tens of
> thousands."

In those days the most rapid and effective mode of communicating a news item from one part of the nation to another was to tell one person a bit of news and soon it was wafted on the wings of the wind all across the nation of Israel. So it was with the song which the ladies' choir chanted at the top of their voices. Unfortunately, the news trickled back to King Saul. At first he was glad to hear such praise and adoration being sung to me, a young shepherd lad, concerning my great victory over Goliath.

As time passed and the excitement of the episode of the "giant slaying" and the subsequent great victory of the army of Israel over the Philistines had died down, King Saul began to analyze what had happened in the preceding days. There was at first the stalemate between his army and that of the Philistines. Day after day that huge fellow whose name was Goliath had taunted the army of Israel with the challenge, 'Send one of your soldiers out to fight with me; whichever one of us wins will cause his army to win the victory over the other nation's army, a nation which will become subservient to the other nation. Yes, day after day that stalemate had continued. Next in the sequence of events which took place in the preceding days there had appeared on the scene that brash young shepherd lad who declared that it was a shame and disgrace for the army of the Lord Jehovah to have to endure the verbal abuse of that huge giant, Goliath. He asked, "Why doesn't one of you soldiers of the army of Israel accept the giant's challenge and go out and fight him?" Neither the king nor the soldiers of Israel gave an answer to the young lad's question. "Well, then, I guess it's up to me," said the young lad. Casting aside the offer of King Saul's armor, he stepped out onto the field of battle in front of all the soldiers of Israel and marched resolutely toward the giant armed with only a sling and a shepherd's staff. As he passed over the little brook on his way to fight the giant, he stooped down to pick up some smooth stones in the brook with which with which to "load" his weapon, a simple sling, Having done that, he continued to march directly toward that big hulk of a man, Goliath. Suddenly he began whirling the sling containing a rock over and around and around over his head and then let go of the small stone. A gasp went up from the soldiers of Israel when suddenly that stone from the sling found its mark in the only unprotected spot on the body of the giant. So great was the blow on his forehead that Goliath tumbled face forward to the ground. Young David quickly ran forward, grabbed Goliath's sword and cut off the giant's head. Yes, that was a wonderful moment for all to witness. Next, in the musings of King Saul there arose in his mind the song that the ladies of Israel had sung. Suddenly he said to himself, "Hey, they paid much greater praise to that young shepherd lad, David, than to me. They are crediting me with the slaying of only a thousand enemy soldiers and praising David by singing that he slew ten thousand of the enemy. Not only is that not true, but it shows that they are more fond of young David than they are of me. I don't like that one little bit!" From that time on a burning jealousy arose in the heart and mind of King Saul concerning me, a simple young shepherd lad who against all odds had been able to slay that huge giant, Goliath. "I need a way to get rid of him," he mused. "However, if I should slay David, the whole country would turn against me. No, I can't do that. I must figure out a way in which he will be slain by the Philistine army so that his death will not reflect on me."

At the time when King Saul was having such feelings of jealousy, I was too young to under-stand the meaning of jealousy and its possible aftermath. Oh, to be sure, I had felt such an emotion back when I was living in the family circle. I was jealous of my big brothers who always seemed to get the choicest of the tasks which my father assigned to us on a daily basis. At that time I was too young to analyze that situation and give to it the academic title of "jealousy"; I simply knew how I felt about that situation concerning my brothers who always got important and challenging assignments of tasks and I always got the lowly task of herding the family's flock of sheep. I thought to myself, "There is no justice in the way my father handles the work assignments. I want something that's considered big and important to be my work assignment instead of always getting the lowly task of herding the sheep!" If my feelings were called "jealousy", I knew then and there that I did not like such an emotion. However, as I said earlier, I was too young to label that emotion either as held by King Saul or myself.

"'Ah, I know a good way to keep tabs on young David's actions and movements around the nation. I shall give my oldest daughter, Merab, in marriage to him. She can keep me posted on what David is thinking and doing. Also, she can get word to me concerning a time and place where I can way-lay him." With that sly plan in mind he called me into his chambers and informed me that he was going to live up to his promise to give his daughter in marriage to the person who could slay the giant. When he announced this to me, my reaction as a young lad could be interpreted in several ways: 'I don't want to marry your daughter', or I was sincerely aghast at the very idea of an unknown lad from a lowly shepherd's family such as I was to marry a young lady who was of the royal family of the king of the nation of Israel. Also, I said, '"Because of that a marriage between the two of us would never work, for she is of royal stock, and I am of the lowliest of families and, therefore, we could never be compatible." Actually, I was just being properly humble but all the while was thrilled at the idea of being able to marry the daughter of a king.

As was the custom there was an allotted time for the engagement prior to marriage, a custom so similar to the custom of a later period in history. As the day drew near for the marriage ceremony to take place, King Saul called me to his court chambers and said in effect, "Sorry about that, but I have changed my mind and am giving my daughter, Merab, to Adriel of Meholah." No doubt the news of Saul's going back on his promise to me that he would give his daughter in marriage quickly made the rounds of those in the king's court. That increased the embarrassment I felt concerning the matter. It was not a matter of a broken romance, because there had been none involved. I had scarcely laid eyes on Merab, so there was literally no love lost there. Eventually word reached the ears of Saul that his younger daughter, Michal, was in love with me and would like very much to become my bride. His reaction to that news was overheard by some of the men who had the ear of King Saul and who reported the same to me. King Saul said to himself, "Well, all right, I'll give her to David as his wife; that will enable me to carry out my promise to young David which I made to him before the slaying of Goliath, and it will please Michal, since she thinks she's in love with young David. She can be my 'plant' or 'spy' inside David's household; she can keep me informed about his schedule and advise me as to when would be a good time to do away with him."

When the king announced to me his plan to give Michal to me as my bride, I again made my little speech of not being worthy to marry the king's daughter, saying "Do you think that it is a small matter to become the king's son-in-law? I'm only a poor man and little known." In other words I was saying, "I have nothing in the way of a dowry or appreciation gift for the king." The king's match maker replied, "Don't worry about that, for the king wants no other price for your dowry for his daughter than one hundred foreskins of the Philistines." In his sly and treacherous plan the king felt that I would most likely be killed in my effort to kill one hundred Philistine soldiers."

When the king's word concerning the price for his daughter was officially relayed to me, I said to myself, "That's something that I can afford. Silver and gold or livestock I do not have, but I can surely slay one hundred Philistine soldiers and bring their foreskins to the king (that surely sounds weird, but the king is a weird person). Just think, I can soon become the son-in-law of a king. What a change from being a lowly shepherd lad. I shall be considered a part of the household of King Saul himself!"

I soon got busy with my plan to provide the requested dowry to present to King Saul for the hand of his daughter in marriage. I and my contingency of soldiers made several forays against the Philistine army. Soon not only had I killed the one hundred Philistine soldiers from whose bodies I removed their foreskins, but I went the "second mile" . . . . I and my men killed another one hundred Philistine soldiers and brought to the king their foreskins. Since he had witnesses to the agreement he had made with me concerning the condition under which his daughter would be given to me in marriage, he had to go through with his promise. Thus, I became the son-in-law of King Saul.

As time passed the king became more and more morose in the fear that I was more popular with the citizens of Israel than was he. He observed that i was winning more battles against the enemy than was any other of his officers, a fact that caused my popularity to increase. Naturally it caused King Saul's jealousy of me to increase also. I'm ashamed to say that my former love and respect for him decreased. However, I still maintained the respect for the Lord's anointed king, because I knew that my personal feelings must not allow a "rift" to occur between the two of us. He was still my king and as such I must always endeavor to treat him as the person I first thought him to be. From early childhood onward I had been taught to revere the "Lord's anointed king", a fact that caused me to put my personal fears and emotions behind me and to show reverence to him.

As was my unconscious habit, I continued to analyze the character of King Saul. Through the passing of time I came to realize that there was yet another facet to the character of King

Saul which I must add to my compilation of such facets. This facet was that jealousy was a prominent one in the picture of his total characterization. Now, don't get me wrong . . . . I did not consciously analyze the character of the king. Rather, I observed from a distance the different foibles of his total makeup which gave to me a mental picture of the one who had been anointed to be king of Israel. Since most of those facets of his personality and character were not as pleasing as they might have been, I tried to resolve that issue by saying to myself, "His 'blue moods' have caused him to be the way he is. He has a psychological problem which seems to have control of his total being. That simply means that we who are serving under him need to give him our best support."

CHAPTER 12

A FRIEND IN HIGH PLACES

My friends in the palace shared with me that King Saul had become increasingly bitter about what he perceived to be happening around him. He was becoming more and more obsessed with the idea that I was a threat to his power over the nation. My friends said that in his more morose moments he envisioned an uprising among the citizens of Israel. He perceived that there was a strong possibility that the Israelites might cause the army to turn against him and sponsor a coup d'etat. He imagined that such an uprising might be led by me. It was hard for me to understand why the king felt that way about me, for I was very, very loyal to him. I honored him as God's anointed king. I felt that he was psychotic and not really responsible for his hostility toward me.

Finally matters came to a head when King Saul's unfounded jealousy of me was brought into the open. My palace friends said that on a certain day he called into his presence his son Jonathan and his court attendants and ordered them to kill me. His attendants left the impression with him that they would be obedient to his command. Jonathan was noncommittal in replying to his father about that command. Later he drew me aside and warned me concerning his father's awful jealousy which had grown so strong that he wanted to have me killed. Jonathan said to me, "I have worked out a plan to determine if my father's command to have you killed was a real and lasting one or if it was a passing mental phase from which he has moved on in his thinking. In the meantime I want you to hide from the sight of the king's men. Tomorrow morning I shall ask my father to go for a walk with me. While we are walking in the field in which you are hiding, I shall ask my father concerning you."

As planned later Jonathan brought up the matter of Saul's command to kill me by saying to him, "Father, David has done you no wrong. He is a loyal subject. He proved that when he put his life at risk in order to slay Goliath. Please don't you do wrong by slaying him or having him slain. Why do you want to kill an innocent man, one who has done no wrong to you but who has been such a great help to you?" King Saul stood there listening to his son Jonathan making a plea on my behalf. After a few moments of meditation concerning his beloved son Jonathan's request, he turned to him and took an oath and replied, "As surely as the Lord lives, David will not be put to death." At that point Jonathan called loudly for me to appear before the king. When I had come into the presence of King Saul and Jonathan, I learned from Jonathan what had transpired. I breathed a sigh of relief, for I was so glad to be back in the good graces of King Saul, whom I greatly respected and revered in spite of his fits of anger and moody ways. What a relief it was to hear from the lips of Jonathan that the king would no longer seek my life and would expect me to continue in his service as an army officer and harp player.

Shortly after that episode the Philistine army again attacked Israel. Saul's army went out to meet the enemy. I led my battalion into battle with a vengeance. I felt that the Philistines were once again defying the nation and army of the Lord Jehovah. Therefore, I felt that I had a personal vendetta against an army that had slain so many of my fellow countrymen in the past days. My blood boiled within me due to the anger I felt toward those heathen Philistines who were once again seeking to conquer the nation of Israel, the chosen nation of the great God of Israel. I challenged the men under my command to give their all as we strove to conquer the enemy. Looking back on that occasion I realize that I fought like a "mad man" because of the intensity of my determination to cause the Philistine soldiers to flee for their lives. It worked! After battling for a few hours we saw our dream come true as concerned the portion of the Philistine army which my battalion was confronting. The soldiers of the Philistine army stopped fighting and started to run from us like frightened antelopes. Upon our return from the scene of battle my men and I, although weary from battle, were exhilarated with our great success. Later my fellow citizens came to me privately and congratulated me on the success of my battalion. They said that my men and I had far outshone the other sections of King Saul's army in the recent skirmish. Being human I was grateful to hear those remarks, but I reminded myself that the praise for the victorious outcome of the battle was due my Lord.

I recall that shortly thereafter I was called to come to King Saul's palace and play on my harp for him. Once again a great depression had descended on him. As I was playing I observed that the king looked in my direction with hatred in his eyes. Naturally I realized that he was not himself and that he might try to do harm to me. I felt that he was not responsible for his actions at that point; for it was obvious to me and to the members of the king's staff that he was not himself that severe depression had settled upon him. As the minutes moved on into hours my fingers were becoming sore from "strumming on" the strings of the harp. Also, I was growing weary and less observant of King Saul's actions. Suddenly out of the corner of my eyes I saw a javelin leaving the hand of the king and rapidly heading in my direction. In my haste to escape the approach of the oncoming javelin I jumped up, knocked over my harp and ducked to my right. I heard a thud as the point of the javelin buried itself in the wall behind where I had been seated.

When I had emotionally recovered from my narrow escape from the unsuccessful effort of King Saul to pin me to the wall behind me, I came to the realization that it was time for me to leave the king's presence. Through no fault on my part my very presence in the room with the king seemed to intensify the king's deep depression evidenced by his effort to assassinate me. I strongly suspected that his staff members had been urged to seek harm to me, and it was obvious that the king would again make a personal effort to do me harm. Therefore, for the sake of my wellbeing I slipped away from the palace under the blanket of darkness.

I had not realized how deep was the king's hatred for me, for in earlier days his hatred had seemed to be a passing thing. However, it was different this time. I was soon informed by some of the members of my own household that my movements were under the surveillance of the king's men. Some of the members of my household learned that the plan of the king's men was that they were to kill me in the morning. My wife, Michal (the daughter of King Saul), warned me that if I did not flee that very night I would be killed the next day. She greatly assisted me in escaping from my home which was being watched. She made a rope with bed coverings and let me leave through a window and down that rope to the ground. As I recall it was very dark that night as I stealthily slipped away under the blanket of darkness. Michal knew that the king's men would come into my house looking for me early the next morning. In an effort to give me time to make my escape from the local scene she took an idol shaped like a man's head from a pedestal there in the house and placed it on my bed. She took some goat's stringy hair and placed it over the head of the idol. Then she piled the bed covers on the bed.

True to the information that had been passed to Michal from the palace, there appeared at my home early the next morning a group of men whom King Saul had delegated to capture me. Michal met them at the door and told them that I was sick in bed. They glanced at the bed and were fooled by the appearance of a man lying there. They returned to the palace and told the king that I was too sick to come to the palace. "You stupid men! Go back and bring that sick son-in-law of mine on his bed to me so that I may kill him!" Those men came back to my house with the purpose of bringing me bed and all to his palace. As they examined the form on the bed they discovered Michal's ruse. She was brought into the king's presence where she stood trembling before her very angry father. "Why did you deceive me like this and send my enemy away so that he escaped?" She quickly responded, "Oh, father, I was forced to do what I did, for he said to me 'let me get away. Why should I kill you?'"

That night as I fled for my safety I knew that I had to go somewhere that Saul would not look for me. "But where could I find such a place?" I asked myself. Failing to come up with an answer to that question, I came to the conclusion that it would be good for me to seek the help of the prophet Samuel. After all he had anointed my head with oil to signify something that at that time I had not comprehended. Surely Samuel would remember me and perhaps could give me some advice as to how to escape from the death grip of King Saul. With that in mind I furtively made my way across the land to Ramah where I hoped that Samuel would be in residence. It was a happy moment when I came into the presence of that powerful representative of the Lord Jehovah. Samuel and I then went to Naioth near Ramah.

It became obvious that King Saul had spies planted throughout the land of Israel. One of them reported to the king that I was in Naioth. Soon he sent some of his henchmen over to Naioth. Before they found me they encountered Samuel standing in the midst of a group of prophets who were prophesying. God's Spirit drew Saul's men into the group and soon they were prophesying along with the prophets. One managed to get away from the group and returned to Saul to inform him as to what had happened to the delegation he had sent to capture me. Not to be outdone King Saul sent another delegation of men to capture me. They also joined the prophets and began prophesying. Again Saul was informed as to what had happened, and he sent a third group to capture me. That group also was caught up with the prophesying prophets. Having had three groups of men to fail to bring me back to him, he said to himself, "Well, I guess it is up to me to get the job done." With that he set out for Ramah to capture me. Upon his arrival he asked the people there, "Where are Samuel and David?" He was told that Samuel and I were over in Naioth of Ramah. While enroute to Naioth God's Spirit came upon him as He had come upon Saul's messengers. He went along the way to Naioth prophesying as he walked. Upon his arrival in Naioth he stripped off his robes and prophesied in Samuel's presence. He lay in that condition all that day and that night. The citizens of the area coined a phrase, "Is Saul also among the prophets?"

Through this experience of endeavoring to escape from the wrath of King Saul I came to see how great is the Lord Jehovah's protective power over those who love Him and who desire to serve Him. Never would I have dreamed what method God would choose to use in circumventing King Saul's attempts to kill me. I was amazed to see for myself how God's Spirit turned the king's messengers into a mumbling, chanting religious people who obviously were no longer concerned about their mission for the king. Even more spectacular to witness was how God's Spirit changed at least temporarily the mind and purpose of King Saul who was so bent on bringing about my demise by turning him into a prophesying "zombie". Just to stand there and witness the power of God to change people for his purpose caused me to breathe inaudibly to God, "How great thou art in all of Thy ways! You changed the wrath of King Saul and his messengers from their evil intent to commit murder into a condition of praise unto Thee!!"

Although I felt that I did not deserve having friends in high places to assist me in a very, very dark hour o my life, I rose up to call them "blessed". More especially did I quietly breathe a prayer of thanksgiving unto Almighty God for His loving protection over me when it seemed that the world had turned against me. God's great representative on earth, the prophet Samuel, stood like a protective wall around me by allowing God's Spirit to work through him to be a great visible symbol of God's divine presence protecting me in that dark hour.

CHAPTER 13
FLEEING TO A FRIEND FOR COMFORT

Yes, as I look back on my early life I can well remember the fact that I had to play "cat and mouse" with King Saul. When he caught up with me there in the presence of the prophet Samuel I was momentarily saved by God's Spirit Who caused the king to join the group of prophets, some of whom were the usual wandering band of prophets and some were the king's men who had been sent to capture me. So caught up in the frenzy of the group of prophets was he that he stripped off his royal robes and in a state of near nudity lay on the ground in a controlled state for a day and a night. That gave me time to flee from his presence. But where could I go that he would not find me? I tried to think as Saul would think about where I might hide. Then it came to me that the very last place where he would look would be in the area of the palace from which I had fled. Back to that area I returned and sought out my friend Jonathan, the king's son.

I realized that Jonathan loved his father very much and therefore saw his good characteristics. Thus, he naturally found it hard to believe that his father would do such a thing as to try to kill me. However, Jonathan loved me very much also, for he considered me to be his best friend. Earlier we had made a covenant between us that we would be true friends for life. With that in mind I determined to get in touch with him and seek his help to solve my plight. Stealthily I got word to him that I was in hiding near the palace. Jonathan came out to see me and talk with me about the situation I was in.

I asked Jonathan, "What have I done to cause your father to be so angry with me? Have I committed a crime against him? How have I wronged him that would cause him to want to kill me? Please tell me so that I can correct such a wrong." Jonathan looked at me in great surprise. "Whatever gave you such an idea? You have done nothing whatsoever to cause him to want to kill you! My father would not kill you or have you killed." I realized then and there that King Saul was privy to the fact that his son Jonathan and I were very close friends, a fact that caused him to refrain from sharing with his son concerning his intention to kill me. He knew in his heart that if he had shared his secret intentions with his son, his son would warn me about his father's plans to bring about my death and would certainly seek to stop him from carrying out such plans and, more importantly, he would have warned me to flee. Even after I shared with Jonathan how the king had tried to take me captive at Ramah Jonathan found it hard to believe that his father would do such a thing.

When Jonathan got over his surprise and shock at what I had said about his father's intentions, he remonstrated against my accusation by saying, "Never! You are not going to die! Look, my father doesn't do anything, great or small, without confiding in me. Why would he hide this from me? It's not so!" I stood there for a moment thinking to myself, his father has carefully withheld from Jonathan his plan to bring about my death. After a long moment of staring into the face of my friend and seeing innocence written on his countenance, I took an oath that what I was about to say was true. Then I said to him, "Jonathan, you've got to realize that your father is very well aware of your and my friendship and thus he knows that he cannot share this matter with you because you would tell me all about it. Also, your father realized that his bringing about my death would cause you a lot of grief. I tell you for a fact that there is but one step between me and death!" For a long moment Jonathan stood there with a look of unbelief written across his face. Finally, he said to me, "My friend, whatever you want me to do for you I shall do it." His tone of voice implied that although he found it hard to believe what I had just told him he would go along with such requests as I might make.

I shared with him a plan that would let both him and myself know if what I had said about King Saul's plan to kill me was true. On the morrow King Saul would be celebrating the Festival of the New Moon at the palace. "If what I had said about the king's intentions to kill me is true, it will become obvious at the festival dinner, for I am supposed to have dinner with your father. However, instead of being at the king's table for the feast, I am going to hide in this field until the evening of the day after tomorrow. If your father misses me at all tell him that I asked your permission to go to Bethlehem, my hometown where all of my clan will be gathered for the annual sacrifice. Now, listen Jonathan . . . . if the king says, 'Very well' and lets the matter drop, then we shall know that I am safe from his wrath. However, Jonathan, if you see that he has become angry over my absence from his feast, we shall know that I am not safe . . . that he plans to harm me." Then I looked Jonathan straight in the eye and said, "In the event that the king is angry with me and I am forced to flee from his anger, I ask you to remember me kindly and to remember that we have come together in a covenant relationship. If you believe me to be guilty of something that has caused your father to be angry with me, then I ask you yourself to kill me without bothering to hand me over to your father for him to kill me."

Jonathan's reaction to my speech about his killing me brought an instant reaction, "Never! If I had had the least idea that my father was trying to kill you would I not have told you?" The vehemence

With which he said that convinced me that it was true that he was not privy to King Saul's plot against me. Then I asked, "How am I going to know what the king's reaction to my absence at his feast is?" "Come, let the two of us go into the field and talk. I swear by the Lord, the God of Israel, that I shall find out from my father what his intentions are toward you by this hour on the day after tomorrow. If he is not angry with you, I shall send you word to that effect. However, if he is angry with you and intends to harm you, I shall surely let you know so that you can flee from the reach of his anger."

Again, he and I renewed our covenant relationship at his expressed request that I be kind to him and his family members if at a point in the future his father's regime should come to an end and that I would be in a place of leadership. I was more than happy to enter into such a covenant with him. While we were standing there together, he uttered the words of the oath he was taking, "May the Lord call David's enemies to account." Then he turned to me and asked me to reaffirm my oath concerning him.

It was a wonderful and serious moment when we took those vows, for we loved each other as we loved our own selves.

Then Jonathan said, "Here is the way that I shall reveal to you the message concerning my father's attitude toward you. On the day after tomorrow about evening go to the place where you hid when this trouble began and wait by the stone Ezel. I shall shoot three arrows to the side of it, as thought I was doing some target practice. Then I shall say to my young servant lad, 'Go, and find the arrows.' If you hear me say to the lad, 'Look, the arrows are on this side of you; bring them here', then come out of hiding to the place where I am standing, for you will surely be safe, there is no danger. However, if I say to the lad, 'Look, the arrows are beyond you,' that means that the king is angry at you, and you must flee for your safety. Oh, by the way, David, remember the matter we discussed earlier, that is, our covenant together. Remember, the Lord is witness between you and me forever."

Much later I learned how the drama of the Feast of the New Moon played out. King Saul sat in his accustomed place by the wall and Jonathan sat in his accustomed place across the table from the King. Abner, the commander of Saul's army, sat next to Saul. My place was conspicuously empty. It seems that the king said nothing about my absence; for he supposed that I was ceremoniously unclean and therefore could not attend. However, on the next day at the meal King Saul asked why "the son of Jesse" had not come to the meal either yesterday or today? Jonathan replied in the manner in which I had earlier instructed him, saying that he had given David permission to attend his clan's feast in the town of Bethlehem, where his clan was meeting. It was reported to me in detail King Saul's reaction to Jonathan's prepared speech. He angrily shouted at Jonathan, saying, "You son of a perverse and rebellious woman! Aren't you aware that I know that you have sided with the son of Jesse to your own shame and to the shame of the mother who bore you? As long as the son of Jesse lives on this earth, neither you nor your kingdom will be established. Now send and bring him to me, for he must die!" Jonathan dared to talk back to his very, very angry father by saying, "Why should he be put to death? What has he done?" So insanely angry was Saul that he threw his spear at his own much loved son in an effort to kill him. That very outburst of anger on the part of King Saul completely erased any doubt in Jonathan's mind that his father intended to kill his good friend, David.

So angry was Jonathan at his father's declaration of his intention of killing me that, forgetting all protocol, he arose from the table and stormed out of the palace. So grieved was he at his father's shameful treatment of his good friend, David, that on the second day of the feast he could not eat anything. According to our prearranged plan for communicating the message concerning the king's attitude toward me, Jonathan took a small lad with him out into the field where I was hiding behind the big stone Ezel. He instructed the young lad to run and find the arrows which he shot. While the lad was running where the arrow was supposed to fall, Jonathan shot the arrow and immediately called out, "Isn't the arrow beyond you?" My heart fell in sorrow to hear that coded message which revealed beyond a shadow of doubt that King Saul definitely planned to kill me. Just as I turned to hurry away, I heard Jonathan shouting, "Hurry, go quickly, don't stop!" By Jonathan's words and by his strident voice I knew that speed in making my "get away" was very necessary. I waited a moment and saw him give his bow and arrows to the lad and could hear him instructing the lad to take those items back to town. After the lad had gone beyond sight, I came from behind the south side of the stone and bowed down before Jonathan three times with my face to the ground in an act of deep gratitude to him for endangering himself to save me. Then we kissed each other and shed bitter tears. Realizing that I might never see my friend again, my weeping was uncontrollable.

The last words of Jonathan to me remained with me for the rest of my life. He said, "Go in peace, for we have sworn friendship with each other in the name of the Lord, saying, 'The Lord is witness between you and me, and between your descendants and my descendants forever.'" The time had come when for the safety of our lives we had to part, he going back to town and I going out into the life of a hunted animal.

CHAPTER 14

USING SHAM FOR SURVIVAL

Under the canopy of darkness I ran for my life from the presence of King Saul and his staff members . . . . yes, and from the king's army which obeyed his commands regardless of how they felt about them. He was determined to kill me although I had been his loyal supporter. It grieved me for him to feel such great hatred toward me. It was hard for me to admit that God's anointed king was not of sound mind and temperament. Yet it was obvious to one and all that it was true. I had felt deep pity for him; now I felt great fear of him. I knew in my heart that if I expected to see many more sunrises I had to steer clear of him and his men. Thus, there I, the celebrated giant slayer and the leader of almost always victorious campaigns, was fleeing for my life from the king of Israel and his army. How difficult it was for me to comprehend that I had suddenly gone from "riches to rags" figuratively speaking. I had no one to whom I could turn for help, no earthly person that is. I knew that the God of my youth about whom I had sung many psalms while guarding my sheep at night was there for me. In this dark hour of my life I indeed turned to Him for guidance through the morass of trouble in which I found myself.

Fleeing from the enemy who had once been my friend was a completely new situation for me. Up to this point in my life I had been accustomed to meeting danger head on. Now my own countrymen were forced by the king to seek me out in order that I might be slain at the king's command. Where could I possibly go that the enemy would not find me? For starters I felt that it would be good for me to seek aid from the priest of God who had his place of worship over in the village of Nob. Surely Ahimelech, the priest, would give me aid and comfort. Traveling slowly in the dark of night I came to the place where he dwelt and where he continually offered up sacrifices unto the Lord. I had assumed that Nob was far enough from the king's palace that no one would be aware of King Saul's effort to catch and kill me. Thus, I was greatly surprised to walk into the presence of Ahimelech and to see his odd reaction to the sight of me. He was visibly trembling with fear. His question to me was, "Why are you alone? Why is no one with you?" Realizing that he must have been forewarned by someone, I said as matter-of-factly as I could, "Oh, the king charged me with a certain matter of great secrecy, saying that I must not tell anyone about my mission or about the instructions which he gave me. As for my men, I told them to meet me at a certain place. I just stopped by to secure from you some bread, five loaves if you have it or whatever amount you might have on hand." Ahimelech answered me by saying that he had no ordinary bread available, that all the bread he had was the consecrated bread which he had just removed from the altar when he had replaced it with bread fresh from the oven. He said, "I could let you and your men have that PROVIDED that they are ceremoniously clean and have been kept from women." I almost snorted at him, saying to myself that my men had had no chance to be with women, that they were obviously ceremoniousally clean. I told him, "My men are ceremoniously clean, for women have been kept from them, because we are on a mission." Priest Ahimelech handed to me the consecrated bread, that is, the bread of the Presence, without further questions.

As I was leaving I learned that King Saul's head shepherd, Doeg the Edomite, had come by the priest's tent earlier and had been detained. Then, I knew why Ahimelech had acted in such a frightened manner when he saw me. Obviously Doeg had told him about the great search for me that was in progress. I posed another request for assistance from Ahimelec, "Do you happen to have some armor here in this tent of worship? In my haste to do the king's bidding I rushed off without my armor." "Well, all I have here is the sword of the giant Goliath, the one which you used to cut off his head. It is wrapped in cloth and is over behind the ephod. If you want it, take it. There is no sword here but that one" "That will do just fine," I replied, "there is no better sword than his."

Knowing full well that the sneaking looking Doeg, the Edomite, would rush off to spread the word that I had been seen at the tent of Ahimelech, I rushed off in the direction of Gath to seek assistance from its king. To my dismay some of the men of Gath recognized me and said among themselves, "Isn't this David, the king of the land? Isn't this the person the women of Israel sing about as they dance?" Then they started chanting the little ditty the women of Israel had sung after my victory over the giant Goliath:

> "Saul has slain his thousands, and
> David his tens of thousands"

I thought to myself, "My, my, how fast news travels over the face of the land from one nation to another even as the winds of a storm. At that rate the news of my fall from favor with King Saul will soon reach the ears of Achish, the king of Gath. What can I do to get out of this predicament?"

Slowly there seeped into my mind the scheme of using the ruse that I was insane and had wandered from the land of Israel to Gath. Reading the minds of the men of Gath, I put on an act in their presence. I drooled over my beard as insane men do and babbled in their presence and with my sword made unintelligible marks on the wooden gates. When I was brought into the presence of King Achish, he said to his men, "Just look at David, the man from Israel. He is as crazy as he can be . . . . he is insane! Why are you bringing him to me? Do you think that I am so short of men under my command that you need to add an insane fellow to my army? Did you intend to bring this madman into my house for me see his crazy behavior?" Seeing their king's reaction to what appeared to be the antics of a crazy man, they lost interest in me and left me to wander around among them and get lost in the crowd. That night I was able to slip unnoticed from their midst and over the wall of the little town. I recall that once I had escaped from the town which I had hoped would be my place of refuge I travelled until I was out of the territory of Gath.

I was trying to be strong in spite of the great adversity which I was encountering, but my heart was about to burst. I cried to God:

"O Lord, hear my prayer,
Listen to my cry for mercy;
In your faithfulness and righteousness
Come to my relief.
The enemy pursues me, he crushes me to the ground;
He makes me to dwell in darkness
Like those long dead.
So my spirit grows faint within me;
My heart within me is dismayed.
Let the morning bring me word of your unfailing love,
For I have put my trust in you.
Show me the way I should go,
For to you I lift up my soul.
Rescue me from my enemies, O Lord,
For I hide myself in you."

Again I was on the run from King Saul and his army. I finally came to the cave of Adullam, where I rested for several days. I was able to survive with the aid of my sling with which I killed small animals not far from the cave. Time passed and after a while word reached my father Jesse and my brothers as to where I could be found. They came along with their servants to seek me out. On the way they had shared in a secretive manner my whereabouts. From over the land there came a bunch of nondescript men, men who had lost faith in King Saul and men who were on the run from his clutches. They wanted to join me and form a band of terrorists against the king. Now, that was not what I really wanted to do, for I still had respect for King Saul (not as a person but as the one anointed to the office of king by God's servant, the prophet Samuel). It was so very hard for me to turn against him. The men insisted that I organize them, a bunch of malcontents, into a group that could protect itself against the clutches of King Saul and of the outside world. There were about four hundred men who gathered around me and insisted that I become their leader. As I looked at them I saw them as a flock of sheep without a shepherd. They sorely needed someone to lead them, to advise them and someone to give them hope is such a perilous time in their lives.

I realized the immense peril that faced my immediate family, that is, my aging father Jesse and my mother. I made a secretive journey to Mizpah in the land of Moab where I approached the king with a request. I implored him to allow my parents to come to his land to live until such time as I could discern what the will of God was for me. He graciously gave heed to my requested and allowed them a safe haven in his land. My brothers became members of my small band of men who tried to keep one step ahead of Saul's grasp.

There I was a man fleeing for his life, running from the presence of King Saul as though I had committed a grievous crime. The only crime of which I was guilty was the crime of being the object of his jealousy and hatred. Knowing that fact allowed me to keep my self respect. However, there I was living in a cave and stealthily wandering about for a bit of food here and a bit there. I said to myself, "David, you who was greatly praised by the women of the kingdom because of having slain the giant, Goliath, and who are highly respected by his fellow soldiers for his great ability on the field of battle . . . . well, now, you must face the situation in which you are at present . . . . *you are a man without a country!'"* That realization caused me to be greatly grieved. My love for King Saul had faded during the past years and my respect for him as a person was gone. However, my respect for him as being the Lord's anointed king remained intact.

I was relieved at the great courtesy shown to me by the king of Moab in the act of granting the privilege of living in the safety of his country to my father and mother. I was assured that they would be safe there under his watchful eye. Knowing King Saul as I did, I knew that he would stoop to any means of getting to me for the purpose of king me, even to taking as prisoners my parents and using them as hostages with the hope of capturing me. Due to the kindness of the king of Moab concerning my parents, I felt that that was problem I would not have to face.

When my family members furtively sought me out there at the cave of Adullam, they did not come empty handed. They brought with them those four hundred men who had become disillusioned by the reign of King Saul. Those men pled with me to allow them to become my "army". Looking at them I felt that they would be almost impossible to "whip into shape" as soldiers. Well, at least they would be a start. On the practical side they would be serving in our little army with no pay .... and for that matter without any assurance as to where their next meal would be found. To have my older brothers serving under me could be awkward even though they had assured me that they would not allow our relationship to interfere with their discipline. Well, I had to admit that this could be the beginning of my little army even though at best it would be a small "rag tag" army. No doubt this was God's way of answering my prayer for His protection and leadership.

CHAPTER 15
CLASH BETWEEN CHURCH AND STATE

Hearing bits and pieces of news from the court of King Saul I came to the conclusion that King Saul's mental and emotional condition was deteriorating rapidly. According to my news sources he had sunk deep in the mire of self-pity. His earlier belief that I was determined to kill him had greatly enlarged in his mind. Because his son Jonathan had shared with me that the state of the king's hatred toward me was such that I needed to flee for my life, he had turned in his thinking to the view that Jonathan had wronged him greatly. And then there was the straw that "broke the camel's back" with the angry king who suffered such depression.

My glimpse of Doeg, the king's chief shepherd, in the tent of the priest Ahimelech when I had stopped there to seek food and armor had made me very, very suspicious that he would quickly inform the king of my visit to the priest's tent. My suspicions became fact a few days later when Doeg, who was standing with the king's officials near him, stepped forward and announced to the king, "I saw David, son of Jesse, come into Ahimelech's tent. I noticed that Ahimelech appeared to be frightened at David's presence. Nevertheless he inquired of the Lord on David's behalf, gave him consecrated bread to eat, and also gave him the prized sword of Goliath." My confidant in the court who heard the conversation between Doeg and the king said that the king's countenance darkened with evil portent. He immediately dispatched some of his soldiers to go to bring Ahimelech, son of Ahitub, and all his father's family to the king's court. In his rage over Ahimelech's having aided me he was determined to make an example of him to all the kingdom. In his depressed mind he considered Ahimelech's act of kindness to me to be a traitorous act. He was determined to let the citizens of the kingdom know what would happen to them if they decided to commit a similar act of disloyalty to him.

Upon the priestly clan's arrival at the palace King Saul called them into his presence there in the palace. He almost shouted in his angry state as he addressed Ahimelech by saying, "Listen now, son of Ahitub." "Yes, my lord," was the priest's answer. Saul stormed out at him, asking, "Why have you conspired against me, by aiding my enemy David by giving him bread, inquiring of the Lord what David should do in attempting to escape from me, and giving him the famous sword formerly used by the giant Goliath? Because of your doing those things for him, he has rebelled against me and lies in wait to do me harm."

I was told by my confidant who was daily in the king's court that Ahimelech, who had earlier trembled in fear when I went to him for help, now assumed an attitude of boldness that was out of character for him. He suddenly had the boldness to try to reason with King Saul who was livid with anger. He said, "Oh King, who among all your servants is as loyal to you as is David, son of Jesse? Remember, he is your son-in-law and because of that if for no other reason he feels great loyalty to you. Don't you recall how brave and loyal he has been in his role of captain of your team of body guards? Haven't you noticed that David is highly respected by the members of your household? That day back in my tent in Nob was not the first time I had inquired of the Lord on his behalf. There was nothing unusual about that, for I had done that on his behalf many times. David is a religious man who is accustomed to seeking the guidance of the Lord Jehovah for guidance in his life. Please don't accuse me or any member of my father's family of treason, for neither I nor any of my family know what you are talking about. We have heard nothing of the situation which you are describing. It is news to us." King Saul refused to listen to Ahimelech's effort to reason with him and announced, "You will surely die as well as all the members of your father's family." Having said that, he turned to his guards who were standing beside him and snarled, "Kill these priests, for they have sided with David against me. The day that he appeared at their tent of worship they knew that he was fleeing from me, but they did not tell me. They are traitors to my kingdom!" The members of the king's guard stood motionless, for they were not willing to kill God's servants. In his red hot anger Saul turned to the evil Doeg and ordered him to strike down Ahimelech and all the members of his clan. So flattered was he to be selected by the king to do his evil bidding that he fell to with vengeance and not only killed the eighty-five men who wore the ephod which signified their priestly status, but he also killed all the citizens of the town of Nob, men, women and children and also all the livestock . . . . sheep, cattle and donkeys . . . . found in the town.

By the grace of God one of Ahimelech's sons, Abiathar, escaped death at the hands of Doeg and fled to me. I gave thanks for his escape and told him, "I well remember that day when I came to your father's tent seeking food and armor. As I was leaving I saw the evil Doeg there and said to myself, "As surely as my name is David, Doeg will lose no time in going to King Saul and reporting to him my visit with your father. Therefore, I am responsible for the death of your father and all your kinfolk. Stay with me and don't be afraid. We are in this great calamity together. King Saul is not only seeking your life but mine also. You will be safe with me." As I look back on that occasion I realize that I was not nearly as sure of our safety from the clutches of Saul as I sounded. I simply felt that I needed to give him some degree of encouragement due to his great fear.

During the days which followed I endeavored to train my small "rag tag" army which consisted of some four hundred men. Some of them had had no battle experience and some had but needed to be trained in the manner which I had found to be the most effective. They showed me what they could do as fighting men. They sparred with each other while they were in training. Some had to have more "pointers" as to the way I wanted them to do battle than did others. Of course the question continued to "crop up" among the men, "How can we fight the large army of Saul with our little army of only four hundred men?" I had to instill in them confidence in their ability as fighters.

One day some time later a messenger brought to me the news that the Philistines were fighting against the men of Keilah and were taking over the grain in the threshing floors there. I thought to myself, "Those pesky Philistines are stirring up trouble against our people again. What will the citizens of Keilah do if the Philistines succeed in conquering the town and capturing all the wheat that has been brought into their threshing floors? Is it the proper thing for me to use my small army of men to rebuff the Philistines?" I inquired of the Lord and His answer was positive . . . . "go"! Realizing that I had no official standing as the leader of a group of men who had joined together for safety and in rebellion toward the king of the land, I felt that it was proper that I should consult with the men of my small army. Their reply was, "Here in the land of Judah we are a bunch of scared men and are running from the clutches of the king. How can we dare to fight the people of another nation?" Again I got on my knees and asked the Lord, "Dear Lord, I come to you again about the wisdom of this little army of mine going out to do battle against the Philistines at Keilah. What is your final response to my question?" Again I received the answer, "Go, for I am going to give the Philistines into your hands." When I shared with my men what the Lord had said about undertaking the mission to Keilah, they agreed to undertake that mission. They were greatly comforted by the Lord's promise that He would give us the victory, and they agreed with me that it was the proper thing to make the attack and seek to save the people of Keilah. True to God's promise we were able to defeat the Philistines and to save the people of Keilah. Naturally there was great rejoicing among the citizens of the small town and among my men also. Training my small army in the art of warfare had really paid off; I was proud of them.

Abiathar, the only one left of the priestly clan, had thoughtfully and quickly grabbed the ephod from the tent of worship and brought it with him when he came to seek refuge with me and my little band of soldiers. I was glad to have that symbol of the presence of God with us.

What I was not aware of at that time was that the news of our victory over the Philistines at Keilah had wafted across the way to King Saul's court. His reaction was not that of happiness concerning the victory of my little band of Israelite soldiers over Israel's constant enemy, the Philistines. Rather, his happiness was brought about by the knowledge that if he rushed over to Keilah with his large and strong army, he could most likely catch me and my little army still in Keilah, a town with gates and bars. He was certain that with his superior forces he could hem us within the confines of the small town. Fear rose up in my heart and mind. I immediately called for Abiathar to bring the ephod to me that I might inquire of the Lord. "O Lord, God of Israel, your servant has heard that King Saul is planning to come to Keilah to destroy it because of my presence in it. My question is this, O Lord. Will the citizens of Keilah forget that my men and I saved them from the Philistines and because of their fear of Saul's big army surrender me and my men to him? I ask you again, will Saul come down against Keilah? O Lord, God of Israel, please answer your servant's question."

The Lord said to me, "He will come down to Keilah." I persisted in my inquiry of the Lord by asking again, "Will the citizens of Keilah surrender me and my men to Saul?" God answered me, saying, "They will." "What am I to do?" I asked myself. "One thing that is certain is that my little army now numbering some 600 men cannot fight the huge army of the king. Therefore, we must leave immediately and keep on the move, going from place to place." Evidently the news of my decision to leave Keilah quickly got back to King Saul, for he did not bring his army down to Keilah.

I was happy to see on the countenances of the soldiers of my little "rag tag" army pride and happiness due to their victory against the Philistine army at Keilah. They had gone into battle because I was able to assure them that God had shared with me that He would be with us and enable us to win the victory. Now, the mood had changed. The news that King Saul and his large army were planning to come down to capture our little army erased my soldiers' air of confidence, changing it to a pallor of fear on their countenances due to that news. I consulted the Lord again concerning the intent of King Saul and learned that, for a fact, he planned to come to Keilah with the expectation of finding our little army still there. Knowing full well that our 600 men could not possibly defeat the huge army of Israel, we knew that the better part of wisdom was to rush away from the scene of our recent victory. We marched from Keilah doing "double-time" style of marching. To an onlooker it might appear that we were a bunch of scared conies rushing away to a hiding place. Such an appearance might be entirely correct as to the facts of the case.

Now it was "high time" to decide about our next move. Should we stay together as an army, or should we disband and each soldier disappear into a cave or some such hiding place? Somehow we had to "wait it out" until King Saul and his fighting men decided that we were nowhere to be found and turned back to their headquarters near the palace. Living off the land as we had to do became even more difficult due to the fear of being seen by the approaching large army of the king. However, I comforted myself by deciding that this waiting period could be a good training period for the members of my little army, for it could teach them many useful tactics concerning defensive warfare. In the period of waiting to see what King Saul's next move was they learned how to "fade into thin air as it were" in causing themselves to be almost impossible to be discovered by the army of Israel. At that time we did not know that our enemy had turned back from chasing us.

CHAPTER 16
SAVED BY THE ENEMY

Ah, how well I remember those days when my little band of men and I had to save our lives by playing a game of "cat and mouse" or "spy and counter-spy". As the weeks and months passed by King Saul's anger toward me mounted and even more so did his effort to find and kill me grew. My men and I had to live the life of the hunted. We were like animals of prey, hiding here and there from the clutches of the king and his large army. No doubt it was obvious to all the citizens of Israel that catching and killing me was more important to him than making was with other nations who were at enmity with our nation. Some of the old sages of Israel were saying that the king's unnatural hatred for me was causing him to major on minors.

Our scruffy little army was so poorly armed and so poorly trained as soldiers that we never considered attacking King Saul and his large army. Common sense told us that we could never succeed in such an undertaking. Also, I had tried during the span of time after they had come under my command to teach the men of my little army that we should never consider trying to take the life of our king, for he was the Lord's anointed. However, I must admit that I was not very successful on that score, for they had had to flee from him for the sake of their lives. Not only did they fear him, but they had rancor in their hearts toward him for what he had done to them and was still trying to do to them. He had caused them to have to flee from their homes and their families, leaving behind all that they held dear. At the present time King Saul gave them no rest, for he relentlessly pursued them night and day. They had to live one day at a time with little thought as to what the future held for them. The present was all they had. It was a matter of being in this part of the country today before fleeing to another part of the country tomorrow. All they could do was to endeavor to keep one jump ahead of the mighty army of Israel.

For a while my men and I found refuge in the area known as "Desert of Ziph", a wide expanse of arid land that dared mankind to exist on it. We had to depend on the generosity of the few citizens who were scattered over the area for "hand outs" of food now and them. We had to have stew made from a few scrawny desert animals which my men were able to catch with crudely made traps or by bringing down a few birds killed by they slings. It was a matter of just existing, of barely keeping body and soul together. To put it mildly a life of moving from one place to another there in the desert area was almost more than human bodies could tolerate. Although they, for the most part, were strong men they suffered not just physical but also emotional trauma during those days of rapid transit from one area to another.

One day a person from the court of the king suddenly appeared in our midst. At first when my men became aware of who he was they were very afraid. Word was passed among them that the son of King Saul had come to them there in the desert. "How odd it was that the king sent his son Jonathan out to visit them in their hiding place," they muttered to themselves. Obviously he had been sent to spy on them. If that were the case (and they were certain in their hearts and minds that it was so) why was I showing such courteous attention to the king's son? They noticed that when Jonathan arrived in our camp that I hugged him as though he were my brother. To put it mildly my men were nonplussed by my warm reception of the king's son.

Realizing the undercurrent of fear that was sweeping through my little army, I quietly passed a message along to them. I sent word that although Jonathan was the son . . . . the flesh and blood . . . . of the king, he had come on a mission out of love and mercy. There at Horesh Jonathan and I shared what each knew about the way the king was trying to do harm to me and my men. Jonathan admonished me for fearing his father, assuring me that the king would not harm a hair on my head. Oh, how I wanted to believe that, but I had to admit to myself that my friend Jonathan's words did not ring true. Oh, don't get me wrong, in his heart he thought that what he was saying was true. Was he naïve or was he lying to me? I came to the conclusion that so great was his love for his father and for me that he could not imagine that there was real danger for me and my men at the hands of King Saul. I respected the son's love for his father enough to pretend that what he was saying was true . . . that his father would never harm me.

My friend Jonathan suddenly spoke as though he were prophesying the future. He said to me, "Some day you will be king over Israel, and I shall be second in command under you. I know in my heart that it will be so . . . . and furthermore my father knows that to be true also. No doubt in his efforts to harm you he is trying to prevent that from happening." Well, maybe that part of Jonathan's discourse with me was correct I thought. Again, we two dear friends made a covenant with one another in the presence of the Lord. After that act of love and abiding friendship Jonathan took his leave of me and my men. As he made his departure I stood looking at his receding figure and felt a mixture of love and honor sweeping over me. He was going back to the court of his father, King Saul, while I was left to the loneliness of the surrounding desert and to a life of a hunted animal. Oh, how in those moments I wanted to believe what Jonathan had predicted about a time in the future when I would have a life of peace and prosperity among the people of Israel!

I broke into song, singing unto the Lord the petition of my heart at that moment:

> "May those who seek my life
> Be disgraced and put to shame;
> May those who plot my ruin
> Be turned back in dismay.
> May they be like chaff before the wind,
> With the angel of the Lord driving them away;
> May their path be dark and slippery,
> With the angel of the Lord pursuing them.
> Since they hid their net for me without cause
> And without cause dug a pit for me,
> May ruin overtake them by surprise . . .
> May the net they hid entangle them,
> May they fall into the pit, to their ruin."

When the dust had settled from the retreating footsteps of my dear friend, I turned back to my band of loyal comrades in arms. We discussed what the future held for us as we sought to keep body and soul together. We decided that we would remain there in the area of Horesh for the time being. How it hurt to think of the way in which the citizens of the town of Keilah turned against me and my men after our fighting to save their town from the onslaught of the band of marauding Philistines. How could they show such a lack of appreciation for what we had done by being willing to hand us over to the king's forces (this having been revealed to me by the word of the Lord)? As I was mulling over the two-faced nature of mankind, unbeknown to me history was being repeated. Just in time word came to me from my confidant in the king's court that the Ziphites from the area of Horesh were plotting against me and my men. Messengers were sent by them to King Saul informing him or, rather reminding him, that I and my little band of men were hiding out in their area in the strongholds of caves and rocky terrain on the hill of Hakilah which was south of Jeshimon. They made a promise to the king that when it suited his schedule that he could come on down to the area of Horesh and its citizens would hand me and my men over to him. When I heard this I wondered to myself if my little band of men had become such a nuisance to the citizens of the area by our tactics for survival that they desired to get rid of our presence from among them. Or, as I continued to mull over the matter I came to the conclusion that the men of Horesh simply wanted to incur the favor of King Saul in order to gain future favors from him. "Oh, how selfish and full of intrigue is mankind," I moaned silently to myself.

It was reported to me that King Saul was very gracious in his reply to the messengers from Horesh. He replied, "Make preparation to carry through on your promise to capture David and his forces, so that when I come all will be in readiness for me and my forces to round them up." However, it was obvious to me that he was not interested in capturing my men; it was just myself that he wanted to get his hands on.

At the time when I heard about the arrangement between the Zithites and Saul concerning capturing me, my men and I were in the Desert of Maon south of Jeshimon. My men and I left that area and went to the mountainous area of Maon and hid there. It wasn't long until word of my general whereabouts was reported to Saul. He came seeking me there in Maon. He and his forces were going along one side of a mountain, while my men and I were on the other side of the same mountain. We were in a big hurry to put a greater distance between his forces and mine. However, try as hard as we could to outrun the forces of Saul, they were gaining ground on us. Just as the situation for us became very dire, Saul received word that the Philistines were raiding the land of Israel and that he needed to return from seeking me. He and his forces were desperately needed back in the area of Gibeah to protect his kingdom. My confidant got the message to me as soon as he could concerning Saul's return to the heart of Israel to protect it from the Philistines.

I uttered a silent prayer of thanksgiving, saying, "Lord, you've done it again! You have stepped in with your arm of protection and have rescued me from the jaws of death. How wondrous are your ways that you would use my long time enemy, the army of the Philistines, to bring about my salvation from certain death. I have been saved by the enemy!!! Thank you, thank you, O Lord!" Then, I burst into a song of praise and thanksgiving to God for His saving us from our enemy:

> "The salvation of the righteous comes from the Lord;
> He is their stronghold in time of trouble.
> The Lord helps them and delivers them;
> He delivers them from the wicked and saves them,
> Because they take refuge in Him.
> Then my soul will rejoice in the Lord
> And delight in his salvation.
> My whole being will exclaim,
> 'Who is like you, O Lord?
> You rescue the poor from
> Those who are too strong for them,
> The poor and needy from those who rob them."

CHAPTER 17

RESISTING TEMPTATION

How grateful were my men and I for having been saved in such an unexpected way. Just when we thought all hope was lost, the Lord used Israel's long time enemy, the Philistines, to attack the forces of Israel. Thus, King Saul and his large retinue of soldiers were forced to leave off pursing me and my men and turn to his national responsibility of fighting off the attack of the Philistines. We quickly left the rocky and mountainous area of the desert of Maon and stealthily moved under the shadow of darkness to a new position. It was in the mountains of En Gedi where there were many large caves in which to hide.

Later, after having defeated the onslaught of the Philistines, Saul gave his full attention to his endeavor to capture me. He carefully chose three thousand good warriors from among all his soldiers to join him in the pursuit of me and my small group of soldiers. Word had been passed to him by some of the citizens who were loyal to him that I and my men were hiding in the general area of En Gedi. He summoned to the palace some of the citizens who lived in that area in order to question them in an effort to determine just where in that vicinity my men and I were encamped. They answered that they had had glimpses of my little band of soldiers in the area of the "Crags of the Wild Goats," an area so named because of its difficult terrain, an area that was mountainous and full of huge rocks and boulders. The by-word among the natives of the area was that it was only fit for the use of mountain goats, for it was too rugged for human beings to use.

In marching through that area King Saul and his army passed by many sheep folds which were located in the flat land under the mountains. What he did not know was that I and one of my men were watching his every move from our vantage point at the mouth of the deep cave high on the side of one of the craggy mountains. Some of my men in their youth had discovered this cave. They told me, "It looks like a small cave due to the fact that just a few feet into the cave there jutts out from the side walls boulders, one on either side, giving the appearance of them being the end of the cave. However, it is one of the largest and deepest caves in these parts." "Fine . . . . we shall hide in the back recesses of that cave." As my men stealthily made their way up the side of that cliff, they came to the cave's entrance. They entered single file into the "black darkness" of the interior of the cave. They were startled by droves of creatures of the night flying out in droves over their heads. Fortunately, my men were accustomed to moving about in the darkness of night, but this posed a new problem for them. The deep darkness of the interior of the cave caused them to stumble over the rough floor of the cave as they carefully felt their way to the back part of the cave. True to the description of the interior of the cave which I had been given by one of my men we discovered that it was indeed a huge cavern. After a few hours our eyes began to adjust to the total darkness within the interior of the cave so that we were able to creep about in it. One of my men was posted at the entrance of the cave, and I was a few feet inside it.

Suddenly King Saul and his soldiers turned in the direction of our hiding place. We realized that should King Saul have curiosity concerning the cave in which we had sought refuge and take a look inside, our lives would be lost. As every human being knows, fear for one's safety can cause almost any one to get "panic religion". Our men were saying what they considered to be their last prayers. I ordered them to move silently to the rear of the cave. As I said earlier, the mouth of the cave did not indicate that it was as deep as we discovered it to be. For that we were grateful to God. Our scout secreted himself behind a big boulder just inside the cave's entrance from which vantage point he could observe every move King Saul's men made and report the same in barely audible whispers to us. "Those three thousand men have been ordered to halt. It appears that they are taking a rest stop. Oh, there on this side of the group I can see a helmet sporting a plume. I believe that is King Saul . . . . can't be sure yet. I saw him some years ago; he was a head taller than most of the men. Yes, the man wearing the helmet with the plume IS King Saul." I interrupted the scout to ask, "What is he doing?" "Uh, oh, no! He's coming in this direction." I moved to the mouth of the cave, being certain to stay in the shadows, I just had to see for myself. Yes, the king was surely coming toward the mouth of our cave. With him was a small group of his soldiers. I hastily gave command to my men who were hiding behind me by motioning them to go deeper into the cave. I observed that the king was saying something to those nine or ten men with him . . . . could not hear his words, but I observed that they all sat down and took out their water jugs and began to drink. The king was coming to our cave alone. I hastily retreated further into the recesses of the cave and hid behind a "jut out" in the wall of the cave. From behind that "jut out" I continued to watch King Saul's movements. He slowly entered the mouth of the cave; its interior darkness momentarily blinded him. He stood still for a moment until his eyes could become adjusted to the darkness. Slowly he moved forward toward us, stopped, took a drink from his water jug and relieved himself. Then in the coolness of the cave's interior he sat down on the floor of the cave and leaned back against the side of the cave. My men and I were as quiet as death, so afraid of being heard were we. We observed that after a bit the king's head slumped forward and there was the sound of very heavy breathing. Obviously he was sleeping. My men whispered into my ears, "This is the day the Lord spoke of when he said to you, 'I will give your enemies into your hands for you to deal with as you wish.'" (I Sam. 24:4) In the excitement of the moment imprudently I crept forward to his very presence and with my sword I cut off a corner of his garment.

A few minutes later I was filled with remorse for having done such a thing as violate the king's presence by cutting off a bit of his royal robe. After the king had awakened from his nap and returned to his men and marched on down the way, I turned to my men and said to them, "May the Lord forgive me for what I have done to my master, King Saul, who is the Lord's anointed. May he forgive us for even thinking that we might kill or capture him while he was asleep, for he is the Lord's anointed one." My men grumbled among themselves loudly enough for me to hear their unhappiness due to my lack of using the grand opportunity placed right before us to kill the King of Israel who was seeking to destroy us. I lectured them on the subject of NOT returning evil for evil. I stressed the fact that as evil as were the intentions of King Saul it did not make it right that we should violate the sanctity of the Lord's anointed servant. I'm afraid that they only saw that occasion when the Lord put our enemy in our hands, and we did nothing of consequence about it as a huge mistake militarily speaking. I stressed to them that we were not the "hunters", our role was to be that of the "hunted" as concerned King Saul. I repeated, "He is God's anointed one!"

When the king was back among his men and had begun marching on passed the area, I stepped to the mouth of the cave and shouted as loudly as I could, "My Lord the King!" Hearing my voice King Saul paused, turned and looked back in my direction. I bowed down to the ground and cried out to him, "Why do you listen when men tell you that I am seeking to harm you? My actions toward you have always been kind. Today you have seen with your own eyes how the Lord has delivered you into my hands when you were in the cave. Some of my men urged me to kill you, but I chose to spare your life. I said to them, 'I will not lift my hands against my master, for he is the Lord's anointed.' See, my father, look at this piece of your robe in my hand! I cut off the corner of your robe, but I did not kill you although I had every opportunity to do so. Now please understand and recognize that I am not guilty of wrongdoing or rebellion. I have not wronged you, but you are hunting me down to take my life. May the Lord judge between you and me. And may the Lord avenge the wrongs you have done to me, but my hand will not touch you. As the old saying goes, 'From evildoers come evil deeds,' so my hand will not touch you."

I was getting fired up in my oratory to the king as I continued to try to reason with him concerning his misconception of my intentions. "Against whom has the king of Israel come out? Whom are you pursuing? A dead dog? A flea? May the Lord be our judge and decide between us. May he consider my cause and uphold it; may he vindicate me by delivering me from your hand."

I heard King Saul ask, "Is that your voice, David my son?" As I watched I saw and heard the king weeping aloud. Then, when he had somewhat regained his composure, he said "You are more righteous than I. You have treated me well, but I have treated you badly. You have just now told me of the good you did to me; the Lord delivered me into your hands, but you did not kill me. When a man finds his enemy, does he let him get away unharmed? May the Lord reward you well for the way you treated me today. I know that you will surely be king and that the kingdom of Israel will be established in your hands. Now swear to me by the Lord that you will not cut off my descendants or wipe out my name from my father's family."

I felt in my heart that the Lord had worked a great miracle that day in the heartfelt repentance exhibited by King Saul. He who had been consumed by hatred for me had made a complete "turn around" in his attitude . . . . he had truly repented and turned from his old attitude toward me. Whether it was due to intuition on his part or due to knowledge given him by the Lord, he predicted that one day I would be king of Israel. Suddenly I remembered that day when the prophet Samuel had turned up a cow's horn filled with olive oil and poured it over my head and had uttered some religious jargon which my youthful ears did not understand. Connecting that with the prediction which King Saul had just made began to weigh heavily on my soul. Was it true that I was destined to be the ruler over the nation Israel?

King Saul and his army of well trained men took their departure from the area as my men and I stood at the entrance of that large cave and watched them marching away from that vicinity. Undoubtedly his men wondered at the strange turn of events. With their own ears they had heard the conversation carried on between the king and myself, a conversation that was shouted by the two involved so that they could be heard over the great distance between the two. When they saw the taciturn King Saul weeping, I observed from my distant vantage point that they all turn their eyes upon him with a questioning countenance. They obviously had never expected to witness such a change in a person's attitude and appearance as they observed in King Saul that day. They had marched from army headquarters out into this "no man's land" sort of terrain with orders that at all costs they were to apprehend me and the members of my rag-tag army and slay us. Following the conversation shouted back and forth between their stern leader, King Saul, and the renegade leader of a small army which had been tucked away in the interior of a large cave, they suddenly got orders to return to the palace headquarters. They had only recently been selected for the new marching army and had not yet learned the ways of King Saul. They realized that they would have to become accustomed to sudden changes in attitudes as well as changes in plans if they were to continue in his army.

CHAPTER 18

HOT ANGER QUENCHED BY THE ACTIONS OF A BEAUTIFUL LADY

Yes, King Saul had shown remorse for his actions against me in endeavoring to find and to slay me. He had listened to false rumors that said that I was trying to kill him and to take over his throne. My actions there at the cave when he was at my mercy opened his eye to the fact that I was not guilty of things which were relayed to him by those false rumors that had been shared with him. He showed great remorse for his past actions against me and my men by weeping profusely . . . and loudly . . . in the presence of his soldiers. However, he did not offer me and my men a place in his army, nor did he make any tangible overtures of peace and reparations toward us. Having observed the mood swings of the king in times past when I was a member of his staff, I came to the conclusion that his remorse was probably temporary. Thus, my men and I felt that the prudent thing for us to do was to continue to live apart from the main stream of social, political and economic life as was practiced by private citizens of the nation of Israel.

Shortly after my men and I had been granted peace at the hands of our king word was passed to all the citizens of Israel that our beloved judge and leader of the nation prior to the anointing of Saul as king and the prophet and religious leader of Israel had died. It was announced that his burial would be in his home town of Ramah. All the citizens of Israel flocked to Ramah to pay their respects and their love to such a faithful and powerful political and religious leader as he had been. I rejoiced that now we could move openly about without fearing danger from King Saul. Therefore, my men and I made our way to Ramah to attend the great memorial service for Samuel.

We now felt that it was safe for us to live more openly, no longer living like bats in caves. We moved southward in the desert of Maon to set up camp. There we found a purpose in life by keeping the shepherds of the area safe from marauding bands of thieves. Our very presence there in the area of the good grazing grounds frequented by many herds of sheep caused bands of sheep stealing thieves to know that they had best ply their trade elsewhere. Most of the shepherds rewarded the protective efforts of my little group of followers by sharing their food and an occasional sheep with us. Word reached us that a very rich man by the name of Nabal, owner of three thousand sheep as well as a thousand goats, was in the process of having his sheep sheared in the area of Mt. Carmel. I realized that our provisions were getting low and that this would be a good time to make a tactful plea to Nabal to share with us some of the food which he had prepared for his sheep shearers. It was the custom in those days for owners of large flocks of sheep to hire "professional shearers" to take care of that job for them. They paid the shearers an agreed on fee per sheep sheared and in addition they fed the shearers a rather sumptuous meal per day. In our hearts we felt that in reality he owed us much for having protected his sheep from danger during the past many months. Therefore, I chose a delegation of some ten men to approach Nabol and deliver my message to him. They interrupted me to say: "Sir, we've heard that he is a surly and mean man. What should we say to him?" "First of all, be very tactful and courteous. Greet him as follows: 'Long life to you! Good health to you and your household! And good health to all that is yours!' I thought that such a courteous greeting might soften him up before he heard the request we were making to him. Say to him: 'We hear that it is sheep shearing time with you. Sir, when your shepherds were across the way minding your sheep we did not mistreat any of them. In fact, all the time they were in the area we saw to it that none of your sheep were missing. If you don't believe us, ask your servants. Please be favorable toward our delegation sent by your servant David. This is a festive time, for the sheep shearing time of the year is a time of great harvest of wool. We have come to ask that you show kindness to our leader, David who is the son of Jesse, by sharing whatever provisions you can spare with him and his men in return for the protective watch care we have given through the year to your shepherds.'"

Nabal cocked his head to one side, shaped his lips into a snarl, and then stormed out at my messengers, "What did you say? Are you saying that this request came to you from a fellow named David, son of a man named Jesse? The very idea! I've never heard of such a person named David nor of a person named Jesse. Many servants are slipping away from their masters; for all I know you and your leader David may be escaped servants. I'm not about to take my bread and water and the meat which I have slaughtered for my shearers and give to men who have come from who knows where?"

My men returned to me with heads hanging low. They rehearsed to me all that had been said by Nabal. For a long moment I sat there in silence, and then I felt anger rising up in my heart and mind. I allowed my anger to get the best of me, causing me to "run ahead" of the Lord. I acted before I prayed things through. I almost shouted as I barked orders to my men, "Put on your swords!" I hastily put on my sword also. I left two hundred of my men to guard our provisions and took the other four hundred armed men with me. We headed straight for the home of Nabal. In the meantime unbeknown to me one of Nabal's household servants approached Abigail, the wife of Nabal, with an urgent message. "A group of men from the army of David, son of Jesse, came to your husband with a request for some food and other provisions. Your husband hurled insults at David's men and sent them away. We servants know for a fact that David and his men protected Nabal's servants who were minding his sheep. Night and day they were a wall of protection around us all the time we were herding our sheep near them. Not one of Nabal's sheep was stolen due to the presence of David and his men in the area. David has a sufficient number of fighting men to come and wipe out Nabal and his servants if he is provoked to anger. Please, madam, think it over and see what you can do to make amends for the mean behavior of your husband, Nabal. Disaster is hanging over our master and his whole household. He is such a wicked man that no one can reason with him."

Abigail thought over the matter, and then quickly "rose to the occasion". She helped herself to a great amount of the provisions intended for Nabal's sheep shearers. She gathered together and loaded on available donkeys two hundred loaves of bread, two large skin bottles of wine, five sheep that had just been dressed, five bushels of roasted grain, a hundred cakes of raisins, and two hundred cakes of pressed figs. She did all of this in a matter of minutes, for she simply helped herself to food intended for Nabal's sheep shearers. She sent servants on ahead with the donkeys laden with the provisions. She then took time to bathe, dress herself in her best looking garments and used on her face such cosmetics as were available to her. Then she got on a donkey and followed somewhat behind the others. She did not have time to think of the many dangers involved in what she was doing. If her surly and mean husband, Nabal, heard of what she was doing he would probably have beaten her within an inch of her life or even divorced her and sent her away. Fortunately the servants and donkeys laden with those provisions simply conveyed to him the message that more food was being sent out for the sheep shearers. Traveling alone when leaving the house would simply indicate to him that she was going over to a neighbor's home to visit with the lady of the house. Obviously she had a good head on her shoulders, for she quickly planned a way that would not arouse suspicion in Nabal's evil and suspicious mind. Another potential danger was that she could have fallen into the hands of marauding bands of evil men. She did not allow the thought of personal danger to hinder her from carrying out her effort to save her household from the hands of an angry David.

As I and his men were marching in the direction of Nabal's home I rehearsed all that had happened: "It's been useless . . . . our protective watch care over this evil fellow's property in the desert so that nothing of his was missing. He has paid us back evil for good. May God deal with me, be it ever so severely, if by morning my men and I leave alive one male of all who belong to Nabal!"

With fear and trepidation Abigail came to a dark ravine with mountainous hills rising up on either side. Her heart beat a little faster, for she knew that bands of men with evil intent frequented such areas as that. Suddenly, there came toward her in the shadows of the ravine hundreds of men, a sight that caused her heart almost to stop beating. Before she had time to analyze the situation I appeared before her; she seemed to perceive me as a man with an air of authority. I rode up to her and introduced myself. She quickly dismounted from the donkey and bowed low before me with her face to the ground. Literally she fell at my feet and announced her identity to me. Then she issued to me a plea: "My lord, let the blame for this unfortunate response of my husband, Nabal, be placed squarely on my shoulders and not on anyone else. Please allow me, your servant, to speak to you; listen to what I, your servant, has to say to you. May my lord pay no attention to what my husband, that wicked Nabal, said and did to your messengers. He is just like his name . . . . his name is 'Fool'. Whatever he does and wherever he goes folly goes with him. But as for me, your servant, I did not see the men you sent. Now, since the Lord has kept you, my master, from bloodshed and from avenging yourself with your own hands, as surely as the Lord lives and as you live, may your enemies and all who intend to harm my master be like Nabal. And let this gift, which your servant has brought to you, my master, be given to the men who follow you. Please forgive your servant Nabal's offense, for the Lord has certainly made a lasting dynasty for you, my lord, because you fight the Lord's battles. Let no wrongdoing be found in you as long as you live. Even though someone is pursuing you to take your life, the life of my master will be bound securely in the bundle of the living by the Lord your God. But the lives of your enemies He will hurl away as a rock is hurled away from a sling. When the Lord has done for my master every good thing He promised concerning him and has appointed him leader over Israel, my master will not have on his conscience the staggering burden of needless bloodshed or of having avenged himself. And when the Lord has brought my master success, remember your servant."

I was amazed at her dramatic yet humble speech to me. I also stood there convicted of the sin which I had planned to commit, that is, slaying Nabal and all the males in his household. Finally I regained my power of speech and replied to the beautiful lady bowed down before me, "Praise be to the Lord, the God of Israel, who has sent you today to meet me. May you be blessed for your good judgment and for keeping me from bloodshed this day and from avenging myself with my own hands. Otherwise, as surely as the Lord, the God of Israel, lives who has kept me from harming those of your household, if you had not come quickly to meet me, not one male belonging to Nabal would have been left alive by day break." Having said that, I gratefully accepted the gifts of food which she had brought to me and my men. Then I said to her, "Go home in peace. I have heard your words and granted your request."

Man that I am, I could not refrain from going over in my mind all that had just happened. Never had I heard a better worded plea for mercy, a plea that was presented to me with such urgency and such dignity. More especially I continued to think about her beauty and her humility. Also, I continued to think about her prophetic speech concerning my future. She seemed to have a divine knowledge of what the future held for me. I had been so mired down in the day to day affairs of guiding my small band of soldiers in our effort to escape from the clutches of King Saul that I had not thought much about what the future might hold. Her prophecy concerning my future brought back to my mind that event that occurred when Samuel poured a horn of oil on my head and spoke some religious words over my young head.

Upon Abigail's return she had planned to tell Nabal all about how she had used her good sense, her charms, and the food that had been prepared for their sheep shears in order to quench my hot wrath toward him, anger which was to have resulted in the killing of him and the men of his household. However, upon her return she discovered that Nabal was entertaining his friends (actually some acquaintances that he was trying to impress . . . . he had no real friends.) He was entertaining those acquaintances in the manner of a king. It was obvious to Abigail that the party had gone on for some length of time prior to her return home, judging by the raucous noise emanating from the banquet chamber. She could hear his drunken voice over the noise of the banquet. Therefore, she waited until the next day when his hang-over had lessened somewhat before approaching him and sharing with him how she had saved his life. Just as she finished her recounting of what had transpired between her and me and my men Nabal's face tuned white, he sat motionless for a few moments, and then he became as lifeless as a stone. Hearing how he had barely escaped death by me and my men, he was obviously frightened beyond measure. He lingered ten days in that condition and then died.

I suspect that Abigail grieved only for the sake of appearances. I had perceived on the day she came to me and pled for mercy for the men of her household that any affection she may have had for Nabal early in their marriage had disappeared. She sent word to me that her husband had died and would no longer be a cause for my anger. Spontaneously I cried out, "Praise be to the Lord, who has upheld my cause against Nabal for treating me with contempt. His death has kept me from any wrongdoing and has brought Nabal's wrongdoing down on his own head."

My first thought was, "Abigail is free from her bad marriage. She is free to marry someone else. I would like that 'someone else' to be me. She is a beautiful woman and she is a wise woman. She could certainly be an asset to me. My marriage to Michal, King Saul's daughter, was overturned by him, for in his anger at me he took her from my house and gave her in marriage to a man named Paltiel. After that I married a woman by the name of Ahinoam. Many men have any number of wives. Surely I can allow myself to have two wives to care for. No doubt Nabal's property will go to a male descendent, since widows do not usually inherit their husband's property. Abigail will need some man to give her a home. I'm infatuated with her. I'm going to ask her hand in marriage."

A bit later I sent a couple of my servants to Abigail to ask her to be my wife. Well, now, looking back on how my proposal was stated to her, I suppose that I wasn't very romantic nor was I very tactful . . . . or just maybe it was the fault of my servants who gave my message to her, for they simply said to her, "Our leader, David, has sent us to you to take you to him to be his wife." I guess for too long a time I had been just in the presence of men, for I had forgotten that ladies like more romance than that. However, that brusque proposal extended to Abigail on my behalf worked. Upon their return my servants told me that she had immediately bowed herself to the ground and said, "Tell David, 'Here is your maidservant who is ready to serve you and wash your feet.'" They told me that she quickly summoned a servant to bring a donkey to her. She, along with five servant girls, hastened to accompany my servants back to my camp. She obviously was ready and willing to become my wife. When she arrived at my camp, she was as radiant as a teenage girl who was about to be married. Her arrival at my camp with the intention of becoming my wife made me a very, very happy man.

CHAPTER 19
A SECOND ENCOUNTER

For a while my men and I enjoyed a time of peace, a time of rest from the game of "cat and mouse" as played by King Saul and his army and me and my little band of some six hundred men. I well remember that occasion when my men and I showed mercy unto the king there in the darkness of the cave nearly a year ago when I cut a small portion from his royal robe as he slept. Upon my revelation to him a few minutes later of how I had had a chance to kill him but did not and of how he had been filled with remorse and left off seeking my life. Those months which followed that event were indeed wonderful days of peace when we could move freely about and enjoy a life of safety.

However, I had come to realize through the past few years how unstable the character of the king was. His personality was changeable from day to day. I had known in my heart that the king's plea for forgiveness for his conduct toward me on that occasion was not a lasting statement of real peace. So deep was his fear of my endeavoring to take over his throne that soon his anger toward me would flare up again. Yes, it was obvious that he was a man of unstable character. His periods of depression and his fear of his throne being usurped by me caused him to rise up again and again against me. Well, here once again he was "out to get me".

I had long since learned that I needed to be as "smart as a serpent and as harmless as a dove". My "observer at the king's court" (I don't like the word "spy") periodically sent word to me of any visible change in the King's attitude. Nearly a year after the episode of my refusing to take his life there in the cave my "observer" sent word to me that King Saul was again on the war path against me. It appeared that the Ziphites were trying to stir up trouble again by sharing with the king the fact that it was known to them that I was hiding in the hill of Hakilah which faces Jeshimon. There was no doubt in my mind but that those "two-faced Ziphites" phrased their information to the king in such a way as to stir up the king's old animosity toward me. Evidently they did a good job of it, for it was reported to me by my "observer" that King Saul had left the palace accompanied by three thousand of his soldiers and were heading toward the Desert of Ziph in his search for me and my little band of warriors. I immediately had some of my men to scout out that area until they found the exact whereabouts of the king and his band of soldiers. They returned with the news that from the vantage point of a high spot on the crest of the Hill of Havilah they had been able to observe the "layout" of the army of King Saul. It was located on the road at the base of that hill. My little band of soldiers and I were encamped in the desert not far from the Hill of Havilah. Having heard from my court "observer" that the king was following me for the purpose of capturing me, I sent out spies to invade his army in an effort to learn that if that was true (later I asked myself why I had bothered to do that, for in my heart there was no doubt that my court "observer" had correctly stated the king's intent). Those who had been sent out to observe the layout of the king's army returned to me with the information that King Saul had definitely followed me and that he and his army were encamped along the road of Havilah at the Hill of Jeshimon.

I decided to face danger "head on". I asked Ahimelech and Abishai, "Which one of you will go with me on my mission to King Saul's camp. I warn you that what I am planning to do will be dangerous?" Abishai replied, "Sir, I will go with you." The two of us arrived that day about dusk and observed for ourselves the "lay out" of the king's camp. In the very center of the camp were the tents of King Saul and of Abner, the commander-in-chief of Israel's army. Abishai and I, hidden from the enemy's view, watched the movements in their camp as night drew on. King Saul retired to his tent for the night and so did Abner. The king had placed his water bottle by the head of his bed roll and had stuck his spear into the ground beside him. We could see through the open air sides of their tents that they appeared to be sound asleep. Soon all the soldiers had retired for the night. I motioned to Abishai to follow me. The two of us crept stealthily forward, weaving our way among the many, many sleeping soldiers. Fortunately, we were able to reach the very center of the camp without having disturbed a single soldier from his heavy sleep. I thought to myself, "The Lord has obviously caused a deep, deep sleep to come upon all the soldiers in the camp, for not a single one is awake and standing guard duty. All are snoring loudly." When we had arrived at the center of the camp and were standing beside the sleeping forms of King Saul and Abner, Abishai whispered to me, "Give me permission to take the king's spear and pin him to the ground by plunging it through his heart!" "No, you must not do that, for who can lay a hand against the Lord's anointed and be guiltless. Just be patient, for as surely as the Lord lives, He will 'strike' the king. Either the king's time will come when he dies a natural death, or else he will be killed in battle. The Lord forbids that we lay a hand on him, for he is the Lord's anointed. Here's what we shall do. Grab the king's spear and water jug, and we shall leave." With those two items in our hands we made our way back through the thousand of sleeping soldiers without awakening a single one of them. Yes, it was obvious to me that the Lord was with us!

We quietly made our way over to the other side of the hill. At the break of dawn I stood some distance across the way on top of a hill silhouetted against the dark purple of the sky and shouted, "Aren't you going to answer me, Abner?" Abner looked as though he were seeing and hearing a ghost. He called out to me, "Who are you who are calling to the king?" I replied, "You are a man, aren't you? And who is like you in all Israel? Well, then, why have you not guarded your lord the king? Someone came in the night to destroy your lord the king. What you have done is not good! As surely as the Lord lives, you and your men deserve to die because you did not guard your master, the Lord's anointed. Look around you. Where are the king's spear and water jug that were near his head?" About that time King Saul awakened and recognized my voice and said, "Is that your voice, David my son?" "Yes, it is, my lord the king. Why is my lord the king pursuing me, his servant? What have I done, and what wrong am I guilty of? Now let my lord the king listen to his servant's words. If the Lord God has caused you to be angry at me, then offer an acceptable offering unto Him. If, however, men have caused your anger to burn toward me, may they be cursed before the Lord! They have driven me from my share of the Lord's inheritance and have said, 'Go, serve other gods.' Now do not let my blood fall to the ground far from the presence of the Lord. It appears to me that the king of Israel has come out to look for a flea, even like a man who is hunting a partridge in the mountains." There was a long moment of silence before Saul called out to me, "I have sinned. Come back, David my son. Because you considered my life precious today, I will not try to harm you again. Surely I have acted like a fool and have erred greatly." I outwardly accepted his apology although in my heart I "took it with a grain of salt" as the old saying goes. I called to him, "Here is your spear and water jug. Send one of your young men up to me, and I shall give them to him to return to you. Remember, the Lord rewards every man for his righteousness and faithfulness. The Lord delivered you into my hands today, but I would not lay a hand on you who are the Lord's anointed one. As surely as I valued your life today, so may the Lord value my life and deliver me from all trouble." In an apparent air of humility King Saul called to me and said, "May you be blessed my son David; you will do great things and surely triumph."

I lingered there on the crest of the hill until I heard King Saul give the order to his men to "break camp and move out". I then turned and went down the other side of the hill and rejoined my men. We went on our way with the knowledge that the king had left off pursuing us but also with the knowledge that it was probably for only a short while. I thought to myself, "King Saul is a person who knows how to repent of his sins, for he has had a lot of practice in doing so. I knew in my heart that his moods controlled his actions and that his moods would probably cause him to turn against me again in a comparatively short time.

I must admit as I stood at the head of the bed roll on which King Saul lay sleeping that I was sorely tempted to allow Abishai to yield to his desire to pick up the king's spear and drive it through King Saul's heart. I have to admit that I am as human as any other person, that I am tempted to do wrong things on those occasions when the old human self pointed me in the direction of such an opportunity as I had that night and on the previous night when hiding in the cave. However, there was that quiet inaudible voice reminding that to yield to such a temptation would be very displeasing to God. On both occasions when I had the opportunity to send King Saul to his eternal reward, I chose to remember that he was the Lord's anointed and as such it was not my place to commit such a crime.

The results which came from having made a righteous choice of action on those two occasions in which I spared King Saul's life proved to have a great result . . . . King Saul left off chasing me and my small army and returned from following after us. Both times immediate peace was achieved by my "taking the high road" of not slaying the Lord's anointed. For not yielding to temptation my little army and I were rewarded with military peace at least for a while.

CHAPTER 20
SAFETY IN THE LAND OF THE ENEMY

My men and I left the scene of our encounter with King Saul and moved on father south in the desert. All the while I pondered the situation we were in, that is, living a life of being pursued by King Saul and his army. The more I thought about the instability of the pattern of life that my men and I were forced to live due to our being intermittently pursued by the emotionally unstable king the more I decided that we needed to make arrangements to go where the king would no longer seek us. Where could such a place be? Well, certainly it would have to be beyond the borders of King Saul's kingdom. And just where could we find such a place?

After weighing all the possibilities of a place that would be safe from the clutches of the jealous king of Israel, I finally came to the conclusion that we needed to go over the border to the land of our perpetual enemy, the Philistines. When I suggested this to my men as a plan of escaping from being intermittently pursued by the emotionally unstable king of Israel, they cocked their heads to one side as if they could not believe what they had just heard from my lips. "What did you say? Go over the border into the land of the Philistines? They have long been the enemy of Israel! How could you suggest such a thing??" After waiting a long moment for them to stop their murmuring, I shared with them my rationale for making such a suggestion. I wanted the decision to be agreeable with my little band of soldiers and not just an executive command on my part. Ever since the little band of men had come together under my leadership I had lived with the realization that they had chosen to come over to my side . . . . it was indeed their choice. In no wise did I consider myself to be their king, not even their commanding general. I was simply one who had gained a reputation as a good fighter. When they had become disillusioned with King Saul they sought me out and looked to me as one who would be an able leader to their little band of soldiers who had gathered together. Since that was the case I always endeavored to be a democratic leader, not a dictator, not an "anointed king" with the God given right to control them. Thus, I wanted to be certain that they would be agreeable to such an odd plan, that is, to go into the lap of the longtime enemy.

"Here's my plan. In order to be able to hide from King Saul in the midst of our long time sworn enemy we shall have to be as wise as serpents and as harmless as doves. That is, we shall have to pretend to be friends of the Philistines and enemies of Israel. Achish, king of Gath in the land of the Philistines, will be proud to have a band of soldiers who are "turn coats" from Israel and who are seeking asylum with them. They will considerate us to be enemies of our own flesh and blood and will, therefore, give us a home and protection among them." "Will we be planning to return to Israel shortly?" I replied, "No, under this plan we shall make arrangements to take our families and possessions with us for a long period. When God sees fit to take the life of his anointed king and leader of Israel, King Saul, perhaps we can safely return to our beloved home land. Until then we should plan to make the land of the Philistines our homeland."

As I had predicted, King Achish of Gath in the land of the Philistines graciously gave permission for me, my men and our families to move over to the area of the town of Gath. Naturally there was a lot of grumbling on the part of my men but more so on the part of their wives. They resented being uprooted from all that they had held dear. They had maintained their homes while their husbands had been "on the run" from the clutches of King Saul. I gathered my two wives, Ahinoam of Jezreel and Abigail of Carmel, my livestock, and household possessions and carried them across the border into the land of the Philistines to the town of Gath. My men did the same. Having been told that we were now enemies of the nation of Israel, the citizens of Gath received us very cordially. When King Saul heard that we had crossed the border over into the land of his long time enemy, the

Philistines, he no longer pursued us. To have done so would have meant that he would have to muster his entire army and fight not just my little band of wandering soldiers but also he would have to fight the army of the Philistines in order to capture and kill me.

I realized that if we settled in Gath, the home city of King Achish, our goings and comings would naturally be seen by him and his officers of the court. I knew that my people should be a good distance from Gath for that very reason. Therefore, as tactfully and slyly as I could I told King Achish that my little group of people should not crowd in on the good people of Gath and cause them to be so very inconvenienced. "Why not assign me and my little band of people to the area of one of your small country towns. We would not be as much of a bother to you and your citizens if we lived some distance from Gath. You know how disruptive it would be to have all of us who have different ways and a different language to be 'plopped down' in your midst. The last thing that we want to do is to inconvenience you and your fine people. It does not seem proper that we, a group of foreigners, live in the royal city along side you and your finest citizens!" Achish sensed that I obviously really desired for us not to be a bother to him and his citizens in the capital city of Gath by crowding in on them. He acquiesced to my request and gave us the little town of Ziklag to be the home city for us "turn coat Israelites". I was very grateful to him for doing that, for we would not be as apt to irritate the good people of the little town of Ziklag as we would have those in the big city of Gath. Far more importantly the peasant people in the small town so far away from the capital city would not pay as much attention concerning the movements of my little band of soldiers.

As time passed my men and I again plied our trade of being soldiers and went out to do battle. We raided towns of the Amalakites, the Geshurites, and the Girzites who lived in the land to the south in the direction of Egypt. I occasionally reported in to King Achish, who seemed to show a friendly curiosity as to what areas we had raided. I would give him the answer he wanted to hear, that is, I would lie and say that we had raided some area in the territory of Israel. It obviously pleased him to hear that his enemy, Israel, had suffered at our hands. On the other hand if we had told him the truth that in reality we had raided areas of the land of the Philistines he would have had his mighty army to surround us there in Ziklag and slaughter us. In order to leave no evidence as to where we had raided we slaughtered every man, woman and child in the areas which we had successfully raided. Believing my report to him that we had made all of our raids on areas in Israel, Achish was highly pleased. He assumed that because of our supposed raids against Israel that we would be greatly hated by the Israelites.

There came the time once again when the army of the Philistines under the leaderhip of King Achish was making arrangements to do battle with Israel. The king called me in and said to me, "You must understand that you and your men are to accompany me and my army as we go to do battle against Israel." That caused me to feel that I had ice water in my veins . . . . the very idea of fighting against my own people. Well, I had dug a hole from which I would have to climb out. I had lied about making raids against towns of Israel when in reality I had been raiding Philistine towns. I had led him to believe that I and my men were "one of them". As the old saying goes, "Be sure your sins will find you out!" Finally, I glibly replied to Achish, "Then you will see for yourself what your servant can do." Was I bluffing or was I bragging? No doubt due to my bold statement and due to the lies I had told him he said, "I'll make you my bodyguard for life!" "Wow", I thought to myself, "What have I done?"

All the forces of the Philistine army had been gathered at Aphek and organized for battle. The army of Israel camped by the spring of Jezreel. Achish's army came out in full force; it was under the leadership of the rulers of the land who marched with their units of hundreds and of thousands. Achish had placed me and my small band of soldiers at the rear of the Phisistine army. Suddenly the Philistine rulers (the territory of the Philistines was divided into geographical section with a king or ruler over each) saw my group of soldiers and turned to Achish and asked, "Hey, what about these Hebrews whom you have placed in our army? Since we are fighting the Hebrew nation it is not safe to use them in our warfare against their fellow Hebrews. In the height of battle they could switch over and leave our army and join forces with their fellow Israelites." Achish told them that we had been with him for over a year and had shown no disloyalty to them. "I have found no fault with him and his men." The Philistine rulers would not listen to Achish. They insisted that my little band of Hebrew soldiers must not go with them into battle. "Send them back to the area you gave them, that is, Ziklag. They must not go with us into battle against the army of Israel. In the heat of the battle they would probably turn against us and go over and join forces with the Israelite army. Right now he is out of favor with King Saul, but there is no better way for him to regain favor with him than by turning on our men and killing them and taking their heads to King Saul. Isn't he the same David who fought against our army some time ago and was so victorious over us that the women of Israel sang a ballad about him, saying, "Saul has slain his thousands but David his tens of thousands?" Achish could not stand up against the Philistine army commanders sufficiently to win his point. Therefore, he called me to him and said, "During the time that you have been living in the land of the Philistines I have found no fault with you, but the army commanders have declared to me that you must not go to battle with our army." "But what have I done," I asked. "What have you found against me since the day I came to you until now? Why can't I go and fight against the enemy of my lord the king?" He answered, "I know that you have been as pleasing in my eyes as an angel of the Lord; nevertheless, the Philistine army commanders have said that you must not go into battle with them. Arise at daylight in the morning and return to Ziklag." There was nothing further that my men and I could do to prove our loyalty to the Philistines, so we followed his instructions and returned to Ziklag. Their army moved out to do battle against the army of Israel.

What a dismal feeling my men and I experienced! We found through that turn of events that we were men without a country. We had been run out of our native land of Israel by King Saul. We had found refuge and fellowship with King Achish of the Philistines and had settled down in Ziklag where we could feel at home even though in a country not our own. We were ready and willing to go to war against our beloved Israel in order to show our gratitude toward our former enemy, the Philistines. I had been very careful to *show loyalty* to the Philistines although secretly my men and I had raided and wiped out some their smaller towns. I have to admit that King Achish "stuck his neck out" on our behalf by arguing that I and my little band of fighting men would be an asset when the Philistines engaged in battle with Israel. He did all he could to convince his army commanders that we were loyal to them, but they would not listen. They overpowered Achish's desire to have us march into battle with the people of his nation. There was nothing else that he could do but to send us back to Ziklag where we were supposed to "sit out" the war between the Philistines and the nation of Israel. It really went against our grain not to be able to do what we were trained to do, that is, fight with all our might.

CHAPTER 21

A SAD RETURN

As my men and I approached Ziklag where we had left our families and our possessions, we could see no silhouettes of our homes in the distance. Hoping that we were having an optical illusion, we moved forward with top speed. Our speed was matched by the rapidity of our heart beats. Unfortunately there was no optical illusion involved. As we drew near to the site of Ziklag we saw with our eyes what our hearts had not wanted to believe. What a sight we beheld! The town of Ziklag had been burned to the ground. Where the little town had stood, there was nothing left but ashes. Suddenly the full realization of what had happened hit us "head on". It has been said that "grown men don't cry". In our case that day that statement was proved to be very false. My men and I literally fell apart. We wept loudly, for we were bereft of our wives and children. Were they killed and burned in the fire, or were they taken captive by some enemy? The sorrow on the part of my men soon began to turn to bitterness which they directed in my direction. It was whispered to me that some of the men were talking of stoning me. Their attitude greatly added to the sorrow over losing my family that was already heavy in my heart. To put it mildly I was in great distress.

When I finally got control of myself I called for Abiathar, our priest, to bring to me the ephod of which he was the custodian. I inquired of the Lord, "Should I and my men pursue the raiding party which burned our little town of Ziklag? If we do pursue them will we be successful?" "Pursue them," the Lord answered. "You will surely overtake them and succeed in rescuing your families from the raiders." We had our answer. We rose up from our weeping and wailing and started out in hot pursuit. Scattered along the way were bits of evidence which revealed the path the raiding party had taken when they carried off our families and possessions. Like the proverbial blood hounds we were able to track the receding raiders and their trophies. We moved rapidly for a great length of time in our anxiety to catch up with the raiding party which had our families in its possession. Finally we came to a deep ravine which was called Besor Ravine, where we were forced to stop and catch our breath. Having marched back to Ziklag from the front lines of battle with Israel and then, without stopping to rest from that long march, we had begun "marching on the run" as we feverishly pursued the evil raiding party somewhere ahead of us. After a few minutes I called out, "Forward, march!" To my dismay I saw that many of my men were struggling to get up but were dropping to the ground. I called out, "Halt!" After hastily checking the condition of my six hundred fighting men I discovered that at least two hundred of them were physically unable to put one foot in front of the other. There was nothing to be done but to leave them there to recuperate to the point of useful service later. With the four hundred men who were still reasonably able bodied we began to move across the Besor Ravine. When we came out on the other side we saw a man lying along our path. I had him brought to me so that I could question him. He was obviously sick and very, very weak. My men fed him from the rations in the pouches which they were carrying. Then, upon questioning him, I discovered that he had been without food and water for three days. After he had drunk water and had eaten the rations which my men provided I began to ask questions of him. "To whom do you belong, and where do you come from?" In a very weak voice he replied, "I am an Egyptian, a slave of an Amalekite. When I became too ill to travel he abandoned me." I then asked him what towns they had raided. "We raided the area of the Kerethites and the territory belonging to Judah and the area named for Caleb. Oh, yes, and we raided and burned the town of Ziklag." Then I asked him to lead us to the raiding party which had abandoned him. He replied, "If you promise on oath that you will not kill me or hand me over to my Amalekite master, I will lead you to where the raiding party is."

He led me and my men in a stealthy fashion so as not to give a warning to the Amalekite raiding part concerning our approach. Sure enough and true to his word he led us to a spot within sight of our prey. Much to our surprise the band of Amalekites were not in a close military formation with their prisoners (our families) in a tight enclosure as we had expected to find. Rather, they were scattered over a meadow eating and drinking and carousing. Obviously they were celebrating by enjoying the great amount of booty which they had captured from their raids on the towns of the Philistines and Judah. Silently I motioned my four hundred warriors to rush into the midst of that reveling group of Amalekites. Each of my men zeroed in on a warrior and began to fight man-to-man as he had been trained to do. We had arrived at the scene of the enemy's revelry at dusk-dark at which time we began to fight the enemy with all our "might and main". Since our families were being held prisoners by the enemy, our incentive to slay the members of the raiding party was at an all time high. For nearly twenty-four hours we fought furiously with the full intent of killing every warrior in the Amalekite raiding party, an enemy which had caused us such grief. By the evening of the next day we had reached our goal. Not one of the members of the evil Amalekite raiding party was left alive with the exception of four hundred young men who fled on camels. I was very proud of my four hundred men, for not one of them turned aside from our task of slaying the enemy in order to search for their families among the people scattered over the meadow. Now that our goal had been reached, exhausted though we were, each of us began the search for his family members. We wandered over the area frantically calling the names of our wives and children as black darkness settled around us.

The next day we did an inventory and discovered that not a single member of any of the families was missing . . . . all had been accounted for. Then we checked for our possessions which had been taken by the raiding party. As we started the homeward trek we gathered all the livestock which had belonged to us along with livestock which had been taken by the Amalekites on some of their other raids. Some of that plunder my men assigned to me and drove them ahead of us, saying, "This is David's plunder!"

After a few hours of slow traveling due to the women and small children and the great amount of plunder we had taken we came back to the Besor Ravine. There we were reunited with the two hundred men who had been physically unable to go into combat with us against the Amalekite raiders. A bit of repercussion occurred on the part of the four hundred men against the two hundred men who had been unable to fight and had been left behind. The men who had fought so vigorously declared that the ones who had been physically unable to fight against the raiders should not be given any of the plunder. They were adamant about that. Then and there I felt the need to establish a policy for present and future needs. I called the men before me and declared that all six hundred men should share and share alike in the division of the plunder. In doing this I had to lay my life on the line, for the four hundred warriors could not understand my line of reasoning. I had to explain that the two hundred soldiers who had been left behind had planned to go with us, but they had been providentially prevented from entering into the fray. Besides that they protected our property while we were fighting. After a while the mutterings of the four hundred men stopped.

Even before we began building homes for our families on the burned out site of Ziklag, I began making friends with the citizens in several towns in Israel by sharing some of the plunder we had gained in battle with the Amalekite raiding party. I thought to myself, "You never know when you will need such friends. Beside that they were kind to me and my men when we roamed about in their territory.

Chapter 22

In Need of "Burned Bridges"

King Saul joined those who were grieving for the prophet Samuel whose death occurred some years after Saul had become king. It was Samuel who had anointed him as the first king of Israel. He realized that it had been against Samuel's better judgment to establish an earthly king over Israel. Actually Samuel had been hurt by the clamor of the citizens of Israel for a king to lead them. They wanted to be like the other nations of the world who were ruled by earthly kings. Samuel considered it to be a slap in his face for them to behave in that fashion. For years he had ruled the people of Israel by the will and wisdom of Almighty God, that is to say that he had been a wise and righteous judge under the leadership of Jehovah God. There had been a succession of judges prior to Samuel. Many of them had been successful military leaders in addition to the usual task of judging the citizens of Israel. Like Samuel they had served in that capacity rather successfully, for they had been in tune with God's leadership. In spite of the fact that at times Samuel had rebuked Saul because he had been unwise in some of the decisions he had made, Saul revered him. He knew that Samuel had the ear of the Lord and thus made Godly decisions. He admired Samuel for those righteous decisions which he made on behalf of Israel. Another reason that Saul attended the burial of Samuel was that it was good politics to be seen there.

In the early part of his reign Saul had outlawed mediums and spiritists in the land of Israel perhaps in an act designed to please the prophet Samuel. In a sense he was "cutting the opposition" to Samuel, or so he thought. I was informed by my friend in the court of King Saul that there came the time when the Philistines again "got the itch" to do battle against Israel. It was their custom to do battle with Israel on a recurring basis. Such an occasion arose when the army of the Philistines came out to wage war against Israel. It was arrayed against Israel once again, this time making camp at Shunem. King Saul gave orders for his forces to make camp at Gilboa. When he learned of the size of the army of the Philistines, he literally trembled in his boots. He needed to know whether it would be possible to have a successful encounter with such a huge army. He instinctively wanted to consult a medium, but he suddenly remembered that he had driven mediums and spiritists out of the land. What was he to do? He surely needed help in discerning the future. He inquired of the Lord as to the outcome of such a battle, but the Lord did not hear him, that is, He gave no answer through dreams, through the Urim, or through prophets in the land. In desperation he turned to his attendants and instructed them to find a woman who was a medium so that he could go and inquire of her. They replied, "There is one in Endor." He asked himself what he could do about that now that he had outlawed mediums and fortune tellers in the land of Israel. They evidently had gone under cover to avoid prosecution by him. Well, certainly he could not reveal his true identity to those practicing such an art when he went into the presence of one of them to seek the information which he desired. Therefore, he took off his kingly robes and dressed as an ordinary man. He took two of his men and went out into the darkness of night to visit the medium in Endor. She invited them into her home and told them to be seated. When she asked him to state his business he asked her to consult a spirit for him. "Bring up the one I tell you to." She replied, "Surely you are aware that what you are asking me to do has been outlawed by King Saul. Are you here to set a trap for me in order to bring about my death?" Saul swore to her by the Lord that she would not be punished for consulting a spirit for him, a spirit whom he would name. "All right, whom shall I bring up for you?" "I would like for you to bring up the old prophet Samuel." When she succeeded in bringing him up, Samuel revealed to her that the man sitting in her room was King Saul. She screamed at Saul, "Why have you done this to me? You are Saul who has outlawed my work as a medium." "Now, now, remember the oath I took a moment ago, so don't be afraid. What do you see?" "I see a spirit coming up out of the ground?" "What does he look like?" "An old man who is wearing a robe is coming up out of the ground." By that description Saul knew that the "spirit" was Samuel, and he immediately got down with his face to the ground. Samuel said to Saul, "Why have you disturbed me by bringing me up?" "I am in great distress; the Philistines are fighting against me, and God has turned away from me. No longer does He answer me either by prophets or by dreams. Therefore, I have had the medium to bring you up so that I can enquire of you what I should do." As he had done in life Samuel gave Saul a rather harsh reply. "Seeing that the Lord has turned away from you and has become your enemy, why are you consulting me? The Lord has done what he predicted through me that He would do. He has torn the kingdom of Israel out of your hands and has given it to one of your neighbors, that is, to David. Because you did not obey the Lord by carrying out His great wrath against the Amalekites, he has done this to you today. The Lord will hand over both you and the nation of Israel to the Philistines. Tomorrow both you and your sons will be with me. The Lord will also hand over the army of Israel to the Philistines." Immediately Saul prostrated himself on the ground because Samuel's message filled him with great fear. His strength was gone because he had eaten nothing for the last twenty-four hours.

The medium went over to Saul when she saw the helpless condition he was in. "Listen to me, I, your maidservant, have obeyed you. I took my life in my hands and did what you told me to do. Now, please listen to me your maidservant and do what I tell you to do. Here is some food which I want you to eat so that you may have strength enough to go on your way." "I will not eat!" The men who had come with him also urged him to eat, and he listened to them. He arose from the ground and sat on the couch there in the living room. The medium went out to the stall at the back of her house and butchered the fatted calf which she had kept there. She quickly made some unleavened bread. She set the hot food before Saul and his men, and they ate, after which they arose and went out into the night.

CHAPTER 23
A PROPHECY FULFILLED

Since my little band of soldiers and I were not allowed to participate in the forthcoming battle with the mighty army of the Philistines against Israel, I could only wait and listen for any echo that might come drifting across the way to Ziklag. I was like a fish out of water, that is, I was so very anxious about the outcome of the battle that was being waged between the army of my adopted nation and my native nation. The commanding generals of the Philistine army were probably correct in their assessment of my loyalties. They assumed that if they allowed me and my little band of soldiers to go into battle alongside them at some point in the heat of the battle our real loyalty would cause us to turn from them to the army of our native land, Israel. At that point in time we were so grateful to the Philistines for allowing us to find safety within their borders that we were sure that would never happen. But as the old adage puts it, "Blood is thicker than water". Well, it was obvious that neither side wanted us to be a part of their fighting force, so all we could do was to wait and see.

The army of the Philistines in a few short years had become a huge one which enjoyed the reputation of being a mighty force. In times past their army had not been successful against King Saul and his army, but now they were confident that the situation would soon change. There seemed to be a spirit of great confidence among the Philistine soldiers. It was a "can do" attitude, an attitude that had not been true in days past. Achish, their king, was kinder and more personable than most of the near eastern rulers. He had given great authority to his army commanders . . . . almost too much he muttered to himself at times. In other words the morale of the Philistine soldiers was at an all time high. Their commanders had put their soldiers through rigorous training for hand-to-hand combat. The seasoned warriors complained (behind the commanders' backs of course) that they were being treated like raw recruits. At the same time, however, they had a great sense of satisfaction that they were serving in a well trained army.

On the other hand the army of Israel had been traveling under the assumption that it was indomitable. They reasoned that their past victories over the Philistines gave them the upper hand. One could say that they were resting on their laurels and felt that no further training was needed. Also, King Saul had not given proper attention to the matter of conducting a "continuing education" in warfare, for he had been too engrossed in chasing me and my little band of malcontents. What a shock it was to him when he went out to do battle against the Philistines and looked across the distance to see the enemy arrayed in such strength. From their vantage point the Israelites declared that the horde of enemy soldiers was as numerous as the sand of the sea shore. It was small wonder that King Saul's heart sank within him. As I learned later it was on that night before the great battle that he was so greatly troubled as to its outcome that he resorted to seek out the medium known as the "witch of Endor". As I described earlier in my memoirs the king had to be very stealthy about that, because he had earlier outlawed the use of mediums. When I heard about what happened that night, I almost felt sorry for King Saul. When the medium called up the spirit of the dead prophet Samuel, he heard the prophet tell him that because he had turned against the Lord God the Lord had turned against him. The spirit of Samuel told him that his sons would be killed in battle the next day and that he would die also. It was hard for me to imagine what state of mind King Saul was in the next day when he began to do battle with the mighty army of the Philistines.

What a fiercely fought battle that was there at Mount Gilboa! The Philistine soldiers fought like roaring lions. They pushed forward en masse like a living wall of swinging swords. Never had the Israelites seen much less encountered such a fighting force. Obviously the Philistine soldiers had been instructed to seek out King Saul and his sons and slay them. It was a mystery as to how they were able to identify the royal sons of Israel who were intermingled with the rest of the Israeli soldiers . . . . but they obviously did. Perhaps King Saul's sons had been thoughtless enough to wear their royal robes or perhaps a royal insignia. A shout in the language of the Philistines could be heard, "I've killed one!" A bit later there was the roar of another voice above the din of warfare, "I've killed another one!" A while later a third voice called out, "I've killed another!" They had been so well instructed about the family of Saul that they knew that they had to kill Saul's three sons in order to "wipe out" the seed royal. A shout went up among the troops, "That does it! We've killed them all!" King Saul had been secreted in the center of a knot of his soldiers in order both to hide and to protect him. However, their plan did not work, for an arrow shot by a member of the Philistine army's band of archers found its way into the body of Saul, wounding him critically. I heard that because of the great pain caused by the severe wound he had received he instructed his young armor bearer to draw his sword and run it through the king's body. The poor young armor bearer stood there on one foot and then on the other in frozen indecision. "Kill my king? Never!" was the thought running through his young mind. Seeing that the young man was too terrified to obey him, King Saul took his sword and fell on it and died. He knew that the moment it was discovered by the enemy soldiers that he had been critically injured; they would delight in "making sport" of him before "finishing him off". To him it was the lesser of the two evils. The young armor bearer followed the king's action and took his own life.

On that fateful day King Saul and his sons, Jonathan, Abinadab, and Malki-Shua were all slain. The forces of Israel were scattered by the onslaught of the Philistine army. When the Israelite civilians along the Jordan River Valley and those across the Jordan saw what had happened to the army of Israel they abandoned their towns and fled. The next day the Philistine soldiers returned to the scene of the battle of the previous day and began stripping the clothes off the bodies of the Israeli soldiers and gathering their possessions. As they were doing that they came across the bodies of King Saul and those of his three sons lying on Mount Gilboa. They cut off the king's head and stripped off his armor. His armor they put in their heathen temple, the temple of the Ashtoreths. They fastened his body to the wall at Beth Shan along with those of his three sons.

When some of the braver soldiers of Israel heard what happened to Saul and his sons, how it was that their bodies were fastened to the wall at Beth Shan, they slipped stealthily through the darkness of night and crept up to that wall and took down the royal bodies. They took the bodies to Jabesh where they burned them so that they would not be recognizable when the enemy sought to recover them . . . . and they surely would. The bones which were left from the burning they took and buried under the shade of a tamarisk tree there in Jabesh. Regardless of how they might have felt personally about King Saul, they knew that they must show proper respect to a fallen leader. For seven days they fasted in his honor.

CHAPTER 24
HOW THE MIGHTY HAVE FALLEN!

What I just described in the preceding account of the fierce battle between the army of the Philistines and the army of Israel was hearsay information, for I was not anywhere near that battle. Instead my small band of soldiers and myself were in the opposite direction raiding towns and villages of the Amalakites. I gave my men orders to take a brief rest break from the throes of warfare and give respite to their weary bodies. For two days we all enjoyed resting and being with our families there in Ziklag. On the third day we were disturbed from our rest by the arrival of a stranger in camp, a man whose clothes were torn and there was a lot of dust on his head. Had he been in a dust storm or was the dust on his head a sign of his being in mourning. Evidently he asked one of my soldiers where I was, for I happened to look in his direction and saw my soldier pointing to me. The man made his way to me and fell on the ground, prostrating himself before me as a sign of paying honor to me.

Giving him a long look I asked from whence he had come. "I have escaped from the camp of the Israelites." "Tell me what happened." "Well, it was like this; King Saul's men fled in fear of the army of the Philistines. Some of them fell and died due to the wounds which they had received in the battle. Three of King Saul's sons were in the group that died also. King Saul himself was critically wounded and later died at his own hands." I stood there watching that fellow's facial expression and his body language in an effort to determine if he was telling the truth. Finally, I asked him, "How do you know that Saul and his son Jonathan are dead? Can you prove that what you are saying is true?" "I surely can. You see it was like this; I just happened to be on Mount Gilboa. I glanced over to my right and there was King Saul himself; he was leaning on his spear, using it as a brace to hold his body upright. I looked behind me and realized that the chariots and their drivers were rapidly approaching and were almost upon the king. All of a sudden King Saul started looking in my direction and calling out to me. I obediently replied, 'What can I do for you, sir?' He stared at me with eyes that were glazed over with pain. Then he asked, 'Who are you? I don't recognize you.' 'I'm an Amalakite, sir.' He replied, 'Come over here to me and stand over me; use my sword and kill me. I am mortally wounded; I do not want those heathen Philistines to make sport of me before killing me. I am in the agony of death, but I'm still alive.' Well, seeing as how he could not survive his wounds and that he was going to die in a short time, I figured the kind thing to do was to put him out of his misery. Also, seeing as how he was a great king, and I was just an ordinary man who was a foreigner, I had no choice but to obey him. You are staring at me as though you don't believe me. I've got proof." Having said that, he lowered a knapsack that had been slung around his neck and reached into it. Slowly he pulled out two articles and said, "See, here is King Saul's crown which he was wearing in battle and here is an armband with the royal insignia on it . . . . I took from his arm. Now, are you convinced that I did what I said I did?"

Hearing what the Amalakite said and seeing the proof that he was telling me the truth when he said that King Saul and his son Jonathan were dead, I immediately began to tear my clothes as a sign of deep sorrow. My men followed me in that gesture. We all mourned and went without eating until evening. We were weeping because of the death of God's anointed, King Saul, and for his highly respected son, Jonathan. Also, we were showing sorrow and respect for the defeated army of Israel. Although we had been ostracized from Israel, our native land, we had the highest sympathy for it.

The next day after mourning all the preceding day I began to take care of some unfinished business, that of judging the dusty stranger who had brought the sad message on the preceding day. I called him before me and asked him, "Where are you from?"

"I'm an Amalakite, sir." I made a mental note, "He is an enemy whose people we have been fighting." Then, I began an informal trial with him as both the "witness" and the "criminal". "Why were you not afraid to kill the Lord's anointed?" Then I turned to one of my men and told him to kill the Amalakite who was standing there with a smug look on his face probably because he expected me to reward him for having killed the person who had caused me and my men to be ostracized from Israel. I addressed the Amalakite with these words, "Your blood be on your own head. Your own mouth has testified against you when you said, 'I killed the Lord's anointed'. Quick as a flash my man drew his sword and killed the Amalakite.

I then withdrew from the presence of my men and into the solitude of my house. I sat down and reviewed my friendship with Jonathan. I remembered those youthful vows which we had taken in which we had promised that come weal or woe our friendship would last until death parted the two of us. In those moments of remembering Jonathan a song rose to my mind which I quietly sang to myself:

"Your glory, O Israel, lies slain on your heights.
How the mighty have fallen!
Tell it not in Gath,
Proclaim it not in the streets of Ashkelon,
Lest the daughters of the Philistines be glad,
Lest the daughters of the uncircumcised rejoice.
O mountains of Gilboa, may you have neither dew nor rain,
Nor fields that yield offerings of grain.
For there the shield of the mighty was defiled,
The shield of Saul—no longer rubbed with oil.
From the blood of the slain,
From the flesh of the mighty,
The bow of Jonathan did not turn back,
The sword of Saul did not return unsatisfied.
Saul and Jonathan—they were loved and gracious,
And in death they were not parted.
How the mighty have fallen in battle!
Jonathan lies slain on your heights.

"King David: 'My Life as I Remember It'"

I grieve for you, Jonathan my brother;
You were very dear to me.
Your love for me was wonderful,
More wonderful that that of women.
How the mighty have fallen!
The weapons of war have perished!"

CHAPTER 25
GOING HOME

After a period of mourning over the deaths of King Saul and of my dear friend Jonathan, I settled down to a quiet time in which I began to think of what I should do now that I was no longer on the run from King Saul and, therefore, had no need to hide out in enemy territory. I no longer thought of the Philistine nation as being my enemy, for its king had been very kind to me and my band of men. He had allowed us to have the town of Ziklag in his country to be our dwelling place. We had been allowed to bring our families over into his land and set up housekeeping on his turf so to speak. That having been said I had to admit that there was a longing in my heart to be back in my homeland of Judah. Having grown up in the area of Bethlehem, I felt that there was no place like my old home area. No doubt my men were feeling the same way though they did not openly express it.

I went to the Lord in prayer about what I should do. "Should I remain in Ziklag in the land of the Philistines or should I return to my roots?" After a period of earnest prayer concerning the matter I felt that the Lord was telling me that I should return to Judah. That having been settled in my thinking, the next question that I posed to the Lord was, "Where in Judah should I settle?" The Lord responded by pointing me in the direction of Hebron of Judah. The women in our little conclave expressed dissatisfaction at having to pull up stakes and move with the children, the cattle, and all their earthly possessions again. They said, "It seems like it was only yesterday that we got here and tried to make a home in this place." However, they were obedient to the decision which I and my men had made to go back across the border into the land of Judah. Soon they showed enthusiasm at the thought of moving back into their native land. The great question was, "How will we be received by the followers of the late King Saul? Will they meet our band of soldiers and their families with pleasure or displeasure?"

Well, for good or bad, we broke camp and started the long trek to the east, heading back into the land of our former enemies. We encountered no confrontation from the people of Judah as we entered their land and headed for the area in which I grew up, the area of Hebron. We had not been very long in that area until we were approached by a large band of rough looking soldiers. We were stressed by the sight of them. The men of our little band came forward and placed themselves between their families and possessions, and those rough appearing men. When they had arrived at a spot in front of me and my people they let it be known that they had come in peace. I asked them to state their business. They nodded in the direction of their obvious leader who stepped forward and began to speak. "We have come to you on a mission from the people of Judah. As you no doubt know we lost our King on the heights of Mount Gilboa where he suffered death in the battle with the Philistines. We have come on behalf of the nation of Judah to ask you to become our king. We remember how as a young lad you showed great heroism by slaying the giant Goliath. We remember, also, how you led regiments of our soldiers into many a victorious battle. We are sorry for the way you were treated by our late King Saul. We are asking that you overlook that and that you become the king of our nation, Judah. We think that there is no other warrior like you."

I thought to myself, "Ah, now I begin to see why the Lord advised me to return to the land of Judah. He knew all the time that this would happen. It was He who had the prophet Samuel to anoint me as king when I was but a lad and while Saul was still king. He is carrying out his plan of so many years ago," I said to myself. The men of Judah who were standing before me were obviously waiting for an answer from me. In my heart I knew that their request was of the Lord who had planned this all along. Finally I gave answer to them by saying that I would accept their invitation to become their king and that by the help of the Lord Almighty I would endeavor to be worthy of such an honor and such a responsibility. Those men, the obvious chosen representatives of the nation of Judah, presided over the ceremony of anointing me as "King of Judah".

Oh, what thoughts ran through my mind during that little ceremony in which I was set aside as the chosen one to lead the little nation of Judah. I recalled those long and lonely nights out under the stars when I served as the shepherd of my father's herd of sheep. I recalled how I sprang to the rescue of my sheep when a marauding animal approached them. I recalled how God had empowered me, a mere lad, to slay the giant Goliath. I remembered how I had led regiments of King Saul's soldiers into victory over the enemies of the nation. I certainly remembered my years of leading a little band of men as we moved from one hiding place to another as we were pursued by the powerful King Saul. Now, all of that foundational training was climaxing in the responsibility that was being thrust upon me as the new King of Judah! Was I capable of handling such a responsibility?

Well, there I was, a newly anointed king. What should I do first? I should take care of some unfinished business I decided. I had learned that it was the men of Jabesh Gilead who had stealthily retrieved the bodies of King Saul and his sons and had given them a final burial safe from the hands of the Philistines. That was a great thing they did as they endeavored to do what they could to honor the remains of the fallen king of Judah, King Saul. I felt that the proper thing to do was to give to them the thanks of the nation of Judah by sending to them some chosen men to deliver my message to that effect. My message was, "The Lord bless you for showing this kindness to Saul your master by burying him. May the Lord now show you kindness and faithfulness, and I too will show you the same favor because you have done this. Now then, be strong and brave, for Saul your master is dead, and the house of Judah has anointed me king over it." Not only was that the proper thing for me to do in remembrance of King Saul, but also it was a strategic way for me to announce to them that I was the new king of Judah. To do this was good diplomacy as I endeavored to take over the reigns of government for the little nation of Judah.

My time of happiness and honor bestowed on me by the act of anointing me to be the new king of Judah was short lived. Trouble was brewing to the north through the action of Abner, the late King Saul's army commander. He took it on himself to make Ish-Bosheth, Saul's surviving son, the king of Israel which consisted of all the other tribes of Israel. Abner and the men of Israel who were loyal to Ish-Bosheth came down to the pool of Gibeon where they took their seats beside it. Joab, whom I had appointed to be my army commander, and my men serving under him also went out to the pool of Gibeon and sat down on the opposite side from Abner's group. Abner, a brash sort of fellow, challenged Joab to have a duel between twelve of his men and twelve of Joab's men. They were to fight hand-to-hand there in the sight of the rest of those present. My commander agreed to accept the challenge. It was an ugly sight. Twelve young men from each opposing group paired off to fight to the death. Those young men were foolish enough to feel that they were doing an honorable thing. Each grabbed the other by the hair of the head with one hand and with the other hand thrust his dagger into the bowels of the other with the result that both were killed. (From that time on that place was known as the "Field of Daggers".) When those young men's daring hand-to-hand combat was over the two armies took up the fight. What a fierce battle that was! Finally when the battle was over it was obvious that my army under Joab was the winner.

Abner and his forces fled from the scene. One of Joab's brothers, Asahel, who was noted for his ability to run swiftly, chased after Abner. Hearing the pounding of feet behind him, Abner guessed that it was the fleet footed Asahel and told him to stop chasing him. "I don't want to have to kill you. If I did kill you, how could I face your brother, Joab?" However, Asahel doggedly continued the chase until he came alongside Abner at which time Abner rammed so hard the butt of his spear into Asahel's abdomen that it came out of Asahel's back. What a gruesome sight that was! Every one of my men stopped when they came upon that awful sight. After a long pause they continued in hot pursuit of Abner and his followers. Just as the sun was setting they approached the hill of Ammah. The men of the tribe of

Benjamin stopped fleeing and formed ranks and made a stand on top of the hill in defiance of Joab and his men. Abner who had taken command of the Benjamites called out to the approaching Joab and addressed him saying, "Must the sword devour forever? Don't you realize that this will end in bitterness? How long before you order your men to stop pursuing their brothers?" Those conciliatory words of Abner hit home to the heart of Joab, who answered Abner with these words, "As surely as God lives, if you had not spoken, the men would have continued the pursuit of their brothers until morning." Joab sounded retreat on the trumpet with the result that all his men came to a halt, and their attitude toward the forces of Abner cooled for the time being.

We learned later that Abner and his men continued their forced march through the night to the east where they crossed the Jordan River and continued all morning until they came to Mahanaim. When the score was tallied up my men had killed three hundred and sixty of Abner's soldiers. Our losses numbered twenty men which included Asahel, the fleet footed brother of Joab.

CHAPTER 26
THE BEGINNING OF MY DYNASTY

Sad to say, the "truce" at the end of Joab's chase of Abner and his men did not last long. There was a continuing struggle between the tribes of Israel and the new nation of Judah. I sensed that the underlying desire of the majority of citizens in each of the two entities was that there once again could be a united nation under one ruler. Naturally the tribes of Israel assumed that they should assimilate the younger and smaller nation of Judah into its fold. Judah, though greatly outnumbered by Israel, had the dream of seeing a united nation with me as Judah's king being the king of that desired unified nation. Periods of peace between the two nations did not last very long, for eventually one group would call the bluff of the other. As a result war between the two factions would soon begin again.

For me this was the longest period of comparative peace that I had experienced since my fight with Goliath, an event that cast me in the role of a soldier in the eyes of my compatriots. I was still half man, half boy, but nevertheless I was thrust into the life of a warrior. Now as King of Judah I felt that at last I could have a period of tranquility in my life. My desire was to begin to have children by my two wives, Ahinoam and Abigal. True, I had been married to Michal, the daughter of King Saul, but he had taken her away from me and given her to another man. As king of Judah I now could settle down in permanent living quarters with my wives. As a person with the position of King I would be able to support many wives. As had long been the custom of men who could afford it, several wives per man was considered "good". After all, women were almost considered to be the property of their husbands. In such an arrangement the husband was expected to provide well for his wives. They were expected to bear him many sons through whom his dynasty would endure. Single women only in rare instances owned property in their own right. They had little honorable means of support. It was considered by them to be a blest thing to be married to a husband regardless of how many wives he might have.

After a while of comparative peace and tranquility in my life I had became husband of several wives in addition to Ahinoam and Abigail. These were Maacah, daughter of Talmai who was King of Geshur, Haggith, Abital, and Eglah. After a while each wife presented me with a son: Ammon, the son of Ahinoam; Kileab, the son of Abigail; Absalom, son of Maacah; Adonijah, son of Haggith; Shephatiah, son of Abital; and the sixth was Ithream, son of Eglah. As was obvious to all I had taken time to become a family man. I was so very proud of these sons and dreamed of the day when they would grow up and follow in my footsteps by becoming great warriors.

Unfortunately, for the next six or seven years there was continual battling back and forth between my nation of Judah and the nation of Israel. Secretly, I could see that the opposing army was growing weaker while the army of Judah was growing stronger. Joab had proved to be a good commander of my army.

It was the gossip of the day that Abner, commander of the forces of Israel, was adding glory to himself rather than to his King, Ish-Bosheth. In every way possible he down played the importance of the king and built himself up in the eyes of the people. It was told me that one day it was reported to King Ish-Bosheth that Abner had had sexual relations with Rispah, one of King Saul's concubines. My source of information said that when Abner was questioned about his misdemeanor his anger flared up and he shouted at King Ish-Bosheth to the effect, "Is this the way you reward me? Do you consider me to be a 'dog's head'? I have been loyal to you; there have been many times when the thought occurred to me to betray you into the hands of Judah, but I didn't. Now you are reprimanding me, the commander-in-chief of your army, for such a little thing as assuming the right to take over with the right of access to the dead King Saul's concubine? I refuse to be insulted by you. Thus far I have been loyal to your father, the late King Saul, and now to his family and extended kindred. Let me tell you this, may God deal with me, be it ever so severely, if I do not turn from allegiance to you and start assisting Judah's king, King David, to achieve the place that the Lord promised on oath to him. I shall henceforth give my allegiance to King David and assist him to become the King of a united kingdom, that is, Israel and Judah combined." King Ish-Bosheth said nothing further to the very angry Abner; for fear that his anger of the moment might be carried out as he had threatened.

After seething with anger for a while Abner began to put feet to the threat which he had made to Ish-Bosheth. He contacted me by sending messengers who delivered this question, "Whose land is the territory occupied by Israel and Judah? If you will make an agreement with me, I shall help you to bring all Israel over to your command." After thinking this over I sent word back to Abner by his messengers, "Good! I will make an agreement with you, BUT there is one proviso. Don't appear before me unless you bring with you Michal, daughter of King Saul." Backing up my statement to Abner, now traitor to Israel, by sending word to King Ish-Bosheth demanding that he send to me Michal, for whom I had paid a dowry of a hundred Philistine foreskins. There was no doubt that the king was very fearful that Abner would turn against him as he had threatened, so he made haste to carry out my demand. As you can see, I was not putting all my eggs in one basket, that is, I was not depending on Abner alone to meet my demand. I also made the demand of the King of Israel himself. My demands bore results. The king gave orders to take Michal away from her husband, Paltiel. Obviously there had been a real love match between him and Michal, for it was reported to me that he followed after her weeping until Abner ordered him to go back home.

CHAPTER 27

AN UNEXPECTED TURN OF EVENTS

Abner, Commander of the Army of Israel, proved to be what I had long suspected . . . . a self-serving type of fellow. As mentioned earlier he had rushed in following King Saul's death and proclaimed Ish-Bosheth, King Saul's son, the king of Israel. I learned later that such action on Abner's part did not necessarily express the feelings of the people of Israel. I also learned later that many of the citizens of Israel felt in their hearts that they would like to see me become their king. Many of them knew that years earlier I had been anointed by the highly respected prophet, Samuel, to be king of the total nation of Israel and Judah combined. There was a strong indication that Abner saw in Ish-Bosheth a man who was weak enough in spirit that he could be used as a "figure head king" through whom the strong willed Abner could actually "call the shots" in ruling over Israel. To put it mildly Abner was a brash, hot headed sort of fellow with very conniving ways.

Be that as it may I later saw in Abner a conspirator whose political clout in Israel could serve well my purpose in attaining my goal of becoming the king of all twelve tribes who resided in the land of Palestine. As you may have observed when you read the early part of the account of my life's journey that I was an opportunist. To put that statement into a spiritual light I thought of my actions simply as taking advantage of the opportunities that the Lord put in my path so that I might achieve my goals in life, the most important of which was to become the king of Israel and Judah combined. Well, be that as it may, I was surprised to hear the message which Abner sent to me that he was willing and ready to hand to me the great Kingdom of Israel. He was ready to make an agreement with me to that effect. I was requested to send word to him concerning my reaction to his offer.

After a short time of giving thought to Abner's offer I sent messengers to him saying that I would accept his offer to hand over the northern kingdom to me. However, my statement of acceptance was contingent on one matter. He must bring to me my first wife, Michal, daughter of the late King Saul. As you will recall she was taken from me by her father and given to another man, Paltiel. Through the years I had wondered about her and had longed to have her back in my possession. Perhaps my statement may have sounded to you as though I thought of Michal as being a piece of property which was stolen from me. I suppose in a way that was how I felt about her. My pride had been hurt in that earlier transaction when King Saul took her from me. As much as anything I wanted revenge from King Saul even though he was now dead.

I learned through the "grapevine" method of communication that Abner began the process of turning over Israel to me by calling in the elders of Israel and conferring with them. He reminded them that they had wanted me instead of Ish-Bosheth to become their king at the death of Saul. He said, "For some time you have wanted to make David your king. Now do it! For you will recall that the Lord promised David, 'By my servant David I will rescue my people Israel from the hand of the Philistines and from the hand of all their enemies.'" Abner gave the Benjamites a special personal hearing, for they had assumed a place of leadership in Israel at the end of Saul's life. Following that he came down to Hebron to relate to me the steps he had taken to bring to fruition what he had promised to me. When he, along with twenty of his men, arrived at my headquarters for a conference, I had a feast prepared for them. After all, the least I could do for Abner was to show my deep appreciation in this way for what he was about to do.

At the conclusion of the feast Abner excused himself along with his men by saying, "Let me go at once to assemble all Israel for my lord the king, so that they may make a compact with you, and that you may rule over all that your heart desires." I bade him and his men farewell and sent them on their way. They had just left when my army commander, Joab, and the men of his raiding party arrived back from a raiding party hot, dusty and tired. Obviously my men had been very successful in that raid, for they brought back much plunder. In the early days of the kingdom of Judah this was the method by which our little nation sustained itself. When provisions began to get low, my army made a raid against one of our enemies, engaging them in victorious warfare. The possessions of the conquered group were taken from them and were brought back to enrich the coffers of our little nation. Upon Joab's arrival back in Hebron he was immediately informed by the people that Abner and a group of men had visitied with me and that I had honored them with a feast and sent him away in peace. Joab's face flushed with anger. He came into my presence with a scowl on his face and anger shooting from his eyes and blurted out to me, "What have you done? Abner, the leader of the nation Israel with which we are at enemity, came into your presence, was honored with a banquet, and was sent away by you in peace. Why on earth did you let him go in peace? Now he is gone from our grasp. You know very well the kind of fellow Abner is. No doubt he came over here on the pretext of friendship with you, but most likely he came to deceive you by making rash promises to you and for the purpose of observing the movements of your army and also for the purpose of learning everything you are doing? You ought to have known better!" Joab and his brother, Abishai, were very, very angry at Abner for slaying their brother, Asahel, a short time earlier.

Without my knowledge Joab took matters into his own hand by sending a band of messengers to catch up with Abner and bring him back on the pretext of wanting to confer with him about their future work together in a united kingdom. Innocently enough Abner returned so that he and Joab might confer. Upon Abner's return to my headquarters Joab gave the appearance of showing Abner great hospitality. After hospitable greetings had been shown to his "guest", Joab drew him aside as though to be out of earshot while sharing some classified information. When out of sight of their men Joab drew his dagger and plunged it into the abdomen of Abner who died few moments later.

Joab had been away from my presence with his raiding party and thus was not privy to what Abner was arranging concerning bringing over the tribes of Israel to become my subjects. Joab had acted in hot-headed passion in avenging the death of his brother without seeing the whole picture. What he did in that act of vengeance against Abner would destroy the period of peace between Israel and Judah that both nations had been enjoying for a while. More especially Joab's hot-headed action in taking matters into his own hands before he had learned the good use I had planned to make of Abner would prevent the plan from going into fruition. Well, I was more than somewhat perturbed by what had just happened. Joab's action against Abner would most likely bring enemity between the nations. Abner's and my plans would probably not materialize. I took turns being hopeful and being despondent. I attempted to bring order out of chaos resulting from Joab's action. A lot of political prowess was called for, so I began to swing into action. I made a big show of grief over what had happened to Abner with the hope that I could prove to Israel that what had happened between Joab and Abner was a personal matter and not one involving myself and the members of my court. I managed to get word back to Israel that I was innocent of the crime, that it was entirely the work of Joab who was seeking vengeance against Abner who had slain his brother. I let my displeasure at the action of Joab be made known to the elders of Israel by uttering a curse against Joab and his kin in which I said, "May his (Abner's) blood fall upon the head of Joab and upon his entire father's house. May Joab's house never be without someone who has a running sore or leprosy or who leans on a crutch or who falls by the sword or who lacks food!"

I ordered a big funeral held for Abner. I gave instructions to Joab to take on the stance of mourning for Abner by observing the custom of showing that one was in mourning by tearing his clothes and by walking in front of the coffin of Abner as we made our way to the burial spot there in Hebron. I walked behind the coffin in an attitude of mourning. At his tomb I wept aloud and had all those in attendance at the funeral to weep aloud also. I knew full well that our act of mourning would be relayed to the citizens of Israel who would realize that Abner's murder was neither mine nor Judah's desire. I even sang a hymn of lament at his grave:

> "Should Abner have died as the lawless die?
> Your hands were not bound,
> Your feet were not fettered.
> You fell as one falls before wicked men."

Following my hymn of lament all the people wept over the grave of Abner again. Following the funeral I fasted. My people urged me to eat something, for I had eaten nothing since the news of Abner's murder had reached me. They were greatly concerned about me and continued to urge me to eat, but I refused by saying:

> "May God deal with me, be it ever so severely,
> If I taste bread or anything else before the sun sets!"

I noticed that all my people were observing my actions and seemed to be greatly pleased by them. When reported to the leaders of Israel I was told that my show of grief pleased them also. Obviously I had achieved my purpose in dramatizing my grief over Abner's death, for the people of Israel accepted the fact that I had had nothing to do with it. I further emphasized that fact by saying to the men of my court:

> "Do you not realize that a prince and a
> great man has fallen in Israel this day?
> And today, though I am the anointed king,
> I am weak, and these sons of Zeruiah are too
> strong for me. May the Lord repay the evildoer
> according to his evil deeds!"

Chapter 28
Misguided Helpers

Hardly had I and my people in Judah recovered from the death of Abner, the would-be traitor to King Ish-Bosheth, than another unexpected turn of events occurred. Two men of Israel took it upon themselves to hasten the day when all obstacles to my becoming their king were removed. Evidently they belonged to those in Israel who had become disillusioned with their king. Word leaked out across the border from Israel that its citizens had taken notice that Ish-Bossheth had become an even more timid and inadequate ruler after the death of Abner, his army commander on whom he had leaned. He was not aware that Abner had struck a bargain with me concerning my becoming king of Israel. All that he knew was that Abner on whom he leaned for guidance and strength in governing Israel had been murdered.

There were two men who plotted to bring about the death of King Ish-Bosheth. They were Baanah and Recab, who were the sons of Rimmon of the tribe of Benjamin. At midday on a very hot day the two of them went into the palace and pretended to be going to the inner part to get some wheat which was stored there. When they were certain that no one was watching them, they entered the bed chamber of the king where they found him lying on the bed asleep. As was his habit he was taking a noonday nap. Stealthily the two of them approached the bed, took out their concealed daggers and stabbed the king in the stomaChapter To prevent the king's outcry from being heard they placed their hands over his mouth. When it became obvious that he was dead, one of them pulled out his concealed sword and cut off the king's head. Slipping it into a bag so that any person who might observe them leaving the premises would suppose that they were carrying a bag of wheat. They left with an innocent demeanor so as to prevent anyone of the palace servants taking notice of them. Traveling at a slow pace until they had reached the outskirts of the town they made their way out into the countryside. By that time it was beginning to get dark. They mounted their donkeys which they had tethered to a tree earlier and made their obstinate beasts of burden move more rapidly than they usually did. They traveled all night and later the next day they arrived in Hebron and came seeking an audience with me.

The two of them bowed before me until I acknowledged their presence. Now, let it be said that God had gifted me with the ability to read a person's character by his facial expression and by his whole demeanor. Well, as I surveyed those two who stood before me, I observed that they were hot and dusty. That conveyed to me the knowledge that they had traveled a long way in haste. I observed that they had an ingratiating smile on their faces. Instinctively I sensed that they had committed some crime. When the customary greetings were over, I told them to state their business. Both spoke at once in their excitement over the great gift which they were planning to present to me. Finally, one took over as the spokesman for the two of them. He said very proudly, "Here is the head of Ish-Bosheth, son of Saul, your enemy who tried many times to take your life. This day the Lord has avenged you, my lord the king, against Saul and his offspring." My heart seemed to stand still for a long moment. The news was too much for me. True, King Saul had tried many, many times to take my life, but also true I never lost my allegiance to him who was God's anointed. In spite of all the hatred he had shown toward me I never lifted a hand against him even though I had several opportunities. Also true, he had caused me to live the life of a hunted animal, for I was a "hunted one". There arose in my memory all the past trials and tribulations which King Saul had caused me to bear, yet there also arose in my memory my sacred pledge of allegiance to him whom I saw as the "anointed King" who had been placed upon the throne of Israel by God. Thus, there was a long moment before I had an opportunity to recoil from the mental scenes of the past and turn to the present situation. I spoke to the two men standing before me who were holding a sack containing the head of the murdered king of Israel. It was almost more than I could do to contain myself sufficiently to the point that I could address my message to them. In essence I said to them, "There was an earlier situation in my life when I lived over in the land of the Philistines in the town of Ziklag that corresponds to what has just happened here. A man came rushing into my presence with what he considered to be very good news to present to me. In a spirit of glee he announced the news that King Saul was dead. He thought that he was bringing good news to me, for he had heard how King Saul had chased after me as though I were an animal of prey. Well, he thought wrong. King Saul was 'God's anointed' and no matter how he had treated me I respected him for his position. Guess what! I rewarded that bearer of such news by having him killed. Now, I ask you how much more should I do to you two who have come to me telling me that you have killed and cut off the head of the king of Israel, King Ish-Bosheth?"

There stood those two traitorous murderers before me with a startled look on their countenances. They had supposed that I would richly reward them for the message and the proof of that message in the bag they carried. They had assumed that I would be delighted to learn that they had removed an obstacle which had stood in the way of my becoming king of Israel. With a look of dismay they heard me call in my body guards and issue orders to them to take the two traitors outside and kill them. Those of my court who heard my reaction to the message of the traitors to Israel were greatly puzzled. They murmured among themselves, "One would have thought that King David would have been overjoyed at the news which he has just received. Doesn't the fact that King Ish-Bosheth is now dead open the way for King David to become king of Israel? We know for a fact that most of the people of Israel have been wanting David to become their king. What a strange reaction. Well, one thing is certain; it is obvious that he firmly believes in the sacredness of the role of being an anointed earthly king of the Lord Jehovah's people!"

I had my body guards to cut off the feet of the messengers to symbolize that they had brought an evil message. I also instructed them to cut off the hands of the two messengers to signify the evil those hands had done in killing the king of Israel. In order to make known to my citizens of Judah and especially to the citizens of Israel my great displeasure over the slaying of King Ish-Bosheth I had the bodies of the two traitors hung on a wall in a very public spot, the pool of Hebron, where all the people would see them. In a spirit of lament I had the head of king Ish-Bosheth buried in the grave of Abner. At this point I thought it unwise to send his head back to Israel to be buried with his body. I knew that it would take much time for the news of my reaction to the slaying of their king to reach them there in Israel. Therefore, they would likely misunderstand and thus react unkindly to those who might have been assigned to return the head of the king to Israel. I felt that the slaying of King Ish-Bosheth could easily be blamed on me and the people of my kingdom at first. Thus, I had publicly shown my sorrow over what had happened and my great displeasure over the two who had caused it to happen. Due to the intermingling of the citizens of Israel and Judah I knew that my reaction to the murder of their king would soon be spread by word-of-mouth among the citizens of Israel.

During the past seven years there had been many things which had occurred that could have resulted in war between the two nations. I did my best to address each situation with great diplomacy to prevent such from happening. Yes, I admit that my goal was to become the king of a nation that included both Israel and Judah. However, I realized that it would not be by war between Judah and Israel that I could attain such a goal. Israel's army was huge as compared with my army there in Judah. All the while I lived to the best of my ability in such a way as to gain the respect of my people for the way in which I ruled over them. My hope was that the respect and love which my people had for me might influence the people of Israel to feel that I would make a good king for them also. I felt that DIPLOMACY was the key to achieving my goal.

CHAPTER 29

MARCHING UNDER THE BANNER
OF THE LORD

After moving in and settling down in my large new home (the palace for the king of Israel) I began to enlarge my personal interests. I looked around and found other ladies whom I desired to have as my wives or as my concubines. They needed to have husbands, and I needed to have more sons to add to my family. As time went on several more wives and subsequently moresons were added to my family. Oh, of course there were daughters also born to my wives and concubines, but according to the custom of the day they were not usually counted. When grown they would marry and become members of their husbands' families. My sons who were born into my family after settling down in Jerusalem were: Shammua, Shobab, Nathan, Solomon, Ibhar, Elishua, Nepheg, Japhia, Elishama, Eliada, and Eliphelet.

Trouble with the Philistines was of ongoing concern. They were a nation of people whose way of life was to make war almost annually against the surrounding nations. Their income was largely derived from plundering the armies which they conquered. When they heard that Israel and Judah had united to form a single nation and that I had been anointed king, they donned their armor and marched over in the direction of Jerusalem to do battle with my army. I had secretly hoped that they would give me more time to solidify my armed forces before they made another foray in our direction. Not so! They continued in their "warring ways" and marched over to try their mettle against united Israel. From early life I had had the custom of praying about any problem that faced me. This was a problem indeed! I went to the Lord in prayer saying, "Shall I go out and attack the army of the Philistines who are arrayed in the valley below? Will you hand them over to me?" The Lord responded, "Go, for I will surely hand the Philistines over to you." With that assurance of victory I led my army forward into battle. We soundly defeated the enemy. I sang a song of victory,

> "As waters break out, the Lord has broken
> out against my enemies before me."

The place of our victorious battle came to be called "Baal Perazim", which means "the Lord who breaks out". The Philistines retreated in such haste that they left their idols. My men gathered them up and hauled them off.

Some time later the Philistines had either forgotten their great defeat at the hands of my soldiers, or they thought that they had found a new tactic by which they felt that they could defeat us. Whatever their thinking on the subject might have been, they recouped their armed forces and once again marched against Israel. Again I inquired of the Lord if my army should march out to do battle with them. His answer was "Yes, but don't march out directly facing them; instead go around behind them to where you see that patch of balsam trees. Wait until you hear a sound in the tops of the balsam trees like that of an army marching before you; then begin your attack against the Philistines. The sound which you hear in the balsam trees means that I the Lord am going ahead of you. When you hear that sound move forward quickly, because I the Lord will have gone out ahead of you to strike the army of the Philistines." Thus, under the banner of the Lord Jehovah the army of Israel marched forth as directed. It fought bravely, striking down the enemy from Gibeon to Gezer. What a powerful leader is the Lord!

Peace, peace at last. While so busy defending the new nation of united Israel, I had had to neglect some things which I had been contemplating doing for the sake of Israel, things which were of a spiritual nature as opposed to military affairs. Prominent among those things was the matter of bringing to the capitol city of Jerusalem the Ark of the Covenant. It was sacred to the minds and hearts of our people. From their infancy they had heard about the Tent of Worship which was made by Moses during the wilderness wanderings of our people. Moses had made it under the detailed directions of the Lord Jehovah. It was the place of worship for the children of Israel during their wilderness wanderings. They had also heard that the Ark of the Covenant was in the section of the tent which was the holiest spot. It personified the presence of the Lord. It was called by the Name . . . . the name of the Lord Almighty who is enthroned between the cherubim that are on the ark. It had been kept in the house of Abinadab, the priest, during the past years. My desire was to bring the sacred Ark of the Covenant up to the city of Jerusalem to be the center of worship of the Lord Jehovah.

Two young men were appointed to perform the sacred task of moving it to its new home. They were Ahio and Uzzah, sons of Abinadab. It was to be brought on a new cart drawn by oxen. Ahio walked in front of it, and Uzzah walked alongside it. A great parade was formed as an escort for the sacred ark. Music for the parade was furnished by all sorts of instruments: harps, lyres, sistrums, tambourines, and cymbals. The people along the way were rejoicing over the fact that the Lord Jehovah whose presence dwelt in the sacred ark would soon be dwelling in their midst in the city of Jerusalem. In the midst of their rejoicing they temporarily forgot the holiness of the ark until there was a full demonstration right there among them. As the ark and the entourage passed by the threshing floor of Nacon the oxen stumbled and the ark rocked back and forth on the cart. Uzzah, who was walking along beside it, instinctively reached out and grabbed hold of the ark to steady it and thus to prevent it from falling off the cart. To the horror of everyone the young man suddenly dropped dead. The music stopped abruptly and the revelers stopped in stony silence. What had happened? Oh, to be sure, all of us could see that the young man had died, but why? Suddenly the truth was revealed to us that the great holiness of God, whose presence was represented by the ark, had been abused. Though his intentions were good Uzzah, mortal and sinful, had committed an irreverent act . . . . he had dared to touch the holiness of God as it were. My humanity was heavy upon me in that moment. I became livid with anger at the Lord for what he did to Uzzah. Uzzah had meant well. Why did the Lord take such a drastic way of rebuking him for touching the holy ark? The place where this happened became known as "Perez Uzzah", i.e., "outbreak against Uzzah." Looking back on that event in later years, I was horrified at myself, a sinful man, for daring to be angry at righteous God. Years later I came to realize that God used the death of Uzzah to teach us that sinful man must not dare to be that familiar with holy God. I learned that unholy man must not try to humanize holy God in our thoughts, i. e., not to try to bring Him down to the level of humanity.

What happened that day caused me to have a holy fear of the presence of the Lord. I asked myself, "How can the ark of the Lord ever be brought into the city of Jerusalem?" That caused me to decide that it would not be wise to bring into a city full of people with unclean hearts the sacred ark of the Lord. In order to have time to come to a proper conclusion as to what should be the place for the ark to rest I issued the order for it to be carried to the home of Obed-Edom the Gittite. Surprisingly he did not seem to fear its presence in his home. Close observation revealed that the Lord was richly blessing Obed-Edom and his entire household. After three months word to that effect was brought to me saying, "The Lord has blessed the household of Obed-Edom and everything he has, because of the ark of God." I decided that Jerusalem could certainly use such a blessing as had been showered upon the temporary host of the ark. I issued an order that the ark was to be brought into the city of Jerusalem. The great rejoicing which earlier had been shown over the moving of the ark was begun all over again. Trumpets were played to announce in an official way its approach to the gates of the city. There was rejoicing on every hand. This time I was determined that we would make it a completely sacred trip. When the oxen which were pulling the cart had gone forward six steps, it was stopped so that there could be a sacrifice of a bull and a fattened calf. For this sacred occasion I wore a linen ephod. In the midst of all the singing and rejoicing I danced in my worship of the Lord as I sought to reveal my great happiness over this sacred event. It seemed that all of the inhabitants of the city of Jerusalem and those of the surrounding area were involved in this meaningful parade. All felt the happiness of the presence of the Lord as signified by the presence of the ark. Along side the procession were those who played musical instruments with the trumpets being predominant. They seemed to be signifying the opening of the gates of the city.

What a day of rejoicing that was! As the procession entered the gates of the city there was an even greater sound of rejoicing due to the arrival of the holy ark of the covenant. Slowly and in a great spirit of reverence those in the procession accompanied the cart on which the ark rested to the tent which I had prepared for its resting place. All of us realized the sacredness of this moment in which the symbol of God's presence had come to rest in the heart of our recently united nation of Israel and Judah or simply "Israel" as we had come to call it. We felt then and there that Almighty God would henceforth be the ruler and guide of our new nation. From henceforth His holy presence would hover over the city of Jerusalem which would cause all of us who were dwelling in it to feel that it had truly become the "City of God". As the ark was placed in the spot in the tent which had been prepared for it a great hush came over the multitude of people surrounding the tent. In our hearts we knew that this was a great moment in the history of our new capital city which we had named Jerusalem and in the history of our newly reunited and revitalized nation. Our hearts were filled with the happiness that at long last God's presence as symbolized by the presence of the ark of the covenant would be near us all the time.

Then I offered burnt offerings and fellowship offerings unto the Lord on behalf of the people.

In the spirit of the moment and due to the fact that I was clothed in a part of the priestly apparel (the ephod) I presumed to perform these sacred rituals in the new tent of worship in the presence of the ark of the covenant. Hithertofore, this was the task of the high priest, but during the many dark years (spiritually speaking) since Samuel's death there was a dearth of priests who had been consecrated to the Lord's service. When I had finished this service of worship I presented gifts to all the people present, gifts of a loaf of bread, a cake of dates and a cake of raisins.

CHAPTER 30
THE SPOILING OF A HAPPY OCCASION

Later my happiness over the great occasion of bringing the ark of God into the city of Jerusalem was marred by one I had assumed to was sharing my happiness over the arrival of the ark into Jerusalem. My first wife, Michal, who had been my wife but who had been taken from me and given to another man by her father the late King Saul and whom subsequently I had had forcibly taken from that husband to come back to become my wife again, confronted me in a spirit of anger. It seems that as the procession which escorted the Ark of the Covenant into the city of Jerusalem had arrived at the gate of the city Michal looked down from the vantage point of a window in the city wall and saw me dancing before the Lord. She observed that I was dressed only in an ephod. In that day "ephod" might refer to a sacred object, perhaps a part of the priest's clothing, or it might refer to that part of the priest's sacred garments worn on sacred occasions. I had usurped the ephod . . . in this case a sort of priestly apron . . . . to be my "uniform" to wear on the occasion of the bringing into the city of Jerusalem the Ark of the Covenant. It was a short apron which did not limit my actions as I danced mightily before the Lord. It seems that Michal greatly disapproved of my mode of dress and of my dancing before the Lord. Whereas my sole intent was to worship and praise the Lord on that great occasion, Michal my first wife, interpreted it another way.

When I arrived at my home following the festivities of the day, Michal met me at the entrance and began to berate me. She screamed out at me with sarcasm in her voice, "How the king of Israel has distinguished himself today, disrobing in the sight of the slave girls of his servants as any vulgar fellow would do!!!"

No doubt she was referring to the fact that I had not worn my kingly regalia on the festive occasion just completed. In my heart I had determined that I would not appear before the crowd of people in my royal attire as though I would have been attempting to impress them with my own importance rather that directing their thoughts and attention to the King of Heaven, the Lord Jehovah, before whom we were marching, playing instruments, shouting and singing . . . . all to His glory. If my ephod was skimpy to the point of not hiding my legs, it was for the purpose of allowing me full movement as I danced mightily before the Lord as I endeavored to prove to Him my love and adoration. After hearing her tirade and pausing to consider a proper response to her, I finally replied with these words, "It was before the Lord and for the Lord that I was dancing. You remember who the Lord is? He is the God of heaven who chose me rather than your father or any of his sons to rule over His people Israel. I, the chosen one, will celebrate before the Lord in the way I feel to be most appropriate. For His sake in the future I shall become even more undignified than I was today. I shall humiliate myself even more in order to elevate Him in my presence and in the presence of His people. As concerns the slave girls of whom you spoke, I imagine if the truth be known they hold me in honor for the way in which I conducted myself this day!"

Michal could never forget that she was the daughter of King Saul and that I was the son of a shepherd. From the time that her father, King Saul, had given her to me in marriage she had looked upon me as being a "nobody". She never seemed to be sad that King Saul took her away from me and gave her to another man, a man who evidently loved her and treated her nicely. She was cool toward me from the time when she reentered my life, that time when I had her forcibly taken from her second husband and brought back to me. She had shown no affection toward me since then. Coolness on the part of a mate brings about that same attitude on the part of the other mate. From that point onward Michal and I just tolerated each other. Although women of my day wanted and expected to have children, Michal never did.

CHAPTER 31

A PROMISE FROM GOD

Once again there came a time when I could take a breather from warfare against Israel's enemies, first and fore most of whom were the Philistines. At such times of peace I was able to turn my attention to the contemplation of things spiritual. From those early days when I was a shepherd lad out on a hillside on a starlit night watching over my sheep I have always enjoyed communing with my heavenly Father. As a young lad I did not fear the darkness of night nor any marauding animals sneaking up to attack my flock of sheep. I did not get lonely even though all I had to talk with were my sheep. I knew that I had a heavenly Shepherd who was right there watching over me on those dark nights. I talked with him as though He were a human being who was sitting beside me. That was because I felt in my heart that He was answering my questions no matter how boyish they were and that He took my thoughts seriously. My God and I walked together, talked together, and felt such closeness. Actually I felt closer to my heavenly Father than I did to my parents, for I could tell Him things which I would not tell my earthly parents. Certainly I felt closer to Him than I did to my six big brothers. If I had confided in them some of my innermost thoughts, they would have laughed at me, made fun of my thoughts, and teased me unmercifully.

That early habit of communing with God carried over into my adult days. I greatly enjoyed quiet moments of communing with my God. It was so good to be able to slip away from those hurly-burly times when every one of my subjects seemed to be clamoring for my attention to their problems. As time went on it grew increasingly hard to find a moment in which to meditate. Nathan, a man of God, came to be a person on whom I could lean and from whom I could learn the thoughts of God. I soon learned that he would tell me the truth even when it hurt. He obviously "had God's ear", for from time to time he brought a message from God to me. It meant so much to me to have him to lean on in discerning God's will in matters both personal and national.

In a lull between times of warfare I turned my attention to the matter of providing a permanent house in which the ark of the covenant could dwell, that is, a house for my God. I went to God in prayer concerning that matter. I relayed to Him my feeling that it was not right for me to dwell in my new palace which had been constructed from cedar lumber from Lebanon and from the neighboring marble quarries while He was still dwelling in a tent. I turned to my friend and counselor, Nathan, and said, "Here I am, living in a palace of cedar, while the ark of God remains in a tent." I implied that my heart told me that it was not right for the situation to be so. I felt that it was my privilege but more especially my obligation to provide a proper earthly house for the Lord Jehovah. Nathan replied to me, "Whatever you have in mind, go ahead and do it, for the Lord is with you." Good old Nathan . . . . the connotation of his statement was that he felt that I would do the right thing concerning this matter.

Evidently what I had said about building a proper house for the Lord weighed on his mind and heart through the remainder of that day. That night he had a message from the Lord concerning my intentions. The Lord told him, "Go and tell my servant David, 'This is what the Lord says: Are you the one to build me a house to dwell in? I have not dwelt in a house from the day I brought the Israelites up out of Egypt to this day. I have been moving from place to place with a tent as my dwelling. Wherever I have moved with all the Israelites, did I ever say to any of their rulers whom I commanded to shepherd my people Israel, 'Why have you not built me a house of cedar?' Now then tell my servant David, 'This is what the Lord Almighty says: I took you from the pasture and from following the flock to be ruler over my people Israel. I have been with you wherever you have gone, and I have cut off all your enemies from before you. Now I will make your name great, like the names of the greatest men of the earth. And I will provide a place for my people Israel and will plant them so that they can have a home of their own and no longer be disturbed. Wicked people will not oppress them anymore, as they did at the beginning and have done ever since the time I appointed leaders over my people Israel. I will also give you rest from all your enemies."

The Lord continued His address to Nathan in this manner: "The Lord declares to you that the Lord Himself will establish a house for you: when your days are over and you rest with your fathers, I will raise up your offspring to succeed you, who will come from your own body, and I will establish his kingdom. He is the one who will build a house for my Name, and I will establish the throne of his kingdom forever. I will be his father, and he will be my son. When he does wrong, I will punish him with the rod of men, with floggings inflicted by men. But my love will never be taken away from him, as I took it away from Saul, whom I removed from before you. Your house and your kingdom will endure forever before me; your throne will be established forever."

After meditating on the Lord's message to David through him, Nathan came to me and reported what he had heard from the Lord. At first I was shocked to hear the words of the Lord which had been delivered to me by His servant Nathan . . . . who was I to hear such words of love and praise of me? I felt so unworthy of the Lord Jehovah's blessing on me, a blessing that was extended to my descendants. As I meditated on His words, I sensed that he was establishing an everlasting covenant with me and my descendants. There was a sense in which He seemed to be establishing an earthly kingdom of some duration but more especially a spiritual kingdom that would one day bless the nations of the world. I was awed by God's words as delivered to me by Nathan the prophet. Indeed! Who was I to be shown such favor by Almighty God?

After the shock had worn off a bit I collected my senses about me and left the palace and went into the presence of the Lord in the tent where the Ark of the Covenant now resided. There I sat in reverent meditation before Him. Finally these words came from my lips as I communed with Him: "Who am I, O Sovereign Lord, and what is my family, that you have brought me this far? And as if this were not enough in your sight, O Sovereign Lord, you have also spoken about the future of the house (descendants) of your servant. Is this your usual way of dealing with man, O Sovereign Lord?" In other words I was asking my Lord why I was singled out for such divine favor. "What more can I, David, say to you? For you know your servant, O Sovereign Lord. For the sake of your word and according to your will, you have done this great thing and made it known to your servant."

"How great Thou art, O sovereign Lord! There is no one like you, and there is no God but you, as we have heard with our own ears. And who is like your people Israel—the one nation on earth that God went out to redeem as a people for Himself, and to make a name for Himself, and to perform great and awesome wonders by driving out nations and their gods from before your people, whom you redeemed from Egypt? You have established your people Israel as your very own forever, and you, O Lord, have become their God. And now, Lord God, keep forever the promise you have made concerning your servant and his house. Do as you promised, so that your name will be great forever. Then we will say, 'The Lord Almighty is God over Israel!' And the house of your servant David will be established before you."

"O Lord Almighty, God of Israel, you have revealed this to your servant, saying, 'I will build a house for you. So your servant has found courage to offer you this prayer. 'O sovereign Lord, you are God! Your words are trustworthy, and you have promised these good things to your servant. Now be pleased to bless the house of your servant, that it may continue forever in your sight; for you, O Sovereign Lord, have spoken, and with your blessing the house of your servant will be blessed forever.'"

CHAPTER 32

MEMORIES OF MY MILITARY

CAMPAIGNS

"How those memories ever fill my soul!" What does an old warrior have at the end of life's journey but his memories? Looking back over my past life I realize that I spent the majority of it endeavoring to establish Israel as a strong nation. If I do say so myself, I did succeed in reaching my goal. Before I become boastful, however, let me say that any success that I had in doing battle against the enemy was due to the will, the power, and the presence of the Lord my God in each of my battles. Personally speaking, in order to have succeeded in doing such a goal it was necessary that I spend a good portion of my life in warfare. In the ebb tide of life old soldiers like to sit in the shade of a tree on a hot day and reminisce concerning the battles in which he participated and the success of each of them. If he is truthful he will also call to mind those campaigns which did not end the way he had planned. Looking back over my life I am no exception to any other warrior . . . . I do like to think back over those years of warfare and relive each battle.

As King of Israel I felt that it was my role to lead in the various campaigns in which Israel was engaged. When young I "chomped at the bit" to be in the thick of battle. As time moved on the strength of my youth was on the wane, but I would not admit it. My desire to be in the forefront of each battle remained the same as in the days of my youth. On one occasion it became obvious to my men that I was no longer the mighty warrior that once I was. In well chosen words and in a spirit of great deference they said to me, "Thou shalt go no more out with us to battle, that thou quench not the light of Israel." (II Samuel

21:17b) They revealed to me that my role as king was not only that of a warrior and ruler but it was also that of a symbol of all that the nation of Israel stood for. In my latter years I heeded their words and not my desires . . . . I remained in Jerusalem when my army went out to do battle under the able leadership of the army of Israel's commander-in-chief, Joab. He had proved himself in battle after battle. Therefore, I felt somewhat at ease about how things were going in each battle, for I knew that Joab would rise to the occasion. I sat in the palace and waited for the arrival of the messengers whom he sent to share with me news as to how the current battle was going.

After a period of comparative peace with the adjoining nations war broke out again. The Philistines again came forth to do battle with Israel. This time the army of Israel was able to defeat them soundly. I took from them as a prize of war the area of Methegh Ammah and added it to the growing boundaries of the nation of Israel. Of course I knew that it would be only a matter of time before the Philistines would again try its mettle against Israel.

The nation of Moab over to the southeast of Jerusalem in the area adjoining the great Salt Sea were constantly irritating Israel and was a source of great nuisance. Finally when I felt that Israel had had enough irritation from the Moabites my army invaded their nation. I felt that it was necessary to take drastic measures to convince them that Israel was not a nation to be "toyed with". I ordered that their soldiers who survived the battle be made to lie down in formation on the ground. My soldiers were to measure them off with a length of cord. Every two lengths of them were to be put to death, while the third length was allowed to live. When word of this drastic treatment of the Moabite soldiers reached the ears of the ruler of Moab, he admitted defeat at the hands of the army of Israel and accepted the terms I laid down to his nation. Those terms stated that Moab was to become a vassal state under the dominion of Israel and as such was to bring tribute year by year to Israel. Yes, by humane standards I admit that I had used very drastic measures by which to bring the Moabites under subjection to Israel, but I felt that such drastic measures were required to "make believers" out of them and to cause them to be at peace with Israel.

Later I learned that Hadadezer, the son of Rehob, king of the nation of Zobah, was on his way to take back his rule over land extending to the Euphrates River. If he should succeed in doing that he would become much too powerful for Israel to handle. I knew that it was a matter of immediate importance that I stop him his tracks. Therefore, we attacked him and overcame him. As a result we were able to take from him rich plunder. Counted in that plunder was a thousand of his chariots, seven thousand charioteers, and twenty thousand foot soldiers. I knew that we had to disable the chariot horses in order to prevent their being useful to the enemy in the event they should recapture them. Therefore, I had my soldiers to hamstring all of them with the exception of a hundred which would be useful to my army when fighting on the plain. Chariot warfare was not of value when fighting in the hill country.

Word was brought to me that the Arameans of Damascus had come to the aid of Hadadezer. This was a problem to my forces indeed. However, my army rose to the occasion and went forth to engage them in combat. I have never seen my soldiers fight more fiercely than they did that day. When the heat of the battle was over it was discovered that we had slain twenty-two thousand of them. The result of this great victory was that Israel gained control over all the Syrians, and they became subject to me. As a vassal state they were required to bring tribute to the coffers of Israel. In order to maintain control over that new area which had been added to Israel's borders I had garrisons built in the area surrounding Damascus. Among the things of value which were captured from the Syrians were shields of gold and much bronze. These items were brought to me in Jerusalem. These were dedicated to the Lord.

When King Toi of Hamath heard of the victory of Israel over the Syrians, he was very pleased, for they had been a "thorn in his side" for many years. In appreciation of my victory he sent his son with gifts to show his high esteem to me and to my nation. Those gifts were articles of gold, silver, and bronze. These gifts were dedicated to the Lord. Already there had been obtained many rich articles of gold, silver and bronze which had been taken from the nations which my army had defeated such as Moab, the Ammonites, the Philistines, Amalek as well as those from the Syrians.

Another fierce campaign was the one with the Edomites in which my army was victorious. There in the Valley of Salt my men were able to count the bodies of eighteen thousand of their soldiers. In the eyes of the nations of the day to defeat the Edomites was a great honor. Perhaps this victory when coupled with the other victories of Israel was the reason that among my people and even among the surrounding nations I had gained the name of being a great warrior. As I saw it that reputation belonged to my able and loyal soldiers. More especially any honor which was being given to me and my soldiers in reality should have been given to the Lord Jehovah, who had been responsible for our gaining our victories in battle.

In order to maintain power over the nations which had been conquered by Israel I ordered that garrisons be built in those areas and staffed by my soldiers. It was the duty of those soldiers stationed in those garrisons to quell any attempted uprisings among the conquered people.

CHAPTER 33
REMEMBERING A COVENANT

In a lull from the stress of wars and internal problems of government I sat one day and thought back over my early life. Naturally I remembered those days which I spent on many a hillside with my father Jesse's sheep. I remembered how I wanted to grow up so that I would be assigned to a task other than that of a lowly shepherd. Being the youngest son of Jesse's seven sons it fell my lot to care for my father's sheep. Not only did I remember my distaste for that task, but I also remembered that because of the life of loneliness with only sheep for fellowship I drew nearer to my God than I would have otherwise. Those nights of looking up at the sky and seeing all those stars twinkling back at me caused me to be very aware of the great creator God who had set all of them in place.

As my time of reverie progressed I remembered my early life in the palace of King Saul where I had the duty of calming him during those times of his inner torment by playing on my harp. Especially did I remember my friendship with King Saul's son, Jonathan. I remembered what close friends we had become in spite of the fact that he was the son of a king and I was the son of a shepherd. I had found him to be a person of pure character and a heart of love for all that was good. Our friendship continued to be strong even in those times when his father, King Saul, exhibited insane jealousy of me. We made a covenant one with the other to remain friends and to be faithful to that vow until death. I recall so vividly the last time I saw him. I was hiding in a nearby field when he came out with a young lad and pretended to be doing archery practice. He gave a prearranged signal indicating that I must flee for my life because King Saul was planning to hunt me down as though I were a wild animal. That's the last time

I ever saw him, for I followed his instructions and fled in haste from the wrath of King Saul. It was with great grief that I learned some years later that he, along with the king and a sibling, had been slain by the Philistines.

Thinking back over the covenant Jonathan and I had made with each other, I realized that I had almost forgotten it. That thought pricked my conscience with a great sense of guilt. Of course I knew that death in battle had taken my friend from me, but it dawned on me that I ought to make an effort to learn of any relatives of him or of other members of the family of King Saul. In spite of his seeking to kill me, causing me to hide in the caves and crevices of the surrounding mountains like a animal of prey, I had always shown reverence for the anointed of God, King Saul. Now I felt that it was high time that I should seek to put that reverence into action by trying to find members of the former royal family and to see what I could do to show my respect to them on behalf of the late King Saul.

It took some sleuthing on the part of my staff to find the answer to the question I posed to them: "Is there anyone still left of the house of Saul to whom I can show kindness for Jonathan's sake?" After much inquiring among the people who had served under King Saul, there was found a person by the name of Ziba, a person who had served in the former royal household. He was asked to appear before me. At the appointed hour the door opened and a person entered and came toward me with his head hanging downward. I asked that person, "Are you Ziba?" Seeing that he appeared to be very ill at ease . . . . actually, very afraid, I had to ask that question in a very modulated tone with even a bit of deference to put him at ease. His answer was short and to the point, an answer that showed much humility. It then occurred to me that he was accustomed to King Saul's erratic behavior, a fact that most likely had cause him to fear that I was of the same sort. It was even quite likely that he feared that I was trying to do harm to him in retribution for the way the former king had treated me (I assumed that those who had served close to him would have heard how I had been treated by my predecessor on the throne). I hurried on to ask the question which was on my mind, a question which would surely cause him to know that

I was not concerned about him. That question was: "Is there no one still left of the house of Saul to whom I can show God's kindness?" Immediately there swept across Ziba's face a look of relief. Because of my question he could surmise that I was not interested one way or another in him but that I sincerely wanted to learn if anyone of King Saul's household was still alive. No one whom I had previously asked concerning that matter had any information.

His face revealed a very relieved look as he hurried to answer my question. "Sir, to the best of my knowledge there is only one person of royal blood. He is the son of the late Prince Jonathan." My heart beat more rapidly at the mention of the name of my beloved friend, Jonathan. "Tell me about him. Was he injured in that great battle against the Philistines, a battle in which King Saul, Prince Jonathan and his brother were killed?" "Oh, no sir, he was not injured in that battle or in any other, for you see he has never been able to fight the army of Israel?" "What do you mean? Surely the son of my brave friend Jonathan would be a warrior!" "Sir, as I just said he has never been able to do battle against any of our enemies because he is a cripple." There was a long pause in which Ziba probably observed the sadness on my countenance at the thought of the son of my dear friend being a cripple. He continued, "When the Philistines were invading the whole area during that great battle, the nurse maid who was responsible for the care of the small lad picked him up and fled for their lives. For some reason she dropped him. As a result his feet and legs were severely injured. He has been crippled ever since." "What's his name?" "Sir his name is Mephibosheth." "Where is he now?" "He is at the house of Makir, the son of Ammiel, over in a little place called Ammiel in the area of Lo Debar."

I lost no time in sending for him and having him brought to the court. It was obvious that Mephibosheth was ill at ease. Could it be that he was afraid that I wanted to kill him and thus be rid of the last of the royal line of my predecessor, King Saul? When I looked up from some legal papers which I was perusing and saw him sitting on the floor with his crooked feet and legs somewhat askew from his body, my heart broke within me. Yet, he bowed before me as best he could in order to show great humility to me. How could this have happened to the son of my dear friend, Jonathan? "Mephibosheth," I said to him. In almost a whisper he replied in a "cowed manner," "Your servant." I noticed that his whole body was shaking in fear of me. Immediately I said to him, "Don't be afraid, for I will surely show you kindness for the sake of your father Jonathan. I will restore to you all the land that formerly belonged to your grandfather, King Saul, and you will always eat at my table."

Still trembling and fearful but with a look of great surprise because of my promises to him, he humbly prostrated himself before me, "What is your servant that you would notice a dead dog like me?" Immediately I called Ziba from the back of the room to come forward. When he stood before me, I told him what I had said to Mephibosheth about the land of his grandfather being given to him. Then I told Ziba that from henceforth he and his sons and servants were to work all that land which I had just given to Jonahan's son. I made a mental note that the land should be worked really well, for Ziba had plenty manpower to do that task, for he had fifteen sons and twenty servants. Ziba was overcome by my message to him. He was overcome with joy and replied, "Your servant will do whatever my lord the king commands his servant to do." I learned that Mephibosheth had a small son named Mica. I told him that he and his son were to be my honored guests at my personal dining table in the palace each day from then on. Because of that honor he and his son moved into the town of Jerusalem in order to be near my palace so that he would not have to walk in his crawl-like manner to the palace to eat.

Yes, I made both Mephibosheth and Ziba very happy by my remembering my covenant with Jonathan, beloved friend of my youth. In treating Mephibosheth with kindness I felt that I was actually showing that kindness to Jonathan. I was blessed in my spirit by remembering Jonathan in this way. I felt that I had lived up to the covenant I had made with him so long ago.

CHAPTER 34
THE RESULT OF MISUNDERSTOOD KINDNESS

I recall an occasion in my younger days when I was trying to do the right thing, but my effort was totally misunderstood. Word came to me that Nahash, King of the Ammonites had died and his son, Hanun, succeeded him on the throne. The news brought to my mind an occasion when Hanun had been kind to me. I felt that an appropriate thing for me to do was to send a delegation of my men who were versed I appropriate protocol to Hanun and express to him my sympathy for the loss of his father. My intentions were good, but unfortunately they were misinterpreted. I heard by the "grape vine" that some Ammonite nobles who served as advisors to their young king Hanun told him that surely he would not be so foolish as to believe that the real purpose of my delegation to his palace was to express sympathy on my behalf. "Why, it is obvious to us that those in King David's delegation are here to spy out the land so that they will know what strategy to use in conquering us!" Hanun's inexperience caused him to listen to his me and to follow their advice.

Hanun had his men cut off half of the beards of each member of the delegation and to cut their robes off halfway up their buttocks. What shame and embarrassment my men experienced at the hands of the Ammonites! Word was brought back to me shortly thereafter concerning this incident. Anger burned within me concerning how the Ammonites had treated the members of the delegation whom I had sent to show my sympathy to their new king at the loss of his father, the late King Nahash. I sent instructions to the men of the delegation to remain in Jericho until their beards grew out again; then they were to return to Jerusalem.

Word of my wrath about the shameful treatment they had administered to my men found its way back to King Hunan. He realized what an evil thing he had done, but more especially he realized that it was certain that I would not take his treatment of my men "sitting down." It was obvious that I would not let that matter rest until my army had engaged them in battle. Fearful that his nation was not strong enough to withstand the army of Israel he got busy and hired some mercenary soldiers. Word got back to me that the Ammonite king had secured the services of "soldiers for hire" with which to augment his strength in battle. He hired 220,000 Aramean foot soldiers from Beth Rehob and Zobah, a thousand soldiers from King Maacah, and twelve thousand from Tob.

When the Ammonites heard that my army under Joab's leadership was intent on coming over with the full army of Israel, they hurriedly drew up their battle plans. It was decided that the Aramean mercenary soldiers and the men from Tob would be placed in the open field some distance from their city gates. The army of the Ammonites was placed at the entrance of the city gate. This strategy caused Joab and his army to have the enemy before him and back of him. This situation called for real military finesse on Joab's part. He selected some of his best fighting men and assigned to them the task of fighting with the Arameans, who were stationed in the field. The others he placed under the leadership of his brother, Abishai, and arrayed them in front of the city of the Ammonites. Abishai was instructed by Joab that if the battle against the Arameans got too rough for him and his men that Abishai and his soldiers were to leave their position at the city gate and join Joab in the fight against the Arameans and vice-versa. Joab gave all the men a pep talk in which he said, "Be strong and let us fight bravely for our people and the cities of our God. The Lord will do what is good in His sight."

When Joab and his men advanced against the Aramean soldiers in the field they fled. Being hired soldiers they were not concerned how the battle came out.... they were only concerned about saving themselves. The Ammonites, seeing the Arameans in flight, retreated to within their city gate. With the battle ending in favor of the Israelites, Joab and the soldiers of Israel returned to Jerusalem rejoicing. All of us knew in our hearts that the Lord had given us the victory

Hardly had I and my army settled down into a routine of peace when word came to me that the Arameans had regrouped and were planning to do battle again with Israel. This time King Hadadezer's army led the Arameans. He evidenly figured that this would give courage to the army of mercenaries who had run from the army of Israel a short time earlier. When I received that news, I had the army of Israel to march forth and cross the Jordan River to do battle with them. Before the Arameans had a chance to flee once again my soldiers had slain seven hundred of their charioteers and forty thousand of their foot soldiers. The head of their army, Shobach, was among those whom we slew.

The final result of this great battle was that the many Aramean vassal kings realized that their armies had been soundly defeated by the army of Israel. They decided that their only alternative was to make peace with the nation of Israel and become subject to it. It was good to know that the Arameans were afraid to help the Ammonites any more. Surely this would have the effect of a lasting peace with the Ammonites!

CHAPTER 35

THE AWFUL RESULTS OF ONE LUSTFUL LOOK

There came that time when I no longer went out on the battlefield. My body was no longer as strong or quick of motion as it once was. I still had the desire to be in the midst of each battle which the army of Israel fought. It was a case of "my spirit was willing but my flesh was weak." However, there was more to it than that. My advisers shared with me that the citizens of Israel had come to look upon me as the symbol of their nation, a symbol which they did not want to be endangered. In addition to that I personally realized that the matters of state were increasing to the extent that they took most of my time. Therefore, I came to the point that I sent my soldiers out to do battle under the leadership of Joab instead of myself. However, each time Israel was at war with one of its enemies I pined to be with it, leading it into the middle of the fray as in the days of yore.

Usually during those times when my army was engaged in a battle I kept myself busy back in the palace with matters of state so that I would not feel so keenly the loss of my vim, vigor, and vitality that had formerly propelled me onto the field of battle with patriotism burning in my heart and energy in my limbs. There came that day in the spring of the year when I sent my army into battle with Israel's perpetual enemy, the nation of the Ammonites. On a day during that war I suddenly felt at cross purposes with my conscience. I had sent Joab out to lead in the warfare, but I felt that I should be there in the midst of the fray. Oh, to be sure, there were plenty of business matters of state that I should be handling, but on that particular day I rebelled against doing my duty as king. Instead I went up to the deck on the roof of the palace and lay down on a sleeping mat to take a nap in the warm spring sunshine. My nap was more fitful than peaceful, for my dreams were of things which should not be a part of my mind and heart. Suddenly I awakened, yawned and stretched my arms. I stood up and walked back and forth on the surface of the palace top deck. Finally I stopped pacing and stood behind the three and a half foot high wall which formed a banister around the deck. My gaze swept over the surrounding city of Jerusalem. I thought to myself, "How much the city of Jerusalem has grown since I and my army defeated the Jebusites and took over their city. Dwellings and market places have sprung up to the point that the area within the walls of the city has been completely covered. It's so good to stand here and view all the works that my hands (figuratively speaking) have done in Jerusalem. I'm very proud of what has been accomplished here within the great walled city of Jerusalem. It's so good to be able to stand here and gaze at all of it."

Suddenly, my attention was caught by a very unusual sight. "Am I really seeing what I think I am seeing??? From this height I can see over into many of the private courtyards of the private homes. What am I allowing myself to do??? I'm acting like a 'peeping Tom'. I should not be doing this. Oh, just look at that particular backyard! There is a woman taking off her robe right there before my eyes! She is obviously taking advantage by bathing in the warm spring sunshine which is in abundance in her court yard. Oh, good, no but one me can see her, for the walls of her courtyard are so high that none of the neighbors can see what she is doing. The few homes that have housetop decks are so low that if there happened to be anyone on them they could not see what I am seeing. My, my, what a beautiful woman she is! My conscience tells me that I ought to stop gazing in her direction, BUT my desire is to watch her every move as she bathes. I can't stand it! The sight of her nude body is more than I can stand. I want to see her up close. I have strong lustful feelings toward that woman. I don't know who she is, and I don't care . . . . I want her!" I had a servant to inquire furtively as to her identity. He returned with the news that her name was Bathsheba, the daughter of Eliam. Then he added that she was the wife of Uriah the Hittite. "Oh, too bad! She is married to a leading soldier in the army of Israel. Well, I happen to know that he is out in the field of battle where he is engaging in warfare with the Ammonites. He probably won't be back home for a long while. Anyway, I won't let anything stand in the way of my having access to that woman." I then sent a servant to tell her to come to the palace, for the king was commanding her presence.

In the meantime there was a strong fight going on inside my mind and heart. My conscience said, "Drop the matter; think about another subject." However, burning lustful feelings swept over me and became so strong that they controlled my mind and heart. The power of Lucifer began to lay out an evil plot in my mind that destroyed my better judgment. A voice within me cried out, "I've got to have her. She may be someone's wife, but I'm king . . . I have the right and power of position that affords me the opportunity to do what I want to do, be it right or wrong." Suddenly the power of proper judgment left me.

Soon there came into my presence that ravishing looking young lady . . . . the most beautiful woman I had ever seen. Lust sprang up in my mind and heart and before I knew what I was doing I invited her into my private chambers and made known to her my burning desire. Whether she was afraid to rebuff the "great King David" or whether she really desired to do my bidding I did not try to discern. All I know was that quite sometime later my lustful passion had been satisfied, and I sent her back to her home. I thought to myself, "What an enjoyable experience . . . . and no one will ever know about it. No doubt she will be reluctant to speak to anyone about it. She told me she was married (a fact that I had already discovered), but I noticed that she seemed to be ready and willing to acquiesce to my desires. Could it be that she had the same lustful feelings toward me that I had toward her? Her soldier husband had perchance been away a long time? Perhaps when he was at home he showed no affection toward her." Well, all that was beside the point. I had taken advantage of the opportunity to satisfy my lustful desires. I really wasn't concerned about the emotions that had played in her heart while we were sleeping together . . . . I was just happy that that experience had greatly pleased me and had well satisfied my sinful emotions. Ah, I had always heart that 'stolen fruit tasted best'. Following that experience I knew that that old saying was true. Actually I felt very smug about that experience. I had been with another man's wife and had enjoyed the experience very much. As I thought about what had just happened in my bed chamber, I murmured to myself the old saying, 'All is well that ends well.' With that behind me I realized that I should get back to checking on the business matters of Israel.

But, alas, all was not well. There came a message from Bathsheba. The message was a simple statement which said, "I am pregnant." When I saw those three words on that piece of parchment, I felt that I had ice water running through my veins. I turned away and faced the wall, so that the messenger could not see my reaction. Panic took hold of me; I stood there trembling. Those words which had run through my mind earlier . . . ."no one will ever know about it," came tumbling down around my ears and grabbed my heart. That adage . . ."be sure that your sins will find you out" . . . grabbed my panic stricken conscience.

Finally I was able to compose my thoughts enough to send Bathsheba's messenger back to her house. He had hardly left the palace before I endeavored to solve this great problem. Soon the fact that she was pregnant would become obvious and all her neighbors would start counting the time that her husband, Uriah the Hittite, had been away in combat. The women of Jerusalem always looked so innocent and serene as they moved about in the market place and along the streets, but I had it on good authority that behind the walls of their homes or over their back fences they shared with each other all the 'dirty linen' about their neighbors which they had heard or imagined. Yes, soon Bathsheba would be the talk of the town, for those busy tongues of the good ladies of Jerusalem would be wagging about her pregnancy without the benefit of her husband's presence at the calculated time of conception. I had asked myself, "What will Bathsheba do when she is confronted and questioned by those gossiping ladies? Will she remain silent about who the father of her baby is? Not likely! They will wear her down to the point that she will almost shout from the housetops of the town that King David is the father of her unborn child." That concerned me deeply, for since I had been anointed king of all Israel the people of the kingdom had looked up to me not only as a great warrior who was their protector, but they had looked up to me as being their model of right conduct. My image in their eyes would be shattered. I could not allow that to happen. I made a quick decision. I sent word to Joab, "Send to me Uriah the Hittite." No doubt this would raise a red flag or two in the mind of Joab, but I would have to run that risk. One thing I could count on was that Joab would follow my bidding whatever it was.

While waiting for Uriah to come back into Jerusalem from the scene of battle, I plotted my strategy. I would question Uriah about the well being of the army's commander-in-chief Joab, about the state of health of the troops, and the progress of the battle. Surely that would give him the idea that he had been randomly chosen to bring me news from the battle front. Then I would graciously tell him that he needed to take a little time for an "R. and R." at his home with his wife since he was surely weary after the most recent skirmish and after the long walk from the battlefield back to Jerusalem to bring me the news from the battle front. He left the palace, and I assumed that he was on his way to his home. To add to my façade of appreciation for Uriah I sent a messenger with a gift for him. I thought to myself, "Now my worries are over. Uriah will sleep with his wife and everyone (Uriah included) will believe that the baby that has been conceived when Bathsehba and I slept together was his child. All is well!"

Unfortunately all was not well. Things did not work out as planned. If I must say so, I don't recall ever encountering such a dedicated soldier as was Uriah. Or was he just plain stupid? He declined my suggestion that he go down the street to his home and have a conjugal visit with his wife. Instead, he slept at one of the entrances of the palace where the palace servants slept. When asked why he refused such a privilege as had been arranged for him . . . . an R. and R. with his beautiful wife . . . . he replied, "The ark and Israel and Judah are staying in tents, and my master Joab and my lord's men are camped in the open fields. How could I go to my house to eat and drink and lie with my wife? As surely as you live, I will not do such a thing!"

Well, my strategy did not work out as I had planned it. I tried again. I sent a message to Uriah saying, "Stay one more day, and tomorrow I will send you back." He agreed to stay another day or so. I had him to eat at my table. I had my servants to ply him with a great amount of wine until he was quite drunk. Even so he could not be persuaded to go home to his wife, Instead he again spent the night at the entrance of the palace on his mat with the king's servants. I thought to myself, "Nothing has worked in my effort to get him to sleep with Bathsheba. I shall have to take more drastic measures."

I wrote a note to Joab with certain instructions concerning Uriah. I knew that the message would not be read by Uriah for two reasons: (1) he was too conscientious a person to read other people's messages, and (2) he was unschooled and therefore could not read the message if he had so desired. Desperate situations require desperate measures! In that note I instructed Joab to put Uriah in the line of battle where the fighting was fiercest and then have his soldiers to withdraw and leave Uriah defenseless. Surely that would send Uriah to his eternal reward!!!

This time my plan worked. I admit that in handling the situation as I had done in my effort to cover up my great sin of adultery, I had committed an even greater sin, that of having an honest, dedicated soldier killed. Actually for all practical purposes I had committed murder! But all would soon be well, for I would marry Bathsheba, the 'grieving widow of Uriah'. Soon the two of us were married and in the eyes of the world I had done a gracious thing by taking to wife that grieving widow.

CHAPTER 36

WHEN THE PREACHER VISITED ME

Well, so far so good with my last devised plan. Uriah the Hittite was killed in battle. A great funeral was conducted for him. His widow grieved loudly. The drama devised for covering up my sin of adultery with Bathsheba was played out before the citizens of Israel even as I had planned it. Joab had led the Israelites in a battle tactic that was not his usual style. He led his army to within shouting distance of the wall of the city of the Ammonites. He had been taught by warriors of old that a good Commander-in-Chief would never lead his forces to go close to the wall of the city being attacked. It was well known that the archers from the vantage point of protection by the city wall could rain down arrows upon the attacking force. Joab this time had deliberately done just that. When the battle was raging fiercely, Joab quietly gave the sign to most of his men to withdraw some distance. Uriah was so caught up in hand to hand combat with a group of the Ammonite warriors that either he did not hear Joab's command to pull back (it was obvious that Joab did not want him to hear) or else he was so intent on fighting three or four tough Ammonite soldiers that he refused to move to a position toward the rear. Whatever the reason, Joab had accomplished my wish to have Uriah slain.

Like any good Commander-in-Chief Joab sent to me by his couriers a detailed account of how the battle had gone. He said to them, "When you have finished giving the king this account of the battle, the king's anger may flare up, and he may ask you, 'Why did you get so close to the city wall to fight? Didn't you know they would shoot arrows from the wall? Who killed Abimelech son of Jerub-Besheth? Didn't a woman throw an upper millstone on him from the wall, so that he died in Thebez? Why did you get so close to the wall?' If he asks you this, then say to him, 'Also, your servant Uriah the Hittite is dead.'" Obviously Joab knew how I, old warrior that I was, would react to the report which he sent, so he told the couriers to be sure to inform me that Uriah had been slain. My reaction was as he had predicted, but my anger was quickly abated when the couriers casually added, "Oh, yeah, Joab said to tell you that Uriah the Hittite had been killed." That was a coded message to me letting me know that my instructions concerning Uriah had been carried out.

It was obvious that the couriers were waiting for my message to Joab, so I said rather piously, "Tell Joab not to be upset about Uriah's death; the sword devours one as well as another. Press the attack against the city and destroy it. Say this to encourage Joab."

Well, it was good to hear for a fact that Uriah was dead. Now there was nothing standing in the way of carrying out my plan to cover up my sinful act with Bathsheba. Yes, "All is well that ends well."

After a proper period of mourning on Bathsheba's part, I made a big show of taking unto myself a new wife, the widow of Uriah the Hittite. The citizens of Jerusalem murmured among themselves that the widow Bathsheba was a "fine woman" and that it was so kind of their king to take her as his wife. What better tribute to Uriah could the king give than by taking the fallen warrior's poor defenseless widow into his harem to care for her during the remainder of her days? Secretly I gloated to myself that I had just proved that I could not only fight my way through a hard battle, but I could also fight my way through a maze of details in order to cover up my sin of adultery. I figuratively beat my chest and exulted like the king of the apes. I was one relieved and happy person because all had worked out so well through my strategy to prevent my evil sin of adultery from being found out by the people of my kingdom. It was beside the point that I had committed an even more heinous sin, that is, the sin of having a good and innocent man murdered. Yes, I had to admit to myself that through my conniving I was just as guilty of his death as if I had stabbed him through the heart with a dagger. "But," I murmured to myself, "in order to save my standing among my people I had to do that. It was a matter of 'first things first'!"

In due time a baby boy was born to Bathsheba. Oh, how good it was to see her so radiantly happy over the arrival of the baby. I had to admit that he was a fine looking infant. Of course I was accustomed to seeing my wives' happiness over the arrival of our many children. This time there seemed to be something special about this particular baby. Just what was it? I thought to myself that I did not have time to "grieve over spilt milk". There was too much in the way of national affairs that had to be handled for me to take time to meditate on my past evil actions. I truly rejoiced over the baby's arrival in spite of all that had transpired just prior to his birth. Perhaps that was what made him seem so special to me. I chose to look at the sunny side of my past actions and not dwell on those things I had committed on the dark side of the equation. I repeated to myself what had become my theme song, "All is well that ends well!

One day a short time later a palace attendant came into my chambers with the announcement that Nathan the prophet had come to call on me. "My lord, it seems that he has a request of make of you. He mumbled something about your making right a wrong that seems to be bothering him," said the attendant. I bade the attendant to usher the prophet into my presence. I had come to know and respect Nathan during the past years. He seemed to be a man of God. I felt that he was a man who took his prophetic role very, very seriously. In fact I felt that Nathan was too serious by nature . . . that he ought to "lighten up a bit". "Oh, well,' I mumbled to myself, "he is a good man who takes his work as a prophet of the Lord Jehovah very seriously. I would not want him to be any other way, for serious demeanor is the stuff of which a good prophet is made."

After a bit of small talk Nathan moved the conversation to the problem that was bothering him. I nodded in assent to his request that he might freely share with me the problem that was bothering him. He began to tell me that a great wrong had been done to a poor man by a rich man. It seems that the poor man had no flock of sheep; all he had was one little ewe lamb to which he had become very sentimentally attached. He had made a pet out of it. Why, he even let the little lamb sleep in his bed with him. One day a traveler came and sought lodging for the night in the home of a local rich man. Well, the rich man said to himself, "I know that it is expected of me to entertain my guest at dinner this evening. That has long been the custom among my people to house and feed traveling men who seek shelter in our homes for the night. I don't mind the work involved on the part of my servants in preparing a nice meal for the traveler who is my guest for the night, but I do object to using one of the sheep from my large flock for that purpose. I need each sheep in my flock to produce a large quantity of wool which I am planning to sell on the market at sheep shearing time. Call me stingy if you like, but I just can't give up one of my own sheep for this purpose." The rich man's head steward leaned over and whispered in his ear that a poor man who lived down the roadway a short distance had a lamb that would be young, tender, and just the right size for the evening's meal. "The other day when I passed that man's house I saw the little lamb out in the yard; it was following the poor man around like a little puppy." With the snap of his finger the rich man ordered his steward to go and fetch that lamb and prepare it for the evening meal.

At that moment Nathan stopped abruptly and waited for my reaction to his story. I felt the blood rushing to my face even as I became livid with anger at the injustice that had been done to that poor man. As soon as I could gain sufficient composure, I blurted out, "As surely as the Lord lives, the rich man who did this deserves to die! He must pay for that lamb four times over, because he did such a thing and had no pity." When I had simmered down from my outburst of anger, I looked at Nathan in anticipation of his sharing with me the name of the evil person who had done that deed.

There followed a long pause and finally Nathan said very quietly, "You are that rich man of whom I spoke! This is what the Lord, the God of Israel, says, 'I anointed you king over Israel, and I delivered you from the hand of Saul. I gave your master's house to you, and your master's wives into your arms. I gave you the house of Israel and Judah. And if all this had been too little, I would have given you even more. Why did you despise the word of the Lord by doing what is evil in His eyes? You struck down Uriah the Hittite with the sword and took his wife to be your own. You killed him with the sword of the Ammonites. Now, therefore, the sword will never depart from your house, because you despised me and took the wife of Uriah the Hittite to be your own. This is what the Lord says, 'Out of your own household I am going to bring calamity upon you. Before your very eyes I will take your wives and give them to one who is close to you, and he will lie with your wives in broad daylight. You did it in secret, but I will do this thing in broad daylight before all Israel.'"

I sat there in a state of shock. My head was spinning and my heart was pounding. My famous question which I had asked myself in the aftermath of my two sins, "who is to know about my sin", was harshly answered by the word of the Lord through his prophet, Nathan. There crept over my being a great sense of shame and intense grief. Nathan had caused me to see myself as the Lord saw me . . . . a rank sinner who was an adulterer and murderer. For the first time in a very long while I saw myself as a person who is unclean in the sight of God. Hither to fore I had felt keenly the presence of the Almighty God. Suddenly I sensed that He had removed his holy presence from me because of the heinous sins which I had recently committed. Nathan's little parable described what I had done . . . . I who had many wives had taken from Uriah the Hittite the only wife which he had, and to cover that sin I had ordered his murder. "Woe is me; I am a great sinner in the sight of Almighty God. I see myself and I don't like what I see. I am so sorry for the sins I have committed, and I want forgiveness from Holy God for them." Before Nathan left my presence no doubt he had observed my obvious horror over my sins. I felt that I deserved to die because of my sins. Before departing from my presence Nathan quietly said, "The Lord has taken away your sins. You are not going to die. But because by doing this you have made the enemies of the Lord show utter contempt; the son born to you will die." I vacantly watched Nathan's departure, as I sat staring into space in frozen silence. My strategy to cover my sins from the knowledge of my subjects may have been very effective, but at that moment I could care little for such a victory. It made me say to myself, "Forget what the citizens of the kingdom would have thought about what I had done . . . . that no longer concerns me. What now concerns me is that I have not been able to cover my sins from the all seeing eyes of Almighty God. I now realize that He had been watching every step I had made as I had left the pathway of righteous living and had gone off after my lustful pleasure. Oh, how can I bear the curse which Nathan had said would be visited on me in the near future! How can I bear the great grief that God is going to place on me . . . . the death of my newborn son now, and in the future my wives will be taken from me and 'used' before the eyes of the public by a person 'close to me'?" Still ringing in my ears was Nathan's voice as it spoke for God, "The sword will never depart from your house."

Then and there I felt that I must fall on my knees before righteous God, the God who had led the children of Israel out of bondage into the Promised Land, the God who had helped me, a simple shepherd lad, to be able to slay the great giant, the God who had brought me out of comparative oblivion and set me on the throne of Israel, the God who had been my daily companion, the God who is above all gods, the only true God . . . . yes, I felt a dire need to pour my heart out in bitter repentance before my God and imploring Him to forgive me of my great sins of adultery and murder. The tabernacle was not private enough for my purposes, for there were people going in and out all hours of the day. Therefore, I went into my private chambers where it would be just my God and I. Falling on my knees I poured out my heart in a bitter confession of my sins and a heartfelt request for cleansing from them. Later I wrote out in poetic verse a heart broken confession of my awful sins and an earnest plea for forgiveness and placed it among the other psalms which I had composed:

"Have mercy on me, O God, according to your unfailing love;
According to your great compassion blot out my transgressions.

Wash away all my iniquity and cleanse me from my sin.
For I know my transgressions, and my sin is always before me.
Against you, you only, have I sinned and done what is evil in
your sight,
So that you are proved right when you speak and justified
when you judge.
Surely I was sinful at birth, sinful from the time my mother
conceived me.
Surely you desire truth in the inner parts,
You teach me wisdom in the inmost place.
Cleanse me with hyssop, and I will be clean; wash me, and I will
be whiter than snow.
Let me hear joy and gladness; let the bones you
have crushed rejoice.
Hide your face from my sins and blot out all my iniquity.
Create in me a pure heart, O God, and renew a
steadfast spirit within me.
Do not cast me from your presence or take your
Holy Spirit from me.
Restore to me the joy of your salvation and grant me a willing
spirit to sustain me.
Then I will teach transgressors your ways, and sinners will turn
back to you.
Save me from bloodguilt, O God, the God who saves me, and my
tongue will sing of your righteousness.
O Lord, open my lips, and my mouth will declare your praise.
You do not delight in sacrifice, or I would bring it;
You do not take pleasure in burnt offerings.
The sacrifices of God are a broken spirit; a broken
and contrite heart,
O God, you will not despise.
In your good pleasure make Zion prosper; build up
the walls of Jerusalem.
Then there will be righteous sacrifices, whole burnt
offerings to delight you;
Then bulls will be offered on your altar.

When I arose from my knees a feeling of peace swept over me. "The Lord has heard my prayer for forgiveness. He has forgiven me of my two awful sins, but He will exact a penalty from me even as He told me through the lips of the prophet Nathan. Praise be to my Lord and my God, the Almighty One! Yes, I praise Him from the depth of my wounded heart and from my broken and contrite spirit."

CHAPTER 37

A DEATH IN THE PALACE

The great joy on the part of Bathsheba and myself as well as on the part of the people of Jerusalem over the birth of our little son was short lived. Shortly after the visit of Nathan the prophet the first of those awful judgments which he predicted appeared to be ready to take place. One morning a messenger came to my chambers and told me that Bathsheba had sent word by him that our new born son was ill. I dropped what I was doing and rushed over to her chambers there in the harem. She was distraught with grief; her eyes were red and swollen. She was trying to soothe the cries of the baby boy cradled in her arms. She was softly singing a little lullaby. I rushed over to her side and kissed her and took the baby from her arms and tried to soothe it. Naturally I was very awkward in trying to do that, for I had not had much experience along that line. When my other children had been born I was younger and was endeavoring to play the role of a great "he man" who would not do what women are supposed to do. Oh, to be sure I had visited the older children at or shortly after their births, that is, if I was not engaged in a battle somewhere at the time. Most of those babies were now growing into the teenage stage and did not care to be bothered with my presence. To my sorrow I realized that I had never taken much part in their upbringing. Rightly or wrongly I had figured that when they became almost grown I would teach them the fine art of doing battle in the proper style. Until then I felt that it was their mother's task to take care of them. Was it due to the fact that I was older and more sentimental now than I was in my early days? Or was it due to the fact that this baby was so very special because of the circumstances surrounding his birth? Or was it due to the fact that I was so very much in love with the baby boy's mother, Bathsheba? Well, whatever the cause needless to say I was stricken with sorrow when the baby I was holding in my arms gave every evidence of being very, very ill. His little body was hot with fever. Fresh on my mind were the words which the stern prophet Nathan had uttered concerning my infant son . . . . "The baby will die!"

After several minutes in which I endeavored to soothe the baby I realized that I was not very effective in doing that. I put him back into his mother's arms, stood looking down on the two of them, turned and left the scene. It would not be the manly thing to be seen weeping, so I hurried from the nursery so that my hot tears could flow down my cheeks unseen. I went back to my quarters, but it was not to take care of the nation's business affairs. Rather it was to prostrate myself before the Lord my God. There I lay crying out in a tortured voice to God on behalf of my infant son. No eloquent words fell from my lips. Rather, they were simple petitions uttered by me for God's mercy to be on my little son. My soul was in such anguish that I was not aware of time. After a while my attendants became worried about me when they did not see me out and about the palace area checking on matters of state. They came to my quarters, pausing when they came near enough to hear my heart wrenching cries for God's mercy to be shown on my infant son. They backed away and quietly gathered in a cluster down the corridor out of earshot and discussed what they had heard from my private chambers. Time passed. All was quiet in the other parts of the palace. There were no sounds of laughing and talking among the palace staff. When they realized that I had not come to the great banquet hall where I and the men of my staff were accustomed to dine, their concern for my welfare grew. They whispered among themselves, "He has spent all day prostrated on the floor of his room calling out for God's mercy. The head steward dared to go into his presence to urge him to come and partake of some food. The King told him to get out and not bother him. The King needs his food. How can we persuade him to leave his praying and come and eat?" Everyone just shook their heads, for seemingly no one had an answer to that puzzling question.

So distraught in prayer was I that I was not aware of the passing of time or of all the whispering that was going on among the members of the palace staff who were so worried by my behavior. They had never seen me act in that fashion. I could have told no one truthfully whether the total cause of my grief was due to the remorse over God's awful curses pronounced on me through the prophet Nathan, or was it just due to the thought of losing my infant son to the jaws of death? Looking back by hindsight I would say that no doubt it was both due to remorse over my sins and the prediction of the prophet Nathan that the baby would die because of my two acts of sin. Perhaps it was a mixture of the two, but I had never been so grief stricken before. The weight of a mountain seemed to be pushing down on my heart. "My baby son, my little son! Why, Lord, why? Lord God of Israel, I know that you have the power to heal my little son from this great illness. Please hear and heed my prayer that he can be restored to health! Please, please forgive me of my great sins of adultery and murder which have caused the illness of my little son!" Over and over these pleas were uttered from my grief stricken heart.

So intent was I on the matter of praying for my little son that I had no desire for food nor for contact with my people. My sole purpose was to pray to God to spare my little son's life. I lay prostrate on the floor of my chambers with no thought of bathing or caring for my body. All that was of concern to me in that period of time was for the welfare of my little son. Oh, the curse that God had put on my baby! I realized in my heart that God was placing the price of my sin on my innocent little baby, not on me who was so guilty of those two great sins . . . adultery and murder. I cried out, "Lord, let me be the one to pay the price of my sins; I am the one who should die, not this innocent child. My guilt is ever before me!" Day after day I remained in the depths of prayer. The passing of time meant nothing to me. I was vaguely conscious of the whispers which seem to float in the air over me. Those whispers seemed to be saying, "The king needs some food; how can we get him to eat?" I regretted that my despondent behavior was upsetting to my beloved attendants, but I could not help myself.

Later I learned how concerned the people of Jerusalem were over our little son's illness. Some even dared to come into the palace and approach Bathsheba and to whisper to her their concern for the baby, and some even dared to share remedies they had used on their babies when they were sick. Even my wives in the harem showed concern for the illness of the baby of the young and beautiful Bathsheba. Hither to fore they had been rather unkind to her due to their jealousy over her being added to the large group of wives I already had. They felt that I had forsaken them in order to give all of my attention to Bathsheba. However, when the baby was born they paid their respects to her and congratulated me on adding a pretty young wife to the sisterhood of my wives and on having another fine son. They expressed their great concern by saying, "It's too bad that the baby was so premature at birth . . . . at least two months early even though he is a nice size baby (they were simply going by the number of months since I had taken Bathsheba to wife)." Some of my wives showed enough compassion to Bathsheba to lend her a helping hand.

I continued to fast and pray day after day. My body was growing weaker though I was not really conscious of that fact since I had remained in the prostrate position. So intense was I in my earnest prayers to God for mercy on my little son that I had no sense of reality. My voice was so hoarse that my prayers were scarcely above a whisper. After seven days of calling out to God I became a bit more aware of the movements and whispers of my attendants who were close by. Suddenly I overheard one of them saying, "We've got to tell him!" I paused in my prayers and asked, "Is the child dead?" "He is dead," they replied almost inaudibly. Obviously they were highly concerned about my reaction to that news.

Upon hearing that my little son was dead I arose from my prone position with the aid of the attendants . . . after those seven days in that position I was very, very stiff. I went into my bed chambers and bathed and even put on some fragrant lotions and changed into clean clothing. I asked that food be set before me, and I ate with a ravenous appetite. Again I overheard the voices of the attendants as they whispered among themselves.

"His actions now are very odd indeed. Upon hearing that the baby is dead he is 'coming alive' again. What do you make of that?" Finally they approached me and asked in awed voices, "Sir, why are you acting this way? While the child was alive you fasted and wept, but now that the child is dead you arise and eat. That is in reverse of how most of us react." I looked at their concerned faces and finally explained to them why I was acting in what they thought was a strange way. "While the child was still alive I fasted and wept. I thought, 'who knows, the Lord may be gracious to me and let the child live. But now that he is dead, why should I fast? Can I bring him back again? I will go to him, but he will not return to me."

After bathing, dressing and eating some food, I began to think in a more normal fashion. I said to myself, "Yes, the baby is gone from the earthly scene. There is nothing I can do for him. I prayed as best I knew how during those seven days of his illness but with no apparent results . . . . well, no visible results. However, a spiritual result has proved once again to me that God says what He means and means what He says." Still ringing in my ears were His fatal words which were conveyed to me by Nathan, "The baby will die". His prophetic words which were uttered by Nathan the prophe were carried out in the manner in which He spoke them. I asked myself, "Will God carry out His other threats which Nathan conveyed to me?" My heart feared that He would be true to His word in those cases also.

Then my conscience spoke to me saying, "David, you have been very selfish. You have left Bathsheba to suffer alone during the ebbing away of our baby's life. What have you been thinking? You have been very self-centered even though you thought you were doing what was best . . . . praying night and day for the baby. Poor Bathsheba!" I left my chambers and rushed over to be with her and to comfort her as best I could as she mourned over the baby's death. I followed my usual way of communicating with my wives . . . I paid her the honor of spending the night with her in her chambers.

In due time another baby was born to Bathsheba. Judging by his lusty cries he was a strong, healthy little boy. Bathsheba's sorrow had turned to joy; "I have a man child once again, a very healthy one!" I rejoiced with her and so did the citizens of Jerusalem when they heard the good news. "Now the king's new wife will be comforted. We are happy for her. What do you suppose the baby will be named?" In due time a decision concerning that matter was reached and the result was announced, "His name is to be Solomon." Evidently the Lord looked with favor upon our new baby son, for He sent word by Nathan that the baby should be named Jedidiah, a name that literally meant "loved of the Lord". I took that to mean that the Lord had now allowed my past sin of adultery and murder to be atoned by our first baby's death and that the name suggested by Him was the way in which He was revealing that the life of little baby boy Solomon would be blessed by Him.

As I mentioned earlier Joab, my commander-in-chief, had a way of assisting me in my "off the record" activities. Earlier when I had sent word to him to go against his military training and fight near the wall of the city of the Ammonites in order to bring about the death of Uriah the Hittite, he abated my anger at the news of his bad military tactic of fighting near the city wall by adding the cryptic little phrase, "... and Uriah the Hittite is dead." It was obvious that he "saw through" my scheme, but instead of rebelling at my orders to him had acquiesced to them. Now Joab sent a message to me concerning the progress of another battle and the need for my assistance in carrying it through to a satisfactory conclusion. He had successfully attacked Rabah of the Ammonites and captured its water supply. Now the city must be besieged in order to capture it. His note to me was short and to the point, "Now muster the rest of the troops and besiege the city and capture it. If you don't, I'll capture the city and it will be named after me." Joab dared to presume on our friendship and issue that not-so-veiled threat. I took the bait, mustered the remainder of the entire army, and made the attack on the city. It was successful. The city was captured.

It was a big moment when Joab took the crown from the head of the defeated Ammonite King and placed it on my head. The crown was very heavy, for its weight was about 75 pounds. It was made of pure gold and set with many precious stones. I posed for a while with it resting on my head, but soon I took it off and relegated it to my store room of treasures. We took a great amount of plunder and brought out of the city the Ammonite citizens who had not fled prior to our siege. They were consigned to jobs such as workmen with saws, iron picks, and axes, and with brick. We handled the citizens of all the other Ammonite towns which we had captured in the same way. In due time I, along with my army, was able to return to Jerusalem and enjoy a time of rest and fellowship with my large family.

CHAPTER 38
LOVE AND INTRIGUE

As the days went by I often recalled with shame and sadness that occasion when my lustful gaze and my human desires overcame me, causing me to turn from following after the will and way of my Lord Jehovah and falling into the morass of sin. In those solitary moments when I remembered how I had allowed myself to weaken and to yield to the temptation of the evil Lucifer I shuddered and moaned to myself. It later became obvious to me that the one moment of stolen pleasure with Bathsheba had put a blight on the remainder of my life. God's curses delivered to me by the mouth of the prophet Nathan had already begun to come to fruition. My beloved baby son born to me by my beautiful Bathsheba had died just as God had said that that he would. Oh, the depth of despair which that brought into my heart and life!

With the passing of time I began to feel normal once more, especially after the birth of Bathsheba's second son. I rejoiced in the arrival of little Solomon. He was an exceptional child it seemed to me. Oh, I know, every father thinks his child is unusually smart, but others who observed the growth and development of little Solomon remarked to one another that he was a special kind of child . . . . so intelligent!

My love for little Solomon unintentionally took my mind away from my grown sons. They were fine lads when one stopped to take notice of them. On those rare occasions when I did take notice of them I beamed with pride. They had grown to be young men, but sad to say, I didn't really know them. The same was true of my daughters. I had been so busy as a warrior and later as the King of Israel that I had depended on my wives to shape and mold my children. If there was any credit due concerning their development into manhood or womanhood I must confess it should all go to their mothers. That wasn't to say that I didn't love them, it was just to make note of the fact that I had been removed from their lives both emotionally and physically while they were growing and developing. On those occasions when I thought about my role of "absentee father", I was sad. Quickly, however, I would console myself by saying, "Well, that was just the way it was due to the circumstances that surrounded me. I often envied the life I had experienced back in my childhood home. My father Jesse was an ever present father, a "hands on" parent who was there for his boys. As a little lad I may have thought to myself that he was too close to the scene, for he was a keen observer of all the antics which my brothers and I "pulled off" for fun or just due to plain spitefulness toward one another. Well, I surely had not been that kind of father! At times I felt that I knew my subjects there in the kingdom of Israel better than I did my own family members . . . . a sad feeling indeed!

Of all my sons I would have to say that young Absalom was the most handsome. He was blessed with heavy and beautiful hair. One day while in my presence he boasted that when his hair became so heavy that it was a burden to him he had it cut off to a very short length. He said that out of curiosity he weighed the hair that had been shorn from his head and found it to weigh five pounds. Everywhere he went it was observed that not only did the young ladies look admiringly at him but that the adults did also. The young men of Jerusalem secretly admired Absalom's good looks, but the emotion they experienced was that of great jealousy.

Another of my sons was Amnon. To the casual observer and also to me he appeared to be a calm even tempered young man. Later it was revealed that he was a head strong person who felt that it was his right to get what he wanted when he wanted it. That fact became obvious on one occasion when he yielded to an awful temptation. That is not to say that I was aware of what happened on that occasion . . . . I was made aware of it only after the sin he committed led to another grievous sin being committed. When I learned all at once about those two sins which had been committed, I shivered and shook due to my great grief over them. The sin of adultery on the part of one son followed by the sin of murder on the part of another son caused me to relive those two sins which I had committed earlier in my life. Actually, their sins seemed to be a reenactment of my own two sins. Was God visiting upon me the payment for my sin of adultery and murder through the sins of my two sons?

As I previously said, I was shocked and emotionally wounded when I heard an account of what transpired on two occasions in the lives of my children. Amnon was guilty of a grievous sin, the sin of raping his half sister, the beautiful Tamar. It seems that he had become very, very infatuated with her. He could not think of anything but her. He wanted very much to have relations with her. She was an innocent virgin and had no idea concerning the thoughts which were running through his mind. She only gave him a passing glance. After all, he was her brother, and, therefore, he surely would not have such sinful thoughts toward her. He was getting nowhere in his lustful desire to be with her. He became so obsessed with his lustful desires that he was not himself. How could he manage to get Tamar's attention? He could not figure out a way to do so.

One day, Jonadab, his close friend who was also his first cousin, observed Amnon's downcast countenance. "Why do you, the king's son, look so haggard morning after morning? Share with me the reason for that." "Well, I will tell you. I'm in love with Tamar, my half sister who is Absalom's whole sister, but I can't get to 'first base' with her. She won't give me the 'time of day'." Almost immediately the "wheels started to turn" in Jonadab's shrewd mind. After a while he said, "I've got a plan for you to follow; here it is. Pretend that you are very ill. Get in bed and look the part of a very sick man. The family members will be very, very sympathetic. I strongly suspect that when the news of your "sickness" reaches the ears of your father, the king, that even he will come to check on you and see if there is anything you need. I realize that he is usually an absentee father, but I'm sure that he will come visit you. Do as I have said and play the sick ploy to the hilt." Amnon thought to himself, "That's a strange way to achieve my goal, but I believe Jonadab is shrewd enough to have a workable plan. I'll let him tutor me step by step as I go from that point."

Sure enough when I, King David, heard the news that Amnon was quite ill and had taken to his sick bed, I came to check on him. "Son, what do you need to make you feel better?" "Well, father, I just can't seem to tolerate food. Therefore, I am getting weaker and weaker. The thought occurs to me that if I could have some food prepared and cooked right here in my bed chamber so that I could watch that action, it might tempt my appetite. I don't want one of the servants to do that; I would like to have my sister Tamar to prepare the food in my presence. I understand that she knows how to cook even though she doesn't ordinarily do so. When she has finished the preparation of the food, I can eat it from her hand." "That's a good idea," I replied, "it just might cause you to take some nourishment." So concerned was I about my son's illness that it did not occur to me that there was anything strange about his request.

I spoke to Tamar and suggested that she carry out Amnon's request that she prepare some food where he could see it being done and for her to "hand feed" him due to his weakness. It was obvious to me that he did not trust the servants; perhaps he feared that they might take advantage of his weak condition and try to poison him. With that I left and hurried back to the palace to attend to affairs of the state. Little did I suspect any foul play on the part of Amnon, for he appeared to be much too sick to take advantage of anyone, especially a teenager. Also, it never entered my mind that he was entertaining such lustful thoughts and evil schemes against his sister, Tamar.

I learned a long while after the fact that his evil scheme seemed to be working. Tamar had complied with my suggestion and dutifully went over to Amnon's home. Immediately she was alarmed by the condition which her brother seemed to be in. There he lay on his sick bed uttering every now and then a moan or a groan, she cheerfully announced that she had heard that he was sick, so she thought it would be good to come over to his house and cook some of his favorite food right there before his eyes. Just maybe that would cause his appetite to build up for the meal. After she had prepared it she placed in on a plate and handed it to him, or at least that was what she tried to do. He shook his head weakly and mumbled that he was too weak to hold the plate and eat. "Oh, that's perfectly all right, I'll feed you as if you were a small child again." With that she stepped over to his bedside when suddenly he grabbed her and said, "Come to bed with me, my sister." In dismay she screamed, "Don't do that, my brother. Don't force me . . . such a thing should not be done in Israel. It's a wicked thing you are asking of me. Stop and think about me. If I yielded to you it would cause me to be so disgraced that I could never be rid of that deed. Just look at you! If you did this you would be like one of the wicked fools of Israel. You are above doing such a deed . . . . you are the son of the King of Israel! If you must have me, speak to our father, King David; I know that he will not keep me from being married to you!" Amnon at that point was so filled with lust that he thought that such lust could be best satisfied by forcing his sister to have sexual relations with him. Being stronger than she was, he pulled her into bed with him and raped her.

That evil act on his part had a strange reaction. Suddenly he hated her more than he had been infatuated with her. He pushed her away and yelled, "Get out of my sight; I hate you!" Tamar tearfully remonstrated saying, "No, to send me away after this awful thing you have done to me would be a greater wrong than what you have already done!" She clung to him beseeching him to take her to be his wife and turn that awful sin into an arrangement that would cover the sin of rape . . . at least that's the way she felt at the moment. Amnon called out in a loud voice to a male servant, "Come and put this woman out of the door to my room and lock and bolt it so that she cannot get back in!"

Tamar left the house of Amnon and went back to her house where she revealed to the world her dire distress. As was the custom of that day when a person was in great sorrow, she cut up the beautiful ornamented robe which she and the other daughters of the king wore. She put ashes on her head and went away, weeping as she went. When her brother Absalom saw her condition and heard her uncontrollable sobbing, he asked, "Has that Amnon, your brother, been with you?" Obviously he had put two and two together. He had heard her say that she was going to Amnon's house to prepare him a meal due to his sickness, and now he was hearing her sobbing and was seeing her with ashes on her head and with her beautifully ornamented robe being torn. Tamar's words could not be understood because of her sobs, but she made the matter clear by nodding her head in the affirmative. Absalom simply said to her, "Be quiet. Don't tell what Amnon has done to you. He is your brother and sometimes such things happen between siblings. After all, we can't let this be known, for we are the children of the King of Israel. Were it to become known among the people of Israel it would be a great disgrace to our father." If Tamar had been able to think things through at that time she probably would have sensed that her brother Absalom was not taking the sad event as casually as he appeared to be. However, she simply took his words at face value because she was so overwrought. From that day forward she lived in deep depression in her brother Absalom's house.

Yes, the beautiful Tamar's life was in a shambles so to speak. From that time forward she seldom was seen out of her house. She continued to be a "basket case" for some time to come. That sinful event caused Absalom to seethe with smoldering anger which continued to build up within him. For two years this situation continued. Unbeknown to anyone he was plotting revenge on his brother Amnon. At the end of two years his carefully laid plans for revenge came to fruition. It was sheep shearing time and Absalom's sheep shearers were plying their trade at Baal Hazor which was near the border of Ephraim. Often the owners of large flocks of sheep celebrated the occasion by having a party. He sent out invitations to all his brothers, that is, all my sons. Then he came to me there in the palace and graciously extended to me and my officials an invitation to attend the party. In fact he insisted that I and my officials attend. I replied that if we went that it would be a great burden on him, for there were a lot of us. He continued to urge me to attend, and I continued to say "No." Secretly I felt that my sons would have a lot better time if I were not present. In other words my presence would probably put a damper on the spirit of the party.

Finally Absalom said, "If you won't agree to come please allow my brother Amnon to attend and my other brothers also."

I assured him that all of my sons could attend, even though it would take them away for a few days from the duties which I had assigned to all of them. Little did I suspect that Absalom had carefully devised a plot to kill Amnon. He had instructed his servants to supply a lot of wine for all to drink, especially Amnon. "When he gets "deep in the cups" (drunk) listen for this order which I shall give to you, "Strike Amnon down," you are to kill him there and then. Oh, I know you are afraid for your lives; to kill any innocent man is unlawful, but to kill the son of King David is something to be reckoned with. Of course you are afraid of the consequences of that crime. Just remember, you can tell my father the king and all of the soldiers that you were simply following my instructions. The blame will fall on my shoulders."

The murder of my son, Amnon, went off as planned. All of the other brothers and the other guests were suddenly shocked out of their drunken stupor. They ran and jumped on their mules and rode away as fast as their steeds would carry them. Each thought to himself, "I may be the next one to be murdered if I don't make haste to get away."

A servant who had witnessed the murder of Amnon obviously either saw the act of murder or heard about it just after it had happened. As with any situation the bearer of sad news sometimes is prone to enlarge on the story. Part of his report to me was true; the rest he assumed had happened. His report to me went like this, "Absalom has struck down all your sons, Oh, King David. Not one of them is left alive." The shock was too great for me. I tore my clothes as a sign of deep mourning and prostrated myself on the ground. My servants tore their clothes and stood around me. Shortly after I had received the tragic news of the death of all my sons, my nephew, Jonadab, said to me, "My lord should not think that they killed all the princes; only Amnon is dead. This had been Absalom's expressed intention ever since the day Amnon raped his sister Tamar. My lord the king should not be concerned about the report that all the king's sons are dead. Only Amnon is dead."

A bit later the clatter of the hooves of many mules was heard. There approached all of my sons with the exception of Amnon and Absalom. They were wailing loudly, and I joined them as we all grieved for Amnon. Absalom had fled from my jurisdiction over to Geshur, where he remained for three years. Oh, how I mourned over Amnon's death. Now I mourned over the absence of Absalom. I longed to see him, but I had to forego acting on my personal feelings. After all he was guilty of murder. As king I could not condone what he had done, for when I had presided over murder cases occurring in the past in Israel I had never shown leniency to the murderer. Thus, it was fortunate that Absalom had fled to Geshur, for there he would not be subject to a murder trial here in Israel. He was simply a guest of the people there. If he had remained in Israel and "faced the music" so to speak, a murder trial would certainly have involved my oversight. As bad as it was for Absalom to be absent from his homeland and from his family, it was better than being brought to justice in Israel.

CHAPTER 39
A FATHER'S GREAT SORROW

In the days following that tragic episode in which my beloved son Amnon was murdered and Absalom was lost to the family circle, I spent much of my time grieving over the death of one son and grieving over the absence from the family circle of another son. I realized that I had to be very firm in the way in which I responded to the situation. With the passing of time I became a bit more reconciled to the situation. I had slowly stopped showing my grief outwardly though I continued to grieve in the privacy of my bed chamber there in the palace. Common sense had dictated that I must be seen by my loyal subjects as keeping a steady hand in running the "ship of state" in spite of what had happened. It was hard, hard, hard!

As time following that tragic event passed day by day, month by month, and year by year, I suddenly realized that it had been three years. Yes, it had been three years since I had seen my handsome and much loved son, Absalom. He had remained in Geshur where he felt that he was safe from criminal action which he would surely have received if he had returned to Israel. By that time I had become somewhat reconciled with the fact of Amnon's death. Surely I had mourned for him during those years following the tragic event, yes, I had mourned for him until that point in time when I grew accustomed to the fact of his death. Now, I realized that I was greatly missing fellowship with Absalom. The edge of my shock over that tragic event which had resulted in Amnon's death three years earlier had been dulled. My thoughts by this time had turned to the absence of Absalom. Each day I found myself greatly desiring to have him back in the family circle. I missed him so very muChapter

My mourning over his absence did not escape the observant eyes of Joab, who had come to the point in our relationship wherein he could "read me like a book". Quite often he would endeavor to bring to pass things which he knew that I desired to be done. In doing so he worked behind the scenes to accomplish those things in an effort to make it appear that I was responsible for making those decisions. In this instance he began to work things around so that I would suddenly find myself inviting Absalom to come back to Jerusalem. To accomplish that, he knew he would have to handle me "with kid gloves". He was aware of my longing to see him, of my stern attitude toward him due to the crime he had committed, and of my trying to "walk the straight and narrow" way in handling this family matter so that my subjects could not say that I had made a great exception in Absalom's case.

In order to accomplish his scheme Joab sent a messenger to Tekoa with the instructions to bring back to Jerusalem a certain "wise woman" who had the ability to act. Upon her arrival he shared with her how she was to figure in the plot which he had devised. He instructed her that she was to act the part of a woman who was in deep mourning. She was to dress in mourning clothes, use no perfumes or fragrant body lotions. She was to give the appearance of being a woman who had been in deep mourning for the dead for many days. "When you have put on the clothes of a mourner and have succeeded in appearing to have been in deep grief for many days, go into the presence of King David and say what I tell you to say."

When she had reached the point that she felt she could play the part of such a person as Joab had described to her, she went into the palace where she appeared before me and fell to the ground in a great show of reverence for me. Then she cried out to me, "Help me, O King!" Immediately I felt compassion for her, and I quickly asked, "What is troubling you." "O King, I am a poor widow; my husband has been dead for some time. I had two sons. They got into a fight in the field; no one was there to stop them. One struck the other and killed him. Now all of the kinsmen have risen up against me because I have not acted in this matter as they demand that I should. They are demanding that I hand over the son who committed the crime that they may put him to death for the crime of murder which he committed. O King, they are demanding more than that justice be done . . . they desire to kill the remaining son in order to put to death the surviving heir of my husband and take the property for themselves. They desire to put to death the only 'burning coal' I have, leaving my deceased husband neither name nor descendant on the face of the earth." When I had heard her story, I told her to go on home and I would issue an order on her behalf. In seeming gratitude she uttered her thanks for my decision concerning her problem, saying, "My lord the king let the blame rest on me and on my father's family, and let the king and his throne be without guilt." Greatly impressed by her thanksgiving I replied, "If anyone says anything to you, bring him to me, and he will not bother you again." She continued, "Then let the king invoke the Lord his God to prevent the avenger of blood from adding to the destruction, so that my son will not be destroyed." I replied, "As surely as the Lord lives not one hair of your son's head will fall to the ground." There was a long pause then she looked me directly in the eyes and said, "Permit your servant to speak a personal word to my lord the king." Already she had taken much of my time in hearing her case; now she wanted to have a personal word with me. Well, I suppose I can grant her a bit more time. What could she possibly mean by that request? I simply said almost curtly, "Speak!"

Her next words seemed to tumble from her lips, "In the light of your decision to grant my personal request why have you devised a thing like this against the people of God? When the kin says this, does he not convict himself, for the king has not brought back his banished son? Like water spilled on the g round, which cannot be recovered, so we must die. But God does not take away life; instead, he devises ways so that a banished person may not remain estranged from him." I sat there stunned. I felt the blood rising to my face. That grieving widow has gone too far this time. She has spoken so boldly to the point of almost becoming impertinent to me. Then she continued, "And now I have come to say this to my lord the king because the people have made me afraid. Your servant thought, 'I will speak to the king; perhaps he will do what his servant asksl Perhaps the king will agree to deliver his servant from the hand of the man who is trying to cut off both me and my son from the inheritance God gave us." Then she uttered words obviously designed to assuage any anger which may have risen in my heart. "An now your servant says, 'May the word of my lord the king bring me rest, for my lord the king is like an angel of God in discerning good and evil. May the Lord your God be with you.'"

After a long pause I said to the woman, "Do not keep from me the answer to what I am going to ask you." "Let my lord the king speak," she replied. "Isn't the hand of Joab with you in all of this?" I thought to myself, "This is exactly the way in which Joab operates; instead of coming to me personally and telling me what he thinks I ought to do, he chooses a method of getting across to me what he thinks I ought to do, a method which he hopes will not reveal his hand in all of this." The widow looked at me for a long moment, then replied, "As surely as you live, my lord the king, no one can turn to the right or to the left from anything my lord the king says. Yes, it was your servant Joab who instructed me to do this and who put all these words into the mouth of your servant. Your servant Joab did this to change the present situation. My lord has wisdom like that of an angel of God—he knows everything that happens in the land."

I strongly suspected that Joab was lurking just outside the door of the throne room, so I called in a loud voice, "Joab! Joab, come here!" Almost immediately he entered the room with a red face, an obvious reaction to being caught in the elaborate scheme. "You have used this woman to be your mouthpiece. You put all those words into her mouth to repeat to me as though they came from her heart. Very well, I get the point. You think that I should bring Absalom back to his home in Jerusalem. Very well, I will do it. Go; bring back the young man Absalom. However, he must go to his own house; he must not see my face." By way of thanking me for carrying out his request delivered by way of the "grieving widow' he prostrated himself on the ground to pay me honor. He blessed me and said, "Today your servant knows that he has found favor in your eyes, my lord the king, because the king has granted his servant's request."

Joab lost no time in going to Geshur to bringing Absalom back to Jerusalem. However, it was not a complete victory for

Joab due to the fact that I did allow him to be brought into my presence just yet. I felt that his full return to my good graces was not warranted yet. Emotionally speaking, I was not ready to look upon him in the light of the crime he had committed against my other son, Amnon. Also, I felt that I would need to take one step at a time in the matter of returning him to full favor in my sight, for I knew that the citizens of the kingdom were watching carefully as to how I handled the situation.

Absalom was very happy to be allowed to come back home and to live in his own home there. Three sons and a daughter were born to him. He named the daughter "Tamar" in honor of his sister who had been raped by Amnon. Two years went by and still he had not seen his father. He asked Joab to come to his house for a visit. He planned to use Joab to intercede for him that he might enter into his father's presence. However, Joab refused to assist him in that matter. After a while he asked Joab to come to his home with the same purpose in mind. Again Joab refused. The headstrong Absalom devised a scheme to get the attention of Joab. He gave instructions to his servants to go out into Joab's field of barley which adjoined his own field and set it on fire. He said to himself, "This act will get Joab's attention." Sure enough Joab was soon seen knocking on Absalom's front door. The two stood there looking at each other for a short while. Joab posed the obvious question to Absalom, "Why have your servants set my field of barley on fire?" "For the simple reason that I could not get your attention otherwise. Twice I sent word to you to come to my home that I might persuade you to intercede on my behalf to my father, the king. You would not. It would have been better for me if I had remained in Geshur instead of coming back to Jerusalem. I want to see my father in person. If I am guilty of anything, let him put me to death. This time Joab was obedient to the wishes of Absalom, that is, he came to me and told me what had happened.

In the light of what had just transpired I sent word to Absalom to come into my presence. He lost no time in coming to the palace. He bowed down before me and prostrated himself in my presence. Tears welled up in my eyes and my heart rejoiced in seeing my son once again. I reached over and gave him a loving fatherly kiss.

CHAPTER 40

TREASON FROM AN UNEXPECTED SOURCE

"Treason" is an ugly word! In whatever situation it occurs it brings disappointment in the one who commits treason. It brings great anger on the part of citizens when an individual or faction in the society of a nation turns against all that the nation stands for. That's generally speaking. In the case of the treason which occurred in my beloved nation of Israel it spelled heartbreak to me because my son Absalom was the one who led a coup against me. It also cost me and the loyal citizens of Israel a near death experience.

Little did I dream that when I allowed my son Absalom to return from exile in Geshur that he would prove to be an ungrateful person and a thankless son. Word was brought to me by members of my court that Absalom had become proactive in the politics of the kingdom. However the word from my informers was carefully couched in language that would not convey negative thoughts against him. I suppose that they felt that it would be lacking in respect for my feelings if they even intimated that he was building a case against his own father. Therefore since I did not have the whole picture of his actions I was naïve enough to be happy that he had settled down from his youthful antics and was developing into a man. I was very happy that he was becoming interested in the politics of the nation. At that point I could never have believed that he had evil intent against me. It was much later when he brought into the open his intent to take over the kingdom of Israel and become its ruler that I could see the truth through my tear stained eyes.

When the truth concerning Absalom's scheme finally became obvious, that is, that he planned to depose me as king and take over the rule of Israel, I was crushed emotionally and physically. My legs became weak and rubbery and my eyes became dimmed by hours of weeping. Why, oh why would my son treat his father as he was doing? Did he not know that I loved him so very much? Could it be because of the way I had handled his murderous act by allowing him to remain in exile so long in Geshur? Could it be that my refusing to see him during those years when he first returned from exile may have been interpreted by him as too severe a punishment on my part and also a lack of love for him? Whatever the cause for his turning against me and my kingdom, he fully determined that the kingdom of Israel should be his to rule as he saw fit.

Absalom began his scheme to take over my throne and become a youthful and vigorous king in my stead by rising early each day and going outside the city gate and sitting by the side of the road that led into Jerusalem. As each man passed by on his way into Jerusalem Absalom called out to them and asked from what town they came. Usually the passerby bowed to the ground before Absalom in recognition of his princely personhood. Immediately Absalom would reach out to him and take his hand and lift him up and kiss him. So personal and cordial was he in his remarks that soon the passerbys unloaded their grievances to him. "I wanted an audience with King David, but I know for a fact that I can't get near him, so I'll have to settle with a conference with one of his staff members." Absalom rose to the occasion by saying, "If only I were appointed judge in the land everyone who has a complaint or a grievance would be heard. They could come to me and get justice." It is a known fact that any happening small or great that occurs in a town soon becomes common knowledge. Finally word of Absalom's antics soon spread even into the palace and right to my throne.

With the passing of time Absalom became the "talk of the town". By his antics he soon ingratiated himself into the hearts of the citizens of Jerusalem. Without realizing it their affections were turning to the young and handsome son of the king. They would whisper among themselves, "He is the kind of king we need. He is young and energetic and has an ear for our problems. Why, he has said over and over that if only he were king the people would get a rapid hearing concerning their grievances.

Looking back on that situation from the perspective of "hind sight" I realize that I should have taken action and nipped his antics in the bud. As concerned matters of state I usually took quick action to quell anything that appeared to be a treasonous problem in the land. However, I saw Absalom's actions as that of a young man who was keenly interested in Israel's affairs of state and was endeavoring to get a handle on them. Actually, I was so happy that he was showing a keen interest in such matters. None of my other sons seemed to have even the slightest interest in politics. Of course if I had known then what I knew later I would have come out of my rosy haze of love for and pride in him and would have taken action to quell his high handed effort to take over my kingdom. As they say "hindsight is twenty/twenty". In fairness concerning my apparent blindness to the festering sore in the politics of the nation brought on by Absalom, I was cloistered in the confines of the palace and missed a lot of "talk" that made the daily rounds in Jerusalem. By the time that the news of his schemes finally came to my attention it had been carefully censored by those closest to me. They were evidently trying to spare my feelings. Also, they probably assumed that what appeared to be a threat to the safety of my role as king would "go away" in due time.

When I heard that Absalom had acquired a chariot and some fine horses to pull it and had hired fifty men to run ahead of him as he drove here and there, I said to myself, "That's Absalom! He has always been dramatic in everything that he did. He always was one to call attention to himself. I supposed that there was no harm in his doing that. I was never one to call attention to myself in such dramatic ways. He must get that part of his nature from his mother! My parental love blinded me to what was happening behind the scenes. Looking back on that situation from the perspective of these last years of my life I should have been able to see through Absalom's antics. However, there is a lot of truth in the old adage, "Love is blind."

Some four years following his return from exile in Geshur where he had been accorded a welcome by his grandfather, Talmai, who was king of Geshur and whose daughter, Maacah, was married to me and was the mother of Absalom, approached me and requested permission to return to that area and carry out a vow that he had made while in exile there. His vow was, "If the Lord takes me back to Jerusalem I shall worship him back here in Hebron." Thinking over his request for a while, I could find no reason for denying it. In fact I was pleased that he remembered his earlier vow and wanted to carry it out. To my way of thinking such a request revealed real character on the part of my much loved son. Again, my parental love for him blinded me from seeing or even sensing that something was amiss with his request. Actually, I was pleased to realize through this request that my son was a religious man, a fact that I had never seen in him prior to this time. Therefore, I gladly granted him his request to return to the area of his early vow and to carry out the terms of his vow. Little did I sense his ulterior motive.

When it was too late I learned that this was just another one of his schemes to achieve his plan to seize my throne. How could I have known that Absalom had laid out a plan of such large proportions? How could I have realized that this was part of his scheme to advance his selfish desire? It was much later that I learned the horrible truth. Even before I had granted his request to go back to Geshur, he had secretly sent messages to the heads of the tribes of Israel which said, "As soon as you hear the sound of the trumpet give this message to your people to say, 'Absalom is king in Hebron!'"

It was later that I learned that he did not go alone, for he had issued special invitations to some two hundred men of Israel to be his guests. It must be said that those men who were invited were not privy to the real reason back of their invitations. They simply thought that they were to go to share in Absalom's carrying out his vow. There were to be sacrifices offered which would be followed by a great feast. Thus the invitation pleased those men who were invited to that grand occasion. Little did they suspect the real motive behind the invitation which they had received. In the midst of the sacrifice and subsequent feast he secretly sent a message to Ahithophel to join with him in the sacrifice and feast. What seemed to be an innocent gesture in extending the invitation to Ahithophel, Absalom was actually flattering him to the point that he would join forces with him. This was indeed a "low blow", for Ahithophel had been my trusted counselor. Later when I heard that he had joined forces with the rebellious group I was greatly hurt by his treasonous act, for I had trusted him as my advisor and friend. Slowly the rebellion conceived by Absalom was growing in strength.

After a while I finally absorbed what was taking place in my kingdom. Distressful news was brought to me by a loyal subject who had been in a position to observe what was taking place in the enemy camp. His news was short and succinct, "The hearts of the men of Israel are with Absalom." He simply told me what I had suspected for some time. Nevertheless I sat in frozen silence for several minutes. Then I sprang into action and called my officials to me. "Come! We must flee, or none of us will escape from Absalom. We must leave immediately, or he will move quickly to overtake us and bring ruin upon us and put this city to the sword." Loyally they answered, "Your servants are ready to do whatever our lord the king chooses."

With more rapidity than seemed possible my entire household and I moved out of the palace and out of Jerusalem. Oh, I did leave ten of my concubines behind to take care of the palace. We could not move at a very rapid pace due to the women and children in the group. The soldiers at my command marched past us. Among them were the Kerethites and Pelethites and the six hundred Gittites who had remained with me from the days when I was hiding from King Saul. They had been so faithful to me all during the years following that period in my life. Like myself they were getting some age on them. All of these men marched ahead of me and my wives and children. I turned to Ittai, the Gittite leader, and asked, "Why should you come along with us? You should go back and stay with 'King Absalom'. You and your men are foreigners as far as the Israelites are concerned. You are exiles from your homeland. You only came here recently. There is no reason for you to stay and wander about with us. You and your fellow Gittites go back. May kindness and faithfulness remain with you."

His reply warmed my heart greatly, for he said, "As surely as the Lord lives and as my lord the king lives, wherever my lord the king may be, whether it means life or death, there will your servant be." Tears welled up in my eyes upon hearing his statement of loyalty. Ah, those days when his six hundred men and I were being hunted like wild animals by King Saul were days that tried our very souls! Those were days when the Gittites and I fought together against the men of my own nation due to the phobia of King Saul who thought that I was endeavoring to take his throne from him, a fact that could not have been farther from the truth. During those days when we were being driven from one hiding place to another we bonded together as brother with brother. When I finally regained my composure I simply said, "Go ahead with the Israelite men who are loyal to me. March on!"

Traveling away from Jerusalem into the unknown was like a funeral procession. The citizens of Israel who remained loyal to me were lined up along our route of travel and stood with bowed heads and tears flowing from their eyes. We crossed the Kidron Valley and slowly moved on toward the desert. The high priest Zadok and the priestly tribe of the Levites were in the line of march. They were carrying the Ark of the Covenant with them. At a certain point' they set down the Ark, and Abiathar offered sacrifices until all the people had finished leaving the city. Sadly I told Abiathar to take the ark back into the city, saying, "If I find favor in the Lord's eyes, He will bring me back and let me see it and His dwelling place again. But if He says, 'I am not pleased with you,' then I am ready; let Him do to me whatever seems good to him."

Then it occurred to me that Zadok, the priest, had been known to have the ability to see into the future. I said to him, "You and Abiathar take your two sons, that is, your son Ahimaaz, and Abiathar's son, Jonathan, with you back into Jerusalem and remain there." I felt that they would be more useful to my cause if they remained there where they could see and hear what was going on with Absalom's military plans and could relay the information to me. I slowly climbed up the Mount of Olives barefoot and weeping and with a covering on my head, a sign to one and all that I was in deep mourning. All the people with me also covered their heads and were weeping as they went. As I slowly ascended the Mount I was silently praying that God would turn the counsel of Ahithophel, the traitor who was now following Absalom, into foolishness. As we arrived at the summit there was Hushai the Arkite standing there with his clothes torn and dust on his head, another custom of those in mourning. I said to him, "If you go with me you will only be a burden to me, but if you really want to help my cause remain in Jerusalem and say to Absalom, 'I will be your servant, O king; I was your father's servant in the past, but now I will be your servant,' then you will be in a position to help me. You can help me by frustrating the advice of Ahithophel, my former counselor. Also, the two priests, Zadok and Abiathar, and their two sons will be in the palace. Keep your ears open to anything you hear concerning Absalom's plans and send that information to me." Hushai arrived back in Jerusalem none too soon, for just as he entered the city Absalom and his retinue were also entering the city.

CHAPTER 41
THE TRAIL OF BITTER TEARS

After my retinue and I had gone a little ways from Jerusalem and on past the Mount of Olives, I encountered Ziba who was the steward of Mephibosheth. I noticed that he had with him a string of donkeys loaded with some two hundred loaves of bread, a hundred cakes of raisins, a hundred cakes of figs, and a skin of wine. That sight piqued my curiosity, so it was natural that I asked him why he had brought all of those items. He quietly replied, "The donkeys are for members of your household to ride on, the bread and fruit are for your soldiers to eat, and the wine is to refresh those who grow faint in the desert." Then I asked him where was his master, Mephibosheth, son of Jonathan and grandson of King Saul. Ziba replied, "He is remaining in Jerusalem with the hope that your son, Absalom, will restore to him the kingdom which was formerly that of his grand-father, King Saul." That news hurt me to the core, for the sake of my good friend Jonathan I had invited Mephibosheth to eat at my table for the rest of his life and had given him a sizeable piece of land for the support of him and his household. "What kind of gratitude is that? He has come to the point that he no longer is loyal to the 'hand that fed him'. He plans to fawn over Absalom with the hope that he will restore the kingdom to him, because he was the only surviving descendant of King Saul." Then I turned to Ziba and said, "All that belonged to Mephibosheth is now yours." (Of course that statement was based on my belief that I would regain my throne sometime in the future.) Ziba humbly replied, "May I find favor in your eyes, my lord the king."

As my people and I slowly traveled away from Jerusalem we approached the area of Bahurim. Out of nowhere there came a loud mouthed man by the name of Shimei. He was a very angry person, for he was uttering curses at me and my officials. I learned that he was of the family of the late King Saul. As he drew nearer he began tossing pebbles at me and my officials even though I was surrounded by my soldiers and my special guards. Then he began shouting, "Get out! Get out, you man of blood, you scoundrel! The Lord has repaid you for all the blood which you have shed in the household of Saul, in whose place you have reigned. The Lord has handed the kingdom over to your son Absalom. You have come to ruin because you are a man of blood!" Naturally I was stunned and very hurt that the loud mouthed man was taking out his spite on me and accusing me of things of which I was not guilty. About that time my man, Abishai, rushed to my side and said, "Why should that dead dog curse my lord the king? Let me go over and cut off his head." Perhaps I was unkind in answering him as I did, for I told him, "What do you and I have in common, you son of Zeruiah? If he is cursing me because the Lord said to him 'Curse David,' who can ask, 'Why do you do this?'" I turned and addressed Abishai and all his officials, "My son Absalom, who is of my own flesh, is trying to take my life in order to become king of Israel. How much more, then, this Benjamite! Leave him alone; let him curse, for the Lord has told him to. It may be that the Lord will see my distress and repay me with good for the cursing I am receiving today." As I and my people moved along the way Shimei continued to go along the crest of the hill and continued to shout curses at me and to throw pebbles and dirt at me. Finally my retinue and I arrived at our temporary destination completely exhausted. Oh, what a difference there is between youth and age in one's ability to travel! This was a much appreciated "rest stop" in our march out of Jerusalem.

My plan of planting informers (or should I say my "spies") in Jerusalem to work on my behalf in the new government under my son Absalom was "swinging into action" nicely. In a day or so my informers got the message to me that my friend, Hushai the Arkite, had gone immediately and ingratiated himself with Absalom by approaching him and bowing low and saying, "Long live the king! Long live the king!" Absalom, with a snarl in his voice, asked Hushai, "Is this the love you show your *friend*? Why did you not go with your *friend?*" Hushai knew that Absalom was being sarcastic, but he answered very matter of factly, "No, the one chosen by the Lord, by these people who support you and by all the men of Israel . . . his I will be, and I will remain with him. Furthermore, whom should I serve? Should I not serve the son? Just as I served your father, so I will serve you." Obviously Absalom "took the bait" from Hushai, for he said to him in good faith, "Give us your advice, Hushai. What should we do?"

Later Absalom asked the same question of Ahithophel, who complied by giving him some revolting advice, "Lie with your father's concubines whom he left to take care of the palace. By doing so word will soon spread throughout Israel that you have made a stench in your father's nostrils and the hands of everyone with you will be strengthened." Ahithophel was pleased that Absalom took his advice readily, for Absalom's men pitched a tent on the roof of the palace, and he lay with his father's concubines in the sight of all the people of Israel who were stirring about in the city. That juicy gossip soon spread to all the people in Jerusalem who had not happened to see the event for themselves.

Both I and now Absalom thought that Ahithophel's advice was like that of one who got his advice straight from God. Ahithophel was seemingly full of advice for the young would-be king. He gave another bit of advice to Absalom. "If I were you I would choose twelve thousand men and set out tonight in pursuit of David. I would attack him while he is weary and weak. I would strike him with terror, and then all the people with him will flee. I would strike down only the king and bring all of his people back with you. King David's death will result in all those who are with him returning to you. In handling it this way all of those who are presently following him will return to you." This plan seemed to Absalom and all the elders to be a good one.

However, Absalom wanted to hear from Hushai the Arkite as to what he thought was the best plan to pursue. He told a servant, "Summon also Hushai the Arkite, so we can hear what he has to say." While on his way to talk with Absalom, he was thinking to himself, "Now is my opportunity to confuse the advice given by Ahithophel." When he was ushered into Absalom's presence, he was informed concerning the advice which Ahithophel had given him as how best to proceed. Then Absalom asked, "Should we do as he says? If not, give us your advice." Hushi replied, "The advice which Ahithophel has given you is not good at this time. The reason I say that is because, as you certainly know, your father and his men are great fighters who are as fierce as a wild bear that has been robbed of her cubs. In addition your father is a very experienced fighter, a mighty warrior who will not spend the night with his troops. Already he is hidden in a cave or some other place where he will be impossible for your warriors to find. Also, if he should attack your troops first, whoever hears about it will say, 'There has been a slaughter among the troops who follow Absalom.' Then even the bravest soldier whose heart is like the heart of a lion will melt with fear, for all Israel knows that your father is an accomplished fighter and that those with him are very brave. Therefore, I advise you: Let all Israel from Dan to Beersheba, an army that will be as large as the sand on the seashore, be gathered to you, with you yourself leading them into battle. Then we will attack King David wherever he may be found, and we will fall on him as dew settles on the ground. Neither he nor any of his men will be left alive. If he withdraws into a city, then all Israel will bring ropes to that city, and we will drag it down to the valley until not even a piece of it can be found." After hearing from each of the two advisers Absalom announced to the elders, "The advice of Hushai the Arkite is better than that of Ahithophel." It was obvious to Hushi and to David that the Lord had determined to frustrate the good advice of Ahithophel by causing Absalom to favor the advice of Hushai in order to bring disaster on Absalom.

Hushai was very happy that Absalom had made the decision to follow his advice, advice that would frustrate Ahithophel's better advice. Quickly Hushai slipped around and told Zadok and Abiathar, the priests, "Send messengers over to David and tell him what Ahithophel advised Absalom to do, and tell him what I advised him to do. Tell David, 'Do not spend the night at the fords in the desert; cross over without fail, or the king and all the people with him will be swallowed up.'" Two of my men, Jonathan and Ahimaaz, were staying at En Rogel. A servant girl was to go and inform them, and they were to go and tell me that they could not risk being seen entering the city. Unfortunately a young man saw them and told Absalom. So the two of them left quickly and went to the house of a man in Bahurim. He had a well in his courtyard; they climbed down into it. His wife took a covering and spread it out over the opening of the well and scattered grain over it. No one knew about that hiding place When approached by Absalom's men who asked if she had seen them, she answered very matter of factly, "Oh, those two you are asking about did pass through here, but they were last seen crossing over the brook. That was sometime ago, so I would imagine that they are quite a distance from here by now." She was quite an actress, for she told the lie so very convincingly. The men in the search party hurried on and searched for quite a while, but finding no one, they turned back and went into Jerusalem. When it was evident that the search party was long gone, Jonathan and Ahimaaz crawled out of the well and hurried on to deliver their message to me. "Set out and cross the river at once; Ahithophel has advised such and such against you." So I and all the people with me set out and crossed the Jordan; by daybreak no one was left who had not crossed over the river.

When Ahithophel realized that his advice had not been followed, he saddled his donkey and set out for his house in his hometown. He put his house in order and then hanged himself. Thus in that manner he died and was buried in his father's tomb. I and those in the group who were still loyal to me went to Mahanaim. In the meantime Absalom with his fighting men, a group so large that most of the people of Israel referred to it as being "all the men of Israel", (which was somewhat of an exaggeration) crossed the Jordan River. Earlier Absalom had appointed Amasa, a first cousin of Joab's, over his army in place of Joab who had served as commandant of my army. He had remained faithful to me. Absalom and his retinue camped in Gilead.

To my surprise and delight there appeared on the scene Shobi, an Ammonite, Makir of LoDebar, and Barzillai, a native of Gilead. Their donkeys were weighed down with such stuff as bedding, pots and pans for cooking, wheat and barley, flour and roasted grain, beans and lentils, honey and curds, sheep, and cheese from cows' milk to present to me for my followers' needs. They said to me, "The people have become hungry and tired and thirsty in the desert. There will be very taxing days ahead. We trust that these items of food will revive them and enable them to travel on where you lead them." I wept with gratitude before these three faithful members of my kingdom. What they had just done refreshed me more than the groceries which they had so graciously given to us.

In the quiet moments at eventide I had a bit of time in which to review the recent turn of events. I was still in a state of shock that my own beloved son, my handsome son Absalom, had wooed and won the affection of the people of Israel to himself. As the long time king of Israel I had always tried to be a godly leader before them. My advice and judgments in all the legal cases which had come before me had been as fair and equitable as I knew how to make them. I had tried to show the people of my kingdom that I loved them with all my heart. Had I been naïve in my assumption that they respected and loved me in return? Where did I go wrong? How could my son Absalom turn against me as he had done? Oh, to be sure, I knew that he was a restless sort of person, that he was very dramatic in his actions, and that he was very ambitious for himself. Yes, I had recognized all those traits in him, but I never dreamed that they would lead him to a desire to win over the nation of Israel from me and become its leader. Many years ago I had been anointed as king of Israel and had not been removed from the throne by the will of God. Though now a much older person than when I assumed the throne, I preferred to think of myself as a seasoned warrior and a wise and experienced ruler. Had I been hiding from the truth in a state of euphoria? Had I chosen to see the true situation in my kingdom through rose colored glasses? In my heart I knew that I had intended everything for God's honor and glory and for the good of my subjects.

In those moments of reverie and of a review of the actual situation as it presently existed, I simply shuddered and shook. How could the state of politics in Israel have come to this? There I was the leader of Israel who was now "on the run", a leader who was now being led by his faithful followers of the old days. If I would have admitted it, I would have asked the Lord how I could I have been naïve enough to have failed to see what was coming. More to the point I should have realized that I needed to be down on my knees covered in sackcloth and heavily sprinkled with ashes praying to the God of Israel to save me and my faithful followers from the dilemma in which I found myself. However, at that point I found myself to be too numb from grief and shock to perceive all that had suddenly happened to me and to my faithful followers. In my more lucid moments I realized that my family and those who continued to support me were in a dire circumstance. There we were fleeing from Jerusalem and its environs endeavoring to save our lives from those who were seeking to destroy us. We were out in a territory which was foreign to our people, and supplies were very, very limited. We could not be sure from whence our next jugs of water would be obtained. We had no assurance that there would be food for our bodies on the next day. All that we could be certain of was that we were being hunted down like animals of prey. We realized that our lives were very expendable at that point in time. All that I could advise my people to do was to pray that God would hear our cries for his mercy to be shown to us.

CHAPTER 42

THE MOURNFUL END OF
THE REBELLION

After much hurried preparation for the encounter between the forces of Absalom and those of mine, the day came when the battle took place. It seemed very odd to me that those of the rebellion chose to have the conflict with my army to occur in the forest rather than in the open fields and valleys. Perhaps, however, it was not so much a choice of location as it was a happenstance. Also, let it be said that there was very little open land on the east side of the Jordan that was suitable for doing battle. In preparation for the time when my army would meet face to face with the mighty army of those under the command of Absalom I had divided those in my army into three parts. One part was to be under the leadership of Joab, the faithful commander of my army, a third part was to be under the direction of Abishai, the brother of Joab, and the final third was to be under Ittai, the Gittite.

That decision having been made I declared to my army that I would be leading them in person, saying that "I myself will surely march out with you." As with one voice my men shouted, "No, no, you must not go with us; here is the reason we say that. In the event that we are forced to flee before the huge army of Israel, they will zero in on you. They won't care about us, no, not even if half of our army should die. You will be the one about whom they care. To capture and to slay you will mean to them that the war will be over. You will be worth ten thousand of us. It would be better now for you to give us support from the vantage point of the city." I knew in my heart that they were correct in their thinking about the matter, so I finally agreed to remain in my quarters in the city, saying to them, "I shall do whatever seems good to you." I had full confidence in the three who were in charge of the three divisions of my army. When the time came for them to march out into battle, I stood at attention by the gate as my men marched out of the city in groups of hundreds and thousands.

As each of the three commanders of my army (Joab, Abishai and Ittai) passed by I called out to them, "Be gentle with the young man Absalom for my sake." I noticed that each of them gave me a rather curt nod by which they acknowledged that they heard me, but that they did not necessarily agree with my command to them. Looking back on that incident I should have tried to see the situation from their perspective. Their view was that Absalom had been responsible for causing a great rift in the life of Israel and that he was a conceited and ambitious young man who cared for no one's feelings other than his own. His desire to rule Israel at all costs was more important to him than all the damage he was doing to the unity of the nation. Oh, if only I could have seen the situation from their view point. As it was I could only be concerned for the safety of my beloved but rebellious son, Absalom. My "father love" outweighed all other factors that had brought to pass the darkest day in the Kingdom of Israel since I had become king.

Young Absalom, though very inexperienced in the field of battle, was personally leading his army. He was riding a donkey at the forefront of his troops as they engaged my men in battle. Unfortunately he had failed to realize just how low the limbs of the trees in the forest were. That coupled with the fact that he was riding at top speed ahead of his army, looking back over his shoulder and calling back to his troops to speed up as they fled from the attack of their enemy, caused him to fail to see a particularly low hanging limb on a tree just ahead of him. As a result the long thick hair of his head was caught and entangled in the fork of the limb, resulting in his being suspended in mid-air, while his donkey continued to race on through the forest. A young man of my army rushed back to inform Joab of the situation, leaving Absalom suspended in midair. Joab said in effect, "Well, what did you do about it? You know that the young prince is 'enemy number one,' and the situation you saw him in was a great opportunity to kill him." "Sir, if I had done what you say I should have, I would have caught a lot of flack from my superior officers. If that had happened you leaders would have withdrawn from me, leaving me to face the music alone." "Do you mean to say that you saw Absalom hanging right there before you, and you left him alone! If you had stricken him down, I would have had to give you 10,000 shekels of silver and a warrior's belt!" "Even if a thousand shekels of silver were weighed out into my hands, I would not have lifted my hand against the king's son. In our hearing the king commanded you to 'protect the young man Absalom for my sake'. If I had put my life in jeopardy . . . and nothing is hidden from the king . . . . you would have kept your distance from me afterward." Joab, ignoring my request of him, rushed over with some three javelins in his hands and thrust each one of them into Absalom's heart as he hung on the limb of the tree. Ten of Joab's armor-bearers surrounded Absalom, struck him and finished killing him. Joab sounded the trumpet, and his troops stopped chasing after Absalom's army. Joab's army took Absalom's body and dumped it into a large hole in the forest and piled large heap of rocks over him. During his lifetime he had erected a large stone pillar and had erected it in the King's Valley as a monument to himself. He said to himself, "I have no son to carry on the memory of my name." He named the pillar after his name, that is, "Absalom's Monument".

Knowing how greatly Absalom's army outnumbered my army, I was very surprised that the army of Israel suffered a great defeat at the hands of my men. It was estimated that the army of my enemy suffered the loss of some 20,000 men that day. It was said that more of those casualties were caused by the forest (low hanging limbs) than by the sword. Another reason was most likely due to the fact that Absalom's army was filled with rather new recruits who had had very little formal training in the art of military science. On the other hand old Joab was a well trained and seasoned military leader. A large number of Absalom's troops fled back to their homes and endeavored to be absorbed unobtrusively back into the society of their home areas. Most of them gave evidence of shame as seen on their countenances. And so they should have, for they had been guilty of turning their backs on a "rock of Gibraltar" type of king in order to jump on the band wagon of a conceited, very proud and very ambitious young would-be king.

But back to the results of Joab's slaining of Absalom: I was waiting there in my quarters for news of Absalom. True, his army had suffered a resounding defeat, but what about him? Had he survived the battle? Was he in good shape? I anxiously sat out in the open facing the west from which direction a runner could be soon be seen coming and bringing the latest news. I was numb with worry. Actually the weather was warm to the point of being hot, but I was sitting in my chair and shivering. Worrying over my rebellious son had brought on the effects of a chill, a condition usually relegated to the effects of a fever. Would the runner never show up on the horizon? Why had they not sent a messenger to me earlier with the news which I was so anxious to hear? Had they forgotten my concern over the outcome of the fierce battle and of how my beloved son Absalom had faired in that fierce battle? After having sat there for many hours at last I saw some dust rising in the distance. Was that the dust from a runner who was bringing to me good news? How I wished that I could have been present when the very efficient Joab finally got around to the business of informing me as to what had happened to my son. If I could have had an overview of that event, I would have heard Joab calling a Cushite to him and instructing him to make haste and take the message of what he had seen concerning the final minutes in the life of Absalom to me. Hardly had he given that assignment to the Cushite trained runner than there came to Joab Ahimaaz, son of Zadok, pleading with him to allow him to run behind the Cushite. Joab replied, "My son, why do you want to go? You don't have any news that will bring you a reward." Ahimaaz answered him, "Come what may, I want to run." Joab simply replied, "Well, then, run if you must!" Joab thought to himself that for Ahimaaz to do that would be redundant, but on second thought he decided that it was a good idea, for the Cushite might not be able to bear up under the strain of the race and fall by the wayside. If by chance that should happen then the message would get through to me by the word of Ahimaaz.

Ahimaaz obviously was more familiar with the terrain of that area than was the Cushite runner, for he ran by the plain and thus outran the Cushite. I was sitting between the inner and outer gates straining my eyes to see any sign of a runner in the distance. The watchman went up on the roof of the building in order to see farther into the distance. After a while he spied a man running alone. He called down to me saying that he had spotted a lone figure running in our direction. Perhaps I reasoned that the significance of what we were seeing was that which I so earnestly wanted to be true. I shouted up to the watchman, "If he is alone, he must have good news." Soon I could see that the man was drawing ever closer to where we were. Suddenly the watchman reported that he saw another man running at a great rate of speed. I responded to the watchman that the second runner must be the bearer of good news also. The watchman called down from the roof top, saying that it seemed to him that the runner who was in the lead ran like Ahimaaz. I responded, "He is a good man. He will have good news for me."

While still a hundred or so yards away he called out to me, "All is well!" My interpretation of his statement was what I wanted with all my heart to believe, that is, that all was well with my son Absalom. When he had arrived before me, Ahimaaz prostrated himself before me on the ground and said, "Praise be to the Lord your God! He has delivered up the men who lifted their hands against my lord the king." Impatiently I said, "Fine, fine, but what about my son Absalom? Is he safe?" If I had been thinking more clearly I would have noticed that Ahimaaz gave a rather vague answer, that he seemed to be choosing his words too carefully. Finally he said, "I saw great confusion just as Joab was about to send the king's servant and me, your servant, but I don't know what it was." Impatiently I instructed him to stand over to one side of me where he would wait until the Cushite runner had arrived at which time I would hear his version of what happened and what the ultimate result was. When the Cushite arrived he called out to me, "My lord the king, hear the good news! The Lord has delivered you today from all who rose up against you." In my eagerness to hear about Absalom I made no comment to his announcement about the good result of the campaign.

Instead I impatiently asked, "Is the young man Absalom safe?" In figurative language he gave his answer to my question, "May the enemies of my lord the king and all who rise up to harm you be like that young man." When my mind absorbed the meaning of the Cushite runner's answer, I broke down in tears and moved from the presence of the few who were assembled there and went up to the room above the gateway and wept bitter tears. Even as I was rushing to the privacy of the upper room I cried out in emotional agony, "O my son Absalom! My son, my son Absalom! If only I had died instead of you . . . . O Absalom, my son, my son!" Although I had heard how hard it was to lose a child, and had already experience such a loss when Absalom had slain his brother because of his adulterous affair with his half-sister Tamara the present experience of it was almost more than I could bear. This experience of the loss of a child was far more painful than the earlier one due to the situation that had accompanied Absalom's death. The bitterness that accompanied the circumstances of his death added to the great sorrow which I was feeling in those moments. Also, a sense of failure on my part to guide my son in the right direction had no doubt caused him to be the rebellious, self-centered, egotistical, murderous, and proud young man that he had turned out to be! Oh, how I had failed him in his teenage and young adult years! If I had been there for him, perhaps I could have shaped him into the fine man that he could have been." Grief overcame me. I secluded myself from the public, surrendering myself to my great grief.

CHAPTER 43

STRONG WORDS TO A
MOURNING KING

In those days following the reception of the glad/sad news brought to me by the two runners I was in a daze, a mournful blue daze. The happiest news imaginable had just been heard from the lips of the Cushite runner who said, "My lord, the king, hear the good news! The Lord has delivered you from all who rose up against you." His announcement revealed to me that a miracle had been performed by the Lord God, for my army had been dwarfed in size by the army of Absalom. My army was fighting a very defensive battle against the huge opposing army that was on the offensive with every probability of winning this first big battle of the war between the "new army" against the "old army" of Israel in the great civil war which was being fought. In many cases it was a war in which a brother was pitted against his brother. With an utter lack of confidence in a positive outcome for that battle I had great misgivings. Most of all I was an emotional wreck brought on by the sudden turn of events in which a rising young star on the political scene of the nation of Israel had usurped the affections of a goodly number of its citizens, had quickly built a large army, and had marched toward the capital city of Jerusalem with the full intent of wrenching the throne from me. The main thing that had put me in such a state of emotional gloom was that the brilliant young leader who had succeeded in stealing the loyalty of the people away from me was my son of whom I had been so very proud.

But so much for the "good news" from the two runners. The "bad" news was what came from the lips of the Cushite runner when I asked him pointedly as to what was the situation with my son Absalom. In almost poetic language he replied, "May the enemies of my lord the king and all who rise up to harm you be like that young man!" To me that was the worst news that could have been delivered to me. My heart sank in sorrow, my world turned upside down, and my outlook for the future turned into salty tears. I felt that life no longer had any meaning for me, that my future was behind me, that I just wanted to crawl behind a huge rock and let my life slowly ebb away. I went into isolation so that I could mourn alone until there were no more tears welling up into my eyes and where my sobs could be heard only by me. At that point I felt that my period of mourning would continue until the day that my soul and body would part company.

I was so absorbed in my own sorrow that I had no thought of what was happening among my valiant followers. I learned later that they came from the battle front with a spirit of victory permeating their entire beings. In fact they could hardly contain the happiness and joy that was theirs due to the great victory they had achieved. However, when word was quietly spread among them of my personal tragedy and great sorrow in the death of their enemy, my son Absalom, they began to "slink" around in public as though they had committed a great crime in bringing about his death. They began to feel that they had lost the battle and the whole war due to the way I was mourning over the death of Absalom. Now, that would have been the expected conduct on their part if they had lost the war, but as it was they had under the Lord's leadership won a brilliant victory. The victory of my warriors over the enemy soon lost its vigor after they had heard about my deep mourning.

Joab, ah, yes dear Joab! For years he had been guiding me behind the scenes. He could be obnoxious at time, conniving at times, but he was perceptive at all times. I recall that because of the episode in which I was involved with the beautiful Bathsheba I had some "close calls" politically speaking. I recall that those close calls were quietly and skillfully handled behind the scenes by Joab so as to avoid an open and flagrant conflict with my subjects. All along there had "cropped up" other situations in which he had worked behind the scenes to prevent a crisis in my kingdom. However, this time he seemingly had lost patience with me and my conduct in the aftermath of the slaying of Absalom. When he personally and deliberately jabbed those three spears into the body of my son in spite of the fact that I had told him and my other two commanders please to spare Absalom's life, he had completely ignored my order to do so. For that I could not forgive him. His action on that score really magnified the pain and sorrow which I felt so keenly following his dastardly action.

Seeing the dour effects that my private conduct was having on my loyal followers . . . . especially on my victorious soldiers . . . . Joab knew he had to do something to "jerk" me out of my dour mood. Therefore, he came uninvited and unannounced into my private chambers in the house I was using as my headquarters and found me to be still in deep mourning. Hither to fore, he had addressed the issue which he felt that he must straighten out with me by speaking to me in a very humble way concerning the matter. Evidently this situation irked him more and had more possibilities of harming the kingdom than those earlier situations, for this time he was very abrupt and blunt with me. Yes, he was almost scornful in speaking of my actions of being so mournful and failing to show great appreciation for the good work which my soldiers had done in putting the army of the rebellion to rout.

As he came bursting into my living quarters there in the palace, he was almost shouting at me, saying, "Today you have humiliated your men who have just saved your life and the lives of your sons and daughters and the lives of your wives and concubines. You love those who hate you and hate those who love you. You have made it clear today that the commanders and their men mean nothing to you. I see that you would be pleased if Absalom were alive today and all of us were dead. Now go out and encourage your men. I swear by the Lord that if you don't go out, not a man will be left with you by nightfall. This will be worse for you than all the calamities that have come upon you from your youth till now." I turned and stared at Joab through my tear stained eyes; he had never spoken to me in that fashion. He was entirely out of order to be speaking to me so sternly, for it was not the proper way for a subject to speak to his king. Anger flashed up on my countenance like streaks of lightening across the night sky. After a few moments in which I slowly came out of my state of lethargy brought on by my deep grief, I realized that what Joab had said to me was what I needed to hear. Indeed, I had failed to see the whole picture. I had failed to see things from the perspective of my soldiers and others who had put their lives on the line for my sake. I became quite ashamed of myself for having been so selfish as to mourn the death of one who had sought my death and failing to rejoice with those who were rejoicing over my army's miraculous victory over such great odds.

I lifted myself off my bed, dashed water on my face with the hope that in doing so I would lessen the puffiness around my eyes and wash the tear stains from my cheeks. I went out to the gateway of the city where I was presently using as my headquarters and took my seat. Word soon spread throughout the city that I was in my accustomed place for hearing the needs of my people. Soon the people came out of their homes to see me. They came rejoicing. They offered sympathy to me over the death of Absalom (perhaps it was not heart-felt sympathy, but they knew that it was the proper thing to do). Then they began to talk all at once as they told about the miraculous victory which our small army had been able to bring about. Some made reference to Gideon's small army winning over the millions in the army of the enemy, for they saw in the recent battle that God had intervened and had shown His power by allowing the small army to win over the huge army of Absalom.

I had to call on all my strength in order to be able to put on a good front before my people. My heart was still aching over the loss of my beloved Absalom, but I had to rebuild the confidence of my people in the future of my renewed kingdom. There I was a great distance from Jerusalem living as a stranger in a strange land. I needed to reveal in my demeanor a great confidence in my kingdom as being the true kingdom of Israel. I needed to exhibit a spirit of forgiveness to those who had turned from me to follow after Absalom. Following the big battle in which they had lost in a decisive victory on the part of my soldiers, they had slunk back into their homes in Jerusalem. Most of them had reentered the city under the shades of the darkness of night due to their shame of having played the traitor to their former king and more especially the shame of having been so badly trounced by a much smaller army.

In the following days the people within Jerusalem began to bicker back and forth among themselves as to the stance they needed to take in order to "face up to the future" as regards their allegiance to me or to the memory of Absalom. The ones who had remained quietly loyal to me had to rethink their situation. Could they assume a forgiving stance toward Absalom's followers who were now seen as being traitors to my kingdom? Naturally there was a good bit of animosity between the group who had been traitors to my kingdom and the group who had been tried and true to me all the while. Could the two groups be reconciled to each other and move forward together as though the rift had never occurred? There was much to work out between the traitorious group and the group who had been loyal to me all the while. I knew in my heart that if we were to experience such reconciliation between the two groups it must begin with me. No, I had not caused the civil war to occur . . . . far from it, but I would have to take the lead in bringing about a healing influence among all my people. I would either have to be a good actor, or I would have to be truly forgiving of the group that had played the traitor. Hopefully I could manage the latter.

I realized that I must move back into Jerusalem and reoccupy the living quarters in the palace along with the members of my large family. Also, I must lose no time in resuming the office space where I had been accustomed to taking care of the business matters of the nation. I realized that I needed to let it be seen by the citizens of Israel that I was now back on the job as the king of a united nation. I knew that I had to exhibit a positive attitude as I went among all my people. A very forgiving spirit toward the followers of Absalom had to be shown by me as I moved about among the citizens of Israel, because "deeds are more effective than words" in getting the message across that I desired to bring about a cohesive spirit among all the people regardless of their actions in the past.

Since early childhood I had always endeavored to show a forgiving spirit to all those who had irritated me. During my early years whenever my big brothers took occasion to tease me unmercifully . . . . and those occasions were rather frequent . . . . I knew that they had the advantage of size over me, so I had better not try to use my fists to address the issue. Not allowing myself to go about sulking over their treatment of me, I simply made myself forgive them for their mistreatment. The result was that I had a much happier disposition than otherwise I would have had. Those early lessons stood me in good stead in this situation. Instead of holding a grudge toward those who had been guilty of treason toward me, I found that it would be better to greet them with a smile and some pleasantries .... and pray to the Lord that he would cause my façade to become heartfelt and true.

It was easy to recognize which of the citizens had been loyal to me and my regime and which had been on Absalom's side during the past conflict. The former group came into my presence as I sat there in the gate with broad and happy smiles on their faces and a happy tone in their voices as they spoke to me. The other group came into my presence with heads bowed and spoke in low tones to me from a very humble countenance. Perhaps I overdid it, but I gave those of the latter group more time, attention, and kindness than I did the former, for I felt in my heart that they needed such attention more. I took the long range view which was that I wanted to rebuild my "shattered kingdom" back to its former condition. I knew that it would take much time and energy to do this, but I knew in my heart that it was worth it. In hoping to achieve this goal I was willing to expend as much time and attention as my energy (greatly limited by the aging of my body and mind) would allow. It was my desire that the once united and powerful Kingdom of Israel would once again be looked upon by the surrounding nations in that light. Yes, it would be worth it all to rebuild Israel into a solidified nation with the reputation of being a strong nation under the leadership of its God, the Lord Jehovah. To that end I plotted the course toward the restoration of a strong and unified nation. There were the small details of what had to be done by me as king such as going back to my headquarters in Jerusalem and restoring the former mode of the personal lives of my extended family in the palace. That having been done, I would need to address the things that had to be done to mend the political fences among my people.

CHAPTER 44
HOMEWARD BOUND

"Yes," I said to myself, "it is now time to return to Jerusalem, the beloved capital city of the nation of Israel, a city which many decades earlier I brought into being as the center of the great nation of Israel." It was truly a "home going" experience, the prospects of which brought mixed emotions. I longed to be back in my palace and back doing my work as the king of Israel. However, there was one catch to it. I felt that propriety called for an invitation to be extended to me by a united nation. At that particular point in time there was a great lack of unity, for old feelings were hard to die. Oh, to be sure, I could summon my victorious army to lead me and my household back into the capital city and move me into the palace. However, I realized that such was not the best way to do it. I needed to hear that the remnants of the two factions needed to come together in a spirit of unity and make it a heartfelt desire on the part of both groups to have me to return to Jerusalem and resume my duties as king of a united nation. This would need to be a political and emotional decision on the part of both factions. Certainly there was more to it than just the trip back across the River Jordan and on to the great walled city of Jerusalem.

Those who had sided with Absalom and his group obviously felt themselves to be in a very, very awkward position. The soldiers of that group had fought so valiantly against me . . . but had lost. In their hearts they were likely asking themselves, "Where does that leave us soldiers who fought under Absalom against his father, king David?" The business men, tradesmen and other non-military men and their families who had given their allegiance to Absalom either openly or with some persuasion were also asking themselves, "Where does that leave us?" No doubt the future seemed to be a big blur to them. Without Absalom there to lead them in opposition to me, they suddenly felt that maybe the one who had earlier led their fathers to fight the Philistines so successfully, who had taken over the reigns of government and had led the nation into being recognized as a leader among the nations of their day wasn't such a bad person and such a weak leader after all. In other words without Absalom and his "cheering section" they had lost their passion for his cause.

I discovered that throughout all the tribes of Israel the people were all arguing with each other, saying "The king delivered us from the hand of our enemies in our early days. Yes, and he is the one who rescued us time after time from the many onslaughts of the Philistines. Where is our memory of the victories which he gave us, where is the hand that nurtured us in the infancy of our nation? What has happened to him now? Well, we all know the answer to that question . . . . we caused him to flee to the other side of the Jordan River. We all thought that his son Absalom was going to be such a powerful man who could lead us to greater heights of glory for our nation, BUT where is he now??? He is dead, quite dead, and therefore is not going to be able to lead our nation into the future. We do not well in sitting here without a leader. Why do you say nothing about bringing good king David back to Jerusalem to lead us as he once did?"

At the same time I was growing more and more antsy over getting back to Jerusalem. "Maybe they need some leadership to accomplish that," I said to myself. Therefore, I sent a message to the two priests I had left in Jerusalem when I fled the city, that is, Zadok and Abiathar. The message was this, "Ask the elders of Judah, 'Why should you be the last to bring the king back to his palace, since what is being said throughout Israel has reached his ears there in those temporary quarters on the east side of the river Jordan. Remember, you are the brothers of King David, his own flesh and blood. So why should you be the last to bring the king back?' Say to Amasa, 'Are you not his own flesh and blood? May God deal with him, be it ever so severely, if from now on you are not the commander of his army in the place of Joab.'" Ever since the news that Joab had deliberately disobeyed my orders and killed my beloved flesh and blood, my beloved son Absalom, I said to myself, "I cannot tolerate the commander-in-chief of my army, Joab, to enter my presence. Beside all that he has all too often taken on himself tasks that have irked me . . . it's time for him to 'go'". Therefore, I made that decision concerning giving him Joab's position. My ulterior reason was that Amasa would "snap to action" when he heard of my plans for him.

Maybe earlier in my career I had been accustomed to giving orders to my people in the manner in which I had commanded my soldiers, and had not used diplomacy. In my old age I realized that I should be more diplomatic in the way I handled the affairs of state, that I should consider people's feelings by being more tactful. Slowly I was able to win back the hearts of my people so that they once again respected me and decided that I had been a good king in spite of what Absalom had said about me. They sent word to me, saying, "Return, you and all your men." What happiness that cryptic message brought to me!

After receiving that message I lost no time in moving my family and my retinue westward to the Jordan River. In the meantime the men of Judah had come to Gilgal with the purpose of coming over and meeting me and bringing me and the members of my household across the Jordan River. Among the great crowd were two men who had figured greatly in the retreat of myself and my faithful citizens from Jerusalem to the east side of the river Jordan. One was Shimei who had hurried down with the men of Judah to meet me. To put it mildly I was astounded that he had done that, for I recalled that he was the one who had shouted at the top of his voice curses on me as we marched away from Jerusalem in a state of genuine mourning. I would have thought that when things turned out as they did he would have run from my presence and hidden in some secluded spot such as a distant cave. Now when I learned that he was coming to meet me I decided that he was suffering from a grave mental problem. When he had crossed to the east side of the Jordan he ran to me, fell down at my feet with face to the ground, and said to me, "May my lord not hold me guilty. Do not remember how your servant did wrong on the day my lord the king left Jerusalem. May the king put it out of his mind. For I, your servant, know that I have sinned, but today I have come here as the first of the whole house of Joseph to welcome my lord the king back to Jerusalem." Hearing Shimei's speech to me, Abishai stepped up to me and asked, "Shouldn't Shimei be put to death for cursing the Lord's anointed. My reply was not what Abishai expected, "What do you and I have in common, you son of Zeruiah? This day you have become my adversary! Should anyone be put to death in Israel today? Today I rejoice in the fact that once again I am king over Israel. Should anyone be put to death in Israel today? Today I realize that the Lord God has once again made me king over Israel?" I said to Shimei, "You shall not die." I made that promise to him on oath.

Another with the group that was traveling with Shemei was Ziba, the former steward in the household of the late King Saul. Seeing him I recalled that he had told me how faithful he had been to me in spite of the fact that his present boss, Mephibosheth, grandson of King Saul, had turned to Absalom. Accepting as true what Ziba had told me about Mephibosheth's disloyalty to me in favor of Absalom, I had said hurriedly to Ziba, "You shall have all the property which I gave to Meshibosheth, who has spurned my kindness to him by turning away from me and following after Absalom." When I saw that Mephibosheth was in the welcoming crowd, I conferred with him, asking, "Why didn't you go with me instead of becoming a follower of Absalom?" I hardly had the heart to ask him that question, for during the days of the conflict until that moment he had not taken care of his crippled feet or trimmed his mustache or washed his clothes from the day of my hurried departure until the day I returned. With measured speech he answered my question thusly, "My lord the king, since I your servant am lame, I said, 'I will have my donkey saddled and will ride on it, so I can go with the king.' But Ziba my servant betrayed me. And he has slandered your servant to my lord the king. My lord the king is like an angel of God; so do whatever pleases you. All my grandfather's descendants deserved nothing but death from my lord the king, but you gave your servant a place among those who eat at your table. So what right do I have to make any more appeals to the king?" Having believed Ziba's version of the story, I had wrested the property which I had earlier given to Mephibosheth from him and had given it all to Ziba. After hearing Mephibosheth's version of the story as to why he had not gone with me into exile, I took back half of that property from Ziba and gave it back to Mephibosheth.

Another one of the crowd of men I spotted was Barzillai, a very wealthy man. He had come down to assist in moving me and my entourage across the Jordan River and to bid me and my people a good trip on to Jerusalem. I was so pleased to see him there to assist me in the move that I spontaneously said to him, "Cross over with me and stay with me in Jerusalem, and I will provide for you." Barzillai graciously responded by saying, "How many more years will I live, that I should go up to Jerusalem with the king? I am now eighty years old. Can I tell the difference between what is good and what is not? Can your servant taste what he eats and drinks? Can I still hear the voices of men and women singers? Why should your servant be an added burden to my lord the king? Your servant will cross over the Jordan with the king for a short distance, but why should the king reward me in this way? Let your servant return, that I may die in my own town near the tomb of my father and mother. But here is your servant Kimham. Let him cross over with my lord the king. Do for him whatever pleases you." I responded to his gracious refusal of my invitation with tears in my eyes and gratitude in my heart, saying, "Kimham shall cross over with me, and I will do for him whatever pleases you, his master. And anything you desire from me I will do for you." As I moved on I thought to myself, "One seldom encounters so great a person as is he." I kissed Barzillai and gave him my blessing, and he returned to his home.

Finally that glad moment arrived in which my family and followers were to cross over the river. Now let it be said that the River Jordan was not very wide and not very deep in most times of the year, but to people of the arid land on the west side it was rather a formidable sight. Most of my people had only been familiar with springs scattered over the countryside. Thus, anything referred to as a "river" was an awesome sight. True, in the rainy season there were at times a great abundance of water flowing from the Sea of Galilee into the Jordan, resulting in a swift current and a greater depth. In such times for women and children it was rather difficult to swim or "thrash" one's way across. After all the people had crossed over, I crossed over and joined them. Soon there arrived on the scene huge crowds of men who were late in getting the word of the "great crossing" and were quite perturbed that my plan for crossing on that day had not been made known to them. Their tone revealed that they felt left out of being there to assist me and my people in making the crossing. They asked, "Why did our brothers, the men of Judah, steal the king away and bring him and his household across the Jordan, together with all his men. We feel left out of this wonderful opportunity to show our love for our king." The men of Judah answered the men of Israel, "We did this because the king is closely related to us. Why are you angry about it? Have we eaten any of the king's provisions? Have we taken anything for ourselves?" I thought to myself, they are acting like a group of young boys on the play ground. Then the men of Israel answered the men of Judah, "We have ten shares in the king; and, therefore, we have a greater claim on David than you have. So why do you treat us with contempt? Were we not the first to speak of bringing back our king?" I thought to myself, "Well, it is clear to me that I am back among my people. Hear all that arguing among themselves? They are acting like a bunch of children. Perhaps part of their argument was for me to hear, thinking that I would be greatly impressed by their show of devotion to me." The men of Judah responded in a harsher manner than before, but by that time I had heard enough from them and closed my ears to any further argument.

Just as we were drying off and getting ready to continue on with the journey to Jerusalem, a troublemaker named Sheba, a Benjamite, had been standing by hearing the argument between the men of Judah and the others. Suddenly he put a trumpet to his lips and blew on it in order to get the attention of that angry mass of people who were shouting at the top their of lungs. The piercing sound of the trumpet penetrated the ears of the mass of angry and shouting men to the extent that they left their sentences floating in midair. Most of them had fought in many battles and thus were trained to stop in their tracks at the sound of the trumpet. Before they could begin shouting at each other again, Sheba called out at the top of his voice, "We have no share in David, no part in Jesse's son! Every man to his tent!" As with one accord they fled from my presence and out across the land ahead of us.

With that turn of events my blood almost congealed within me. How could I go forward in the face of such a disaster? My joy at being invited back to continue my reign dissipated into the air. I sat on my donkey and watched the men of Israel deserting me to follow Sheba, a loud mouthed troublemaker. My positive attitude about being restored to the kingship of all Israel suddenly turned into a very negative attitude. What to do? Well, I would just have to go along with those who were still with me and try to make the best of it.

CHAPTER 45

HOUSE CLEANING TIME

From the time I left Jerusalem in haste to escape Absalom's army until the victorious ending of the conflict much time had elapsed. There was also much time spent in exile while waiting to be received back in Jerusalem to continue my reign as king of Israel. During that time of waiting much happened to change one's attitude and perspective. More than dust had accumulated in the palace during my absence although during my absence much literal dust had accumulated. The palace had to be cleaned from top to bottom. It is true that I had left in the palace ten of my concubines to do that task and to keep it in spotless condition. Unfortunately those ten concubines had become stained with immorality due to Absalom's acting on bad advice. The episode in which he committed immorality of the roof with those ten concubines before the eyes of the citizens of Jerusalem had changed for all time to come my relationship with them. Oh, I am the first to realize that they were most likely forced into those acts of adultery (though it was reported to me that on the occasion of the rooftop "exercise" they seemed to be enjoying consorting with the young and very handsome Absalom). Who were they to stop those moments in the arms of Absalom they reasoned. Well, be that as it may, I could not stand the sight of them now. I moved them out of the palace and into a separate building and placed them under guard as though they were common criminals. Regardless of how I personally felt about them and their open act of adultery for all Israel to watch, did not matter. What did matter in the eyes of my subjects was that I must no longer have any contact with those ten women who had been defiled by the rebellious young Absalom. I knew that my reaction to them was being watched by all the citizens of Jerusalem and environs. To have taken them back to their accustomed place in palace life and in my former relationship with them would have brought the wrath of the citizens down on my head. Therefore, I felt it best to handle the situation with them as I did.

To get back to my home in the palace and back into my role as king was bittersweet. The ten tribes' dispute with the tribe of Judah had alienated a goodly portion of subjects from allegiance to me. Would that severed relationship be restored to its former standing with me? I feared that such would not be the case. Thus, my kingdom had shrunk in size to a fraction of its former self. I had figured that there would be hard feelings between the two factions and that the least little thing would cause a big rift between the sides with differing loyalties. Yet I was not prepared for such a great division between the two sides as had just occurred. The glory of the great Kingdom of Israel had been greatly diminished. I was happy to have been welcome back to my throne, but I was very sad that my former kingdom had been so radically split. The strength of the nation was only a fraction of the man power of its former self. What could I possibly do to bring it back into the old nation that I had built into a nation that was to be reckoned with by the other nations of the world. When I had time during my task of rebuilding Israel to its former strength and glory to think about the former status of Israel with its great walled capitol city of Jerusalem shining from the top of the mountain out across the stretches of arid desert, I could not contain my emotions. It was indeed a sad situation that confronted me upon my rturn to former place as its king.

Then I turned my attention to the "affairs of state". I instructed Amasa, my new commander whom I put in place of Joab, to summon the men of Judah to come to me within three days and told him to be here also. When more than three days had passed and Amasa had not returned nor had the men of Judah appeared before me, I turned in another direction by which to carry out my plan of catching Sheba who had led the men of the ten tribes of Israel to turn from me. I said, 'Sheba will do us more harm than did Absalom. Take your soldiers and pursue him before he finds some fortified city in which to take refuge. Abishai's men along with the Kerethites and the Pelethites and all the mighty warriors went out under the command of Abishai. They marched out of Jerusalem to pursue Sheba.

CHAPTER 46
TAKING TIME TO PRAISE THE LORD

Once again the nation of Israel was at peace, a fact that gave me time to recall the blessings of the Lord to me personally and to Israel in general. In my declining years I began to think backward to those earlier years when I went to battle against the surrounding nations and came out of those battles victoriously. Oh, how good the Lord was to me in the days of my youth when I was in one battle after another. I decided that now it was time to pour out my heart to the Lord for all the blessings he had showered on me and on the nation of Israel.

I sang to the Lord . . . . yes; I still liked to sing the psalms of Zion many of which had come from my own heart . . . . a new psalm, a psalm of praise to His holy name. This psalm was in commemoration of the many, many times in which He had delivered me from the hands of the Philistines and the people of the other nations with whom I had been engaged in combat. Certainly it was also in commemoration of His sparing me from the wrath of King Saul who had done his best to find me and to slay me. I played on the harp with my stiff and aging hands and sang with my broken voice this psalm to the Lord:

"The Lord is my rock, my fortress and my deliverer;
My God is the Rock in whom I take refuge'
My shield and the horn of my salvation.
He is my stronghold, my refuge and my savior;
From violent men you save me.
I call to the Lord who is worthy of praise,
And I am saved from my enemies.

He parted the heavens and came down;
Dark clouds were under His feet.
He mounted the cherubim and flew,
He soared on the wings of the wind.
He made darkness His canopy around Him—
The dark rain clouds rain clouds of the sky.

The Lord thundered from heaven;
The voice of the most High resounded.
He shot arrows and scattered the enemies,
Bolts of lightening blazed forth.
The Lord thundered from heaven;
The voice of the most high resounded.

He reached down from on high and took hold of me,
He drew me out of deep waters.
He rescued me from my powerful enemy.
From my foes, who were too strong for me.
They confronted me in the day of my disaster,
But the Lord was my support.

The Lord has dealt with me according to my righteousness;
According to the cleanness of my hands he has rewarded me.
For I have kept the ways of the Lord;
I have not done evil by turning from my God.
All His laws are before me;
I have not turned away from His decrees.
I have been blameless before Him.

To the faithful you show yourself faithful,
To the blameless you show yourself blameless,
To the pure you show yourself pure,
But to the crooked You show Yourself shrewd.
You save the humble,
But Your eyes are on the haughty to bring them low."

There were a lot more stanza of that psalm of praise within
me, but my tired old voice was "cracking" to the point that

I wanted no mortal to overhear my psalm of praise. Even the Lord might misinterpret my deep emotions due to the broken tones I was using to express my love and appreciation to Him. Needless to say I had so greatly desired to praise Him with the spirit of happiness and with the desire of lifting Him up with the praise that was in my heart and soul. Unfortunately, what was intended to be a continuation of the hymn of love and praise which coming from my vocal chords had begun to sound to the listening ear like a discordant curse. Therefore, I decided that I had better continue singing my hymn at a later date.

As I continued to reminisce over the past days of my life I began to recall the men with whom I had fought. Several stood out in my memory as being men who were great warriors and men of great character. I recalled Josheb-Basshebeth, a Tahkemonite, who was chief of "The THREE" as they were referred to with respect and awe. Now, there was a man who was a mighty man of valor! I recall that on one occasion he fought so valiantly with his spear that he killed eight hundred men.

Next to him was Eleazar, son of Dodai the Aholhite. I recall that he was with me when we taunted the Philistines who were gathered at Pas Dammim for battle. Fear struck the members of my fighting force, and they retreated. Eleazar, however, stood his ground against the Philistines, striking them down one right after the other. Finally his hand grew so tired that it seemed to be frozen to his sword. The Lord used him to bring about a great victory that day. Oh, let me add that the army of Israel returned to Eleazar's side BUT NOT TO FIGHT! They returned for the sole purpose of stripping the bodies of the enemy soldiers for what loot they could find.

Next in my thoughts was Shammah, the son of Agee the Hararite. He was a fierce fighter. For instance, when the forces of the Philistines banded together in a field of ripe lentils, they put up such a fierce appearance that the Israelities fled. Yes, they all fled from the lentil field except Shammah. He stood his ground there in that lentil field, defending it and striking down the Philistines with such great strength that there was a great victory there that day.

I recall an earlier occasion when I was hidden in the cave of Adullam, while a band of Philistines was encamped on the plain below in the Valley of Rephaim. I could not help but think of how thirsty I was. The water in the container there in the cave with me just did not seem to satisfy my thirst. I sighed and uttered aloud a desire that was overheard by one of my men, "Oh, that someone would bring me a drink of water from the well near the gate of Bethlehem." Having grown up in that area, I remembered that there was something about the water in that well which made It seem to be better than water from any other well. Unbeknown to me three of the men from my contingent of men slipped away and stealthily made their way through the Philistine soldiers stationed near the well at Bethlehem's gate, drew water from that well and stealthily made their way back through the enemy soldiers to me there in the cave. They proudly told me that the water which they had brought to me was from the well near the gate of Bethlehem and handed to me a big goard dipper full of that cool water. I did a strange thing just then, a thing that even surprised me. I refused to drink that good water, but instead I poured it out on the ground as an offering to the Lord, saying, "Far be it from me, O Lord, to drink this! Is it not the blood of the men who went to fetch this water to me at the very risk of their lives?" The expression on the faces of those three men was that of shock, anger, and dismay. "After what we went through to get that water he has poured it out on the ground," they exclaimed to the other soldiers there in the cave. After they had had time to think it over, they realized that I had done a sacred think by refraining from drinking water that had cost so much. Instead, I had offered it as a drink offering to the Lord.

Another mighty warrior was Abishai, the nephew of Joab. On one occasion he fought three hundred men, killing all of them. He became as famous as "the Three". He was held by some to be even greater than the three warriors who formed that famous trio.

Benaiah, son of Jehoiada, was a valiant fighter from Kabzeel. He was known throughout Israel for the many great exploits he had done. On one occasion he had struck down two of Moab's best warriors. On a snowy day he went down into a pit and killed a lion. On another occasion he struck down a very, very big Egyptian; although the big Egyptian had a spear in his hand Benaiah went lunging toward him with only a club in his hand with which to do the hand-to-hand fighting against the huge man. Quicker than eye can see he snatched the Egyptian's spear from him and killed the huge man with his own spear. These and many more were the exploits of Benaiah. He was considered by most of his compatriots as being as mighty a warrior as were the famous "THREE". It was a known fact that he was held in greater honor than any of the other "Thirty" (another larger group than the famous "Three" but not quite as famous). I paid him the great honor by putting him in charge of my bodyguard.

I have referred to the group of "The Three" and the other group of outstanding warriors known as "The Thirty". Actually, however, there were thirty-seven mighty warriors in all, although some four of them never got the honor they deserved. All of these men had gained the reputation among the Israelites as being outstanding warriors. The news of their various exploits had traveled by word of mouth among their fellow warriors and fellow country men. Perhaps in some instances their exploits had been "enlarged" a bit in the thinking of the people, but it can be well said that they all deserved membership in that unofficial fellowship. All Israel took great pride in referring to them as the mightiest of all warriors.

In these latter years of my life I have had time to remember the main events which occurred to me along life's journey and to rejoice in them. Oh, to be sure, there were other episodes in my life of which I am not very proud. I must admit that as I reminisce over the many episodes in my life there are some that I had just as soon forget. I shudder when I think of some things which I did during my active years of life's living. From the perspective of my mature years I see so many mistakes that I made, mistakes which I now attribute to youthful pride and to the weakness of humanity which weighed so heavily on me. An evil spirit at times seemed to hover over me, causing me to allow caution to go on the wings of the wind and to cause evil desires to hold sway in my innermost thoughts and actions. Yet, there was always my desire to obey the laws of God which I had been taught by my mother and my father during my young and formative years. It was my desire to conduct my life in a way which would be pleasing to the Lord Jehovah. Yet there were times when human lust, pride and arrogance gained the upper hand in my actions. Following such episodes I was filled with great remorse which caused me to cry out, "Oh, my Lord God, against thee and thee only have I sinned!" So close was my relationship with my God that when I ruptured that relationship by doing wrong to my fellow man my first thought was how I had injured that sacred relationship between my Lord and me. Although I may have caused injury to the body, heart, and soul of a fellow human being, I hardly noticed that because of the great grief that welled up in my heart over the injury I had done to the holiness of my Lord and God through my act of sin. In my outburst of remorse over a sin which I had committed against a fellow man, I was not so much concerned with the injury I had caused that person or persons as I was the injury which I had caused to the heart of my God. In such instances I felt such remorse over my breaking the fellowship with my God that I had enjoyed so greatly. When I got to that point in my moments of reminiscing over my past life, I abruptly turned from the past to the present in order to put a momentary end to my great grief which those memories had caused.

CHAPTER 47
THE SIN OF PRIDE

I recall with deep regret that occasion when I began to think more highly of myself than I should have. There was that time when Israel had finally taken its place among the nations in our part of the world. It had become a nation to be reckoned with. The neighboring nations such as Moab and the nation of the Philistines had learned not to cross paths with Israel with evil intent. It was a period of peace in which my people had time to enjoy their business and family lives. The hustle and bustle of the city of Jerusalem was something to behold. The sights and sounds that emanated from it were the sounds of peace, commerce, and happiness of neighborly fellowship among its inhabitants. I could sit on the palace's roof top porch and look out over the great city of Jerusalem and take pride in what I saw. In such times my pride of accomplishment welled up within me, for I truly believed that I had been the agent of change. Was it not I who had transformed the comparatively small and weak city of the Jebusites into a well fortified city, Jerusalem, which now served as the center of government and commerce of the great nation of Israel? Was it not now thought of as the "city of David"? Was not my palace here in Jerusalem the envy of the neighboring kings? Had I not built the army of Israel into a formidable force which was the envy of the surrounding nations? Yes, I had accomplished so very much in my lifetime. By this point in my reign I began to think of myself with great pride due to my accomplishments.

I knew in my heart that I had built up a "standing army" which was the envy of the surrounding kingdoms. I began to wonder just what were the possibilities of raising a sizeable army for use in times of an attack by an enemy? Finally an idea that had been festering in my heart and mind for some time began to take shape. I decided I needed to know just how many able bodied men could be quickly recruited from among the men of Israel to be added to my "standing army" in the event of an onslaught by an enemy nation . . . . or nations. I called Joab to come for a conference with me. I shared with him my plan to take a census of all the able bodied men in the kingdom, men from who I could muster a great army at a moment's notice. After hearing my thoughts on the matter he was silent for a long while. Finally he spoke aloud the thoughts which evidently had been circling through his mind. "Your majesty, do you really and truly want my opinion concerning your plan?" "Well, of course I do. I consider you to be the greatest army commander among all the commanders of the nations in this day and age." "I appreciate your words of commendation, but, sir, I do not want to hurt your feelings." "Get on with it, Joab!" "Well, sir, what you are suggesting goes against the past ways of our nation." "What do you mean by that statement?" "May the Lord multiply His troops a hundred times over. My lord the king, are they not all my lord's subjects! Why does my lord want to do this? Why should he bring guilt on Israel? Sir, we people of Israel have always considered that the Lord Jehovah is the real commander of our army, not you or me. Does he require a huge army with which to conquer the enemies of Israel? Do you not remember how He had Gideon to cut his fighting forces down to only three hundred soldiers from a force of thousands? Do you remember why He had Gideon to go to battle with only three hundred men?" "Well, I, uh, suppose I do?" "Well, sir, why did God give Gideon such instructions?" "Well, uh, I guess it was because He wanted Gideon and the people of Israel to realize that with His presence and power fighting alongside Gideon's little group of three hundred men that the glory of the victory would point to Him who has all power." "Exactly, O King David. The God we worship is ready and willing to use His great power by fighting alongside our 'standing army' of only a comparatively few soldiers as long as our cause is just. Would not the act of doing a census by which to learn how many men could be mustered from all of Israel show Him that we do not trust Him to use His power with which to lead our nation to victory over the enemy?" "Well, I don't see it that way. Have I not led the army of the nation of Israel to victory time and time again? I plan to continue to do that, and I shall feel much more comfortable having a great army with me. Call it a lack of faith, but that is the way I feel about it!" "Sir, you are the king . . . I'm not. However, mark it down that I don't think that it is right to take a census for such a purpose. I think you will be showing a great lack of faith in God's power to lead a small army to victory as He has done in the past." "Well, you have had your 'say', but I'm going ahead with my plan to have such a census made!" "I repeat, you are the king. The decision is yours." After I had dismissed him from my presence, I watched his receding figure. I thought to myself, "Joab is indispensable to me, but there are times when I feel that I could strangle him with my bare hands! All down through the years of our association together there have been instances here and there when he has had ideas different to mine and has had the temerity to express them ever so candidly. There had been times, also, when he acted against my decisions because he felt he knew better than I did about the proper thing to do. Yes, there had been times when I considered him to be an onerous old rascal who dared to differ with me. The King of Israel! Well, regardless of what Joab thinks about my plan of taking a census of all the able bodied men of Israel, I'm going to carry out that plan!!!"

Regardless of how repulsive my orders to him to expedite my plan to take the census were, Joab went out from my presence to commence the task given to him. He led the census takers throughout Israel in accomplishing the task. There arose throughout the nation negative responses on the part of the leaders under Joab such as, "Hey, that is going to be a lot of work!"; "That is going to be a time-consuming task"; "I think that it is the wrong thing to do." Such were the comments of those leaders who were overheard by some of my "inner circle" of leaders who reported it to me. I stiffened my back bone and carried through on the task of having the census taken. Yes, it turned out to be a tedious, tasteless, time consuming task, but my wishes in the matter were carried out. Joab and his assistants in the project first moved eastward and crossed over the Jordan River. They first went through Gad and on to Jazer. Next they went to Gilead and the region of Tahtim Hodshi, and on to Dan Jaan and westward on around toward Sidon. Then they went toward the fortress of Tyre and on southward through the towns of the Hivites and Canaanites. Finally, they went on to Beersheba in the Negev of Judah.

After they had gone through the entire land, they came back to Jerusalem. The task had taken nine months and twenty days which confirmed the prediction uttered by many that it would be a time consuming task. When the task was finished, Joab came back to me to report the results. "Sir, the report on the census that my men and I have just finished is as follows: "There are one million, one hundred thousand men who are able bodied enough to handle a sword properly. The count includes all such men in both Israel and Judah. That number includes four hundred and seventy thousand in Judah." Joab's report was not totally accurate, for he did not include the men of the priestly tribe of Levi nor of the tribe of Benjamin. I learned later that he had intentionally not numbered the men of these two tribes, because taking the census had been so repulsive to him. This was just another of Joab's ways of getting back at me for being made to take the census against his belief in the matter.

Those who had predicted that taking such a census would be a "time consuming task" proved to be correct in their prediction. It took nine months and twenty days to complete the task. The task seemed endless, for there were so many facets to it. The men in the ten tribes which were counted had to come before Joab and his helpers who interviewed them and who took stock of their physical condition. A scribe had to be present each day as the men passed before the inspectors in order to write down the name of each man and the decision as to his physical fitness for handling a sword in battle. Needless to say all of this procedure went against Joab's "grain". Most of the time he sat at his improvised desk with a scowl on his face as the men of each tribe came by. He was not one to hide his feelings in situations concerning which he did not agree. This was certainly one of those situations.

The report of available man power among the men of Israel was very satisfying to me. I learned that there were in Israel eight hundred thousand able-bodied men fit for carrying a sword in battle and in Judah there were five hundred thousand men for a total of one million and three hundred thousand. I received the report with great pride. I thought to myself, "Now I have the power to resist any nation that sends its forces against me. In fact I have the power to go to war against even the strongest nation that I desire to attack. Yes, sir, now I've got ample power if and when I choose to call all of the able bodied men in Israel to come forward to fight a battle against any nation that I choose. I'm proud of myself for having undertaken this "census project". Now I know where I stand in terms of warfare!"

Over a short period of time my feelings of great pride in the potential fighting power of my nation as revealed by the census began to taper off. There crept into my conscience a feeling that what I had done in having the census taken was not pleasing to the Lord Jehovah. What was causing this feeling? Was it the memory of Joab's hostile attitude to the matter of taking the census? Well, that might have entered into my change of attitude about it, but it was more than that. I definitely felt in my heart that I had displeased the Lord. As I studied the matter I had to admit that just maybe Joab's earlier statement of his feelings caused me slowly to realize what I had done. Indeed, I now realized that I had turned from my faith in God's leadership and power in our battles to man's might and power. I further realized that it evolved from the pride I had in myself and in my leadership of the nation of Israel. Yes, it boiled down to the fact that I had taken my eye off of the Lord and His benevolent mercies toward me and the nation of Israel and had looked at the power of man's military strength, that is, the strength of Israel's military might.

Finally, after letting my conscience "simmer" over the matter of the census taking, I finally became conscience stricken. I got on my knees in prayer before the Lord and called out to Him, "I have sinned greatly in what I have done. Now, O Lord, I beg you, take away the guilt of your servant. I have done a very foolish thing." That night I was so very restless while endeavoring to sleep. I realized more and more how very foolish I had been in allowing my faith to turn away from the power of my God to the power of mankind. It began to gnaw at my conscience to the extent that I was in turmoil while waiting for an answer from the Lord as to my prayer for forgiveness.

CHAPTER 48

THE PENALTY OF SIN

The sin of personal pride which expanded into a spirit of arrogance had indeed led me to commit an act that revealed where my faith lay . . . . in myself as a result of my success as king of Israel. When I finally came to realize what I had done in placing my faith in myself and in my fellowman instead of in the Lord Jehovah, I became very ashamed of myself and sought to do penance for it. After a heart broken prayer offered up to the Lord I got up off my knees with an unrequited desire to be back in the good graces of the Lord.

What I did not know was that the Lord had appeared to Gad, my personal "seer" or religious advisor, the very next day after my prayer of repentance and had given him a message to bring to me. When he strode into my private chambers I greeted him, and In as cheerful a tone of voice as I could muster, I asked if he had a message from the Lord for me. "Indeed I have, my lord the king. Just this morning the Lord God gave me a message for you." I caught my breath and tried to answer in a casual voice as I asked, "And what might that be?" Gad's countenance remained very, very solemn as he replied, "The Lord instructed me to bring this message to you . . . 'Go and tell David, this is what the Lord says: 'I am giving you three options. Choose one of them for me to carry out against you.'" I had prayed for forgiveness, but I did not know that God's forgiveness had a tangible cost to me. Scarcely breathing I said in an almost inaudible voice, "Tell me what they are."

"All right, here they are: (1) Three years of famine in your land; (2) three months of fleeing from your enemies; or (3) three days of plague in your land? Now then, think this matter over and tell me which one you will choose so that I can relay your choice to the one who sent me, that is, the Lord God of Israel." I was silent for a long while until I finally gave this answer to Gad, "I am in deep distress. Let me and my fellow Israelites fall into the hands of the Lord, for His mercy is great; but do not let us fall into the hands of men."

As a result of that decision the Lord sent a plague on Israel as punishment for the great sin I had committed due to my pride. It began that morning and ended according to the time designated. It was awful! The citizens of Israel died "like flies". Seventy people from Dan to Beersheba died. The angel of death stretched out his hand to destroy Jerusalem, but the Lord was grieved over the calamity brought on by the plague and said to him, "Enough! Withdraw your hand." By that time the angel of death had reached the threshing floor of Araunah the Jebusite. When I realized the extent of the plague and that it was attacking innocent people who had had no part in the sin which brought it on, I cried out to the Lord, "I am the one who has sinned and done wrong. These are but sheep. What have they done? Let your hand fall upon me and my family." The lesson I learned through this experience was that it was harder to see innocent people paying for my sins than it would have been to have paid for it with my own life.

On the day in which the Lord stopped the plague Gad came to me with another message from the Lord. "You are to go to the threshing floor of Araunah and build an altar to the Lord on it." I immediately went as the Lord had commanded with the full intent of building an altar to Him there. When Araunah looked up from his work of threshing the grain he saw me and my men coming in his direction, he rushed out to meet us. When he arrived at the place where we were he bowed down with his face to the ground in obeisance to me. Then he asked, "Why has my Lord come to his servant?" "To buy your threshing floor," I replied, "so that I can build an altar to the Lord on it so that the plague on the people may be stopped."

Araunah cried out, "Oh, let the lord my king take whatever he needs to offer up a sacrifice to the Lord. Here are oxen for the burnt offering and here are threshing sledges and ox yokes for the wood for the fire. O king, Araunah gives all of this to the king."

Obviously the Jebusite felt so honored that the king of Israel had approached him about the matter of obtaining his threshing floor that he rambled on in his great excitement. Then he added, "May the Lord your God accept you through the offering."

I greatly appreciate the attitude of Araunah and his offer of his threshing floor and all the necessary items for the burnt offering, but to take it as a gift from him would not satisfy my feeling of what it took to make an acceptable offering to the Lord my God. I replied to his very generous offer by saying, "No, I insist on paying you for it. I will not sacrifice to the Lord my God burnt offerings that cost me nothing." I felt in my heart that to have done so would have made the offering of no value whatsoever to me. I firmly believed that an offering should cost the worshipper a price in order to make it "his offering" to almighty God.

I paid Araunah fifty shekels for the threshing floor, the animal of sacrifice and the wooden instruments with which to use as firewood. When the altar was built and the animal of sacrifice was in place over the wooden harness, a fire was lit and the sweet fragrance of the sacrifice wafted its way upward toward God. Word was slowly passed around the kingdom that the awful plague had ceased.

In the days following the end of the plague I sat on my throne immersed in deep reverie over the sin I had committed, a sin that is common to mankind, the sin of putting one's self before the person and power of Almighty God. I had learned the hard way about the cost of such a sin through the attack of the death angel on my loyal citizens.

This lesson taught to me in such a hard manner certainly made a deep imprint on my heart and life. I discovered that arrogance and pride on man's part were at enmity with our Lord God. He must be the center of our worship with no room left in our hearts for self worship. The upside of this experience really put me in my place, that is, it made me more humble before God and man than I had ever been before.

CHAPTER 49
PLANS FOR BUILDING THE TEMPLE

While I was wallowing in self pity over the fact that I was no longer physically able to lead the army of Israel into combat as in former times and over the matter of having brought on Israel a great plague for my arrogance, I suddenly realized that there was a great project that I was still physically able to enter into. There had been fleeting moments in which the idea of that project had entered my mind, but the cares of the daily business of the kingdom soon erased that idea from my mind. Perhaps it was my trip to the threshing floor of Araunah where I offered up a burnt offering of repentance for my arrogance in placing my plans for running the kingdom above those of the Lord. To be more exact it was for carrying out the census of the able bodied men of the kingdom so that I could glory in the man power of the nation. Because of that God had sent a grievous plague on my people. Through the offering of repentance God had "stayed" the sword of the death angel that was going through the kingdom bringing death to my people. Yes, it was there at the threshing floor of Araunah where I had a great spiritual experience. I came out of that experience with the definite feeling that it was high time that a temple worthy of the Lord God Jehovah should be built. Eagerly I placed before the Lord my desire to build that temple. I was heart broken when His answer came back to me that I had too much blood on my hands, that is, that all during my life I had been engaged in slaying the enemies of the kingdom of Israel. I was not to be the builder of a house of worship and peace; that task was to go to my successor on the throne of Israel. At that point I reasoned within myself that the kind of temple that I really wanted to see being built in Jerusalem was a majestic building that would justly reflect the awesome majesty of our God. So be it that the task would need to be done by my successor; my desire was that such a building be erected regardless of who might get the credit.

Well, the Lord had told me in blunt language that He accepted the idea of such an edifice of worship being constructed, BUT IT WAS NOT TO BE BUILT BY ME! He made it clear to me that the erection of such a building was to be the task of my successor. So be it! However, there was nothing to prevent my gathering materials from here and there with which my successor could construct such an edifice. After reasoning the matter out to that effect I began the project of gathering such materials as would obviously be needed for the building of such a magnificent structure as I envisioned. From Lebanon lumber could be secured. The cedars of Lebanon were known for their long straight trunks from which great rafters for the ceiling and rich paneling could be secured. Fortunately there had been that time when the kings of Tyre and Sidon had realized that they would be better off to make peace with Israel and to establish peaceful trade with her in order to be able to secure food stuff from her productive land. Thus it would be a matter of letting the leaders of that area know that I was interested in securing from the a great deal of choice lumber from them and of their complying with my requests. The terms of trade could be established in a friendly and honest way as had been proved earlier.

Through our merchants who plied the waters of the east I was confident that much gold, bronze and other precious metal could be obtained for use in the decoration of the various parts of the great temple. I enjoyed thinking ahead concerning what would be needed for the building program which my successor would be ordained of God to carry out in the future. Yes, those precious metals could be gathered from various parts of the world and stock piled for future use in the building of the great temple of the God of Israel. And so it was that I satisfied myself concerning the building of a temple to the Lord by gathering materials for my successor to use in erecting a magnificent house of worship there in Jerusalem.

Being only human with all the dreams and desires of a normal person, I could not help but be greatly disappointed by the decision of the Lord that I was not the person to do the task. However, I realized that the Lord was correct in his statement that I was a man who was known for shedding blood. In the early days of my life when I was allowed to get into the fray of one battle after another at a very early age largely due to the notoriety I had gained by my having slain the great giant Goliath, I became a person addicted to doing battle with Israel's enemies. That became a way of life for me. As I matured into manhood, my attitude toward warfare was not quite as "gung-ho" as it had been. As I watched my family grow with the result that I felt that I was needed by them to the point that I should not take any more risk than necessary. Yet, there were many, many battles during my mature life that had to be fought by me as the head of the army of Israel. I say all this in order to agree that I had been involved in many bloody battles; battles which I fought like a mother bear defending her cubs . . . . and enjoyed doing so. Yes, I have to admit that the Lord Jehovah was correct in His view of me as a man of "blood".

In my mind's eye I could visualize the temple of the Lord which was to be built on a promontory in Jerusalem so that it would be the focal point of the walled city of Jerusalem. I could look into the future in my vision of what was to come and see a magnificent structure slowly rising from its foundation and stretching skyward. This afforded me much happiness which helped to cover the great sorrow I felt at not being allowed to make that dream come true.

CHAPTER 50
CHOOSING MY SUCCESSOR

It was such a depressing feeling to realize that my manly vigor was slipping away. At first it was barely noticeable, but little by little it was obvious that it was not "slipping away, but it was "running away" at a rapid pace. I had always prided myself on my physical strength and prowess. In the early days when I was a shepherd lad there had been wild animals which I could slay with my bare hands. Then there were the youthful days when I felt no fear in marching out to meet a man who had put paralyzing fear into the heart of every soldier of Israel. In that instance my youthful attitude toward that huge man whose name was Goliath was simply, "Here is just another opportunity for me to allow others to see what wonders the God of Israel can do through a person of faith." My slaying of Goliath seemed like a rather insignificant accomplishment, but it caught the eyes of King Saul and all the soldiers of Israel. In battle after battle I had felt the strength of the God of Israel empowering me to fight the good fight against the enemies of our beloved nation, Israel. I always felt that I was marching into each battle under the power and presence of my god, the Lord Jehovah.

Yes, it was obvious to me and most likely to all those around me that my strength was ebbing away at a rather fast pace. Also, it was obvious to me and I suspect to those around me that now I no longer walked with any degree of steadiness on my feet. My staff members were too kind (or afraid) to show what they were thinking; they continued to treat me as though I were young and very virile. Well, that was true on the surface, but when they thought that they were beyond the visual range of my dimming gaze or beyond the earshot of my dull hearing there were scarcely audible whispers among them as they went about their duties in my area of the palace. My days were spent propped up on pillows on my large throne chair until it became obvious to them that I needed to lie down for a while. As mentioned elsewhere in my memoirs the office staff carried on the business of the kingdom in such a way that it would appear that I was making all the decisions and doing all the correspondence normal to the duties of each day. In reality my staff members were furtively writing out documents as they thought I would have wanted them to be worded and then bringing them to me and explaining them to me (on those days when I was awake enough to be aware of what they were telling me). Then they pointed to the place where my signature was to be placed and saw to it that my signature was legible. I suspect that there were times when they simply forged my name when it appeared that I was "too far gone" to be able to do so.

Well, what should be done about it? The business of the kingdom had to move on in a proper manner. I was still alive and therefore still the king of Israel. In my more lucid moments I realized that my successor had to be chosen soon and that the choice had to be made known to the people of the kingdom. I gave much thought to the matter of who should be my successor. I had always felt that I would appoint Absalom to follow me on the throne of Israel. Though not the oldest of my sons he had shown great ability in war and in pleasing the people of the kingdom. But alas, he had taken matters into his own hands and had almost taken my throne by force. All seemed to be going in his favor until he was slain by Joab (in my heart I still find it exceedingly difficult to forgive Joab for slaying Absalom, although I know that it was the expedient thing for him to do). Well, which of my sons should I elevate to the throne? Oh, there was Adonijah who had some potential for the role of king, but I had discovered that he was "hot headed" and not very teachable. And there was young Solomon who showed great wisdom for a person so young as he. However, I did not recall having given him any consideration for that post. Oh, to be sure I had noticed that he seemed to have wisdom that was beyond his years . . . . but he was *so young!* In the recesses of my memory there seemed to be a faint recollection of having discussed the possibility of his being my successor, but

I really could not remember what was said and to whom I may have expressed such a thought. As I pondered the matter during my more lucid moments, I realized that the only other person in my bed chamber with me was Abishag the Shunamite who had been selectled by my staff for the primary purpose of keeping me warm. My blood seems to run cold within me. The decided opinion of my staff was that she could be in bed beside me to keep me warm and to minister to my personal needs during the day. She had been chosen because she was found to be the most beautiful young woman in the kingdom. To put it bluntly she was chosen to be my personal nurse and my "bed warmer" at night. What a temptation that nightly arrangement would have been to me in my younger years. I would have had to suppress my lustful feelings if this arrangement had taken place back then. Now there was nothing of that nature going on . . . . she was simply there to serve as a nurse to me.

One day there was admitted to my bed chamber the lady with whom I had my adulterous tryst, the lady whom I was able to marry only by having her husband, Uriah the Hittite, slain in battle. Through my dimming vision I looked at her. Though mature, Bathsheba was still a beautiful woman. As I sat looking at her the memories of the past flooded my thoughts. She made obeisance to me by bowing low. I hastened to give her a nod of acceptance to my attention. She arose and stood there before me in a very hesitant manner. Even to my dull senses it was obvious that she had a request to make of me but was afraid to do so. I mumbled to her, "Speak up, woman." What she said startled me greatly.

"My lord the king, did you not swear to me your servant: 'Surely Solomon your son shall be king after me, and he will sit on my throne?' Why then has Adonijah become king?" Yes, I was very startled on two counts by the statement she made to me: (1) she said that I had promised her that her son Solomon would sit on my throne after me; that shook some of the cobwebs out of my brain to the point that I seemed indeed to recall having told her that; and (2) what she said about Adonijah having been made king . . . . made king by whom? Certainly not by me! That was the first I had heard of that.

Intrigue and counter intrigue were being played out right there under my nose, and I was not aware of it. As I learned after the fact, Adonijah, my son who was the son of my wife Haggith and who was a bit younger than Absalom, had decided that it was proper that he should become my successor. With that in mind he enlisted the support of Joab and Abiathar the priest. However, he did not succeed in getting the support of Zadoc the priest and Benaiah and Nathan the prophet as well as Shimei and my special guards. His mode of gathering his forces was by the political ploy of making a big offering of sheep and fatted calves at the Stone of Zoheleth which was a place where offerings had long been made. He invited all his brothers except young Solomon and all the men of Judah who were royal officials. Nathan called Bathsheba aside and asked her, "Have you not heard that Adonijah has become king without our lord, King David, knowing about it? Both your life and the life of your son, Solomon, are in danger. Let me tell you what to do." He rehearsed with her the action she should take and what she should say to me. She followed his instructions to the letter by coming before me with her plea that I put Solomon on the throne as my successor. She added a word of urgency by saying, "My lord the king, the eyes of all Israel are on you to learn from you who will sit on the throne of my lord the king after him!' That is when she shared with me the news of Adonijah's attempt to take over the throne, saying that it was being made known in Jerusalem that Adonijah was in the process of placing himself in the position of being my successor as king. While she was still speaking to me Nathan the prophet entered my outer chambers and was announced, "Nathan the prophet is here." I nodded to my chamberlain to send him in. He entered and bowed low before me. Then he began by asking in a very innocent tone, "Have you, my lord the king, declared that Adonijah shall be king after you, and that he will sit on your throne?" He did not wait for me to answer his question but continued on in a very excited manner, "Today he has gone down and sacrificed great numbers of cattle, fattened calves, and sheep. He has invited all the king's sons except young Solomon, Joab and his commanders of the army, and Abiathar the priest. Right now they are eating and drinking with him and saying, 'Long live King Adonijah!'

But I your servant and Zadok the priest, and Benaiah, and your servant Solomon he did not invite. Is this something my lord the king has done without letting his servants know who should sit on the throne of my lord the king after him?"

Nathan, a prophet whom I greatly respected as being a prophet who was guided by the Lord Jehovah in all that he did and said, showed his concern about Adonijah's endeavor to take over my throne by intrigue. Obviously Nathan had it straight from the Lord Jehovah that Adonijah was not the proper son to take over my throne at my death but that young Solomon was his choice of the person who should rule over Israel at my demise. Therefore, Nathan revealed a strategy for counter-intrigue in order to have Solomon and not Adonijah placed on the throne.

By that time what had been told me "seeped" into my foggy brain. I commanded, "Call in Bathsheba." When she had entered again into my presence, I said, "As surely as the Lord lives, who has delivered me out of every trouble, upon my oath I will surely carry out today what I swore to you by the Lord, the God of Israel. Solomon your son shall be king after me, and he will sit on my throne in my place." By that time I was out of breath. A radiance swept over Bathsheba's countenance as she again bowed low to the ground before me and said, "May my lord King David live forever!" The Lord cleared my brain enough for me to take action to get the ball rolling on my plan to have Solomon anointed king of Israel. "Call in Zadok the priest, Nathan the prophet, and Benaiah son of Jehoiada." When they appeared before me I said to them, "Take my officials with you and set Solomon my son on my own mule and take him down to Gihon. When you arrive there, have Zadok the priest and Nathan the prophet anoint him king over Israel. Blow the trumpet and shout, 'Long live King Solomon!' Then you are to go up with him, and he is to come and sit on my throne and reign in my place. I have appointed him ruler over Israel and Judah." Benaiah responded by saying, "Amen! May the Lord, the God of my lord the king, so declare it. As the Lord was with my lord the king, so may He be with Solomon to make his throne even greater than the throne of my lord King David!"

Then Benaiah, Zadok, Nathan, the Kerethites, and the Pelethites put into action my plans for making Solomon to be my successor. As instructed they put Solomon on my mule and escorted him to Gihon. Zadok took a horn of oil from the sacred tent which had been dedicated to the Lord Jehovah and in the presence of those who had assembled there anointed Solomon to succeed me on the throne of Israel and Judah. Then they sounded the trumpet and all of the retinue shouted at the top of their voices, "Long live King Solomon!" Then, a parade of sorts began going forward with the musicians playing flutes and all the people present rejoicing loudly and sincerely. So great was the sound from the throng ofpeople in the parade that it seemed that the earth shook with the noise.

Just as Adonijah and all his guests were finishing their feast, the tumultuous sound from the group surrounding Solomon was heard by them. Joab asked, "Hey, what is the meaning of all that noise we are hearing?" Hardly were the words out of his mouth when Jonathan, the son of Abiathar the priest, arrived. Adonijah greeted him by saying, "Come in. A worthy man like you must be bringing good news!" "Not at all!" he replied. "Our lord King David has made Solomon king. The king has sent with him Zadok the priest, Nathan the prophet, Benaiah, the Kerethites and the Pelethites. They have put Solomon on the king's mule; also, Zadok and Nathan have anointed him king while they were yet at Gihon. From there they have gone up cheering, and the city resounds with it. That's the noise you are hearing. Also, Solomon has taken his seat on the royal throne. Furthermore, the royal officials have come to congratulate our lord King David, saying, 'May your God make Solomon's name more famous than yours and his throne greater than yours!'"

Well, the intrigue on the part of Adonijah had been played out to the bitter end but failed in its attempt. The counter intrigue begun by Nathan the prophet who worked through Bathsheba and finished by me had worked beautifully. Solomon was now on the throne. Having summed up the last bit of energy I could muster in order to carry out the counter intrigue, I now lay on my bed in an almost lifeless condition. But there was something I was compelled to do . . . . I bowed there on my bed as best I could in a spirit of worship to Almighty God and said, 'Praise be to the Lord, the God of Israel, who has allowed my eyes to see a successor on my throne today.'"

And what had happened to Adonijah's ill fated effort to obtain the throne for himself??? When those attending his feast heard from the lips of Jonathan what had transpired while they were feasting at Adonijah's banquet, they took leave from the banquet with scarcely a word of thanks to the host and scattered like a flock of small birds when an owl appears on the scene. As for Adonijah . . . . well, he knew that his effort to gain the throne caused him in the eyes of Solomon and his associates to be considered a traitor to the kingdom. He thought to himself, "What can I do to save my life? Oh, I know what a lot of guilty people do; they go into the sacred tent and grab hold of the horns of the altar. Well, in the eyes of the new king and his followers I no doubt am considered to be very guilty." With that he quickly made his way to the sacred altar where he grabbed hold of the horns of the altar. A bit later Adonijah's action was reported to King Solomon, saying, "He is afraid of you, King Solomon, and is clinging to the horns of the altar. He says, 'Let King Solomon swear to me today that he will not put his servant to death with the sword.'" The decision made by the new king, King Solomon, reflected both compassion and justice, for he replied to those who relayed to him Adonijah's fearful plea

"If he shows himself to be a worthy man, not a hair of his head will fall to the ground; but if evil is found in him, he will die." Officials were sent to take him from clinging to the horns of the altar and to bring him to King Solomon in person. He bowed down before the new king who told him, "Go to your home!" Greatly surprised to hear the new king giving such a simple "sentence for his transgressions", Adonijah lost no time in obeying him.

CHAPTER 51

SOME UNFINISHED BUSINESS

Well, judging by the way I felt physically most days, I thought that I was about to draw my last breath. Not only was that my supposition, but it also seemed to be that of my staff and others I chanced to see moving around. They went about on tip-toes and whispered to each other. I imagined that they were looking forward to a big "state funeral", one befitting the only king of Israel they had known in their life time. There would be "pomp and circumstance" played out to the hilt no doubt. My experience with my subjects told me that life was hard and more than somewhat dull for them. Anything out of the ordinary provided for them a welcomed break from the old dull routines of their lives. "Well," I said to myself, "I don't plan to give them that satisfaction just yet. Call it pure stubbornness or whatever you choose, but I'm planning to linger on a while longer and see how things develop with my young son Solomon . . . . now "King Solomon" (I still find it hard to think of him by that title). Yes, I could die now with a sense of satisfaction as pertained to the identity of my successor, but there were some things that needed to be attended to under my "behind the scenes" direction to young King Solomon.

Although, I had not really thought of young Solomon as being the one to succeed me on the throne, I was happy with the way it evolved that he should become the next king of Israel and Judah. Yes, he was immature due to his youth, but I saw underneath that youthful façade a depth of wisdom that was uncommon for one of that tender age. I saw the happiness in Bathsheba's face resulting from Solomon, her son, being elevated to the throne. Through the years since my act of adultery with her and the act of murder involved in order to "cover up" that sin, I had had great remorse and felt that I had "wronged" her. Now, in a sense, I had repaid her by having her son to succeed me to the throne.

Although now I was very frail of flesh, my mind seemed to work at least intermittently. In my more lucid moments I realized that there was some unfinished business that I needed to take care of. My dream during the latter years of my reign was that I could build a temple unto the Lord God of Israel, a temple that would not only be permanent as opposed to a tent as was being used at present for that purpose. Also, I dreamed that it would be a building which would be of great magnificence. I greatly desired that its splendor and size would be the "talk" of the people of the nations all around us. I knew that my God, the Lord Jehovah was the only true God and the only God worthy of mankind's worship. More importantly I desired that such a temple here on earth which would be built and dedicated to the worship of Him would be worthy of such a God as He. My head was "whirling" with ideas of what ought to be incorporated in the great temple which in due time would be constructed to the glory of the great God of Israel and Judah.

One can hardly imagine the great disappointment I experienced when the Lord revealed to me that I was not the one to build the temple, the great sacred house of worship for all the people of Israel. He informed me that it would not be appropriate for me to be its builder, for my reputation among the people of Israel and the people of the surrounding nations was that I was a man of war, a man who had made the blood of my fellow man to flow freely in the many, many battles in which I had been engaged. Could the Lord also have had in mind the blood of Uriah the Hittite for whose death I had been responsible because of my love for Bathsheba? Yes, God's denying me the privilege of being the builder of such a structure during my reign was a source of great and grave disappointment. As deeply hurt as I was by God's rejecting me as the builder of His house of worship, I realized that I could still have a part in the building of the great temple that would be dedicated to the worship of Almighty God.

I realized that my son Solomon had so much to learn about the different facets of the task of serving as King of Israel that he would not have time in the near future to give proper consideration to the task of building the temple of the Lord. I was sure that he would eventually get around to it, but being as young as he was he would most likely not feel that such a project was his top priority among the many projects which he would soon be undertaking. Oh, yes, I had to admit that he had a very level head on his shoulders. His wisdom seemed to emit from his personage as a sweet smelling vapor, BUT HE WAS SO YOUNG! What could I do to assist him in the great project of building a great and sacred temple for the Lord God of Israel? Then the thought came to me . . . . surely the Lord would not deny me the privilege of at least having a part in that great undertaking by gathering and stock piling many materials necessary for such a great building project.

One very important and very necessary item that would be needed by Solomon for the building would be great blocks of stone. Well, there would certainly be no problem in finding a source for stone, for all the world knew that there was a sufficient amount of stone in Israel . . . . sometimes it seemed to me that there was a lot more limestone than soil available here in our beloved land of Israel. Yes, stone we had plenty of, but the need was for "dressed" blocks of stone. With that in mind I called in the aliens who lived among us and checked out each one as to where his talent might lie. By doing this there was soon found a great number of foreigners living in our midst who were capable of cutting and dressing (smoothing) those large blocks of stone that would be needed in such a great building project. There were other aliens who had a talent for smelting iron ore from which could be obtained iron suitable for making nails with which to build the doors and other wooden parts of the building. Plenty of bronze would be needed, so I gathered in a huge supply of it, more than could be weighed on the scales of the day. I placed an order with my allies in Tyre and Sidon over on the sea coast for large cedar logs which would be so necessary for the construction of the roof and other parts of the building. Soon the people of Tyre and Sidon were busy cutting and hewing out large logs from the famous "Cedars of Lebanon."

From the great resources of Israel's storehouses there was provided gold for the "gold work" that would be involved in decorating the building, and the store houses also supplied silver for a similar purpose. Realizing that precious stones would be needed for use in decorating the building and the priestly robes, I ordered that there be accumulated onyx, turquoise, stones of various colors and all kinds of fine stones and marble. All of these were supplied in great quantities, for there was no way of knowing how much of each item would be required to take care of the various needs in the over all building program.

I desired to present something that would be a very personal gift from me, for I was so very devoted to the building of the holy temple unto the Lord God. Therefore, I chose to give my personal treasures of gold and silver over and above what was gathered together from outside sources. This amounted to one hundred and ten tons of gold and two hundred and sixty tons of refined silver. I gave these for the overlaying of the walls of the buildings, that is, for the gold work and silver work and for all the work which the craftsmen should decide to do in the building. That seemed to set a good example for the people of the kingdom, that is, for the leaders of families, the officers of the tribes of Israel, the commanders of thousands, the commanders of hundreds, and the officials in charge of the king's work . . . . all of them gave willingly. When their gifts were itemized it was discovered that a hundred and ninety tons plus one hundred and eighty-five pounds of gold, three hundred and seventy-five tons of silver, six hundred and seventy-five tons of bronze, and thirty-seven hundred and fifty tons of iron had been given. Those who owned precious stones gave them to the treasury of the Lord. I observed that the people rejoiced at the willing response of their leaders, for it was obvious that they had given freely and wholeheartedly to the Lord. It goes without question that I also rejoiced greatly to see such a generous donation by all the people to this great cause.

I sent for my son Solomon and shared with him my plan for building a magnificent house of worship, a house that would almost "outshine the sun" in its splendor and beauty, a temple that would indicate to the people of the nations of the world who chanced to see it that the people of Israel wanted it to be known that their God, the Lord Jehovah, was above all their false national gods, gods that could not compare with the one great God whose Spirit lives in the hearts of all people who love and serve Him. I solemnly charged young Solomon with the responsibility of carrying out those plans for the building of a great and splendid temple for the house of worship of the Lord Jehovah, plans which were so dear to my heart.

I said to him, "Solomon, my son, I am about to go the way of all the earth, so be strong, show yourself to be a strong man, and observe what the Lord your God requires, that is, to walk in His ways, and to keep his decrees and commands, His laws and requirements, as written in the Law of Moses, so that you may prosper in all you do and wherever you go, and that the Lord may keep His promise to me: 'If your descendants watch how they live, and if they walk faithfully before me with all their heart and soul, you will never fail to have a man on the throne of Israel.'"

More importantly I endeavored to lay on Solomon's heart a charge that he serve the Lord Jehovah himself and that he lead the people of Israel and Judah to be true followers of the great God of Israel. Also I endeavored to impress on him the fact that the people of Israel were a "chosen people", a people who had been set aside by Almighty God to be His "light houses" to the people of all nations, pointing them to Him as the great Creator God of the universe and the God who desires to show His providential love to all people everywhere. I admonished Solomon that as long as he led the people of Israel to serve and to be obedient to God's commands that the nation of Israel would prosper. If and when it failed to do so, its prosperity and peaceful status would come to an end.

As I was talking with young Solomon about these matters I observed that he was sitting there with a grave look on his countenance with his head cocked to one side as though better to comprehend all that I was saying. In spite of his youth he had the appearance of a person who had already been tested by the tribulations of life, an appearance of one who had already gained the wisdom of the ages through many years of life's living. If I had not known better I would have assumed that his appearance had come from ages of experience. In fact I had to shake myself in order to return to the reality that the young man sitting on the throne in front of me was still but a youth in terms of the years he had lived here on earth. It gave me an eerie feeling to realize that this young son of Bathsheba and myself who was sitting there had wisdom beyond measure, a wisdom that only God could have given him. As I studied his countenance I realized in my heart that the Lord Jehovah had endowed him with a special spirit of discernment so that he would be able to judge equitably all the cases which in the future the citizens of Israel would bring to him for justice.

Chapter 52

Passing the Buck

Lying there on my sick bed in the final hours of my life on earth I reflected on moments in my life when I felt that grave injustices had been committed by members of my staff and by other people whom I had encountered along the way. Retribution should be visited on their hoary heads before they passed on to their final fate. There was Joab who had all too often been guilty of taking matters into his own hands without consulting with me. He had ways and means of knowing about matters which did not concern him personally, matters that were my concern, not his. Oh, to be sure, there were many times when he seemed to sense what was on my mind and heart and quietly went about addressing those issues behind the scenes. There was that time when I was in a stew so to speak. I had sinned by "lying with" the wife of another man, Uriah the Hittite to be exact. I never expected that act of adultery to have any after effects. I recall how my blood ran cold when I received word from Bathsheba that she had become pregnant as a result of our little tryst. Having Uriah to come from the battle field supposedly to bring to me news of how the war was going did not accomplish my purpose, that is, that he go to his home and sleep with Bathsheba. He was such a dedicated soldier that he would not follow through on my suggestion to do that. Finally, I had to resort to sterner measures. I sent a message to Joab who was leading the battle to place Uriah in an area where the battle was the hottest and to withdraw the other soldiers from his side. Of course I did not confide in Joab as to my reason for doing that . . . . didn't have to, for it all came to light as far as he was concerned when later I took Bathsheba to be my wife. Yes, Joab had put two and two together and got the correct answer to my weird behavior concerning my order for him to plan it so that

Uriah would be slain in battle. Thereafter he had a way of leering at me on occasions as if to say, "You had better treat me right, or else, for I've got a secret which, if I were to reveal it to the citizens of Israel, would ruin your great influence on them. Thus, your royal influence would be ruined." "It's bad to be in such a debt to a person like Joab," I said to myself. True, he had been of immeasurable help to me on that score, but his actions following that were a source of irritation to me. It wasn't so much what he did as what he knew about my "dark side" that bothered me. Later on there were other occasions in which he had acted on my behalf (or so he thought) without consulting me in order to take care of some unsavory situations which existed below the surface. To put it mildly on several other occasions he was a great source of irritation by running ahead and acting on his own without getting orders from me or at least consulting with me. Let it be said, however, that often on those occasions what he did resulted in a benefit to me. Yes, many times I grudgingly had to admit that what he had done behind my back resulted in making life easier for me. However, it was not easy for me to make such an admission, and it was not always easy to forgive him in my heart for those actions.

What I could not forgive Joab for was the slaying of innocent blood; that is, slaying his fellow Israelites in times of peace as though they were on the field of battle. I so vividly remember how he took matters into his own hands in the case of the deaths of the two commanders of Israel's army . . . . Abner and Amasa. There had been a battle in which Joab's brother, Asahel, pursued Abner, commander of the forces of Israel, who was retreating. Abner slew him, an act which Joab could not forgive. In the meantime Abner left the side of Israel and went over to the forces of Judah under the kingship of David. When Joab discovered that fact he pretended to take Abner aside for a private conversation. Suddenly he pulled out his weapon and slew Abner. All of this went on behind my back. Joab's slaying Abner who had come to me in peace and left me in peace, was indeed an act which I could not forgive. What he did was strictly against all codes of military conduct. It almost destroyed the plan to have the forces of Israel surrender and join the nation of Judah of which I was king. Joab's act was not only against military code, the slaying of an innocent man, but it almost defeated Abner's plan to join Israel with Judah and thus have them to become one nation.

At the time of Abner's funeral I ordered Joab to put on a good show of mourning even as I did in order to erase some of the ill will from the forces of Israel. I recall that I sang a lament for Abner:

> "Should Abner have died as the lawless die?
> Your hands were not bound,
> Your feet were not fettered.
> You fell as one falls before wicked men."

I walked behind the bier on which Abner's body lay. Also, I ordered Joab to indicate his repentance over his murder of Abner by tearing his clothes as a sign of grief and walking ahead of the body as we marched in a funeral procession to the burial place of Hebron. There I stood and wept aloud. Those present also wept aloud. Yes, on that day my followers and I made a great display of our grief over the slaying of Abner, a former enemy who had turned to the side of Judah.

And there was the slaying of another man, Amasa, who had pledged to help me upon my return to Jerusalem from fleeing from my son, Absalom. I sent word to him that I was going to make him the commander of my army in place of Joab. I sent him to "round up" the men of Judah and come back with them within three days. At the end of three days he had not appeared. Later when he finally met with my forces that were still under Joab's command, Joab acted very friendly with him. He gave Amasa a warm greeting by saying, "How are you, my brother?" In accordance with the custom of men of the day Joab reached out with his right hand and took Amasa by the beard and pulled him forward to give him the customary kiss of greeting, BUT with his left hand Joab (a left handed person) jerked his dagger from its sheath and plunged it into Amasa's belly, leaving him to fall to the ground and lie there writhing in death. This was just another time in which Joab slew innocent blood. He was angry that I was in the process of replacing him with Amasa as the commander of my army.

Also there was the occasion in which Joab slew Absalom, an act I took very personally. It hurt me deeply. I had issued an order that those of my army were not to harm him, but Joab completely ignored that order. For that act I found it most difficult to forgive Joab. While riding his donkey at a great speed in the heat of battle, Absalom went under a low hanging branch of a tree, and his thick and bushy hair had been caught by the tree limb. His donkey continued to gallop forward leaving Absalom dangling in mid-air. I have to admit that from the overall perspective Joab did the militarily correct thing in stabbing my beloved son. However, as stated earlier, I had taken pains to warn all the members of my little army not to harm him. Joab knew what I had said, but he went right ahead and killed Absalom. I tried to understand with my head, but my heart simply could not understand and forgive Joab. This was a private matter, so I did not mention that to Solomon when I was recounting to him Joab's wrong doings.

What more can I say than to say that under the surface Joab and I had a "love-hate" relationship. He did a lot for me during my reign as king over God's chosen people, but under the surface there were a lot of things concerning him which I could not abide. Thus, I felt that he should not die a natural death.

There was another case that needed to be given attention prior to my exit from this world. There was the case of Shemei, who followed me and my retinue, as we were fleeing from Jerusalem when Absalom and his army approached Jerusalem. Yes, he followed to one side and within seeing and hearing distance of me and my little group. He cursed us with all of his might and main. When Absalom was slain and his army disintegrated, we returned to Jerusalem. One of my army leaders strongly suggested that I have Shemei put to death for his treasonous act, saying, "Shouldn't Shimei be put to death for this? He cursed the Lord's anointed." I replied, "Should anyone be put to death in Israel today? Do I not know that today I am king over Israel?" I turned to Shimei and said, "You shall not die." Now I see the situation a bit differently. I turned to Solomon and said, "Solomon, do not consider him innocent. You are a man of wisdom; you will know what to do to him. Bring his gray head down to the grave in blood."

Well, what Joab did in allowing his personal feelings to supercede the good of the nation was unforgiveable. Perhaps I had been "too chicken" (as the world would express it) to address those issues at the times when those events occurred, preferring to delay retribution until a "more convenient time". Well, here I was nearing death's door and those injustices had not been addressed as of yet. I was well aware that personally I was no longer physically able to handle those matters. Therefore, I expressed to Solomon that my wish was that he take care of those "loose ends" for me. I said to him, "Now you yourself know what Joab son of Zerukiah did to me—what he did to the two commanders of Israel's armies, Abner son of Ner and Amasa son of Jether. He killed them, shedding their blood in peacetime as if in battle, and with that blood stained the belt around his waist and the sandals on his feet. Deal with him according to your wisdom, but do not let his gray head go down to the grave in peace."

On a happier note I recalled the great kindness shown to me durng my exile in Gilead by Barzillai. I charged Solomon to show kindness to the sons of Barzillai. He and his sons had provided the necessities of life for me during my stay in Mahanaim of Gilead, for he was a very wealthy man. I had wanted him to come to Jerusalem with me when I returned from exile, but he insisted that at his age he preferred to remain in his familiar surroundings there in the land of Gilead. "I am eighty years old. How many more years have I to live? Can your servant taste or enjoy what he eats and drinks? Can I still hear the voices of men and women singers? Why should I be a burden to my lord the king?" I appreciated so very much his great kindness to me and my retinue during our exile there. Therefore, I charged Solomon in reference to Barzillai's sons, "Let them eat at your table."

The Lord was so good to me in that He allowed me to live out my days on earth long enough to take care of these final details which I felt needed to be addressed. At this point I felt that I could leave this earthly scene and join my forefathers who have gone to their eternal reward. My prayer utter in the closing moments of life was offered in praise to my Lord and King, the Lord Jehovah:

"Praise be to you, O Lord, O Lord God of our father Israel, from everlasting to everlasting.
Yours, O Lord, is the greatness and the power and the glory and the majesty and the splendor,
For everything in heaven and earth is yours.
Yours, O Lord, is the kingdom: You are exalted as head over all.
Wealth and honor come from you; you are the ruler of all things.
In Your hands are strength and power to exalt and to give strength to all.
Now, our God, we give you thanks, praise your glorious name."

It seemed to be getting darker and darker in my bed chamber even though it was high noon. The scurrying steps of the members of my staff were now almost inaudible. No longer did I hear their whispers around my bed. It was getting increasingly harder and harder to breathe. The feeling of mortality was ebbing away even at the same time that a sensation of other worldly peace began to fill my soul. In a few moments I took my flight to the bosom of Abraham.

Epilogue

Looking back on my life I realize that it was evident by virtue of "hind sight" that I was chosen from the beginning to be a vessel of service for the Lord Jehovah to use. He had a purpose for my life that I could not see while in the process of living it. In my final hours on earth I became aware that each step in my life's journey had been ordained of God.

The lonely days which I spent in my youth as a sheep herder had a purpose for my life that I did not recognize at the time. Oh, I recall that when I first began my task of herding sheep I hated it with a passion and grumbled about it to myself (I would not have dared to let my father hear me grumbling and complaining about it). It was so very lonely on those wind swept plains and rocky hill sides where I saw no other human being for days on end. Slowly I began observing the handiwork of the Lord . . . . the sun, the moon, the twinkling stars of heaven. I began to have daily fellowship with the Lord and soon I was no longer lonely, for I walked and talked with God daily. During that early period of my life as a lowly sheep herder God was preparing me for what was to come. It was a time when I came to have a personal experience with the Lord, a time when I enjoyed talking with Him and sensing His loving presence surrounding me. Yes, it was a time when I came to rely on the Lord and to enjoy fellowship with Him.

A "fast forward" to a later time in history was when two other messengers of God went into the desert to spend a period of time with the Lord God in preparation for their life's work. They were Jesus the Lord and Saul of Tarsus (Paul). Following His baptism Jesus withdrew from the presence of human beings into the wilderness where there were only wild animals around Him. His purpose was to commune with His heavenly Father in preparation for His three years of service in introducing the Kingdom of God to mankind. Later an unlikely candidate, Saul of Tarsus, was chosen by the Lord to become a missionary to the Gentiles. Following his conversion experience on the road to Damascus, Saul of Tarsus (later to become known as "Paul") went into the wilderness in order to commune in prayer with the Lord Jesus Christ. He was getting his "marching orders" for the days ahead when he would be serving as a missionary to the Gentiles. During my days as a soldier in the army of King Saul there were many, many times when I withdrew from my fellow soldiers and went aside and turned my face toward heaven and asked the Lord Jehovah for advice as how to handle a campaign against the enemy. Many, many times I "leaned on" the Lord Jehovah for instruction on how to handle many situations as pertained to battle strategy. Also, in my role as King of Israel I leaned heavily on the Lord for guidance in the affairs of state. Later in life when it appeared that my kingdom was being wrested from me, I sought and received the advice of the Lord.

At the end of my life's journey I realized the high esteem in which I was held not only by my subjects but also by many of those in the surrounding nations. With a supernatural view into the distant future I realized that down through the centuries that followed my life span I had been held in the thinking of the people as being above and beyond the stature of most mortal man. That was an undeserved acclaim that I did not condone, for I knew myself to be just a human being who was no better and no worse than others. I carried in my conscience until the day I died two grievous sins, adultery with the beautiful Bathsheba and the murder of her husband, Uriah the Hittite. Any "greatness" for which I was being extolled, that greatness was due to the power and presence of the Lord within me. The main difference between me and any other ruler of Israel was that I depended on the leadership of the Lord in everything that I did. I sought to give Him credit for any achievement attributed to me. Now at the end of life's journey I wish that I had been more faithful to the Lord, day in and day out.